THE CHRONICLES OF UNDERREALM
COLLECTION ONE

ne Bandele, E.L. Drayton, Brenna Gawain, Riley S. Keene, Rhea Newton, Garrett Robinson, Liandra Sy, Eric Ugland

Copyright © 2018 by Legacy Books. All rights reserved.

Cover Copyright © 2018 by Legacy Books.

a work of fiction. Any resemblance to actual persons living or dead, businesses, events or locales is purely coincidental.

duction in whole or part of this publication without express written consent is strictly prohibited.

thors greatly appreciate you taking the time to read their work. Please leave a review wherever you bought the book or on Goodreads.com.

Interior Design: Legacy Books, Inc.
Publisher: Legacy Books, Inc.
Editors: Karen Conlin, Garrett Robinson
Cover Artist: Sarayu Ruangvesh

1. Fantasy - Epic 2. Fantasy - Dark 3. Fantasy - General

First Edition

Published by Legacy Books

I0749311

LEGACY BOOK

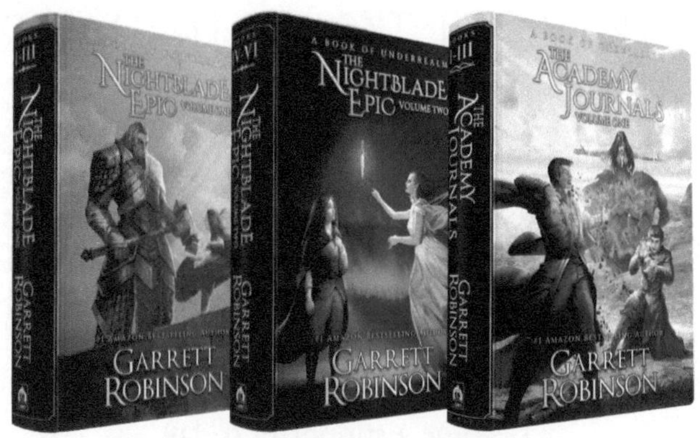

GET MORE

Legacy Books is home to the very best that fantasy has to offer.

Join our email alerts list, and we'll send word whenever we release a new book. You'll receive exclusive updates and see behind the scenes as we create them.

(You'll also learn the secret that makes great fantasy books, *great.*)

Interested? Visit this link:

Underrealm.net/Join

THANK YOU TO OUR PATRONS

The Chronicles of Underrealm are made possible by our supporters on Patreon. These incredible people support each story as it comes out, and in exchange, they get all sorts of incredible perks, in addition to the stories themselves. None of this would be possible without them.

We want to thank YOU by name in future Chronicles of Underrealm. Become a supporter today:

Patreon.com/LegacyBooks

RESEARCHERS

Aeryn, AlmanacPony, Audio Drama Reviews, Beverly Toney, Caroline Wheeler, Chris Sims, Cory Lanning, David Blaskovich, Dianna Andrews, Dylan Chappell, Esdee Ar, Garrett Robinson, George Amin, Ileia Smith, Jamilah Hassan, Jennifer Friedl, Jennifer Peck, Jennifer Thompson, Jesse Smith, John Royer, Kakirtog, the Charr in gold, Karisa Hunt, Karl J. Leis, Leon Kleinveld, Maria Mejia, Mathilde Tamae-Bouhon, Mike Bergonzi, Renee Blaquiere, RJ Womack (Brother Nero), Robert Mattison, Robin Carlisle, Shanna Elyse, Susan King, Violet Rodriguez, William

SCHOLARS

Alex Kanable, Benjamin Hulett, Benjamin Marcus, Bryan Gray, Dakota Heath, Erik Gross, Felix, Gordon Sturgeon, Henrietta, Jason Neu, Jenny Kira Franke, Jim McNierney, Joseph H. Schanken III, Laura Freestone, Lynoth, Marise Boehs, Matty Franklyn, Maureen Army, Meghan Robinson, Paul Tressler, perigaud chloe, Rosie Reast, Sarah, Shanna Banana, Shannon Tusler, Steven Hatfield, SweetTsubaki, Tami Hiner, Thom Millman, Tickle Ivory

CHRONICLERS

Aaron Elena Ender, Abby K, Ailysha, Alys Humfleet, Amber, Andrew Foss, Angie Engelbert, Angie Gwalchmai, Ashley Rodriguez, Blaine Moore, Bradley Burden, Cathleen Mitchell, Charles shropshire, Chelsea & Emily Davis, Danielle Roullier, Dawn Marshall, Devin Whitehouse, Donna LaValley, Dorothy Holzman, Dwight Kuhl, E Lynn Frank, E.L. Drayton, Eric Cerini, Francis Paine, Gabrielle Laruccia, Graham Brown, Hayley Marsden, Jeff Barrows, Jessica Scruggs, Josh Kluender, Julia Shaw, Ken Lulue, Kimberly Grube, Kris Carter, Kristen, Kristie Matheson, Lars Vad Sørensen, Letha Griffin, Liz McElwee, Maree Thompson, Mary Paulk Powers, Matt the Dev, Matthew Hartmann, Michelle Goetz, Mirka Varjus, Mysery, Olivia Helling, Patricia Roth, Peter Bromage, Porter Green, Rachelle Binkley, Rachelle Magil, Raven Evensong, Rich Bonomo, Rico Muerte, Rito, Samantha Jimenez, Saulkin, Scott Acciard, Scott Szabo, Sean Cheasley, Shana Border, Shane Sentes, Stacy Carroll, Stephanie Kellogg, Steven Geyer, Steven Harker, Timothy Kelley, Tori C, Tyandae, Valeria Osom, Weston Ott

INTRODUCTION

The stories in this book are stories of the land of Underrealm.

I created the nine kingdoms of this realm in 2010, and I first published them in 2014, in the novel *Nightblade*. But Underrealm was always intended to be a collaborative effort, rather than the work of one person. The book you hold in your hands is the first realization of that intention.

If you are already a reader of Underrealm, this story will reveal things you've never known about your favorite characters, and introduce you to new characters we know you'll love. But if you've never heard of Underrealm before you read it in the title of this book, the stories will be just as enjoyable.

This book is an anthology. The stories do not have to be read in any particular order. They are not in chronological sequence, and most are unrelated to each other, aside from some characters they share in common. They are presented to you in the order they were published. But for the curious Underrealm reader, if you want to know the chronological order of the stories, the best approximation is as follows:

The Night of Two Kings
The Man and the Satyr
Blood on the Snow
The Hammer of the King
The Legend of Cabrus
The Beast Within
Tavern Crossings
A Night on the Seat
Tides of War
The Sunmane Pass
Chasing Moonslight

If you're new here, welcome to Underrealm. If you've visited before, welcome back. We hope you enjoy your time here.

Garrett Robinson
November 2018

Chronicles of Underrealm

Collection One

LEGACY BOOKS

Tavern Crossings

Garrett Robinson

ONE

21 Yanis, Year of Underrealm 1312

Her black cloak enshrouded her more completely than the night ever could.

Loren of the family Nelda, known to some as the Nightblade, walked west down the main road that crossed the island city of the High King's Seat. Some hours ago, she had strode the opposite direction with purpose, chasing a wizard. But that hunt had returned no prey, and now her steps were listless.

After checking to make sure that the street was empty, she drew her dagger from her belt. It was finely crafted, with twisting black designs on the blade.

Those designs were shifting now.

It was some magic of the dagger that she only partially understood. When she burned the hair of a wizard on the blade, the designs would point in that wizard's direction, no matter how far away they were. But the magic only lasted a few hours. Even now it faded.

Loren had found some blonde hairs in the bedroom of an inn.

She had been investigating an agent working against the High King. When she burned the hairs, the dagger had led her east. The designs still pointed that way. She turned and looked back down the street. Part of her wanted to continue her search. But she had gone all the way to the eastern gate, and the designs had still pointed east. The wizard she hunted was somewhere across the Great Bay, likely in one of the eastern kingdoms.

She leaned against the wall of a building that looked like a cobbler's shop. Both moons hung bright and full above her. Loren half-closed her eyes. For a moment, she could imagine the moons like the pale white eyes of a forest creature glimpsed in the night. In the Birchwood that she had once called home, such creatures would often study her, trying to decide whether she was a threat or a meal. But the scent of humans usually warded them away—and if not, she always had one of Chet's bows.

A pang of longing struck her heart, surprising her. She had never expected she would miss the Birchwood.

Loren pushed away from the wall and walked on.

The High King's palace was not far away. Loren could see its golden spires shining in the moonslight. Chet waited for her there, and part of her longed to return to his welcoming arms. But she felt too defeated, her mood too grim. She had no wish to cast her own dark cloud over him, but she did not know how to rid herself of it.

Voices drifted on the air, pouring from a tavern not far away. On the sign over its door, Loren could just make out a painting of a donkey rearing, its front hooves planted on a great silver bell. There were words beneath the image, but Loren had never learned to read.

Her throat twinged. Perhaps a cup of wine would do the trick. Or two. She probed the inside pocket of her black cloak. Gold weights clinked together, thick and familiar, resting on some pennies and slivers.

There is wine in the palace, said her more sensible side. *If you want to get drunk, you can do it before Chet even knows you have returned.*

But Loren was sixteen, and her homeland was half a kingdom away, and it was the middle of the night. She stood in the greatest city human hands had ever built, capital of the world's mightiest nation, and home to more people from more lands than she had ever dreamed she might see.

Loren took one last look at the palace before heading towards the tavern.

* * *

Ebon of the family Drayden approached the eastern gate. His friends Kalem and Theren walked a half-step behind him.

"Trying to sneak in the same gate does not strike me as a good idea," said Kalem.

"Nothing fun ever strikes you as a good idea," snorted Theren. She ran a hand through her short bob of dyed blonde hair, which stood out stark against her deep brown face.

"Hush, both of you," said Ebon. "The constables will hear us."

"They heard us already," said Theren, "when we snuck out."

"Quiet," said Ebon.

He was already irritable that their night's wanderings had been so fruitless, and his body was injured and weary besides. They had snuck out of the city to investigate markings on a map, the purpose of which they did not know. It sounded mad when Ebon thought about it so plainly. Indeed, he would never have come here if, not only a few days before, his own cousin had not attacked him looking for information. The fight had left him bruised and sore—but it had also filled him with an intense curiosity about the map, and so he had hatched this plan to investigate.

Together they stepped behind a dock piling and looked up at the gate. No constables stood before it, but there were two on the wall above. They did not seem particularly alert. He and his friends had made quite a commotion when they exited the gate, but that had been some time ago.

"Kalem, you should summon a mist," said Ebon. "We will run to the door, and Theren can open it with a spell."

"I cannot," said Theren.

Ebon blinked. "What?"

Theren arched an eyebrow. "The door's latch is on the inside. I cannot see the inside. Therefore I cannot reach it with my magic. Honestly, Ebon, I know you are new to your training, but sometimes I suspect you pay no attention at all."

Panic clutched at Ebon's heart, but Kalem only rolled his eyes, stark white in a face almost as pale. "Oh, very well, Theren. You may end your joke, for I will take the bait. How do you mean to get us back inside the walls, if you cannot open the door?"

Theren gave them a wide grin. "I have no idea."

Kalem stared at her, his smug look slowly dying. "But . . . but . . . what? This was *your* idea! Why would you lead us outside the walls if you had no means to get us back inside?"

She spread her hands. "It was Ebon's *and* my idea. But if you knew I had no way to re-enter the city, you would never have come with me."

Ebon felt his heart drop into his shoes. Kalem's hands twitched as though he very much wanted to strangle Theren—though it would have been a mistake to try, for Ebon had seen her trounce far larger opponents without even using her magic.

"Theren," said Ebon. "If we cannot find a way back into the city, how are we supposed to return to the Academy?"

Kalem moaned and slumped against the piling. "They will find us. We will have to turn ourselves in. And when the Academy finds out what we have done, we shall be expelled."

"Calm yourselves, both of you," said Theren. "We will find a way in. I have before."

"Oh, of course!" said Kalem, brightening at once. "You snuck out once. How did you return then?"

Theren's gaze grew suddenly shifty. "I was with . . . a friend. We helped each other. But she was much stronger in her magic than either of you, and she was a firemage besides."

"An *elementalist,* Theren," said Kalem.

But Ebon's interest had been piqued by Theren's uncommonly vague manner. "Who was this 'friend' you speak of?"

"None of your business, goldbag," she snapped.

Kalem held up a finger. "Wait! I am no elementalist, but a transmuter may be even better."

Ebon frowned. He was new to wizard training, and much of magic was still strange to him. But Theren's eyes brightened, and she nodded. "Better indeed," she said. "The wall?"

"Yes," said Kalem eagerly. Then, seeing Ebon's blank expression, he gave an apologetic smile. "Sorry, Ebon. I mean to say that I can shift stone, creating a hole for us to sneak in through the wall."

The wall was tall, and if Ebon were to guess, he would say it was a few paces thick as well. "Are you sure?"

"Of course!" said Kalem. But his mood suddenly dampened. "Though it weakens the wall a bit, I suppose. Shifted stone crumbles to dust in time. But they will be able to repair it."

"Hearing you talk about mischief is like hearing a cow sing a ballad," said Theren, grinning. "I doubt I will ever get used to it."

Kalem's scowl returned. He gave a sharp motion for them to follow as he stole forwards to the wall. Theren took Ebon's arm and slung it over her shoulder, helping him walk with as little pain as possible.

They came to the wall about a span away from the gate, where the constables would not be able to see them. Kalem crouched by the place where the wall's stones sank into the island's rock, and he placed his hands on it.

"Only a little tunnel," he said. "Just big enough to crawl through."

The boy's eyes began to glow. Ebon felt an itch on his skin like spider's feet. He, too, was an alchemist, and he could sense when that branch of magic was being used.

But when Kalem placed his hands on the stone, nothing happened.

Kalem frowned as the glow died in his eyes. He pressed his hands hard against the stone, trying again.

Still nothing.

"What under the sky . . .?" His words trailed off, and he looked up at them in horror. "Oh, no. It is enchanted."

"What?" said Ebon.

"Spells have been put upon it," said Theren. "They keep magic from affecting it. Only a very powerful wizard could break the enchantment."

"We . . ." Ebon swallowed hard. "Could we not jump atop the wall? The way we did at the Academy to sneak out in the first place?"

Theren looked up, pursing her lips. "I think I can manage it." She grinned. "Though I am surprised to hear you suggest such a thing, Ebon. I thought you did not enjoy heights."

"I do not," said Ebon. "Yet I also do not wish to be expelled from the Academy."

"There may be constables up there," said Kalem. "They could see us."

"I will send you first, then," said Theren. "You can spin mists to hide us when we follow."

"Me?" squeaked Kalem. "First?"

"You shall be fine," Theren reassured him. "Though if you are not, be sure to scream loudly so that we know not to follow you."

"Be nice, Theren," said Ebon. He put a hand on Kalem's shoulder. "You will be fine, Kalem. You are an excellent alchemist. They will not see you."

Kalem sighed. "Oh, very well. But do it quickly, while I still have some grip on my nerves."

"Ebon, give him a boost," said Theren. "On the count of three. One. Two. Three!"

Ebon heaved the boy up. Theren's eyes glowed, and her magic seized Kalem to fling him skywards. Kalem could not help a small screech that quickly went quiet as he mounted the wall. Almost at once, Ebon saw mists spring to life, filling the air above them.

"Hurry," said Theren. "One—"

"Oh, just do it," said Ebon, his throat dry as he lifted his foot. Theren smiled as she helped him jump.

Just as when they had snuck out of the Academy, Ebon felt an unseen force seize him under the arms. He barely restrained a shout of pain as the magic pressed on his bruised skin. It propelled him towards the top of the wall, giving him a moment's sensation of flight.

He reached the lip and threw his arms over it. Ebon grunted as his chest struck stone, igniting a fiery lance of agony.

"Come on," said Kalem, seizing his arms to help pull him up. The boy's eyes glowed with the magic of his mists.

"What under the sky—?" came a strange voice from a few paces away.

Both boys froze. Ebon stared hard into the mist. He saw no one, but he heard heavy bootsteps coming towards them.

"A constable!" whispered Kalem. "They will find us!"

A moment later, there came a *whoosh* of air as Theren vaulted to the top of the wall. Ebon silenced her with a finger to his lips and pointed towards the sound of bootsteps.

Theren's eyes narrowed—and then they began to glow. For a moment, nothing happened. Then at last they glimpsed a form in the mist.

Theren threw out her hands. Ebon saw nothing, but the constable cried out and flew backwards.

"Dark below!" bellowed the constable, her voice muffled by the mist. "Those wizards have returned!"

"They recognize me." Theren sounded immensely proud of herself.

"We were *just* here," said Ebon.

"Even so."

"Shut up, both of you!" cried Kalem. "We must flee! Lower me down!"

He pushed himself over the rear parapet, and Theren's eyes glowed again. Kalem let go and began to float gently towards the ground. But they had forgotten one thing. Kalem's mists were tied to him, and as he went lower and lower, the air began to clear. They would soon be entirely visible.

"Sky above, I did not think of that," said Theren, though she did not sound particularly alarmed. "You had better hurry, Ebon."

"What about you?"

"I will follow just behind you," said Theren. "The jump will be easier for me, for I am neither as fat nor as pampered as you goldbags."

Ebon ground his teeth and pushed himself over the wall. Theren's magic took hold of him at once, and he floated gently to the ground. He looked up nervously—and Theren almost came down on his head. She landed catlike on the cobblestones a pace away, still wearing a mischievous grin.

"Done and done," she said. "This is even better than last time."

"Stop!"

The new shout made them all whirl. A span away, two constables were running down a staircase close to the gate. Both bore torches—and drawn clubs.

"Run!" cried Ebon.

Theren seized his arm to help him, though her grip was like agony on his skin. They pelted down the street. Close behind came the constables, still shouting. Theren turned a few times, trying to create a difficult path to follow. Ebon was grateful Kalem still spun his mists—that and the darkness would keep the constables from being able to see their faces.

But that would not help if the constables caught them. And his steps came slower and slower as his bruises and injuries flared with pain.

"I am . . . too slow . . ." he gasped. "You . . . should go on."

"Oh, shut up," said Theren. But her tone was uncharacteristically grim.

Suddenly Ebon realized he could no longer hear footsteps behind them. He slowly came to a stop. "Are they still there?" he said. "Mayhap they gave up the chase."

"I doubt—"

Theren's words cut off as the constables burst out from a side street.

They were little more than indistinct shapes in the mist, for they had abandoned their torches. But they saw the children and came forwards with clubs swinging.

"Back!" cried Theren.

She released Ebon, and her eyes glowed. The constables flew away to land hard on the cobblestones.

"This way." Theren seized Ebon again and hurried off in another direction. They ran past three more buildings and ducked into a narrow alley. There they stopped, pressing themselves against the alley wall, listening.

A long moment's silence passed.

"They left," said Theren.

"You think they just gave up?" said Ebon.

Theren shrugged. "They tried twice and failed. A third try is always cursed, as they say."

Ebon sighed. "Good enough for me."

"Sky above, that was close," said Kalem, letting his mists fall away to nothing. "Let us get back to the Academy as quickly as we can."

"I have a better idea," said Ebon, sagging against the wall. "I could use a drink."

"Are you joking?" said Kalem, aghast. "Now?"

"I am still injured," said Ebon. "And I nearly collapsed in the chase. Just a quick stop, Kalem, for a moment."

Kalem still looked horrified as he shook his head. But Theren smiled and clapped a hand on Ebon's shoulder, ignoring his groan.

"I think it is an excellent idea," said Theren. "And I know a place not far away with extraordinarily passable wine. The Ass and Bell."

Ebon's brows shot for the sky. "The what?"

Theren grinned. "Judge not its name until you have tasted the fare within."

"We should go back home," said Kalem reproachfully.

"You are free to leave us," said Theren. "But good luck getting back inside the Academy without my magic to help you over the wall."

She smiled at Ebon and took his arm again, helping him down the alley. With a groan of frustration, Kalem followed.

TWO

Mako pulled his dagger from the constable's neck with a sharp tug, sending blood to spatter on the street. The woman gurgled as she died. Her hand grasped his wrist, tugging desperately. A final resistance. Too weak, and far too late.

A pace away, Talib crouched over the other constable. Her knife had been knocked away, but her hands were pressed tight to the man's neck, her thumbs digging into his throat. He grunted and heaved, trying to remove the pressure. His face had gone purple, his eyes bugging out. He gasped and died. Just to be sure, Mako strode over and slit the man's throat. The body did not even twitch.

"You should fetch your knife," said Mako, allowing himself a small smile. "Sloppy of you to lose it."

"I was hardly trying," said Talib lightly, fetching the blade from the cobblestones. "They are only constables."

Constables, yes. But that would be more than enough to ruin everything. Mako could not be sure the constables had recognized Ebon and his friends, in the darkness and the spell-born mists. But if they had, Ebon might have been expelled from the Academy. That could not be allowed to happen.

Not yet, at any rate.

"Well, we had best be on our way," said Mako. "The boy will have moved on."

"Where?" said Talib. She did not ask him how he knew that Ebon would have moved on, just as she had not asked him, earlier in the night, how he knew Ebon was in danger in the first place. Once, she would have, but long years had taught her better. Mako preferred it that way. It was one reason—only one on a long list—why she was his favorite.

"The Ass and Bell," said Mako. "They have extraordinarily passable wine, or so I have heard."

Talib nodded and followed him to a building with a low roof. Mako leaped up on a rain barrel and used it to climb up. Every movement was silent. Even as he began to run along the tiles, his feet made no noise coming down. Talib was just as quiet, for he had trained her well.

What had the dream shown him? He let it play again in his mind. Ebon in the tavern. And a dagger. The dagger was pressed to Ebon's throat, its edge pressing into the boy's skin while he cowered.

A threat on Ebon's life. But the knife did not slash Ebon's throat. That was a good sign, for Mako could only change the visions in his dreams rarely—and at a terrible cost. More troubling was the fact that he could not see who held the knife. He was meant to save Ebon, but he had no idea where the threat would come from.

But Mako had seen something else in the dream—and he had seen it every time, which meant it was important. A figure in a black cloak, sitting at the edge of the room. Try as he might, Mako could never approach them. And where the figure sat, the room grew hazy and indistinct, until it was almost impossible to see.

Was the black-cloaked figure the threat? Mako thought they should be holding the knife if so, but things were rarely so plain. Certainly it seemed they were someone to watch out for.

Mako shook off such thoughts as he and Talib caught up to the children. He must remain in the moment if he hoped to save Ebon's life. He would know the threat when he saw it.

And he would end it.

They caught up to the children and kept pace with them, staying out of sight. Mako had seen the girl, Theren, only a handful of times. It seemed her destiny did not greatly affect his own. But the boy, Kalem, featured more prominently. He would play quite a role in Ebon's life, though the full strength of his influence would not be felt for some time yet.

Mako hid a smile that would have made even Talib shudder.

At last the inn appeared in the darkness. Its windows were lit, and cheery music poured out the front door. Mako stopped on the rooftop across the street, crouching low. Talib shadowed the movement. They watched as Ebon and his friends crossed the street and stepped inside the tavern.

"Shall I—" Talib began.

"Yes," said Mako, a hair too quickly. He was normally better about answering questions before they were asked. "I will watch outside. Ebon will not recognize you the way he would me, but still, try not to let him see you."

"Understood," said Talib. She leaped lightly over the roof's edge to land on the street. Mako did the same, allowing her to draw ahead and slip in through the front door.

Mako walked around the tavern and peered through each window in turn. The place was busier than he would have expected at such a late hour. That annoyed him. More people present meant more possible threats, and a great chance for an assassin to approach Ebon unseen.

As for Ebon himself, he and his friends had taken a table rather near the front door. Even as Mako watched, a barman approached and placed a bottle of wine on the table, along with three goblets. Ebon poured, and they all drank together—the boy, Kalem, with a delicate sip quite unlike the swigs of Ebon and Theren.

Mako spied Talib next, lurking in a corner with a glass of brandy. Though no one in the room would have caught her looking, Mako knew she had every bit of her attention on Ebon's table.

And then, at the bar itself, he saw the figure in the black cloak. They looked womanly, but Mako could not see their face, for the cloak's hood was up. It was made of very fine material. She—if it was a woman—was a powerful merchant then, or mayhap even royalty. Or a servant of either, Mako supposed.

The figure's back was to him. Mako wanted to see their face—to see if he could identify them, if he knew them from somewhere. There was a window on the building's opposite side. He would be able to see from there.

Turning, he stroked towards the building's northeast corner, towards the back door. The front would have too many people, and while he was not a particularly remarkable man at first glance, he still preferred to avoid notice when he could. But just as he reached the back door, a figure came suddenly out of the darkness, and their shoulders collided.

Mako drew back, hand going to his dagger under his cloak. But that was only instinct, and he did not draw. Instead, he appraised the man in half a second. A thin mustache, a scrub of beard. Skinny to the point of starvation, and pale to the point of illness. A plain brown cloak, and beneath it, clothes of blue and grey.

Something twinged in the back of Mako's mind. Dreamsight? Or merely instinct? He could not say. These days, it was harder to tell. But whatever it was, something told him this man was of more note than he appeared.

"Apologies, friend," said Mako. "It is dark here, out of the torchlight." Another lie. He could see as though it were daylight.

The man glared at him. "I am not your friend." And he pushed past Mako, vanishing through the tavern's back door.

Mako wondered if he should have stopped him. But then, Talib would already be inside the tavern. She would be watching over Ebon and his friends. And Mako knew better than to act rashly, without thinking through each consequence.

He pressed on. Soon he reached the window that would let him see the black-cloaked figure. They had their head down, staring into a cup of wine, their hood hiding their face.

And then she looked up.

Mako froze.

She was young. Her skin was light, though somewhat reddened by the sun. Hair as black as her cloak, which he could see now covered plain, worn clothes—a dark green vest over a stained white shirt. But her eyes . . .

Her eyes.

He could see that they were a brilliant green. Likely that was what most people noticed about them. But Mako saw more. In his vision, the eyes glowed. It was something akin to magelight—and yet he could see that it was nothing like magelight at all. And not like those who were Elf-touched, either.

It was . . . different. Different from anything he had seen before.

That realization rooted him to the spot. Mako did not see new things. Not now, not any more. He had peered into most of the darkest corners and holes of all the nine kingdoms. And what he had not seen with his own eyes, he always saw with the dreamsight.

Something new meant something troubling. Something dangerous. Something that made the future uncertain.

Mako gripped his dagger again. The girl might be the one coming for Ebon, or she might not. It no longer mattered to him. She was dangerous.

She would die.

* * *

Lior closed the back door of the Ass and Bell behind him as he entered the back room. He drew his brown cloak tighter over his blue and grey clothing. Had the man outside noticed them? Likely it did not matter. There were few who recognized the clothing of a Shade. Still, he worried.

Two more doors stood before him, one leading to the kitchen and the other to the main room, where he could hear the muted voices of the tavern's patrons. He made for that door and opened it, pausing on the threshold as he took a quick look around.

The ones hunting him could not have found out he would be here, now, but he could never be too cautious. Even a chance meeting with the wrong person could prove disastrous. He would rather not have been here at all. He had only left hiding because his contact had refused to meet in private. She wanted their transaction to occur in as public a place as possible.

Lior sneered. As though she had anything to fear from him. As though he did not risk far, far more by coming here than she did.

Some time ago, he had been given a map. At the time, he thought nothing of it. His masters had entrusted him with far greater tasks, here in the city. The map was an afterthought, a bit of clerical assistance.

Then—not even a week ago—the map had been stolen by wizards. He did not know who they were, or who they worked for. But they must have been highly-placed spies of the High King, to have discovered the inn where he had concealed both himself and the map.

Despite the odds, Lior had done his best to track down the thieves. But he had made no progress before his masters had discovered the map's theft.

The world had gone to madness, then. His masters had not been forgiving. They had not even let him explain what had happened. As if they had no interest in recovering it. It had not mattered to them that he performed every other task he had been given, to the letter. Lior had only barely escaped with his life.

His eyes smarted at the thought. The Shades were his life—had been his life for almost as long as he could remember. They were like family. Rogan, the man who had raised him, was the closest thing Lior had ever known to a father. Doubtless Rogan knew nothing of how he had been cast out. It seemed that even among the Shades, bearers of Underrealm's most sacred burden, politicking had taken sway. Lior could think of no other explanation for why he had been discarded.

He had tried to escape the island, but they were watching the docks. Now he had to find a new place to sleep every night, for no inn was safe from their watchful gaze. His meals were hurried affairs, taken away from any prying eyes. He was nearly starved, and exhausted beyond reckoning. He had not even been able to get new clothes, and he still wore the blue-and-grey clothes of his order—colors he had now come to loathe.

But with luck, that would all change tonight.

He did not see his hunters in the tavern. But he did not see his contact, either. The one who would smuggle him safely off the island. She was not yet late, but she was close enough.

For a moment, he thought about leaving. He already felt far too exposed. But without the help of this smuggler, he had no way to escape the island.

Lior ground his teeth and found an empty table in the corner, from which he could see the whole room. Almost at once, a barman showed up to take his order. "Rum," growled Lior, and the barman hurried away. Lior retreated further under his plain brown hood, his eyes scanning the room for danger—or for his contact.

And then he saw something else entirely. Something that made him shoot straight up in his chair, forgetting stealth for the moment.

At the bar sat a figure in a black cloak. For just a moment she turned, and Lior saw her face. It was pale, and her eyes were a brilliant green. He looked again at the black cloak.

It was the Nightblade. Lior had heard enough stories about her, enough description, that he knew her at once. Every Shade across the nine kingdoms knew Loren of the family Nelda. She had stolen from them, ruined their alliances, and even killed one of the Shadeborn—the undying brutes who were favored by the Lord.

Lior's heart thundered in his chest. He licked his dry, cracked lips. The barman returned with the drink, and Lior paid him, keeping his gaze on the Nightblade.

A plan began to form in his mind.

If he could kill the Nightblade . . . if he could deliver her corpse to his masters . . . they would have to forgive him. If nothing else, they would allow him to reach out to Rogan. Rogan could sort it all out. Lior would be safe once again.

His fingers toyed with the hilt of the wicked knife at his belt. The meeting with his contact was forgotten.

Lior would not have to flee the island. Not after tonight. Not after he killed the Nightblade.

THREE

"There is time yet to discover what the markings mean," said Theren. "You should not worry so, Ebon."

"You do not know whether I should worry or not," groused Ebon. The wine was going to his head, but he had a great deal of practice with drinking. "None of us do, until we discover what the map is for."

"Which we have little hope of doing," said Kalem, sipping delicately at his own drink. "Which is why we should tell one of our instructors. But I have given up hope that either of you will agree to something so sensible."

"You are wise to abandon that hope," said Theren, grinning. She drained the rest of her wine cup and slammed it down on the table. "Sky above, that bottle went fast. I want another, and I am hungry now as well."

"You cannot mean to stay even longer," whined Kalem. "I am going to fall asleep on this table."

"Feel free," said Theren. "I will carry you home if I must. Where is that barman?"

"I saw him go into the back," said Ebon.

"Then I will fetch him." Theren stood.

"I will return our cups, and then I could stand a piss," said Ebon.

Kalem's eyes widened in alarm. "You do not mean to leave me alone?"

"You can come with me if you wish, master goldbag." Theren gave him a mock bow. "A lowly orphan girl like myself could hardly stop you."

She made for the back of the tavern, Kalem on her heels. Ebon scooped up their cups and made his way to the bar. Several patrons sat there. The only gap was beside a figure in a black cloak. Ebon tried to squeeze past them with his empty cups, but this was rather difficult, since he and Theren had done most of the work of drinking the first bottle. At the last second, he bumped the person's elbow, and some of their wine splashed out onto the countertop.

"Ah!" The black-cloaked figure turned and glared at him. She was a girl with pale skin and black hair, around his own age. Ebon was struck at once by her eyes, which were large and brilliant green. But there was something else about them . . . something that seemed to hold him in rapt attention, that made his skin itch the way it did when someone used alchemy nearby.

"I . . . my apologies," he stammered, fighting to free his gaze from hers. At last he managed it, looking down at the cups he still held in his hands. He put them on the counter and reached for a nearby discarded rag. "Here, let me help clean it up."

The girl seemed to hear the sincerity in his voice, for her glare softened. She lifted a hand and waved it airily. "No trouble, I suppose. After all, tonight has already gone so poorly that such a little accident could hardly make it worse."

Ebon snorted without meaning to as he soaked up the last of the spilled wine. "Well, take some comfort in company, then. I have had an abysmal night as well."

That made the girl smile at last, though it was a rueful expression. Even though she was around his age, he thought he saw many old secrets in her eyes—and mayhap painful memories. "I am sorry to hear it, and I hope it gets better. In my experience, it usually does, though the moment itself may darken all hope."

"I have not heard that wisdom before, but I like it," said Ebon. "If the barman were here, I would buy you a drink in thanks—but mayhap I can when he returns. Good eve."

"Good eve," said the girl, and turned back to the rest of her wine.

Trying to put her strange eyes from his mind, Ebon glanced back towards his table. Theren and Kalem had not yet returned. He turned his steps towards the back of the tavern to see what was taking them so long. His clumsiness had not entirely fled him, and he collided with the chairs of some of the other patrons as he wove between the tables. But they were all deep in their cups as well, and they did not seem to notice.

At last Ebon reached the door Theren had left through. But as he paused to pull it open, he took one last glance back into the room.

He froze.

There in the corner sat a man. A thin man with a scrub of beard, and pale—paler, even, than when Ebon had seen him last.

For Ebon *had* seen him before. It was the man from whom they had stolen the map that had led them to the eastern docks.

What was he doing here? Had he remembered Ebon's face? Had he hunted Ebon across the Seat, planning an attack?

But . . . but, no. The man was not looking at Ebon at all. All his attention was focused on someone else in the tavern—though from where he stood, Ebon could not see who. It could have been anyone.

Ebon darted through the door, through the kitchen, and through another door leading to the back room. There he found Theren, who seemed to be rummaging through the tavern's stores of wine in search of a bottle fit for them to drink, and Kalem, who was trying to stop her.

"Wait for the barman, Theren!" said Kalem. "Someone will think we are stealing!"

"I would not steal the wine if the barman were there to pay for it," said Theren in annoyance.

"Stop, both of you!" said Ebon in a harsh whisper. "Someone is here!"

Theren straightened up from the wine case she had been perusing. "Someone? Someone who?"

"The man from the inn on the west of the Seat," said Ebon. "The one from whom we stole the map!"

Kalem blanched. Theren's eyes narrowed. "Are you sure?" she said.

"As I am of anything."

"Show me."

Ebon led them both back through the kitchen, cracking the door just enough to see the man and point him out. Theren studied him with interest.

"We must get out of here!" said Kalem. "What if he sees us? What if he recognizes us?"

"He did not get a clear look at any of us when we first met him," said Ebon. "I walked across the room in plain sight, and he did not seem to recognize me. And look—he seems interested in someone else entirely." And indeed, the man still stared intently into the crowded room, exactly as he had a few moments before.

"Even better," said Kalem. "Let us go before his interest wanes, and he turns it on us instead."

But to Ebon's surprise, Theren grinned. "Go? Are you mad?"

"Are *you?"* asked Kalem in astonishment. "Would you rather stay here and chance him catching us?"

"Catch us?" said Theren. "I am a mindmage. You are an alchemist. What could he hope to do? And besides, we have been wondering about those markings on that map. Who better to ask about them?"

"What?" Kalem's voice went shrill, and his face turned almost as red as his hair. "You *have* gone mad. What do you want to do, sit down at his table and ply him with a drink?"

"Mad I may be, but not foolish," said Theren. "Let us get him alone and capture him. We can force him to tell us whatever we want to know."

Ebon felt a shudder of fear. "Theren, that hardly seems wise. He tried to kill us."

"And he failed. As he will again, if he tries anything. Let us wait for him to finish his drinks, or to use the privy, and then—"

"Look!" said Ebon.

The man rose from his chair and walked across the room towards the bar, which was out of sight from their doorway.

"No good chasing him through the room," said Theren. "Come! Let us go outside and circle around."

"Theren, this is a fool's errand," said Kalem. "We cannot—"

"I grow tired of telling you that you do not have to come," said Theren. "Come, Ebon." And she ran out the back door.

Ebon stared after her, then glanced at Kalem. The boy's face was bloodless again, and he shook his head.

"No, Ebon," he said. "You cannot think she—"

"I must know what is drawn on the map," said Ebon. "But I understand if you want to stay here. Stay hidden, and stay safe."

He ran towards the back door after Theren. And to his relief, behind him he heard Kalem mutter, "Darkness take all reckless fools," as the boy hurried to follow him.

* * *

Loren's second glass of wine tasted better than her first, and the third tasted better still. The wine here was not the best she had, but it was very far from the worst.

Exceptionally passable, she thought, and the phrase seemed to leap into her mind from nowhere. It was an odd feeling, but she dismissed it.

Yet even the wine could not entirely assuage her dark mood. She had thought to capture a wizard tonight, and she did not relish returning to the palace empty-handed. She thought of the boy who had bumped her arm and smirked. At least it seemed she was not the only one having a bad night.

It was a foolish hunt anyway, she thought. *It is not your duty to look into every strange disturbance on the Seat.*

The space beside her had remained empty, but now a girl settled herself on the stool. No, not a girl—a woman. Loren glanced at her. She had dark skin and darker hair, and for a moment Loren's heart skipped, fearing she might be a Yerrin. That merchant family had long held a grudge against her. But her fears soon eased. For one thing, her clothes were not fine enough, though they were hardly plain, either. She wore a dark cloak, more faded and worn than Loren's, and black leather clothing beneath it. And Loren hardly thought a member of the family Yerrin would sit down so easily next to her.

Besides, the woman hardly looked fit to be a merchant. While she was not brawny, she was muscular, in a lean, sleek sort of way that promised more danger than pure strength might have. And though one eye was ruined, with a long scar through it, the other darted everywhere, assessing the tavern's main room.

No, not a merchant. But certainly very interesting.

Loren smiled at her.

"Good eve, friend," she said, raising her cup. "Or near enough to morning, at this point."

The woman glanced at her, looked her over, and turned away. "Good eve. You will pardon me, but I am waiting for someone."

"Yet it seems they have not yet arrived," said Loren.

Again the woman studied her. Her lips drew tightly together. "I am not after whatever you are offering," she said. "If you need it, I can tell you where to find the nearest blue door."

Loren's cheeks flamed. The blue door was the sign of a house of lovers. "I was not . . . I was not offering anything," she said lamely.

"Just because I do not flirt, does not mean I cannot see it when others do." The woman turned away again.

Now Loren was growing irritated. "You misunderstand me. I am bored, and I only wanted to talk. I already have a lover."

"Then talk to her," said the woman, not turning back around.

"Him," said Loren. She closed her eyes and sighed. "Listen. I am sorry. Allow me to make up for it by buying you a drink and then leaving you alone."

The woman paused for a moment before turning once more. She studied Loren even more closely, and finally she sighed. "If you insist. Forgive me if I misread your intent. Though you will have a hard time buying me a drink, since the barman seems absent."

"Then I will leave you be for now, and return when he does to make good on my promise," said Loren. "Fare well."

She rose from her stool and went to an empty table against the wall, deciding it would be too awkward to continue to sit near the grim woman. She sat and leaned the chair back against the wall, sipping at her wine. The conversation—if such it could be called—had done nothing to improve her mood. And even as she watched, the woman at the bar got up, walking off into the crowd. Likely heading off to relieve herself.

Loren glowered into her cup of wine. She thought again of the wizard she had hunted. If only she had at least seen them . . . had seen *anything.* Then she could have brought the information back to the palace, and it could be handled by people of power who were used to dealing with such things. Loren was only a would-be thief, and hardly a spy or hunter at all.

Loren glanced around the room to make sure no one was looking at her. When she was satisfied, she lifted up her cloak to conceal her dagger as she drew it. It could be disastrous to let anyone else see it, but she wanted to take another quick look.

The designs on the blade still twisted and writhed, but slower now, sluggish. The magic was wearing off. They all still pointed in the same direction, drawing her eyes . . .

She sat upright with a start, and the chair, which had leaned against the wall, came down hard on the floor. Loren looked up, getting her bearings.

It was not the wine. The dagger no longer pointed east. Its twisting black spikes now pointed north, towards the back of the tavern.

Her pulse quickened. When she had reached the eastern end of the island city, she had assumed the wizard she hunted was beyond the wall and across the Great Bay. But if they were now north of her . . . they could not be out on the water.

They were in the city.

But the magic was wearing off. Even as she watched, the designs moved slower and slower.

Loren shoved the dagger back into its sheath. She shot to her feet, ignoring the startled looks she drew from the tavern's other patrons, and ran for the back of the tavern.

A door there led into the tavern's back room. She expected to find the barman here, fetching the new keg of ale, but the room was empty. After a quick glance around to make sure no one stood in the shadows, Loren ran out the back door behind the tavern.

The alleyway behind the tavern was dark, especially after the light of the candles and lamps inside. But the last remnants of a magestone still coursed through Loren's veins, and she placed her hand on her dagger. The dagger's magic activated, and the night grew brighter.

Where to? Quickly she looked around, but there was no one in sight except a beggar huddled in a nearby nook, swathed in a threadbare cloak against the night. Satisfied she was alone, Loren risked another look at the dagger's blade.

The designs no longer pointed north. Now they pointed south, and slightly west.

Loren froze. She turned and looked back at the building.

The wizard was *inside* the tavern.

Only, no. Loren looked at the blade again. They were certainly close, but if she guessed the angle right, they were outside. In fact, it looked as if they might be moving around the outside of the building.

Without a second thought, Loren ran east. She would circle around the building in the opposite direction and catch them that way. Sky above, she was going to do it. She was going to find the wizard she had spent the better part of tonight searching for.

She rounded the tavern's northeast corner. Her feet struck something heavy, and she tripped.

Her shoulder struck the cobblestones hard as she slid for almost a pace. Frowning, she pushed up on her elbows. The obstacle had felt heavy, like a full rucksack, or—

Loren's blood ran cold. There, lying against the side of the tavern, was the barman. His throat had been slit. His dead eyes stared at her with an expression of utter confusion.

Before she could stop herself, Loren let out a scream.

FOUR

Mako cursed.

He crouched on the edge of the rooftop just above the alley, watching the girl in the black cloak below him. She had just stumbled over the body of the barman he had killed.

The barman had been uncommonly quiet, and had approached Mako unawares as he lurked outside the Ass and Bell, trying to see where Ebon and Talib had gone to. Mako had been watching Talib have a brief conversation with the girl in the black cloak. Then Ebon had made for the back of the tavern, and Talib had followed. Just before Mako had gone to find them both, the barman had appeared and asked what he was up to.

Mako had not liked the man's tone. So he slit his throat.

But now the girl in the black cloak had found him, and her scream would draw attention. Mako had not seen any constables nearby, but that would not matter. Enough people would come out of the tavern to be a nuisance, and Mako was not so overconfident that he would murder the girl before so many witnesses.

Besides, he had a more pressing mission. The girl in the black cloak was an extra excursion tonight. He still had to find and protect Ebon.

Mako started to rise to his feet, but then he went still. The girl in the black cloak was moving. She, too, seemed to know that others would soon be coming. And she was abandoning the body. Why? She had not killed the barman.

What was she trying to hide? Or, mayhap, what was she trying to do?

After a brief glance around, the girl found a drainpipe on the tavern's wall that flowed down into a sewer grate. She scaled it easily, leaping up the iron wall mounts to the roof. Mako flattened himself to his own rooftop. But then he realized that that might not be enough cover, and so he sidled back and to the side, behind the building's chimney. He paused there, listening as the girl retreated.

Footsteps came pounding from the street below, as he had known they would. Mako slid back up to the roof's edge, watching as tavern patrons came running from around the corners of the building.

"Sky above!" cried one of them. "Someone fetch a constable!"

Mako's mouth soured. Constables were the last thing he wanted just now. But there were close to a dozen people on the street below. Too many for him to silence.

Then, across the main road in front of the tavern, he spied someone else. Someone who had been in the tavern, but had not joined the other patrons investigating the scream. The thin man in blue and grey who had collided with Mako. He stood in an alleyway, watching.

Had he seen Mako kill the barman? That seemed impossible. Mako would have known. And indeed, the man did not seem to be looking at the commotion outside the tavern at all. He looked higher, studying the rooftops, his gaze traveling . . .

Mako realized with a start that he was looking for the girl in the black cloak. What did he want with her?

Too many questions. Too many things unknown. The dreamsight had not left him this blind in many years.

It had something to do with the girl in the black cloak. She obscured events, just as she had obscured his sight within the dream itself.

Suddenly the thin man gave a start. As Mako watched, he slipped out from the alley and hurried towards the far side of the tavern.

He had seen the girl in the black cloak. Mako was sure of it.

And then, even as he watched, three more figures came out of the darkness. Ebon and his friends. They were following the thin man.

Mako growled. What in the darkness below was going on tonight?

* * *

Lior ignored the commotion by the tavern. The Nightblade was plainly visible, scuttling across the rooftops like a cat. He had drawn his knife, and he carried it naked by his side. But he could not climb up to the rooftops without losing her trail. Once she came down, he would end her. That would earn his place among the Shades once more.

The only problem was that she seemed to have no intention of climbing down. She was fleeing the commotion at the tavern, that much was certain. But what had happened there? Had she been in a fight? He wished for a moment that he at at least glanced at what was going on, but it was too late for that now.

At last the Nightblade stopped. She crouched on the edge of a roof, drawing something from within her cloak. She stared at it, but from this distance Lior could not see what it was. A knife, mayhap? He stopped in the alleyway, hiding his own knife within his cloak in case someone approached. Then he leaned forwards and peered through the darkness, trying to see what the Nightblade held in her hand.

The Nightblade looked up. She looked right *at* him. Lior's veins turned to ice.

But no. She was not looking at him, but beyond him. Lior ducked out of sight of her behind a building, just to be safe, and looked the way he had come. There was no sign of anyone there—or had he seen, just for a moment, a black robe vanishing out of sight behind the edge of the tavern?

So. There was someone else out here. Someone the Nightblade was hunting. And if they were her enemy, they might be his ally. Mayhap it was even a Shade. That might be a good thing—if Lior could find and kill the Nightblade first. Then he could turn her over to his brethren with no waiting, and be a triumphant hero before the night's end.

He *must* kill her.

Glancing back out, Lior was surprised to see the Nightblade clambering down off the roof. She slipped back into the alley behind the tavern and out of his view. Quickly he ran to the corner of the building.

He was just in time to see her vanish into the back room, the one that led to the kitchen on one end and the common room on the other.

Lior brought his knife out from beneath his cloak and made for the tavern's back door.

* * *

"He went this way!" whispered Theren, leading them on.

Ebon hobbled after her as fast as he could, the pain from his bruises flaring. "Slow down, Theren," he gasped. "I am going as fast as I can."

"Our prey is moving faster," she quipped. But she dropped her pace.

"Something happened at the tavern," said Kalem. The boy peered into the night, where by dim torchlight they could see a small group gathered in an alleyway, staring down at something.

"Nothing to do with us," said Theren.

"Yes, but—" Kalem stopped in his tracks, his skin going Elf-white. "Dark below," he gasped. "Someone has been murdered."

Ebon's blood ran cold as he stopped at Kalem's side. Even Theren skidded to a halt at that. "What? Who?" she said.

"How am I supposed to know?" said Kalem. "But the crowd parted for a moment and . . . I saw the body . . . and blood . . ."

For the first time that night, Theren looked hesitant. "We will lose the thin man if we do not keep going," she said. But she no longer sounded exasperated with them. It sounded more like she was considering that such an action might be wise.

Yet Ebon was now caught up in the chase. He wanted to know what had been on the map they found, and there was only one way to learn. "Let us catch up to him then," he said, pressing on.

Theren shrugged and took his arm to help him increase his pace. Kalem followed only a moment later.

They just caught the flash of the thin man's cloak as it vanished around the edge of the tavern. But by the time they rounded the corner themselves, he had vanished. The narrow gap between the buildings was empty. Ahead, the alley turned left and right, but the way forwards was blocked.

"Which way?" said Ebon breathlessly.

"We can only guess," said Theren. "At least we have half a chance—some people never get that in all their lives."

"Mayhap he went back to the tavern," said Kalem.

"That seems foolish, what with the commotion now," said Theren. "Come."

They ran to the alley's split and peered left and right. Almost immediately, they saw that the left-hand way ended abruptly less than twenty paces down. There were doors leading into some of the other buildings, but no way back out to the street.

"It looks as if he went to the tavern after all," said Ebon. "The back door, then."

"Let us catch him before he escapes through the front," said Theren.

"But what if he doubles back once more?" said Kalem.

Theren gave a growl of frustration. "Fine. You two go to the front of the tavern. I will stay here and make sure he does not escape this way. He shall be trapped."

Ebon nodded. "Come, Kalem."

"But what are we to do if we meet him?" said Kalem.

"You are a wizard!" said Theren. "Capture him!"

"I am only a third-year, and I am a transmuter besides!" said Kalem. "I cannot batter him about with mentalism the way you can, Theren."

"I will be right here," said Theren. "If it comes to a fight, throw your mists and scream. I will come in at once."

"Come *on,*" said Ebon, seizing Kalem's arm and dragging him towards the front of the tavern.

* * *

Loren burst through the tavern's back room into the main room, nearly mad with frustration. Every time she had checked the dagger so far, it had pointed towards the inn. She wanted to keep it out of its sheath so she could keep a constant eye on the shifting designs, but that would be tantamount to suicide.

The wizard must know Loren was hunting them. They were playing a sort of cat-and-mouse game, with she pursuing the wizard around and through the building, over and over again. But though she was supposed to be the hunter, Loren had the disquieting notion that the wizard was toying with *her* instead.

The main room was empty. Everyone was still outside, clustered around the body of the poor barman. Loren could see the crowd moving through the narrow shutters. She was alone in the tavern.

An animal, frustrated sound ripped from her throat. She ran to the front door and threw it open. The street was empty, but she could see a small group running towards the tavern. One of them wore red leather armor. A constable, come to investigate the murder.

Loren had to leave before they got here. But she could not—*would* not—leave while there was still a chance to find the wizard.

She drew the dagger and looked at its designs beneath her cloak. They were almost still now. The magic had nearly worn off. But they pointed north again—towards the tavern.

And then, even as she watched, the designs stopped moving. And, too, the magestone she had eaten faded away. The night was dark again.

Her magic was gone. But the wizard was still here. Still close.

She had just been in the tavern. It was empty. Her night vision had gone, and she dared not take the time to fish out another magestone. The wizard would escape in moments, if they had not already.

Without a second thought, she pelted around the tavern towards the back alley.

FIVE

Mako watched as Ebon and Kalem slipped into the tavern's back door, leaving Theren behind. Just a moment ago, the thin man had gone in ahead of them, and before him, the girl in the black cloak.

"What in the dark below is going on?" said Talib, appearing beside him as if by magic.

He would have grinned if he were not so confused, if he did not feel so helpless. Talib often tried to surprise him, but he always heard her coming. His senses had help, of course, help that few people knew about, much less had access to.

"I wish I knew," said Mako. And unlike most things he said, it was the truth. He was lost in the dark, the way he had been all those years ago, before the visions started. It seemed clear to him that the threads of fate—the same forces that granted him the magesight—had drawn all these people to this place, on this night. But for what purpose? And what role was he meant to play in it all?

Another thought struck him. "Why are you here?" he asked Talib. "You were supposed to see to Ebon's safety."

"He got away from me," said Talib. "Not far, of course, but enough that I had to come up here to find him again. Do you want me to follow him into the tavern? It is mostly empty, now. He will see me."

"No," said Mako. "I will follow him. But I need you to draw off the girl." He pointed at Theren.

"Draw her off?" said Talib, raising an eyebrow.

"No killing," said Mako, and this time he did allow himself to grin. "Just get her out of sight of the tavern so I can enter it unseen."

"As you say," said Talib, moving off at once. He watched as she dropped to the alley and ran around the side of the tavern. Soon Mako heard the crash of a shattering window, and Theren's head jerked towards the noise.

"Who is there?" she called out.

Foolish girl, said Mako. *You should learn to be a bit quieter.*

Talib dashed across the alley. Torchlight illuminated her for only a moment before she plunged into darkness again.

"Stop!" said Theren. "Ebon! Kalem! I have him!" She pelted off after Talib.

Him? thought Mako. Then he smiled. Theren thought Talib had been the thin man. It was too perfect.

He dropped to the ground, ready to enter the tavern and find Kalem and Ebon there.

Boots slapped on cobblestone, making Mako halt.

The girl in the black cloak came flying into view from the other side of the tavern, thirty paces away. She spotted him in the darkness and skidded to a halt.

"You!" she cried, thrusting a finger in Mako's direction. "Wizard!"

Her eyes glowed at him in the darkness. That peculiar glow. Like magelight, but different.

New.

Frightening.

Mako had his hood up. She would not see his smile. This was an opportunity too good to pass up. Ebon and the thin man in the tavern could wait. He would kill the girl now, quickly, and wipe that worry from his mind. It seemed that, despite all his confusion, the dreamsight had put him right where he wanted to be.

And then the dreamsight took him, and he froze.

The girl still stood there, her finger still outstretched. But time seemed to freeze, and another, ghostly image of the girl stepped forwards, leaving her body behind. She walked straight up to Mako and stopped a pace away, staring at him with those hateful, glowing green eyes. But now the eyes seemed . . . older, somehow. As if they had seen great suffering, or had become windows to a soul that had itself suffered greatly.

"I thought you knew what you wanted, Mako," said the ghostly girl.

"I . . . I do," said Mako.

"Then sheathe your blade somewhere other than my flesh," she said. "I am the Nightblade, and our time is not yet."

"Then . . . then what do I do?" said Mako.

"Leave here, before I see your face clearly," said the girl. "And you might want to look after Ebon. He needs saving, and soon."

The dreamsight vanished, and the world returned to normal. The girl was no longer frozen, but running towards him at full speed.

Mako turned and vanished into the shadows of the alley. Not a trick of the dreamsight, but one borne of long practice using the secret techniques of the Drayden assassins. As soon as he was far beyond the girl's reach, he turned and doubled back towards the tavern, looking for an open window.

* * *

Lior crept through the back of the tavern and into the main room. The Nightblade was nowhere to be seen.

He ran towards the front door, thinking she must have gone hurtling into the street beyond. But he stopped at the last second.

What if it was a trick?

He turned and stalked around the room, knife in his hand. One by one, he peered beneath the tables. She was not hiding under any of them. His frustration mounting, Lior turned and made for the front door to the street once again.

But then one final thought struck him.

Lior looked at the bar.

Slowly, step by step, he approached it.

Did he hear the scuffle of a boot, just out of sight? Or was it his imagination?

His palms had begun to sweat. He tightened his grip on the knife.

Lior leaped around the bar's edge, holding his blade high.

Nothing.

"Dark below," he muttered. He turned, ready to run for the front door. She might have gotten away from him already, but dark take him if he would not at least try to—

The front door shot open. Acting on instinct, Lior threw himself to the ground behind the bar. Above him was a window, shuttered but unlatched. The shock of his landing sent the shutter swinging open, baring the tavern to the cool night air.

Two people entered the tavern. Lior heard the soft sounds of shoes, not the heavy clumping of boots. He froze. Not the Nightblade, then? Or mayhap she had a companion now?

Then the voices spoke, and Lior heard two young boys.

"Where is he?" said one of them.

"How am I supposed to know? I do not even want to be here!" said the other, who sounded much younger—little more than a child.

"Well, come on," said the first voice. "We saw him enter the back room. Mayhap he is still there."

Lior, who had been about to rise, froze.

They were talking about him. They must be.

Were they Shades, come to kill him at last? But how could they be? They sounded far too young.

And yet, the voices sounded somehow familiar . . .

"I want answers," said the first boy. "Come—he is likely in the back room."

"We should go," said the second boy. "Who cares about the map anyway? It could be anything—or nothing. Let us put it from our minds."

The map.

It came to Lior in a flash. When the map had been stolen, the wizards had flooded his room with mist so that he could not see their faces. But he could hear their voices, muffled by the mists though they were. And two of those voices were the same two in the tavern with him now.

His hand tightened on the knife again.

The Nightblade might have evaded him. But the thieves would not. Whether or not this earned him forgiveness from the Shades was irrelevant. He owed his former brethren this much, at least.

Lior tensed, preparing to launch himself from hiding. From the sound of their footsteps, they were almost to the back room. He would surprise them there.

A sharp tap came at the open windowsill above him. Lior looked up.

In the window was the face of a man Lior had never seen before, shaved bald and scarred. The man gave a cruel sneer.

Then his hand flicked forth, and a dagger flew through the air to plunge into Lior's throat.

Blood poured out over his fingers as he clutched the weapon. He tried to scream, but he could not make a sound. In the tavern, he could hear the door to the back room swing open and then shut again. The boys—the spies of the High King—were gone. There was only the cruel face of the man, seeming to hover in the air above him, smiling as Lior died.

Then nothing.

* * *

Loren came to a halt at last, doubling over in the darkness. Her breath burned in her lungs, and the stitch in her side felt painful enough to make her faint.

Whoever she had pursued down the alley was gone. She did not know exactly how they had slipped away from her—and they might not have at all, if she had had a moment to eat another magestone—but she had lost the trail some time ago, and had only kept running in some vague hope of stumbling upon them again in the darkness.

If she were being honest, she was not even sure she had been chasing the right person. The wizard's hair that she had found had been pale blonde. She had not seen the hair of the person she chased.

But if they were not the wizard, why would they run from her?

Then again, why *would* the wizard run from her? They would have no reason to know who she was.

She balled her fists in frustration. It was over now in any case. The magic in her dagger was gone, and she had no more hair to burn. Her little nighttime adventure was over, and she was bone-achingly tired. For the first time that evening, she could not wait to return to the palace and go back to bed.

But as she turned her staggering steps west towards the palace, she paused for a moment and looked back. Whether the wizard had been the one fleeing from her or not, they *were* still in the city. And that meant the Shades had not given up their pursuit of her, or their efforts to strike against the High King.

Mayhap the Nightblade could still do something about that.

Loren continued towards the palace, striding with fresh purpose.

* * *

Mako watched as the children reunited in the alley behind the tavern again. Their voices floated up on the air to reach him where he stood at the roof's edge.

"Where were you?" said Ebon.

"The man burst out of one of the tavern's windows," said Theren. "I chased him for several streets, but he got away from me in the end."

"Are you sure it was him?" said Ebon.

"Of course not," said Theren. "It is dark. But whether it was him or not, he is no longer here."

"Then tonight was just a waste, and we nearly got ourselves killed for no reason," complained Kalem.

"Oh, please," said Theren. "When were you in danger?"

"Well, someone was," said Kalem sullenly. "That poor barman."

"For all we know, that was a drunken fight and nothing more," said Theren.

"Come, friends," said Ebon, shoulders sagging. "I am about ready to collapse. Let us go home."

Theren and Kalem raised Ebon's arms over their shoulders and helped him off down the street. Mako watched them go. Just before they had vanished around the corner and out of sight, Talib appeared at his side.

"A good night's work," said Mako.

"You ended the threat?" said Talib.

"I did."

"Then, yes. A good night's work."

Mako glanced at her. "But still more work to be done."

Talib arched the brow over her good eye. "Now?"

He smiled, answering the unasked question. "In the morning. And it is not a job for you, yet. Why? Do you need to rest?"

Her mouth twisted, hiding something. A smile? A snarl? He could rarely tell with her, something he enjoyed immensely.

"What is this new task?" she asked.

"I said it was not for you. But mayhap it will be, someday."

Talib shook her head. "Very well then. I *will* rest, if you have nothing else for me."

Mako waved her off. She slipped away into the shadows, vanishing into the night.

He turned back to the alley, to the place where he and the girl had glimpsed each other, but only briefly.

His new task could not be given to Talib. Not until he understood it better himself. It was time to reach out to his many, many contacts across Underrealm and learn everything he could about the Nightblade.

The Night of Two Kings

Rhea Newton

ONE

Nayala of the family Uchawi did not know that scholars would later call it—rather poetically—the Night of Ink and Daggers. Nor did she realize that she would one day be known as the last Wizard King. But as the High King's messenger stood in her hall and read the proclamation, she knew one thing above all else: that her life, as well as the lives of all the people in Underrealm, would soon change forever.

Twilight poured through the stained-glass windows of the throne room. Nayala ran her fingers over the gilded ornamentation of her armrest as she basked in the soft evening glow. She liked the way it felt: cold to the touch, but with the promise of something more.

She paid only the slightest attention to the messenger as he read from his parchment. "In this time and for the preservation of the Nine Kingdoms of Underrealm, I do note: that the black stones of power, which are the Magestones, have brought to all my kingdoms only fear and death in these Dark Wars."

Nayala scoffed. She could barely help herself. The High King Andriana the Fearless was ever the hotheaded firemage. An absolutist who possessed not even the slightest whisper of imagination, she could see no use for the stones beyond what her dark flames would touch.

"That the wizards seated upon each of the nine thrones, who are the Wizard Kings, have grown in their greed until they have consumed everything in their hunger."

Andriana was the woman whose negligence had cost Nayala her husband's life. And yet she had such nerve.

"That even now, I myself, who am the High King, feel the insatiable desire for the crystals of power, and that I fear what that desire may yet lead me to do."

Look not upon where your desire might lead, thought Nayala, half wishing that Andriana were here now. *Look rather upon where it has already led. Look upon the countless who have died in your self-righteous crusades against the magestones.*

The messenger who stood before her continued to regurgitate Andriana's rambling decree, which took a good paragraph to reinforce to the potential reader or listener the exact authority of the High King's throne, which had come "in succession unending since High King Roth," and to which "all other kings must kneel."

". . . From this day forth, no wizard shall sit upon any throne in Underrealm."

Nayala went to pick at the stub of her left arm, but stopped herself at the last moment. Bitter memories flooded back, but she pushed them to the back of her mind.

"That any wizard who shall try is a vile traitor, and shall be put to death by any servant of the High King."

Her face grew hard, and her right eye—the blind one—twitched. *The stones will not suffer a dreamer to be High King.*

"That from this day forth, no wizard shall eat the stones of power. That any wizard who shall try is a thrice-cursed abomination, and shall be put to death by any servant of the High King."

Nayala allowed herself a raising of the eyebrows, for even the most composed of kings would have reason to balk at such a sentence. She had expected the decree, of course. But she had not expected it to be so . . . emotive. Andriana the Fearless, champion of the people, grand negotiator and legendary mediator of the dark, terrible wars. What a farce.

"That the nine kings of Underrealm shall abdicate their thrones immediately, for they are all of them wizards, and that is now unlawful."

The king saw her chance.

"This is unthinkable!" She shot to her feet. The High King's lackeys reached for their weapons. "I will hear no more of this drivel!"

The messenger fell into silence, fear creeping across his face. All around them, Nayala's palatial guards levelled their spears at the High King's soldiers, while the court wizards shifted uncomfortably. All except for Uthandi, who stood perfectly still.

"The nine kings of Underrealm shall abdicate their thrones immediately? Andriana the Fearless, indeed. Andriana the Foolish, I would name her. The mere thought of this is an insult to the law."

There were murmurs of agreement in the court. Many of the wizards nodded along with her.

"I will hear no more. Begone." She waved a hand at the procession and sat back down.

"I b-beg forgiveness, Your Grace," stuttered the emissary, "but I was told—"

"I have no doubt as to what you were told," said Nayala. "I do not care. You may leave that message with me."

Silence. Everyone looked to the short young man in the middle of the room, who still stood with the paper in front of him, ready to read from it.

"I cannot," he said, after a long moment. "Forgive me, Your Grace, but I am required to read to you the decree, in its entirety, as many times as is necessary for you to understand it, and then I am to dispose of it."

Nayala did not answer. In her mind, she saw the corpse of her beloved Ranneith, twisted and marred beyond recognition by the blackstone. She recalled the vacuous apology signed in the name of Andriana, whose incompetence was the sole reason for his death. And she wondered how the High King had the gall to call *her* the abomination.

She reached out to the metal of her armrest. The dragon's head was cold and lifeless, and yet so full of potential. Her thoughts reached out to the metal, and found it. In her mind, the gold began to soften and melt, as she molded it to her liking. Her eyes glowed a deep black as the magic worked.

"Allow me to reiterate," she said, coolly, as she focused on the task before her. The solid dragon's head became wet and malleable, and she lifted her hand away from the surface, coaxing it to follow her. "You will leave the decree with me. You will place it at my dais, and then you and your friends will remove yourselves from my palace. You will then leave Feldemar immediately, on pain of death."

She shaped the metal as a potter would, spinning it through her hands until its grooves and notches fit her fingers perfectly, and the metal shaft became a handle.

"You will return to Andriana, the Fearless, and you will tell her exactly this: Feldemar spits on her so-called decree. Her thinly-veiled plan to consolidate power for her weakling son will fail."

The end of the metal she turned into a point, and where it broke from her throne the end became sharp and dangerous.

"Her attempt to control the stones to sate her own hunger will also fail."

Lastly, she reached *into* the metal and changed its very arrangement. The soft and malleable gold hardened, and as she willed it, turned to steel.

"Her audacity will not be forgotten. Moreover, it will not be forgiven."

She balanced the dagger on her fingertip. The dragon's head still adorned its hilt.

"Even a High King must answer to her subjects. Tell her all of that, just as I have said it."

She drew her arm back dramatically, as if to throw the dagger. The procession ducked in anticipation, and someone screamed, but she only laughed and threw it to the floor. Her laughter died as quickly as it had come.

"Get out of my throne room," she said.

The messenger looked nervously around, as if counting the number of guards. He knew that to disobey would be to die. And so he relinquished the parchment, placing it delicately on the floor before him as he backed away.

"Your Grace," he said, quietly, as he bowed and shuffled out of the room.

Nayala glanced at Uthandi, who still stood near the back of the room, watching. The younger woman shrugged when she caught the king looking, as if to say that she was only mildly impressed.

The court broke out into hushed chatter as soon as the High King's man had left. Nayala allowed them to have their moment while she went over everything in her head. Next on the agenda . . .

A much taller man, clad entirely in long green robes and with a hood obscuring his face, entered the room. The Yerrin walked slowly, but fearlessly, much surer of himself than the previous petitioner had been. When he reached the foot of Nayala's dais, he went down to one knee.

"My king," he said. Behind him, a gaggle of servants carried a large lockbox, which they placed carefully on the floor at his side. "Your shipment has arrived."

She gestured to a pair of her guards, who took the box away to secure it in her personal chambers. She caught Uthandi eyeing the box as it disappeared, and thought for a moment that she saw the hunger in the young girl's eyes.

Or mayhap it was just the sunset.

"Rise, Yerrin," she said.

The man stood, but he kept his face hidden.

"The man who passed you on the way out—the High King's courier—do you have any idea as to why he was here?"

The Yerrin gave a slow, almost imperceptible shake of his head. "No, Your Grace." His expression remained still as stone.

Liar, she thought to herself. *You have barely been here a minute, and already you are lying to me.*

"Would you like me to tell you?"

To his credit, the man paused only slightly. "That is for Your Grace to decide."

"He came bearing a decree. This decree is still there in front of you. It comes from the High King Andriana, whose throne came to her in succession unending since High King Roth, and to whom all other kings must kneel, and so on and so forth. Most importantly—most interestingly—the so-called Fearless Decree expressly forbids the use of magestones, the sitting of any wizard upon any throne, whosoever they are, and orders the immediate abdication of all the nine kings regnant. Yes, quite interesting, would you not say?"

"I would say, Your Grace, that this is quite the development, yes."

"And would you also say, my dear friend, that your family had any information about this decree, beyond what you have heard from me today?"

There was another long silence. That was the question he had been waiting for, no doubt, and yet was in no position to answer. Especially not before the entire court.

"I would say, Your Grace, that our family has heard of this decree—very recently—and that we are aware of its implications."

She weighed that in her head for a moment. He showed a surprising amount of honesty. And yet, the throne room was hardly the place to spill all of Yerrin's secrets. Besides that, no one could be allowed to know about her hidden advantage.

"I see that we must speak in private," she said, rising from her one-armed throne. "Come with me, and bring that parchment. The sun is almost set, so I will not be seeing any further petitioners today regardless."

Her majordomo bowed to her in acknowledgement. The rest of the court began to mutter and murmur once again, but they were soon behind her.

Nayala allowed herself one last glimpse at the sunset on her way out. She smiled inwardly, even as darkness fell upon her kingdom.

TWO

The king and the merchant found their way, very slowly, to the back of the palace. Unlike many visitors, he did not compliment its finery or comment on her accoutrements, which said something about the company that he was accustomed to keeping. Rather, they kept to an awkward silence, punctuated only by the clacking of their footfalls on the bare stone.

And so, it has all come to this, mused Nayala as they walked. *Andriana has made her move, the family Yerrin has made theirs. And now it is my turn. Justice, at last.*

After many flights of stairs and long hallways, they came to Nayala's chambers, which were among the highest in the city. She dismissed her guards and invited her guest into the room, noticing the glint of a finely-crafted weapon at his hip as he passed. She repressed a smile and went over to open her balcony door. The cool night's air blew in gently, and with it floated the sounds and smells of the city. Though he tried to hide it, even the Yerrin seemed impressed with the view.

Far, far below, Dahab lay outspread before them. A sprawl of ancient buildings reached from north to south and east to west, an ancient, glittering, unplanned mess of city that never failed to impress. The city's lanterns and fires—small orange pinpricks from up here—carpeted the sprawl, creating a vast swath of lights that joined together to form a soft, flickering glow. The color crept up the side of the mountains whose shadow Dahab occupied, bathing them in its warm, pleasant light. In the distance, somewhere amidst the peaks, the moonslight cast itself upon the spray at the water's edge, where the largest river of Feldemar met the abyss. Where the moonslight met the waterfall, its surface twinkled brightly, so that it seemed a thousand brilliant diamonds were tumbling endlessly from the precipice.

Nayala stood and drank it in for a moment. Having the view was important. It reminded her what she fought for.

"Do you like it?"

The Yerrin did not answer, but she saw the corner of his mouth turning upwards in something akin to a smile.

"Of course you do." She circled the table in the center of the room, picking up a slender bottle and two glasses. "Calentin wine. Will you have some?" She poured without waiting for an answer.

"You do me a great honor," he said, all courtesy and no feeling. He picked up his drink and brought it to his mouth, but barely a sip of the liquid passed his lips.

"Will you take down your hood now? And will you tell me your name?"

He hesitated.

"I recognize you. Ibo, mayhap? Or was it Mebana?"

"We have many names," he said. "It is in the interest of privacy. Today, you may call me Zunala."

"I have not met a Yerrin named Zunala before. But I have seen your face, though you try to hide it. You were not Zunala the last time I saw you."

"I was not," he admitted, slowly taking down the hood.

"Very well. Though I am not sure why you must insist on these anonyms. There are only so many of you running around, as much as you wish that were not true. Only so many faces to memorize. What purpose does a false identity serve, here in my chambers?"

"It is protocol."

"Of course."

There was a soft click as the door opened behind Zunala. Uthandi stepped through and closed it behind her, carefully.

"Your Grace," she said, content to ignore the merchant, who seemed rather bemused. By the look on his face he expected Nayala to say something and admonish her servant. The poor sod had no idea who she was.

"I expect that you have more to say to me, which could not be said outside," said the king, as if nothing had happened. "Now that we are well away from prying ears, I would hear it."

"There is a message," said Zunala, carefully, "but I cannot . . . while she is here, that is, I can say nothing."

Uthandi waited patiently by the door, eyes trained on the merchant. In her hand, Nayala spied a shimmer of light reflecting off of a smooth, dark surface. She smiled and carried on. "A message from the Patron, I suppose? I hope?"

"As I said . . . it is not for her ears."

"From the Patron, then," said Nayala. "No one else is quite so paranoid."

Zunala looked lost. "I do not know what you hope to gain by this interrogation, but I have nothing to say to you while others can hear. If you know him so well, then you will understand that perfectly."

"I do," said Nayala, tilting her head slightly so that Uthandi could see. "That is why I am sorry."

Zunala took a step backwards immediately. He turned on his heels, but Uthandi already had the stone between her teeth.

"You would not harm me!" he cried. "You would not dare!"

Nayala seized her opportunity, and plucked the dagger from its sheath at his hip while his back was turned. Uthandi's eyes flashed with power before turning a deep black. "Stop," she said, calm as could be.

The Yerrin twitched suddenly, as if his body tried to resist her. But Uthandi's mindwyrd would not be so easily broken.

"Now you will answer any and all questions that Her Grace asks of you. Truthfully, and to the fullest extent. Do you understand?"

He nodded.

"Good. Turn and face your king."

Zunala turned sluggishly and faced Nayala once more. His eyes were blank, as if he had been dead for hours. In his hand he still held the glass of wine, but limply, as though he was not even aware of it. She stifled her discomfort.

Frightful magic, she thought to herself, carefully placing the anti-magic dagger on her bedside table.

"We shall lead with the most important question," said Nayala. "What do you—no, what does the Patron know of the Fearless Decree?"

There was a pause as the gears in Zunala's mind began to turn. Basic cognitive abilities came with difficulty when under the influence, it seemed.

"The Patron . . . the Patron struck a deal. He struck a deal with the High King. I do not know the details. Only that his price was high. He was happy. He managed to extort a great deal from her. In exchange for support . . ."

There was a sharp whistling sound as Nayala sucked air through her teeth.

"The Decree will not jeopardize the family," Zunala went on. "Andriana has given him a promise. A compromise. And when the Patron has what he needs from Andriana, he plans to move against her too. Everything else . . . is in the text."

"Just as I thought," said Nayala. Uthandi caught her attention from across the room, eyebrows raised. "How long is it that you have been plotting this?"

"The High King's first messenger came almost a full month ago."

Nayala went over to her dresser and took out a rolled-up parchment, its edges torn and frayed from overuse. She unrolled it and held it up to him. "Is this the first message you received?"

His eyes slowly scanned the words. "I did not see this message. I do not know the answer to your question."

"The messenger, then. A woman of Selvan. Bleached hair, but with black roots. Do you remember her?"

A small pause. Then, recognition dawned on Zunala, clear as day. He could not even try to hide it. "I do. It was her."

"Good." She moved over to the table and held the paper over the flame of a small candle. It was dry, and burned quickly. "Did you see her again?"

"No. Every time, a different courier."

"How many?"

"I do not know. I saw three, but there were . . . there were certainly more. The Patron spoke of them. They were . . . they were always well guarded."

We missed so many of them.

"What is the Patron's plan for the Wizard Kings?"

"He . . . he has not decided. Each is a different problem to unravel."

"What of me?"

"You are dangerous. More so than most. You were to be eliminated." Fear clutched her heart. Though she had survived so many attempts on her life, it always chilled her to hear of another. "The Patron fears you. You have a secret. A power. Something . . . or someone . . . that he does not understand."

Nayala could not help but smile. Uthandi, too, resisted a smirk. It did not bode well that the Patron knew of her. But as of yet, he did not know enough for it to matter.

"Why? Why dispose of the Wizard Kings, and willingly give up the trade, when he has become so rich already?"

"I do not know. I only follow his orders."

"And what do you do, specifically?"

"I carry messages. But by spoken word only, and only one at a time."

"And you had a message for me, did you not?"

"I did."

"And?"

Silence.

"Answer her." Uthandi's voice was cold and steely. Zunala's body jerked when she spoke.

"She . . . she did not ask a question!"

"What was the message?" said Nayala, growing frustrated.

"I . . . I was to give you one warning. Leave Feldemar. Do not return. The family . . . the family will not follow you. Abdicate, and you may yet live out your twilight years in peace."

Nayala scoffed. "I have heard enough."

Uthandi bowed low, and then addressed her slave. "Look at me. Good. In a moment you will leave. You will forget what happened here. All you will remember is that you came here, delivered your message, and left. The king was taken aback, but did not deign to give you an answer. You left, having carried out your task."

"Wait," interrupted Nayala. "Tell him that I agreed to the demand. That I will leave Feldemar, as long as the family continues to supply me with enough stones to stave off the madness."

Uthandi nodded. "As she said. The king agreed to your demands, with her one condition: that she retains the right to buy from you. Most importantly, you did not see me, and you do not know me. You will not remember my face, my voice, or my name."

Zunala nodded lethargically.

"And do not forget your dagger," Nayala added, bringing the weapon over and holding it out for him.

"Take it, and begone," said Uthandi.

The man did as he was bid, with only a small moment of confusion when his fingers closed around the hilt. He then ambled towards the exit, opened it with some difficulty, and disappeared into the hallway, shaking his head as if trying to forget a bad dream. Uthandi closed the door behind him.

"Run the bath," said Nayala. She was staring out the window, trying to judge the time of night by the position of the moons. "We must make our move. Tonight."

THREE

The Wizard King allowed the stress to flow out of her, dissipating into the warm water like a lover's sudor.

She closed her eye.

Her mind floated away, taking all of her burdens with it, whilst her body sank lower into the water. Somewhere in the darkness, Uthandi was undressing.

Nayala waited, allowing herself to feel nothing, see nothing, and hear nothing—except for the soft patter of bare feet on the cold stone floor.

She savored the quiet. The brass bathtub shifted ever so slightly as Uthandi put her weight on its side. Then came the sound of the water parting, and she felt ripples lap at her body. She felt the touch—a hand on her leg, ever so soft, ever so delicate.

She exhaled.

Another hand brushed past her shoulder, as Uthandi gripped the lip of the tub for support, while the first slid down Nayala's leg, finding its way beneath the water to her inner thigh. She felt Uthandi's weight bear down on the tub as the girl leaned forwards. Coarse hair brushed against her nose as the apprentice dipped her head. For one long, grueling moment, there was nothing.

She inhaled.

The pleasure struck her like a lightning bolt.

The king smiled, opened her eye, and stroked the top of her apprentice's head.

"Uthandi," she said. "Do you know where we are headed tonight, my girl?"

Uthandi stopped and looked up, a devilish smile on her lips as she continued her ministrations. "The Yerrin stronghold, Your Grace. Where else?"

The elder wizard fought to keep her voice in check. "And what, pray tell, would be our purpose at such a place?"

Uthandi tilted her head to the side as her grin widened. "I believe, in no uncertain terms, that Her Grace intends to seize the Yerrins and their assets at her earliest convenience. A strike to their heart, if you will."

Nayala was not in the habit of keeping people around based on their good looks alone.

"And how do you figure that?" She made sure to speak slowly, to not trip up on any of her words as the younger woman worked her magic beneath the water. It was imperative that Uthandi knew who was in control.

"You have been waiting for an opportunity," said Uthandi. Her words were punctuated by short pauses, in which she made certain not to shirk from her other duties while she spoke. "That man, that message, they were your opportunity. You knew for weeks that the Decree would be coming. And you knew that the Yerrins would sell you out. The courier we intercepted did not know enough, and so you needed to be sure. Today you received not only confirmation of your fears but, even better, a chance to let your enemies think that they had won. When he returns, he will tell them what they wish to hear. Mayhap, with luck, they will let their guard down. And then . . ."

Nayala writhed suddenly underneath her apprentice's touch. Water went soaring out of the tub as the king arched her back and bucked her hips. Uthandi had most surely timed that deliberately.

Nayala pushed her apprentice away from her, and the woman tumbled backwards with a large splash. Her grin had not faded.

"And then what?" cried Nayala, her voice loud and demanding as she stood up in the tub. She wove her hand through Uthandi's hair and used it to guide her forwards.

"And then . . ." whispered Uthandi, her breath tickling Nayala's thighs, "your Grace shall pounce. Strike like a jaguar, seize the stones, round up the Yerrins when they least expect it."

Nayala gave her the last little tug that she needed. The girl knew what was required of her. "Oh, what a sharp mind you have, Uthandi. So clever, are you not? After all, who would attack and betray their oldest allies because of some foreign High King?"

"Who indeed?" Uthandi was too busy to provide a more detailed response.

"But . . ." continued Nayala, "do you really believe that the Yerrins would be so easily fooled? Uthandi? Uthandi?"

As much as Uthandi might have wanted to answer, she could not, and Nayala knew it. She coaxed the girl on, her grip on the beautiful locks tightening as her body grew tenser.

"Do you think they would not have defenses, secret tunnels, escape routes?" she said through clenched teeth. "In case I had tried to attack earlier, in case I had gotten too greedy? Do you think that over so many years of dealing with one another . . . that we do not know one another? That they would not expect me to attack them?"

Nayala relaxed her arm for a moment, allowing Uthandi time to breathe—and to speak.

"Not at all, Your Grace," she said. The smug smile had returned.

"The warning was not a warning, but a provocation. They expect me to storm the mansions. It will be exactly what they are waiting for."

Uthandi looked up at her in silence. She wore a strange look on her face. Reverence, Nayala might have called it. Awe? Or was it . . . love?

"They will join the High King," said Uthandi, breaking the silence. "The greed of the Wizard Kings will have gone too far. And you will be the unwitting catalyst for their sudden change of heart."

Nayala grinned. "Exactly."

Uthandi smiled and went to continue her job, but the king stopped her short, sure that she would be unable to endure any longer. She pulled on the girl's hair and forced her head upwards so that she could stare into those pretty brown eyes.

"I shall ask you again, Uthandi. What do you believe I intend to do?"

Uthandi lifted a hand to her mistress' leg and began to stroke again, casting her eyes downwards so as to avoid Nayala's glare.

"I believe," she said, her voice barely a whisper, "that you intend to strike at their heart, as I said. Because . . . while the Yerrins may expect you, they could not possibly know of your true plan. A frontal assault would be foolish, and they hope that you would be so reckless, or mayhap blinded by anger. But you have something secret. A hidden power that they do not understand. The reason the Patron fears you so."

"And what is my hidden power?" breathed the king, lowering herself back into the water to sit level with Uthandi. "What is my secret?"

Their lips drew closer as they egged each other on, knowing that the end of their game was approaching. Nayala felt her body tingle at the thought of it.

"Your secret," said Uthandi. "Your simple apprentice. Your loyal handmaiden. A beggar you plucked from the streets." She dropped her voice to a whisper once more. "A mindmage."

Nayala took a deep breath. Her hand played with Uthandi's hair restlessly.

The younger woman savored the silence with a proud grin. "Me."

They kissed like first-time lovers—rough and full of lust—their bodies afire with the tension of their teasing. Their passion threw water from the tub, until they decided to relocate to the bed, where the handmaiden dutifully brought their lovers' game to its fiery conclusion.

It was late by the time they left the bedchambers, clad all in black and silent as the night.

FOUR

The estate of the family Yerrin was a sight to behold, even by the light of the sister moons. There was not one, nor two, but three towering mansions, with a high wall around the compound, a guard on every watchtower and two at every entrance. Palatial grounds that looked better suited to a Dorsean warrior king than to a merchant family—a splendor wrapped in brutality. Or perhaps it was the other way around.

Ages had passed since the building of this place. Many said it was as old as Dahab itself, which would certainly be an achievement to aspire to. But with age came a certain sense of familiarity, and with familiarity came vulnerability. Nayala had dealt with the family Yerrin since she was barely a teenager, and over time, they had a developed a sort of mutual admiration. In time, they had learned many things about her, just as she had learned things about them. Things which included the weaknesses in their defenses, both real and perceived.

Here, in the alley behind a shop where the rain pooled into puddles and rats scurried in the darkness, there was a crack in the wall. Not a literal crack, mind you—the wall here was as well-maintained as ever—

but a chink in the metaphorical armor of the family Yerrin. There were no towers on either side that provided a view of this area of the streets, thanks to the overhang of the butcher's shop next door. Nayala also knew that on the other side of this wall was another blind spot, as well as at the back door to the main house, not a stone's throw away from the wall itself.

Nayala put her palm to the granite. The darkness fled for a brief moment as the king's eye glowed with her power. A mere breath later, the whoosh of rushing water sounded in the backstreets. A small section of the wall dissolved into liquid and joined a puddle on the cobbles. A simple enough task for a master alchemist, but only the first of many.

The two wizards inched forwards in silence. Nayala looked left, Uthandi right. No one was on the other side. They edged through the hole, checking twice and then thrice for a lookout. There was no one. Quick and silent as mice, they sprinted to one of the main building's back doors.

Nayala reached it first, sliding up and gently twisting the knob. Though of course, it was locked.

She glanced at Uthandi, who shrugged.

"Did you expect it to be open?" whispered the mindmage.

"I must use magic again," muttered Nayala. "Too much evidence."

She reached for her powers again, looking down to cover the flash from her eye as the lock melted in her hands. There would be no replacing that one. A wall was easy, but a working mechanism was far too time-consuming to get right. Whatever happened, the Yerrins would know someone had been here.

The door swung open. All that remained of the handle and lock was a hole, dripping with molten brass. They did not even bother to try and close it.

Nayala lowered her voice to a whisper. "I thought mayhap . . . mayhap they would have no need for a locked door at the—"

Voices from around the corner cut her off mid-sentence. She dove into a nearby empty room, dragging Uthandi with her.

"Do you believe that his plan will succeed?" said one of the voices. "It seems ambitious, even for him."

"It seems drastic," replied the other. "I agree with you. But it would only be temporary. The Patron fears for his safety while the war is yet undecided."

"The war?" whispered Uthandi.

"Hist," replied Nayala, still straining to hear the rest of the conversation.

"Yes, exactly. Dahab is not safe," continued the voice.

There was a pause. Nayala thought that maybe the guards had gone out of earshot.

"He is not in Yewamba" was the next thing she heard.

Then there was only silence. The two wizards waited a long while, to be safe.

Not in Yewamba, thought Nayala. She had heard of such a place before—the hidden fortress of the family Yerrin. But she had never found it. *If not there, then where?*

"They *are* afraid of you," said Uthandi, eventually. Nayala could hear the smile in her voice.

"Mayhap. Or mayhap it is merely the uncertainty they fear, as any good merchant should. Regardless, there will be time to brag later. Oh . . . what I would not give to be a weremage now. But I suppose this will have to do."

The dark and empty room shone with magelight for a brief moment as she worked her powers. Their robes of midnight black burst with color as pigments appeared where they had not been before, and the darkness melted away to reveal a deep green. At the same time, the cloth became more ragged and rough as she willed the expensive artisan cotton to change itself. When she was finished, both wizards wore rough spun linen cloaks of Yerrin's green.

"Now walk close to me. Keep your head up, and look the guards in the eyes."

There was a rustle of clothing as Uthandi nodded in the darkness.

"And remember that we are here to capture as many of them alive as we can. If they have an inkling of what might be happening . . . well, they would burn this place to the ground and all the stones with it before they would allow us to take another step."

Nayala led the way. She had been here many times before. They strode down the hallways, holding to the old maxim that most people rarely troubled someone who looked as if they knew what they were doing. They sought someone to interrogate, but it was difficult when everyone seemed to travel in pairs, and the two wizards soon found themselves lost in the upper stories of the mansion.

"We shall just have to take two," whispered Uthandi.

"No," Nayala replied. "It is too risky."

"There is no other recourse. I am more than capable of it. Allow me only to show you."

Nayala grunted, but did not say any more.

They cornered two men guarding an out-of-the way bedroom—probably containing somebody who was at least somewhat important. The corridors up here were slightly narrower, with fewer rooms and thus fewer people to contend with. The views, on the other hand, were extraordinary. There were many open doors and empty rooms, which the two wizards made sure to glance over as they came down the hallway. But the guards must have sensed their strange behavior.

"Do you seek something?" said the taller one. "Or someone?"

"Ah yes," said Uthandi, "please be calm, we will not take long."

There was some apprehension on the man's face, but it vanished almost instantaneously. Uthandi's eyes had already turned to deep black.

"I will simply be asking you some questions, and you will answer them," she continued, casually, in case anyone else was listening in. The guard nodded, almost absentmindedly. "Firstly: whom are you guarding?"

Both men glanced at the door at the end of the corridor. "Annaya," said the shorter one. "She sleeps."

"Annaya?" said Nayala. "The Patron's own sister? Why would she be here, and not in the master suite? She is usually the one to oversee this entire compound."

Of course, the Yerrins were not bound to Nayala's will, and so were content to stare at her blankly until Uthandi stepped in.

"Why does she sleep here, and not in the master suite?" asked Uthandi, with admirable patience.

Four eyes turned back to her. "Because the Patron occupies the master suite," said the taller one.

"No," whispered Nayala. "No, that cannot be."

Uthandi also dropped her voice to whisper. "They are mindwyrded, Your Grace. They cannot lie."

"Then they are mistaken. Surely you understand how risky it would be, Uthandi, to have the most important person in the family staying in Dahab, the night after they provoked me with their sham warning?"

Uthandi looked troubled. The two guards continued staring lifelessly at their master. "I do," she said. "But . . . how—or mayhap more importantly, why—would they be mistaken?"

"Ask them how they know that the Patron is in there."

She nodded, turning back to face her thralls. "How do you know that the Patron is here? Have you seen him?"

Both nodded. The taller one spoke first. "He arrived a few days ago. I saw him with my own eyes."

"I, too."

Nayala shook her head in disbelief. Had they truly been so careless?

"I take it that you know what must be done now, my friend?" she said.

Uthandi grinned. "To the master suite, Your Grace?"

FIVE

Unexpectedly, the master suite was no more guarded than Annaya's room, with only two sentries posted in the corridor. Far fewer than the Patron was wont to employ. Mayhap it was to avoid attention. Or mayhap there were more within.

"How do we get in?" asked Uthandi.

"We will have to kill them," the king replied, "one way or another. I could create an entrance to the room from another direction, but they would surely hear their master's cry for help, and we cannot take the chance that he is sleeping or otherwise indisposed. They will never leave their post, no matter what distraction we create, for they know that such a negligence would be their last. And if we are to kill them, we must do it quietly."

Uthandi inched to the corner and looked down the corridor, smiling. "If I may, Your Grace, I should be able to control them, however briefly."

Nayala gave her an uncertain look. "And what will you do with them?"

The girl slipped around the corner without waiting for permission. "As you said. They must be taken care of."

The guards turned when they saw Uthandi approaching. They

clearly did not suspect that she was up to anything suspicious, merely passing through. That would prove to be their undoing, as they did not have time to call for help by the time Uthandi's eyes began to glow.

"Freeze. You—kill him. Quietly, with your knife. You—stay where you are and do not make a sound."

Nayala watched as the Yerrin whom Uthandi had addressed mindlessly lifted her dagger to her compatriot's exposed throat. She buried her weapon up to its hilt in his neck before ripping it out with a forceful yank. Though Nayala wanted to close her eye or look away, she could not seem to tear herself from the carnage. Blood spilled over the hallway's finery as the guard went down with a gurgle and a few muted coughs. Uthandi made sure to catch and steady him so that he did not make a thud when he landed.

"And now, turn the blade upon yourself."

The woman obeyed, and cut her own throat without a second thought.

Nayala shuddered. Uthandi, drenched in blood, looked back at her. To her credit, the younger wizard did not look at all happy with herself. *It is the first time she has done anything like that*, thought Nayala, as she emerged from behind the corner. "Are you all right?" said Nayala, stepping carefully over the bodies, both of which were still twitching.

Uthandi closed her eyes for a moment and breathed deeply. "Let us continue," she said. Her earlier confidence had vanished.

"Very well," said Nayala. "We must move quickly now. There may be more guards inside. Are you sure you are ready? Good. On my mark. Three. Two. One. Go!"

They burst into the room, hoping to take its occupants by surprise. There were only two, but the first, a bodyguard no doubt, had his sword ready. His eyes quickly fixed on the corpses in the hallway, and then shifted back to the wizards.

"Do not shout!" cried Uthandi. "And put your weapon down."

The guard looked confused for a moment, but he kept hold of his blade. Nayala hurriedly closed the door behind them. At the other side of the room, a tall, bald man leaned casually against the doorframe to the balcony and puffed on his pipe. He wore expensive clothes, all in green of course, despite how garish the color looked on him.

He always did have a terrible fashion sense, thought Nayala.

The mindmage's eyes flashed again. "Do you hear me? Put the sword down. Now."

"Is there a need to be so rude, madam?" said the Patron with a smirk. "He is only performing his duties, after all, to protect me."

The fire in Uthandi's eyes died suddenly, and she looked to her king in confusion. Nayala had no answers for her, of course, but she was adept at getting them.

"What a surprise to see you here, Muwi," she said, hoping the use of his real name might irk him. He showed no such displeasure.

"I could say the same to you, Your Grace," the Patron replied. "I must say I did not expect to see you in my bedroom tonight. But had I known you were so eager for my love—"

"—Silence, Muwi—"

"—I might have slipped into something more comfortable."

"I did not come here to play at words."

"It must be so lonely for you at night, now that Ranneith is—"

"Enough!" cried Nayala, "or I will kill you here and now."

He subsided with a sneer. She was not proud that she was so easy to enrage, but nothing was so sensitive as the topic of her late husband.

"Then again," continued Muwi, as if nothing had happened, "This one is rather pretty, is she not?"

Uthandi glared at him from across the room and visibly tensed her fists. She took a half-step forward, but had a sword leveled at her face before she could go any farther.

Something was wrong. The Patron, even during his worst bouts of anger, had never been so crude.

"No more games," said Nayala, flatly. "We are both here, whether we expected it or not. Let us talk."

The Patron sighed and closed the balcony doors before walking over to sit in an elaborate hide armchair near to the two women. He gestured for Nayala to sit in the one opposite.

He would never normally allow me so close. He knows I can kill him in an instant if I can only touch him.

"I will stand," she said, her mind whirling. "If it is all the same to you."

"It is," he said, waving a hand. He poured three glasses of wine and began to quaff his own. "Suit yourself."

It is a trap, she concluded. Everything she had seen and heard over the night now made sense. Even now, there were probably more soldiers on their way. She took a moment to probe the room with her magic. No enchantments—that was good. She did not have long.

"Why are you supporting Andriana?" she asked.

The Patron let loose a cocky laugh. "Straight to the point, I see."

"If we could get straight to the answer, that—"

"Because she made us an offer. A good offer. Good business demands that one weigh all of one's opportunities, even those that at first glance seem unworkable or drastic."

I could have figured that out without you.

"Are you going to elaborate?" asked Nayala. "Or must we resort to mindwyrd?"

"Try it, and your friend's tongue will be on the floor before she can give a command," said the bodyguard, gruffly.

"Again you threaten me," said Muwi with a sneer. "Could you for once conduct yourself with a little decency, as befits a woman of your title?"

He is wasting your time on purpose, Nayala told herself.

Uthandi tried her magic again, but the guard took a step forwards immediately. "Drop it!" she commanded. "Now! Before—"

She stopped as soon as the point of the blade touched her throat.

"Before what?" jeered the bodyguard.

"Enough!" cried Nayala once more. She took a moment to study the swordsman. A long cloak to hide a magic-proof dagger. No flash of metal from anywhere she could see. He was far more careful than Zunala had been. "We are all of us adults, so let us conduct ourselves appropriately. Tell your dog to stay himself and I will do the same."

They want me to stay, she thought. *They will not risk us fleeing.* She studied Muwi's figure, trying to pick out the location of his own dagger, but she could not see it.

After a pause, the Patron nodded to his guardian, who reluctantly lowered his sword. Uthandi remained motionless, but Nayala saw that she still seethed in silence.

"Why change sides?" said Nayala quickly. "Why now?"

"Andriana promised a great deal. There is nothing to be said about the details, but it will suffice to tell you that the family will continue, as will the trade. For one thing, all Yerrins shall be exempt when it comes to the new law, in perpetuity."

"I wonder how long that will truly last," said Nayala.

"Long enough. I am no fool, I trust you realize. No self-respecting businessman believes decrees from any kingdom which mention eternity. Time is endless, yes, but we are not. But besides that . . . she has given us considerable degrees of influence over the selection of the new kings, so that we might expand our reach across the nine lands. Certain kingdoms are of particular importance, of course."

"*Certain* kingdoms?" asked Nayala.

"Yes," said the Patron with another uncharacteristic smile, "but you need not worry about that. None of it matters anyway. In your eyes, we have betrayed you, and nothing I say will change that."

"You *have* betrayed me," said Nayala, pretending to care.

"This is business, Nayala. This is the modern world. I am sorry to be the one to tell you, but there is no authority but coin in today's world, and no kings but those who own it."

Nayala smiled. "I know that," she said, "I have always known that. I understand completely. I am not even vexed. You should know that about me, Muwi—I find it easy to expect the worst. And you *would* know that, if you were who you appear."

The Patron faltered. Fear began to creep across his ugly face.

"But you are not Muwi," she continued, "because Muwi would never invite me to sit at the same table as him. He would never have so few guards at his door. He would never allow me to use his real name so brazenly. And besides all that, he would never use mine."

"Your Grace!" cried Uthandi. "More guards!"

Nayala had heard the clamor of footsteps already.

"Make sure he survives!" she shouted, pointing at the false Patron, who was now slinking ever lower into his seat.

She threw herself to the floor.

SIX

A SCORE OF SOLDIERS BURST INTO THE ROOM.

The floorboards went up in a puff of smoke.

All of them fell, the Patron still clinging to his armchair. A chorus of shouts and screams went up as they plummeted and hit the next floor only a heartbeat later. There was a cacophony of breaking planks and smashing pots. Paper flew into the air from splintered scroll bins and shattered writing desks. The people in the room were crushed before they could do so much as scream.

The next floor gave way without a second thought. A whirlwind of furniture and bodies—and corpses—fell farther. Nayala felt herself slowing as the shower of wood and paper continued to fall around her.

Uthandi had grabbed on to her mistress and was now easing their fall with the power of her mentalism. At the same time, she catapulted objects into the floors below them at unnatural speeds, causing each level to shatter in turn.

Soon the wreckage came to an end, as the large bulk of people and household furnishings landed in a kitchen on the ground floor. A moment later, the wizards glided to the ground, followed by the false

Patron in his armchair. Uthandi set him down gently in front of Nayala, who smiled mischievously.

When he saw her, he began to babble.

"N-no, please! I am sorry! It was not my idea! He set me up to it! They both did! I-I was just following orders! P-please!"

As he yelled, his body began to change and his eyes shone with a brilliant light. Where he had once been bald, hair grew suddenly into long, tangled curls. His cheeks thinned, and his form grew smaller. When the transformation ended, a woman's face stared back at Nayala.

"There you are," said the king. "Not merely a look-alike, but a weremage." Without hesitation, she retrieved a sword from a nearby body and held it to the frightened woman's throat. "Where is he? Where is Muwi?"

The weremage only tried to cower from the blade, despite Nayala's firm grip on her collar. "I cannot—I cannot say! He will do worse things to me than you ever could."

Do they think me incapable of torture? Nayala did not like it, true, but when circumstance demanded . . .

Another thought came to her just in time.

"Uthandi," she said, calmly, "mindwyrd. She has transformed—that is to say, she used her powers. She does not have a dagger."

The prisoner's eyes went wide. "No!" she cried, but her eyes glazed over soon after.

"Answer the question," said Uthandi. "Where is Muwi?"

"Hedgemond," came the reply.

Hedgemond? Up until that moment it had been inconceivable to Nayala that the Yerrins would want anything to do with that frigid southern wasteland.

"Why?" said Nayala.

"Answer her questions too," said Uthandi.

"He is in hiding," said the weremage. "I do not know what from. Mayhap he believes there is a storm to come."

"Where in Hedgemond?" asked Nayala.

"The Lasanach family castle—Bann Karan. Near Moinna."

Nayala mulled the names over in her head. They meant nothing to her.

A few of the guards groaned. One tried to stand. Uthandi kicked him hard enough to knock him over again. "We should leave, Your Grace," she said.

“Tell her to forget that we spoke after the fall,” said Nayala, “and then we shall leave.”

SEVEN

A FEW HOURS LATER, NAYALA AND UTHANDI SAT FAR ABOVE DAHAB, upon the slopes of the Dahabajo, whence tumbled the sparkling waters of the Habajo falls. Dawn had come, and the sun was already high in the air, casting its rays down upon Dahab, the aptly named Jewel of the North, which responded in kind with a dazzling display of light reflected from the golden trim of its buildings. The city shone like a diamond, even more so than at night. The spray from the falls refracted the sunlight, painting a small rainbow that arched from one cliff face to another.

Nayala liked to go here to think. It had a view that rivaled the one from her bedroom, but without the feeling that she was being watched. As an added bonus, the only noise that anyone could hear this far up was the endless rushing of the water as it cascaded over the edge of the falls.

She had never brought Uthandi here, and the girl seemed almost uncomfortable, as if she were invading a sacred place. Her eyes darted about uneasily.

"I have come to a decision, Uthandi." In truth, Nayala had done so long ago, but recent events now spurred her to act.

"What is your will, Your Grace?"

"Firstly . . . you need not call me that anymore."

"I . . . I understand. You honor me with your friendship, Nayala, I will not—"

"No. I mean . . . what I mean to say is: I am leaving Dahab."

The girl's eyes went wide. "That is hardly something to jest about."

"It is no jest."

"But . . . the legacy . . . Feldemar. The other Wizard Kings!"

"I am not giving up the fight. Feldemar will be in safe hands. My legacy too, I hope. I shall be forthright with you and save you some time. You are my successor, Uthandi. You have been trained to be my successor since I found you, and I think you knew that. You are dear to me, for that reason, and many others. You will lead Feldemar once I am gone. As its king—rightfully, and with my blessing. I must go south, to Hedgemond. I will find the Patron—the real one—and root him out of his hole. If he will not help us in this fight, then I will take his family's stones for myself. Our stockpile will not last forever."

"Allow me to go. You can stay and rule, I will find that weasel and—"

"No. I am getting old, Uthandi, and it is time I moved on. But after today, I can be secure in the knowledge that my kingdom is finally in safe hands. Mayhap . . . mayhap I could convince Andriana . . . we were friends once. But whatever happens, this decree must be resisted. Do you understand? Else it will be the end of us both."

The younger woman nodded with fervor. But still she looked lost, even scared. "I . . . I do not know that I can do it without you."

Nayala took her into an embrace. She had never done that before—it had always seemed too intimate. "You will do fine, Uthandi, my . . ."

What were they, really? Lovers? Friends? Words like that could not adequately describe their bond. And yet . . . for all her charms, Uthandi still could not hold a candle to her beloved Ranneith.

". . . my friend," Nayala continued after an uneasy pause. "Better than fine. You may even do as well as I."

Uthandi chuckled, though it was half-hearted.

After another moment, she spoke. "I would do anything for you, Nayala."

There was a long pause.

"I aim to leave soon," said Nayala, quietly. "I shall leave orders with the generals and the court. You will be crowned immediately. Today, if possible. And Uthandi . . . if I do not return . . ."

"You will," said Uthandi.

"If I do not, then you must continue the fight."

The younger woman nodded fervently, but Nayala's thoughts were already elsewhere.

The weremage's words echoed in her mind. *The Lasanach family castle—Bann Karan. Near Moinna.*

Hedgemond, she mused. *The Yerrins are hiding in Hedgemond, of all places.*

Why?

Nayala did not know. But she was determined to unravel the mystery. Even if it were to send her across the world; even if it would take centuries to find the answer.

And in the end, it did.

A Night on the Seat

Eric Ugland

ONE

The night was heavy, seemingly weighing down the Seat itself. Walls were slick with ice, a white blanket of snow hid the streets, and the clouds were low across the horizon. The air was calm, the lack of wind mayhap the saving grace of the night. Otherwise the chill would have been deadly. As it was, the city seemed to have snuggled deeper under its covers, hiding from the outside world. The streets, even at this hour, would normally have some measure of bustle, those who worked nights moving to and from their jobs. But on this evening, none but the foolish braved the elements. Few ventured out of doors, and then only to make short trips.

Horace Stubhart leaned against a wall, the only guard in his patrol who was willing to weather the weather. His two companions huddled in the hut, sitting around the lonely brazier. Both were from warmer climes, and as the snow had settled around the Seat, they had urged their new Heddish friend to take over some of their patrols. Horace knocked on the window, and the other two guards looked up, their faces clearly showing their misery. Arnaud, the veteran guard, shooed Horace away, indicating it was time for a patrol. For the briefest of moments, Horace wondered if being forced to do all the snow patrols was some sort of hazing, since he was still new to the city guard.

Horace put his truncheon to his head in an informal salute, then whistled a tuneless little ditty and began his stroll along the patrol route. He twirled his truncheon around in a double loop, passing the baton over his right wrist before catching it with his left hand. His grandfather would have been able to do three loops with his eyes closed. Horace often practiced the flashy moves his grandfather had taught him, but no matter how often he tried, he just could not seem to match the old man. Horace came from a long line of guards, though most had been within his home of Hedgemond. Horace was the first to take the extreme step of moving out of the homeland. He had grown tired of being compared to his uncles, brothers, sisters, aunts, cousins, and especially grandfather. A whole host of Stubharts guarded Hedgemond from tip to tail, and in Hedgemond, he was just one more Stubhart guard. But after hearing tales of the High King, her intelligence, her grace, and her loyalty to her subjects, he had to take a chance for something greater. He had to go for a new dream. He was going to be one of the royal guards.

But on this night, at the height of winter, he was just keeping the streets of his new city safe. Making sure doors were locked and lights were out. Chasing away vagabonds and, quite often lately, dealing with drunkards. He found the city big, amazing, and surprisingly endearing, and had quickly come to feel like the city was his. After the attack on the Seat, there were plenty of reasons for people to drink. To forget those they lost. To rejoice in their survival, or even to celebrate a paying job. Drinking often led to brawls in the streets. And once the drunks were out of the tavern, they were the responsibility of the guard. Most evenings, Horace could bet on a full wagon to the drunk tank.

The street lamps struggled against the swirling snow. Horace, feeling confident, tried the triple loop. In his effort to land it, he overextended. The baton brushed against his outstretched fingers and tumbled across the ground. Horace cursed as he tripped over a hidden, uneven cobblestone.

He crashed to the snow in an ungainly sprawl, his armor jingling and jangling. The freezing feeling of snow spread all across his face, as well as an unpleasant wetness as the meltwater seeped into the nooks and crannies of his body. His truncheon bounced across the street and disappeared into a small pile of snow up against a local haberdashery.

Horace got up, shook himself off, wished his fellow guards would grow some fortitude, and trudged into the shadows to pick up his baton. He brushed it off and checked it for nicks and bends. All clear. He felt it was important to keep his appearance as impeccable as possible. He was, after all, an extension of the Seat, and thus, in a rather roundabout fashion, of the High King herself.

A young urchin giggled at him and, when Horace smiled and bowed just a little, the child darted off down an alley. Horace hoped the kid had a warm fire to get to, and he made a mental note to check the alley on his next patrol, just to make sure they weren't still there. Frozen. Horace shuddered. Despite having no children of his own, and having little experience with children, he had a soft spot for them. He rarely punished a child if he could help it, often finding himself in more trouble because of that inclination.

Out of an alley, mayhap twenty paces in front of Horace and on the other side of the street, a young woman scurried with her cloak pulled tight around her. She had tucked her head low under a cowl.

Horace held fast in the darkness for a moment before following. There wasn't a curfew in place, so there was certainly nothing illegal about midnight perambulations. There were plenty of reasons for a person to be out and about in the snow, and yet, Horace felt the urge to tail the hooded figure.

Clearly she had a purpose. And given her occasional furtive looks, chances were that she was engaged in something devious. *How* devious was up for debate. Mayhap she was going from her house to a meeting of traitorous rebel scum planning another invasion. Or it might be someone who'd been taking advantage of all the newly empty homes on the Seat, and her cloak was full of pilfered goods. Regardless, following the woman might just let Horace learn more about the city. And Horace needed such an opportunity. He'd only been here a short time. Mayhap he had just stumbled onto a lucky break.

Horace kept his pace, staying behind the young woman and watching what she did in the snowy street. She had nice boots on, reminding Horace of nobles back in Hedgemond. There wasn't any one particular thing that stood out about the woman's clothes, but the quality of them read as moneyed. They were clearly tailored specifically for her, not just picked out of a stall on market day. And something else, which mayhap only guards were keen to pick up on: he heard the telltale *thwock* of a sheathed blade bumping against a thigh as it hung low off a belt.

A noble out for stroll in the snow at night, thought Horace. Normally he would have gone about his way, continuing on his more typical patrol route. Pass by a number of taverns, make sure the owners weren't having trouble with any of their patrons. This soon after the invasion, the High Seat was still full of workers and tradesmen from outside the city. Most were there to help, nearly all there to work. But some were more interested in making trouble by trying to get a few free drinks from the locals. Recently, a missive had come down from command to be on the lookout for troublemakers in the taverns. But now, with the snow swirling around and making Horace feel like he was back in Hedgemond, he decided he'd rather follow a mysterious woman.

Horace followed her past taverns and homes until they got to a large, walled home sitting separate from the others. The home of someone very wealthy, large and imposing, with ornate balconies and battlements. It almost seemed like a small castle within the city. Grandiose ornamentation belied the residence's fortifications and defensive capabilities.

He looked blankly at the heraldry and cursed himself for not having learned more of it since arriving to the city. Granted, it had been a frenetic time; he'd been forced to jump into the relief effort, arriving when he had. He had come just after the violent invasion of the city. Lucky for him, because the city guard had hired him immediately. And throwing in with the relief effort would look good on the day Horace attempted to make it into the royal guard. There were already citizens who smiled and gave him thanks regularly for his assistance. But it had been exhausting work.

Horace hung back in the shadows, thinking, mayhap, there was an answer. Mayhap this woman was a member of this house, just returning home.

But the woman did not enter the home. She did not knock on the door, nor did she appear to have a key to the building, nor did she want to be seen by the guards, who most certainly were looking out from the arrow slits around the front door. The woman walked around a single time, keeping to the darkness as much as possible, before choosing a shadowed spot for herself. She pulled her cowl low and edged right up to the building across the street until she almost disappeared. Then she watched.

Horace leaned back in his own shadow, pulling his hood up and over his watch helmet to guard against even the slightest glint from the diffuse lamplight. He gripped his truncheon harder a few times and worked his back muscles. He even did a few small stretches, knowing the aim was always to present the threat of violence rather than the actuality. The soldier was trained to strike first, the guard to strike second. Often it put the guard in a worse position, because the better position would be one of surprise.

The woman stood there waiting for some time, as if she was letting the city settle down around her. Horace felt an internal pull to get back to his patrol. And yet, the hooded woman was too much of a curiosity for him to walk away.

And then the hooded woman walked up to the wall and climbed it.

"Well, that is certainly unexpected," Horace muttered to himself.

He stood watching, eyes a bit wide. He would have bet any amount of coin that the wall was not climbable. It seemed perfectly vertical, the stones set together with the tiniest of gaps. And yet, the woman climbed up with little difficulty. As if she were climbing up a ladder, as if it were absolutely nothing out of the ordinary.

Horace stood in the shadow, mouth agape, wondering whether it was unlawful to climb someone else's wall.

The hooded woman climbed up until her head disappeared under a balcony. She spent a moment or two like that, head hidden from the world, before climbing back down just as easily as she had gone up. Then, as if she had done nothing unusual, the woman strolled across the street and into an alleyway. She leaned back, significantly more relaxed.

Horace tried to scratch his head, an action made impossible by layers of cloth and armor. The climb had been so strange, so clearly dangerous. Had the woman fallen from the balcony, the least injury she could have hoped for would have been broken legs. Also, there were robust shrubberies, roughly three feet high, running along the wall below. Shrubberies that had been trimmed recently and aggressively, leaving them pointed and spiky. If the hooded figure had fallen from her climb, she would have been impaled on the branches below, one of the more ignoble deaths Horace could imagine.

Again, Horace thought about going over and confronting the hooded figure. But the woman hadn't done much of anything except some exceedingly minor trespassing. A thought flitted through his mind that she might be the famed Nightblade he had heard tales about. Tales said she was capable of many fabled things. Mayhap this was some business for the High King. But Horace had also heard the Nightblade was no longer upon the Seat.

There was something off about the wall now. It seemed to be ... well, different. But in what way, Horace couldn't exactly say. *It is entirely possible,* he thought, *that I am merely misremembering the wall's initial appearance.* He wanted to go up and touch it, see if there was something about it he should be aware of. And yet at the same time, he felt that there was more to come. That the night wasn't quite over, and something else was just about to happen. So Horace waited. And he watched, keeping his eye on the woman in the shadows.

The woman, meanwhile, kept looking around. She tapped her fingers on the stone wall next to herself in obvious frustration and impatience. It seemed that someone was missing an appointment with her.

As the night went on and the snow seemed to find a new level of fury, coming down with wild abandon as it attempted to bury the city, the woman in the shadows was suddenly not alone. While she huddled in her cloak, seemingly trying to make herself as small as possible, a newcomer suddenly stood proud beside her. Chest out, shoulders back, striking a pose any time he paused in his movements. Take a step, strike a pose. Look up, strike a pose. Peer around the side of a building, strike a pose. He was statuesque and, especially in the snowstorm, gorgeous.

Horace had to admit, he was somewhat drawn to the man. There was a dashing and almost overwhelmingly charismatic nature to him.

The two in the shadows had a muffled and hurried conversation, one they were intensely engaged in. Horace took advantage of their distraction to sidle across the way until he stood just around the corner from them. He was unable to see them any longer, but he could hear their chatter. The woman appeared to be coaching the other on what to say to a lady.

A bell tolled far off, the sound struggling to pass through the thickened air of the High Seat.

"Darkness below! You should speak for me. I do not have the gift of speech you have." Horace was struck by the depth of the man's voice.

The woman responded, "This is your problem. I am merely assisting you in solving it."

"You told me you would help as I needed!"

"Yes, well, I did not quite anticipate the amount of assistance you would need."

"You must help me."

"I am here, am I not? I have not let you flail about on your own." There was a pause, then a long sigh before her voice continued. "What if I hide in the shadows of the bushes below? You stand in the light, easily visible. Then I can feed you words."

"You will tell me what to say?"

"Yes. Though give me a moment to consider what I might say if I had fathered a child with the sister of my betrothed. It is hardly a situation I have encountered before. Now take off that stupid cloak."

Sounds of movement told Horace they were preparing to go over to the balcony. They would surely see him as soon as they cleared the alley.

He only had one avenue of escape. He darted across the street and slid into the shrubberies beneath the balcony, pushing himself as close up against the wall as possible in an attempt to hide. It gave him the opportunity to look at the wall. Now that he was closer, Horace could see slight indentations all the way up to the bottom of the balcony, as if someone had carved handholds in the past and they had since been weathered smooth. Mayhap climbing the wall was easier than he had initially thought.

Below the balcony nearby stood the good-looking, statuesque man, posing again, quite perfectly lit in the dim lamplight. The hooded woman crouched in the bushes, oddly similar to what Horace was doing.

The statuesque man held his pose for a moment. But then nerves seemed to overcome him, for he looked down at the hooded figure.

"Do not look upon me, she must not know I am here," the hooded figure hissed immediately.

"Ah, right," the statuesque man replied.

"Do not speak to me, either."

"Right. But—"

"Why are you speaking to me? What if she comes out right now? She will know I am here, and our charade is ruined!"

"You are quite astute."

The woman growled in frustration. "Quiet."

Finally, the beautiful man seemed to understand, and only nodded in response.

"I am not supposed to be here, remember?" the woman said. "Just you, to whisper your clumsy excuses up to her balcony until she forgives your transgressions."

"Yes, but—"

"No. Remain quiet unless you are talking to her. You have no means of controlling your voice, you always speak at your very loudest. I whisper. Notice how it is quiet compared to your bellowing?"

The beautiful man smiled broadly and pointed at the hooded figure. "Ah, understood."

"Shut up," the hooded figure snapped. "Stop talking to me. Just stand there and look pretty until she comes out of her damn window."

The statuesque man resumed his proper posture, looking impressive as the snow swirled about him, ruffling his hair just so. For a moment there was no sound except the rustle of snow building upon itself. The night was getting a bit chilly, even for Horace, and he wished he had remained in the guard hut next to the glowing brazier.

Overhead came the soft whine: the complaining hinges of a window that was not often opened.

"Valian, my love," trilled a sweet and melodic voice from above.

The statuesque man looked up immediately. And then he looked over at the neighboring balcony above Horace. Then he looked at the woman in the hood, confused. Clearly, he was in the wrong place.

There was a moment of silent confusion, which was then broken by the sharp sound of ripping right above Horace's head.

He looked up. Instead of the blank darkness of the bottom of the balcony, he saw a pair of white slippers and fluttering fur coming very quickly towards him. A hole had opened in the balcony! However, there was no time to contemplate that.

Horace put his arms out and caught the falling woman. It wasn't quite a clean catch—there was quite a bit of grabbing and balancing and Horace nearly falling to the ground—but at least the woman didn't wind up impaled on any of the sharpened branches below. Immediately Horace regretted his quick reflexes, as his back and arms erupted in the exquisite sort of pain only possible when one caught an adult falling from about ten paces.

Horace set the woman on her feet, and they shared a very perplexed look before glancing upwards. Above, a hole in the balcony fluttered in the slight wind, as if the stone were but fabric.

That must be why they call it flagstone, he thought briefly.

The woman in furs screamed.

The statuesque man shrieked, then pointed at Horace and yelled out, "Betrayer! Rogue!"

Horace, for his part, reached up, pulled his hood back and shouted in response, "City guard! Do not move!"

A slim throwing knife sailed straight towards Horace's face. But the woman in furs pulled him out of the way just enough that the knife sliced along his cheek before disappearing into the snow.

The hooded woman drew her long blade. It shone in the moonslight, clearly either a sword that was used regularly but cared for impeccably, or one that had only ever been oiled and sheathed. The statuesque man had a more garish blade; given its gargantuan girth and profusion of pointy bits, it appeared to have been designed mainly for aesthetics, but it looked quite unwieldy for actual combat.

Horace stepped forwards, placing himself between the swords and the young woman, who was confused, but managed to give dark looks to everyone involved.

"You have placed yourself in the wrong ... er ... place!" shouted Valian, the statuesque man. "Prepare to die!"

Valian reared back and then charged, his actions very clearly telegraphing his intention to chop off Horace's head. And, given the immense power behind the prospective blow, those of all his ancestors as well.

Horace's first move was to draw his own sword. He held no illusions about the truncheon's ability to withstand any sword hits. Horace then feinted a block, but instead ducked and smashed his truncheon into Valian's leg.

The big man dropped to one knee, and Horace took the opportunity to give him a strong kick. Valian slid across the snow and collided headfirst into the wall with an impressive *thunk* befitting the man's seemingly hollow head.

By the time Horace turned back to face the hooded figure, she was moving, blade flashing through the night. Horace barely got his own sword up in time to block, making a great clang.

The woman's eyes turned black. Her hand brushed against him, and Horace's armored sleeve fell to the ground.

"Alchemy," Horace hissed, backpedaling away.

"It is called transmutation," the hooded figure growled.

She attacked again, swiftly closing the gap. Horace had trouble keeping up with her; she clearly had extensive sword training. He, on the other hand, had spent more time with polearms and non-fatal weaponry.

In a momentary pause, Horace drew his truncheon and launched a counterattack. The woman smiled and let the truncheon hit her hand.

The weapon became sand, glittering for a moment in the moonslight before showering harmlessly onto her cloak.

"You are outmatched, guard," she sneered. All her yellow teeth seemed to face in different directions.

"Your breath is more of an attack than your blade," he countered.

The figure yelled and swung, a wild overhanded attack. Horace didn't let himself get drawn in. He jumped back two quick steps, and the woman's blade whistled by.

They traded blows, their blades clanging in the snowy darkness. The cacophony echoed off the stone walls. Horace spun to avoid a particularly wild blow and felt something brush across his back. More of his armor fell to the ground. The good thing was that he felt lighter. The downside was that should the hooded woman manage to touch his skin, there would not be very much left of him. He needed to end the fight soon, or perish.

With a deft twist of her blade, the woman locked their swords together at the hilts, bringing their faces close together. Immediately Horace knew his mistake. Her hand was on top of his own. A feeling unlike anything he had experienced before crept along his skin. A cruel smile spread across her face.

"Now you see why we were kings before," the woman said, suppressing an evil laugh, "and why we will rule over you again."

"Not tonight, alchemist," Horace said, and slammed his head into the woman's nose.

There came a very satisfying crunch, accompanied by a guttural grunt of immense pain. For his part, Horace saw bright flashing lights in his periphery, but the brunt of the blow went into the woman's face, and she tumbled into the snow. Blood streamed from her nose. Before she could react, Horace reared back and delivered a kick straight through her yellowed teeth. She fell on her back, unconscious.

Horace looked down at his wrist where the alchemist had grabbed him. The skin was blackened, but color seemed to be slowly pushing back against it. A unique, all-consuming pain blossomed around the area.

A shout for the city guards came from behind him, and Horace spun to see the woman in furs glaring at him.

Horace took a step her way. A knife appeared in her hand, pointed at his chest.

"Hold fast," she said, "and do not think I cannot take care of myself."

Hands raised, he simply said, "I am with the city guard."

"So it appears," she replied. "But it would seem you were somehow involved in this mess, so forgive me if I do not simply trust you because of your uniform."

Another piece of Horace's mail fell off, a lingering effect of the alchemist's touch.

"Or what is left of it," she added.

"No injuries?" Horace asked.

"Look to yourself."

"I am Horace of the family Stubhart."

"Horse? Your name is Horse?"

"Hor-ace."

"Ha. Not much better. Horse seemed a fitting name for a man your size. I am Ateia of the family Aloysia."

She waited, seemingly expecting some response from Horace.

Horace merely smiled. "Nice to meet you, Ateia of the family Aloysia."

Introductions over, Horace pulled off his remaining armor and inspected it. It was ruined. Most of the back and one entire sleeve were missing. But it had done its job, protecting him from the dangers of the alchemist. He looked over at the cloaked woman bleeding into the snow. His spine crawled with the thought of how close he'd been to a thoroughly unpleasant death.

The beautiful man, Valian, lay unconscious in the snow. His motives were clear: seduce the woman from the house. But what had been the goal of the hooded figure? Clearly the death of the woman played into things. Had the hooded figure hoped to frame Valian for the murder?

The clanking of metal boots rang off the walls as the city guard came thundering down the street, showing up in numbers. They liked to make a show of force whenever called for.

The captain stopped his crew and stood, assessing the situation before him. Horace stood ramrod straight and saluted. The captain saluted in return, and nodded.

"What transpired here?" the captain asked, looking at the two bleeding figures and the woman robed in white fur.

Before Horace could answer, armed men and women flooded from the house, swelling the size of the crowd.

Horace drew the captain aside and, in relative privacy, explained the evening's events, starting with following the hooded woman and ending with fighting the alchemist.

"I may have kicked the woman in the teeth while she was somewhat incapacitated," admitted Horace.

The captain nodded. "She deserved it."

He clapped Horace on the shoulder and told him to rest for a minute, then sent one of his men off to the Mystics. Finally he barked an order to his men to stand Valian up. As soon as Valian was on his feet and starting to come around, an older man who had come out from Aloysia manor walked right up to him.

"What do you have to say for yourself, lordling?"

Valian, of course, was only barely conscious, and slurred out a response that could not be understood.

"You, who have asked for my daughter's hand, come in the middle of the night to woo her sister?"

A young woman, looking quite similar to the girl in the white furs, but a bit homelier, strode up to Valian and launched a vicious slap across his face. It was hard enough that the City Watch moved to restrain her from a follow-up attack. The smack seemed to sober the man, and he took a heartbeat to assess the situation in front of him.

"Milord," he said, addressing the older, bearded man, "this is not what it seems. I was merely—"

"Attempting to take both my daughters at once?"

"Of course not," Valian said. Then there was a pause, and it was almost as if the man's head was spinning inside, thinking. He didn't stop at thinking, though, and the words came forth unfettered. "Is that an option?"

Silence. Then a roar from the father, who swung a heavy cane around and thwacked Valian in the head. Valian dropped to the ground again, and the rest of the family leapt into the fracas. There were threats and curses sent Valian's way, and the city guard were forced to block access to the man. They slapped shackles on his wrists and helped him march away.

The men and women of the house began to surround the woman, Ateia, but she held up her hand.

"Guardsman Stubhart," she called out. "It would appear I owe you my life."

Silence held sway over the area. Several stupid responses flooded Horace's head, and he wasn't sure which one to pick.

"Say something, lad," hissed the captain.

"Just doing my job," Horace spat out.

"Not what I would have gone with," the captain mused ruefully.

The woman walked up to Horace, standing mere fingers from him. "It is not a debt I can lightly forget," she said. "Nor do I think your actions fall within the routine duties of the city guard." She paused for a moment, seeming to enjoy making him squirm. "We shall speak again of this, Guardsman Stubhart, and I will begin to make good a debt I fear I will never be able to fully repay."

She arched up on her tip-toes and kissed Horace on the cheek, giving him one private smile before her women-at-arms surrounded her and escorted her back behind the high walls.

The captain clapped Horace on the shoulder.

"Do you know who you saved?" he asked.

"Uh," Horace stammered, thinking this was somehow a trick question, "Ateia of the family—"

"The most beautiful daughter of one of the wealthiest men of Selvan." A wide smile cleaved the captain's face. "What I would not give to have a favor coming from her."

Horace looked wistfully at the house and wondered how far he might stretch such a favor, and if it might extend into the palace. Could this be his way into the Royal Guard?

"Quite a night, Guardsman," the captain said. "Too bad it is not quite over."

Horace followed the captain's gaze as four men and four women in brilliant red cloaks came tromping through the snow.

"Mystics," Horace said softly.

The captain nodded. "Be on your best behavior," he said. "You do not want to wind up going home with them, now."

The Mystics surrounded the hooded woman, pulling her to her feet and wrapping her quite liberally in a shimmering fabric. It took a moment for Horace to realize it was silk. Six of the Mystics hauled the alchemist away. The other two, a large man with a beard and a young intense woman, came over and stood before the captain of the guard.

"Is this who fought the transmuter?" the bearded man asked, pointing at Horace.

"It is," replied the captain.

"Then if you would excuse us," the bearded man said.

The captain bowed ever so slightly, and got his men moving back to their posts.

"Were you touched by the transmuter?" The bearded man's demeanor was solemn with a touch of concern.

"Yes," Horace answered, and showed his wrist.

The woman took Horace's hand and examined his wrist carefully. Then she closed her eyes, which glowed behind the shut lids, and all the pain disappeared from Horace's wrist.

"You are fortunate," she said. "You would not have lasted much longer against her."

"Please explain what transpired this night," the bearded man asked, in such a way that Horace knew it was actually an order.

For the second time that night, Horace explained what had happened, showing the indentations in the wall and the flapping stonework on the balcony, and picking up the various bits of destroyed armor from the snow. At the end of it, the bearded man nodded.

"A good night's work, guardsman," he said. "Have you ever thought of joining the Mystics?"

"No," Horace replied honestly. "It has yet to cross my mind."

"You should think on it," the man said. "It is not every fighter who can defeat a wizard unaided. Should you want to speak with me about it, you would be welcome at our garrison any time."

Before Horace could muster a response, the bearded man walked off into the snowy night.

Horace was alone again. For a moment he marveled at life at the High Seat, where clearly such events were commonplace. He wanted to shout his love for his new home, but at the last moment he realized it was late at night, and the citizens were sleeping. So he settled for smiling instead.

And then he resumed his patrol. He might be joining the Mystics; he might have met a beautiful woman with connections and riches who now owed him a favor; and he might have nearly died fighting a wizard. His life might have changed fundamentally since he had left the guard hut on patrol.

But he still had the rest of his shift to work. Just another night on the Seat.

THE MAN AND THE SATYR

E.L. DRAYTON

ONE

There was hardly a cloud in the sky as the melodic sound of an older man's voice came from an open window.

The satyr, Tiglak, listened closely.

Tiglak had done this many times before, holding this particular stance and listening intently. Now he watched as the man told his tale to a young girl sitting by a fire, her eyes growing wider as the story progressed. This was not the first time Tiglak had heard a tale spoken from this man's lips, for he had been following the human far longer than he would ever admit to another satyr. Tiglak had even heard this particular tale before, but now he observed the girl's reactions as she heard it for the first time.

He did not know why he chose to linger on this particular night. Mayhap it was the soothing rhythm of the man's voice, as if he were telling a true story and not simply spinning a tale for this young girl's amusement. Or could it have been that a part of Tiglak longed to be the hero in the story? Neither explanation felt right. But he stayed, and he watched, and he listened.

As he leaned closer to hear, his hoof slipped. The bush he was leaning upon rustled. Tiglak immediately ducked his head out of sight. Inside the house, the man stopped speaking.

"Wait!" said the girl sleepily. "You have not finished!" There was a pleading tone in her weary voice. Tiglak tried to calm his heavy breathing as he waited for the man's reply.

"I have tarried for too long," the man said at last. "Rescuing young girls and telling them bedtime stories is not all I am meant to do with my life."

Tiglak relaxed his shoulders and slumped under the window. He could tell from the sound of his voice that the man had not moved from where he sat. There was no cause for concern.

"May I know the name of the man who has kept a foolish girl from being trampled again?" asked the girl through a yawn. Tiglak listened closer and risked peeking through the window. He, too, wished to know the name of the man whose stories had fascinated him for many cycles of the moons.

"I am Albern of the family Telfer," the man answered. But it came too late. The girl's eyes had already begun to close, and a yawn escaped her lips. Tiglak saw Albern smile as he watched her slumber. Tiglak suppressed an entirely different expression. He had borne witness to the hapless girl's lack of attention, and he was not surprised to see how easily she had succumbed to sleep. If it were up to Tiglak, he would have let her be overrun by the horse and carriage the first time she had neglected to look where she was going. That would have been a lesson for her, and other humans like her. If she survived, it was unlikely she would make such an error again. If she was killed—well, one less human in the world would be a blessing to any satyr.

Tiglak continued to watch as Albern surveyed the room, scratching his beard as he searched for something. Finally he took two large steps and grabbed a woven blanket, tattered and stained from years of use and lack of proper washing. He threw it open and laid it upon the slumbering child.

"I am sorry, Isabelle."

Tiglak had never heard him say the girl's name before. For a brief moment, he wondered how Albern knew her. Perhaps it was no coincidence that he had happened to be there to save her from the carriage. Tiglak followed Albern only when he could get away from his clan, which was not as often as he liked.

Tiglak's curiosity lasted just a moment too long, and when he regained focus on the room, he found Albern staring back at him.

"Wait," the girl said suddenly, stopping Albern from rushing through the front door. "Will you come again and finish telling me the story?" She yawned once more.

"Mayhap," said Albern.

Tiglak ducked out of sight. He could feel his heart hammering in his ears. He had been seen! If word of this reached his clan, his fate would be far worse than death. He frantically looked at his surroundings, forgetting how he had come there, unable to focus on the best route for escape.

"I walk the same road every day by the moonslight," she said with a smile.

"If you are lucky, I will be there to save you again. But I would not depend on it. Please, watch where you are going."

Isabelle's answer came in the form of a snort.

Tiglak scurried away, feeling certain that Albern would examine the area when he left. As he ran off, hunched almost double to stay out of sight, he examined the positions of the moons and cursed himself. He was late. Again. Every time he snuck away from his clan to watch Albern and listen to his stories, he risked getting caught. The clan would not understand. Even Tiglak did not know how to explain his fascination with the human. He had told himself many times that it was the stories, not the man, that kept him returning.

He rushed through the forest beyond Isabelle's one-room cottage, towards the mountains that were his home. He never looked back—but if he had, he would have seen Albern squinting through the darkness in his direction.

At long last Tiglak reached his clan's camp. He slowed to a walk and tried to steady his heavy breathing, but the attempt was for naught.

"Tiglak, where have you been?" said a satyr. "You missed another wise teaching from the mighty Gragas. He seeks you now."

The satyr pointed just over Tiglak's shoulder. Tiglak did not need to turn around to know that Gragas was approaching.

"Brother Tiglak," said Gragas. "Why do you avoid me like mud on a mountain?"

The satyrs standing around chuckled at Gragas' words. They may not have fully understood what he meant—most satyrs were quicker to anger than they were to wit, and Gragas spoke in strange, musical words that confounded most of them—but they laughed all the same. Failing to laugh at the mighty Gragas' humor was almost as bad as not attending one of his teachings. Tiglak hated the teachings almost as much as he hated the fact that they happened nearly every day. But what he hated the most was being called "brother" by a satyr he hardly recognized anymore.

"I do not avoid you, Gragas," said Tiglak. "I had a more important thing to do."

The other satyrs gasped and backed away from Tiglak. Nothing could be more important than listening to Gragas' teachings—Gragas himself said so often enough.

Gragas turned to the others and, with a smile on his face that looked more sinister than sincere, he asked them to leave. They scattered quickly, not wanting to incur his wrath. A few even walked backwards, bowing as they went to show their reverence. Tiglak shook his head in disbelief.

"I wish you would not miss my teachings. When you do, it makes me look bad to the others." Gragas placed a hand on Tiglak's shoulder. "We were friends, once. What has happened?"

Tiglak shrugged his hand away. "You do not care how they see you. You only care how you see yourself." He had restrained the words for a long time, and now he was angry.

Tiglak and Gragas had been close friends once. Almost brothers. But then Gragas had started speaking about hearing the voice of someone called the Lord speaking to him. Tiglak had tried to ignore it, but as Gragas grew more and more fervent in his teachings, Tiglak knew his old friend would never return. Gragas had always wanted to be the center of attention, even back when they were younger. But this was something different. Something more. Tiglak had begun spending more time alone, wandering the mountainside and the valley below. It was on one of those wanderings that he had happened across Albern.

"I care what they think," said Gragas. "I care, even if you do not believe me. But then, you do not believe in any of my teachings. You would rather listen to a human's lies than a satyr's truth."

"Why do you say that?" said Tiglak, feeling a surge of panic.

"They tell me you listen to a man, when I teach how we must destroy them. If you do not watch out, brother, your sins will kill you—along with all humans."

Tiglak balled his hands into fists. How could this have happened? Whenever he followed Albern, he made sure no one saw him leave, or followed him down out of the mountains.

"I am tired. When you admit your pretense, I might take your advice." Tiglak did not wait for an answer. Let Gragas try to threaten him. He would never think it was right to trick their clan into following Gragas' teachings blindly, and he could tell the elders were becoming fed up as well. The satyrs were starting to take sides between those who followed the elders, and those who followed Gragas. By blatantly not following Gragas, Tiglak was pledging his allegiance to the elders. And he still had enough faith in them to resist Gragas' influence.

TWO

THE FOLLOWING NIGHT, TIGLAK DID NOT LET GRAGAS' WARNINGS DETER him from seeking out and following Albern again. As soon as the moons appeared in the sky, Tiglak snuck away from the satyr camp.

Once he came out of the mountains, it did not take Tiglak long to find Albern walking along a dirt road shrouded by tall trees. It seemed he was on his way to visit the young girl, Isabelle, once again. Walking the familiar path made Tiglak nervous. If Gragas had indeed been following him, he would be easy to find here. Tiglak almost considered turning back.

But something about Albern's behavior seemed odd to him, and it kept him following along. Albern kept stopping short and looking skywards. Tiglak could not see what the human was looking at, but something told him to keep his distance. The trees managed to block much of the moonslight, leaving them in near darkness and making Tiglak question Albern's every move.

He wondered if Albern knew he was being followed. But that seemed ridiculous. Tiglak knew that satyrs were hunters beyond peer.

No mere human could match him when it came to stealth. It was impossible for Albern to know he was being followed . . . and yet . . .

Albern turned on the spot. "Show yourself."

For the first time, Tiglak noticed the human carried a bow and arrows. Albern had a shaft nocked, his bow perfectly still as he peered into the darkness—away from Tiglak.

Tiglak smiled to himself for his moment of fear. The human had heard something else in the darkness.

Then Albern loosed the arrow. Tiglak heard it sail through the air and strike something in the distance. Above the sound of birds bursting from a nearby tree, Tiglak heard someone groan.

Albern heard it, too. He rushed towards the sound, and Tiglak followed, keeping hidden in the trees. Albern reached the place first. When Tiglak caught up, he found the human scratching his head, looking completely befuddled.

The arrow lay on the ground. Tiglak watched Albern raise it towards a stream of moonslight breaking through the trees to get a better look. Blood dripped from the arrow's point. Albern brought it to his nose and sniffed. Tiglak could smell it from where he stood. The arrow was soaked with the blood of a satyr. Albern looked around, trying to locate where the satyr had run off to.

Tiglak had never known a satyr to travel alone the way he had. He feared there might be more of them, perhaps sent by Gragas to follow him. He knew he should return home and try to explain himself—surely the satyr who had just been shot would tell Gragas what they had seen—but something about this human continued to fascinate him.

Albern crouched near the base of the tree. Tiglak leaned in to get a better look. He could see the ground was hard from recent cold days and nights, but there were still slight indentations of hoofprints in the ground. He recognized them, as did Albern who touched the dirt around the prints. From where he stood, Tiglak could tell the tracks belonged to a full-sized satyr. He could not see in which direction they had gone, but it looked like Albern had an idea. He stood, and Tiglak stood at the same time. Albern scanned the woods, his eyes passing over the place where Tiglak stood, just as he had looked straight at him the night before.

Albern slung his bow across his back, wiped blood from the arrow off on his pant leg, and returned it to his quiver. He lingered for a moment, and Tiglak knew he was listening for the slightest sound of movement. When he was satisfied no one was there, he resumed his walk, moving much faster than he had before.

Tiglak had a harder time remaining unseen while following Albern now. Out of nowhere, the human began to sprint. He would stop short and change directions, then cut back the other way, as if he assumed he was still being followed and was trying to lose whoever it was. At one point, Tiglak heard him laugh out loud, and he found himself doing the same. He had not run like this, hunted like this, stopping on a dime and changing directions, since the days when he and Gragas were young, wild and free.

Once they reached the girl's house, Tiglak was nearly out of breath, but Albern seemed unfazed by the run as he took in a deep breath and beat his chest. Tiglak tried to emulate him, but nearly choked instead. Albern peered through the same window Tiglak had looked through the night before. Tiglak could hear humming coming from within and knew the girl was home. As Albern stepped back, he slipped, rustling the bush beneath the window in much the same way it had happened to Tiglak. Albern's face hardened. Tiglak's heart began to race, and he knew it was not only from the quick pace of his run.

"Who is there?" Isabelle asked, sticking her head out the window. When she saw it was Albern, she smiled and rested her elbows on the sill with her head in her hands. "You can use my front door."

Albern looked at his feet. "I know," he replied. He scuffed his feet on the ground, covering any sign of someone else having been there. Tiglak was relieved, but also confused. Why would Albern have done such a thing? Was it just a coincidence? Could Tiglak truly be so fortunate?

"Is everything all right?" said Isabelle.

Albern hesitated before answering. "Everything is fine. I have come as promised, to finish the story." He walked towards the front door. The girl beat him there, holding it open wide for him to enter. The smile on her face was so large, Tiglak wondered if it was as painful for her as it was for him to look at.

"I was careful this time, walking home," she said. "Not that it mattered. There were hardly any horses this time." Tiglak returned to his usual spot just outside the window, shaking his head again. The girl actually seemed upset with the lack of horses to trample her.

Albern sat in the chair by the fire while the girl resumed her place on the floor in front of him. "Do you remember where I stopped my story?" said Albern.

Suddenly, a rock struck the back of Tiglak's head. It fell to the ground with a thud barely audible to anyone but him. He touched the place where it had hit him and looked at his hand, finding a bit of blood. Looking in the direction it came from, he could clearly see the silhouette of a satyr in the distance, flanked by trees and shadows.

Tiglak knew who it was before he began to walk towards him. Gragas held another rock in his hand, ready to throw it.

"I had hoped for your sake, brother, that the rumors were unfounded."

"I can explain," Tiglak said.

But Gragas slapped Tiglak across the face with the back of his hand, leaving a streak of blood. That was when Tiglak saw the wound; a bandage of large leaves barely covered the hole left by the Albern's arrow.

"You will have to answer to the elders for this," Gragas said.

"Since when do you run to the elders? Can you not handle me yourself? Are we no longer brothers?"

Gragas threw the rock he held at Tiglak's feet. "What would you have me do? Lie? You do not even bear witness to the truth I try to teach."

"Please. Say nothing of this. They will kill me."

Gragas did not respond, his face remaining impassive. Tiglak felt anger surging within him, and he spoke without thinking.

"You do not speak truth. There is no Lord—"

Gragas grabbed Tiglak around the throat and squeezed tightly. "The Lord does not like being denied. Their voice tells me what to do and what will come to pass. The sooner you accept what I am telling you, the happier I will be. You used to want to make me happy, once. What has changed?"

From within the house, Isabelle laughed. Gragas loosened his grip on Tiglak enough for him to find some air. "Mayhap you need convincing?"

Tiglak could see evil in Gragas' eyes. "What do you mean?"

"Let us see who speaks truth. Him," he said, pointing towards the house, "or me." He picked up a rock from the ground with his wounded hand, still dripping blood, and threw it at the front door.

"What are you doing? He will see us. Come!"

Tiglak pulled at Gragas' arm, but Gragas did not budge. The front door opened slowly, and Gragas finally gave in, allowing Tiglak to lead him into the shadows and out of sight.

The door finished opening. Albern's bow appeared first as he stepped out cautiously. From where they were hiding, Tiglak could see the rock Gragas had thrown, illuminated by the light coming from inside. Albern knelt to examine it.

"He sees your blood," Tiglak said, looking at Gragas with anger. He had gone so long without Albern even knowing he existed, and now he might never be able to hear the stories again.

"Who is it?" Isabelle's question carried on the wind. Tiglak could see her in the doorway, standing on tiptoe behind Albern and trying to see over his shoulder. Albern kicked the rock away before she could see it and lowered his bow.

"No one. Must have been the wind." He ushered her back inside and closed the door behind them.

"You are crazy. We could have been killed," Tiglak said.

There was no response. He looked at the spot where Gragas had been standing a moment ago. The other satyr was gone. In the distance, Tiglak saw him sprinting towards the mountains.

Tiglak soon caught up to Gragas, who was older and somewhat hampered by his wound. The run reminded him of when they were both younger, how they would race to see who was the fastest. Gragas had always won. There was something about the way the wind whipped through their hair, the strength of their legs as they dug into the dirt, that gave them both a thrill. They looked at each other briefly and knew a race was on.

Gragas nudged Tiglak, knocking him off balance just enough to take the lead. But Tiglak would not give up so easily. He decided to show off by taking a route with more obstacles in his path. He vaulted over fallen trees and used the strength of his arms to swing from branches, until eventually he found himself side by side with Gragas again. They ran together all the way back to the satyr camp. When they finally came to a complete stop, they were both panting and laughing, trying to catch their breath.

"When the elders sentence you to death, I will bear witness, brother," Gragas said, placing a hand on Tiglak's shoulder.

Tiglak felt as though the ground had vanished beneath his hooves. "But I thought . . ."

"The elders allow me to speak of the teachings of the Lord, and in return I tell them of any satyr who sins. You have sinned. I cannot change that."

"Please. What do you want of me? Name it," Tiglak begged.

Gragas looked to be sure no one was within earshot before he answered. "Help me kill the humans. You will prove to me, to the elders, and the Lord, that you are not a sinner."

Tiglak knew what his answer needed to be, though he did not want to say the words. He remained silent for as long as he could before answering. "I will do as you wish."

"It is not what I wish. It is what the Lord wants," Gragas replied as he pointed up to the sky and winked.

For the first time in a long time, Tiglak hated the mighty Gragas.

THREE

THE NEXT MORNING, TIGLAK FOUND HIMSELF SURROUNDED BY SATYRS, all staring at him. Gragas stood at the center of them, a mischievous smile on his face, carrying his ibex axe. It was his mark of strength, a weapon made from the bones and skull of the largest animal he had hunted in the mountains. The Greatrocks were home to many beasts, but few with horns as massive as those the ibex had. To kill one was to prove not only one's strength, but also one's cunning skill at deception, for the ibex never let humans or satyrs get within striking distance. Tiglak knew he was in for a bad day whenever he saw Gragas carrying his most prized weapon, its stone blade shining as it caught the sunlight, nearly blinding him. Even Tiglak did not own such a weapon; he was barely half the size of a full-grown ibex, and killing a newborn did not yield horns worth making into a weapon.

"Arise, brother. There is work to be done."

The others hooted and hollered with excitement. It was easy to bring them together. All Gragas had to do was promise them entertainment and a bloody outcome.

He tried his best to suppress the sadness he felt. Albern was no friend to him, nor would he ever become one. Yet he did not want to kill the human. He tried to reason with himself that there were other places he could hear stories, but it was no use. He had to admit at last: mayhap it was not just the stories he was fond of, but the person telling them.

Tiglak did a quick headcount and saw that Gragas had managed to round up over a dozen satyrs to join his mission. He recognized many as avid followers of Gragas and his teachings. They would blindly follow him into battle and do nearly anything he asked of them. As they set off into the mountains, Tiglak was able to piece together Gragas' plan from the loose-tongued around him. There was nothing you could tell in confidence to one satyr that would not circulate to the whole clan before moonslight.

Gragas intended to ambush Albern and leave him for other humans to find as a message. He said the Lord wanted humans to know that satyrs were returning to take what was theirs. Gragas was good at getting others to follow him, but when it came to his motives, Tiglak knew none of them came from some fictitious voice. These were Gragas' own desires.

At last they reached a modest human home in the middle of a clearing. Gragas paused at the edge of the trees and motioned for Tiglak to stand beside him. "See if your storyteller is home."

Tiglak looked behind him. The other satyrs remained farther back. Their excitement to attack a human was evident on their faces, but they had never come this close to being seen without the protection of the Greatrocks to use for cover. Tiglak was glad for their distance. He did not want to risk their hearing what he and Gragas discussed.

"How do you know he is in there?" Tiglak knew this was where Albern slept, but he did not think Gragas knew as much as he did.

With a smile on his lips and a twinkle in his eye, Gragas said, "You forget, brother. I have the Lord whispering in my ear. He told me this was where I would find who I was looking for. Why do you not do as I command? Should I tell them of your nighttime adventures?" He looked back at the satyrs, who showed signs of agitation. They wanted to get to the fun part of their outing.

Without a word, Tiglak crept towards the home. He had been here before, but only when the sun had gone away and the moonslight served as his guide. He had observed Albern toiling away on the bows he kept in his home. Once Tiglak had witnessed an exchange of coin for one of the bows, and he assumed this was how the man survived.

Tiglak approached a dirt-covered window and hoped that when he peeked inside, he would not see Albern.

His hopes were dashed when he saw the human standing behind his counter, speaking to three travelers. Albern held out a bow to one of them, who looked at it and shook his head, refusing to even take hold of it.

Tiglak's movement caused a slight shadow along the floor that only Albern saw as it fell just behind the travelers. He glanced quickly at the window. Their eyes met for only a moment, but it was long enough for Tiglak to know he had been seen. He ducked out of sight. His heart raced, and he wondered what he should do. Gragas was watching him closely. Tiglak returned to the group, his mind racing with what he should say.

"Is he there?"

Before Tiglak could answer, the door to Albern's home opened with a bang, making all the satyrs scamper out of sight. The three travelers emerged first. One of them held a map in front of his face. The other two were talking to each other about something Tiglak could not hear. While the travelers' attention was elsewhere, Albern peered at the trees and bushes surrounding his home. He had seen Tiglak for certain.

Finally, the human inspecting the map lowered it enough to show his face. "It appears you are correct. We have no choice but to take the route you suggest." His voice was loud and carried easily to the ears of all the satyrs.

"Taking you will not be a problem," said Albern. "What concerns me is your reluctance to travel with a weapon. The Greatrocks are treacherous, even for the most skilled climbers, and satyrs live there." Albern's voice grew louder, as if trying to communicate his words to more than just the three humans who stood before him. "I never travel unarmed when I wander the mountains."

Gragas nudged Tiglak and led him back to where the other satyrs waited, staying low so as not to be seen.

"We are leaving," Gragas announced. He started back the way they had come.

"Why do we retreat like frightened rabbits?" one of the satyrs asked.

"Brothers, the Lord has spoken to me," Gragas said, holding his arms out with great pomposity, the blade of his axe catching the sunlight. He usually made these grand gestures when purporting to deliver a message direct from the Lord. Tiglak rolled his eyes out of habit, as this was not the first show he had seen Gragas put on. "The Lord is quite pleased with what we have witnessed. Instead of killing just one human, we have the opportunity to take four lives. A sacrifice worthy of the Lord, indeed." Gragas looked directly into Tiglak's eyes to ensure he knew that he meant every word. "Come, brothers. We must return to the Greatrocks. There we will take their lives and secure our freedom."

Gragas and the satyrs walked past Tiglak, who stood stiff as a board. What could he do? He glanced back towards Albern's home, hoping to catch a glimpse of him again, but the humans were nowhere to be seen. Tiglak rejoined the others, trailing behind them the entire way, pretending to be just as excited as they were to kill the humans.

The satyrs began to grow tired of all the walking and complained to each other in whispered tones so Gragas would not hear. This pleased Tiglak, who hoped their frustration would cause them to abandon their mission and return to the clan. Without thinking, Tiglak smiled at the thought of Albern being saved due to the satyrs' tendency to grow bored easily.

Gragas stopped short on the path they traveled. "We are here, brothers."

The others looked around, but they could not tell what was so important about this location.

"There is nothing here but a cave," said Tiglak. "Surely you do not expect the humans to enter it willingly? They know we own these lands. They will avoid this path and the cave." The other satyrs nodded in agreement but stopped when Gragas glared at them.

"The Lord would never leave the destruction of humans to chance," said Gragas. "We must make our own fate. There," Gragas said, pointing his axe towards a ledge just above the mouth of the cave. "When I give the signal, you will push those rocks over the mouth of the cave, trapping the lead human inside with me."

"What about us?" whined one of the satyrs. "We came here to kill, not to help Gragas kill."

"Did you not see that the lead human travels with three others? While I kill the leader, I trust the rest of you to take care of the others."

That satisfied them. The other satyrs all climbed the side of the cave and readied themselves behind the piles of rocks. Tiglak's mind raced. Whatever opportunity he might have to save Albern's life was quickly vanishing.

"How do you expect to get him to follow you in there?"

"Simple, brother." Gragas smiled mischievously. Tiglak had seen this look many times before, usually after Gragas managed to talk Tiglak into doing something he knew was wrong. "You will come with me, and you will lure him in."

"I will not," said Tiglak. Gragas gripped the bone handle of his axe, frustration on his face, but Tiglak went on quickly. "What would the others think if the mighty Gragas required help from another? Did you not say you wanted him all to yourself?"

Gragas paused. It seemed Tiglak had guessed right: Gragas was not willing to lose face in front of the others just so he could use Tiglak as bait. He relaxed his grip on the axe and nodded, letting Tiglak join the others. He positioned himself behind a boulder and waited while Gragas entered the mouth of the cave.

Time wore on. The midday sun began to set. Tiglak thought it was taking Albern and the travelers a long time to reach this part of the path, but he remained silent, as he was secretly glad for the extra time. The satyrs grew bored waiting and fell asleep.

Darkness settled around them when Tiglak finally saw four torches alight in the distance. He knew the time had arrived. Tiglak leaned out to get a better look at just how far away Albern was. His weight caused the boulder to move slightly, giving him an idea. One small push, and it would fall easily. He looked around at the satyrs beside him to make sure they were still asleep.

Tiglak looked towards the sky and closed his eyes, whispering words he thought he would never speak. "Help me, Lord."

And with that, he pushed his boulder forwards.

The other satyrs came awake, assuming they had missed the signal, and did what Tiglak had done. Their own boulders crashed over the mouth of the cave. Within moments, the entrance to the cave was completely blocked, as was the path just below them.

"Where are they?" one of the satyrs near Tiglak asked, looking down at the boulders piled on top of each other.

"There!"

In a mad dash, all of the satyrs began to run towards the torch lights. But Tiglak used his speed and agility to beat them all, reaching

Albern and his party before the others. He did not slow his pace as he drew near, even when he saw Albern reach for his bow and pull an arrow from his quiver. Tiglak managed to grab Albern around the waist and, with all of his might, he lifted the man from the ground. Tiglak fled the scene, leaving the three other travelers behind.

Albern was heavier than he looked, and Tiglak was not so strong. He only made it a few long bounds from where he had grabbed Albern before he had to put him down and catch his breath.

Without hesitation, Albern assumed a battle stance. The bow rose in his grasp, an arrow ready to release. He aimed it directly at Tiglak's heart.

"What do you want, satyr? Why have you been following me?"

Before Tiglak could answer, screams echoed from where the travelers had been left behind. Tiglak and Albern stared in the direction of the sound. Both knew exactly what was happening.

"You . . . saved my life?" Albern asked. "Why?"

"I like your stories," Tiglak answered, speaking rough and tripping over the stupid-sounding human words. He did not know what else to say. He had hardly ever spoken to a human before.

Albern started to speak, but Tiglak held a finger up to his lips to silence him. "Listen," he said.

"I do not hear anything," Albern said.

Tiglak knew the silence meant the satyrs had finished killing the travelers. They would be thirsty for more blood.

"You must leave now. I cannot save you twice."

"Wait. What is your name?"

"I am Tiglak."

Albern extended a hand. Tiglak looked at the human's limb, confused.

"Leave now," he repeated. "And if you are smart, you will not return this way again."

* * *

"It is getting late, and I have important work to tend to in the morning," Albern said, rising slowly to his feet.

"Wait, you cannot go!" said Isabelle. "Finish telling me what happened to Tiglak. Was he killed by the other satyrs for saving your life? What happened to the mighty Gragas and his ibex axe? You cannot go until you tell me how the story ends," Isabelle said, folding her arms and pouting.

Albern smiled at her. Then he looked just past her, towards the window, and winked. The girl thought his wink was directed at her, but Tiglak knew better. "Some stories are never ending."

The Beast Within

Garrett Robinson

ONE

9 Maius, Year of Underrealm 1312

Silvin had not deserved pride in a very long time, and perhaps that was why she could spot it so easily.

The messenger who stepped into the common room of the tavern stood straight, shoulders back, chest out, hands on hips. Eagerly he met the gaze of anyone glancing his way. He wore plain clothes and a dark brown cloak, not the red and silver of their order. But he was a Mystic, and a new one, filled with all the arrogance of the neophyte.

Pride, indeed. Silvin hoped he would soon learn to mask it.

The man spent a few moments surveying the room. He passed over Silvin in the corner and kept looking. It was only when she raised her hand and waved to him that he looked back. His brow furrowed, but he came across the room to sit opposite her.

For a moment they were both silent. Silvin had already studied him plenty, but she let his eyes rove over her now—with appraisal, not desire. That was in stark contrast to many others, for her well-worn pants clung tight to her legs, and her leather jerkin showed a thin strip of pale but well-muscled flesh above the waistline. Her hair was done up in golden braids that wove around her temples and ears, and her light hazel eyes had drawn in many a bedfellow through the years. But where these traits caught the attention of the inn's occupants for one reason, they struck the messenger for quite another. He had likely expected a large warrior, like some figure from legend. That was fine. Silvin was used to such expectations, and they had long amused her.

"Sister Silvin?" he said quietly.

"The very same," she said, brushing a golden braid behind her ear. "I have been expecting you, but I thought not to see you until tomorrow."

"I have ridden hard," said the messenger. "The captain said his message was urgent."

Without meaning to, Silvin sat up a bit straighter. "Your message is from the captain?"

"It is. He passed through Redmond, and when he learned where you had gone, he assumed command of the situation at once."

"Then you had better give me his letter."

The messenger reached into his brown cloak, making no attempt to conceal the motion. Several people in the common room took note, and Silvin muttered a curse. It was not like the captain to employ such indelicate agents. Pickings at Redmond must be even slimmer than usual these days.

Into her hand the messenger placed a small scroll, tied with ribbon and sealed with a wax stamp of the Mystic symbol. Silvin broke the seal and unfurled the parchment.

Sister Silvin,

I have been told what you learned about the boy. I would have come myself rather than send a message, but certain unavoidable matters delayed me, for which I apologize. I should arrive the day after you read this. Normally I would ask you to wait, but time will not permit that.

You must find out for certain where the boy is and gain as much information about our enemies as you can. You know what I suspect about them. We must learn if it is true before we act.

Do not attempt a rescue on your own. There are too many of them to risk it.

Keep yourself safe and whole. And remember, always, to maintain control. I know you can.

The handwriting looked like the captain's hand, but there was no signature. Silvin looked up at the messenger.

"This is from the captain?"

A frown. "It is."

"He did not sign it."

The messenger shrugged. "He wrote it at an almost feverish speed. I am amazed he took the time to seal it."

A small twinge of suspicion tickled the back of Silvin's mind—a relic of her childhood that she could not rid herself of, even after all her years wearing the red cloak. Already she could feel her emotions starting to roil and churn within her.

That would not do—not with the mission her captain had entrusted to her. And the letter had his handwriting—Silvin knew it well. With two slow, deep breaths, she calmed herself.

"What is your name?" she asked.

The messenger drew up straight in his seat. "Robin, sister."

"You have done well, Robin. Get yourself a room here, and get some rest. The captain will join us tomorrow."

She stood from her chair. From beneath the table she pulled her swords, two short gladiuses in sheaths of unadorned black leather. These she gathered in one hand before starting off. But Robin seemed put out. He frowned up at her, and his hand jerked as if he had meant to grab her arm, but thought better of it at the last moment.

Not entirely a fool, then.

"Where are you going?" asked Robin.

Silvin arched an eyebrow at him. "To do as the captain commanded."

"Are you going into the forest? I could come with you."

"You could. And that could prove disastrous. Do you trust the captain?"

Robin's eyes shone with a fervent light. Silvin knew it well—it shone in her own eyes often enough, and for good reason.

"I trust him with my life."

"Then stay here," she said, not unkindly. "We all have a part to play. I must play mine alone."

She walked away, ignoring his confused look.

Outside, Silvin studied the sky as she buckled on her swords. The clouds, though thick, did not look any darker than they had when she first woke. All of Selvan had seen much rain this spring, but the storms appeared to have abated for a while. She hoped the weather held up—though upon further reflection, she realized that a light rain might be good for cover, since she was not supposed to reveal herself today.

She sighed and set off for the dark, looming trunks of Brillig Forest, the first of which lay on the horizon.

* * *

The sun, only visible as a brighter glow behind the clouds, was well past noon by the time she reached the trees. But this far south, Silvin knew it would be up for some hours yet. She had come to the Brillig only a few days ago, and she was unfamiliar with its tracks and paths. But she knew enough woodcraft to silence her footfalls and keep heading in the right direction, making for the place where she had first spotted the enemy sentries deep in the wood.

As she went deeper and the sun's light became sparser, she slowed her pace. She was not far away now from where she would find her enemy. Her pulse quickened, and she took deep breaths to slow it.

She would not lose control. She *must* not.

At last she caught sight of one of them: a pale, rangy woman in threadbare green clothing. She wore a thick cloak against the threat of rain. Her black hair was messily cut just a few inches from the scalp, and she picked at her fingernails in boredom.

She did not stir as Silvin passed by, darting silently from tree to tree.

"Fools," whispered Silvin.

Silvin had spent enough time in the forest in the last few days to know that there was only a single thin line of sentries, and then empty woods until she reached her goal. Even so, she kept to the hard ground several paces off the main path, avoiding any wet, mulchy leaves. She did not fear an attack—even if she were spotted, she had her swords—but she was not here to fight. Any skirmish, no matter how small, would put the enemy on alert. They might even decide to leave the forest before the captain arrived, and that could prove disastrous.

After some time, she came to the brink of a high ravine. Its steep wooded slopes fell to a little valley with a flat bottom, and there sat a cluster of buildings. A squat wooden fort sat in the center, surrounded by smaller storage sheds and guardhouses. A rickety wooden wall with a narrow platform encircled the whole camp. The whole place had an air of being off-kilter, as though it were waiting for its own inevitable collapse into firewood.

Normally such a place would have been built at the top of a slope, not down at the bottom where attackers could easily rain arrows from above. But this was no stronghold of kings, meant for pitched battles against determined armies. It had once been a bandit camp. Silvin suspected—as did her captain—that the current denizens of the compound were something far darker.

And far, far older.

Somewhere in those buildings was a captive boy named Rodwen of the family Runda. Rodwen was only a child. He had never done serious harm in his life, least of all to the inhabitants of this compound. But his mother was Rodil, whose sister was Ronen, the queen of Selvan.

That was what had brought Silvin into this forest at the command of her captain. Everyone in the Selvan capital, as well as many Mystics, assumed the boy had been kidnapped for ransom. King Anwar could not fail to pay for his nephew-in-law's recovery, after all.

But Silvin's captain thought the boy had been taken for another reason. A reason involving an unseen war that had flared and ebbed across Underrealm for many centuries and countless human lives.

And if he was right in his guess, then Silvin had a very personal reason to desire Rodwen's safe return.

A skittering, hissing noise sounded from a bush a pace away.

Faster than blinking, Silvin turned and drew her swords. Shards of sunlight made them flash in her hands.

She searched the trees for a moment, her whole body tense. There was no one there. No assassin creeping forwards with a dagger, no archer taking careful aim. Only a bush, and one far too small for a human to hide in.

Could it be a weremage? Silvin supposed it was possible. But to transform into something as small as a mouse or a vole was powerful magic, and Silvin doubted any weremage that strong would be so foolish as to give themselves away.

Her pulse had quickened again. Deep breaths slowed it. She would help no one if she lost control now—least of all Rodwen.

It must have been a rabbit or bird. And if she had thought she heard a voice in the noise, it was only her imagination.

Silvin rolled her shoulders and turned back, surveying the compound again. She had her job to do. She would find where they were keeping the boy, and she would get a count of their foes. Then she would return to the town. It was no simple task, but Silvin was a knight of the order, and a dark-damned good one. This was hardly the most dangerous assignment in her years of wearing the cloak.

Slowly she stalked down the side of the ravine. Less than a span away was a well-tended road leading down, but she knew it would be folly to go that way. There would be guards at the bottom, and anyone in the compound could spot her easily. Therefore she slid from tree to tree, sometimes falling back on her hands and proceeding in a sort of awkward, upside-down crawl.

In half an hour, she had reached the bottom. Soldiers ambled around outside the compound wall, tending to the myriad daily tasks of living. Some gathered firewood, while others fetched water to boil and drink. They were aimless and unwatchful, and Silvin avoided them easily, looking for a place where she could sneak into the compound. There were three gates, but each was guarded. Though the soldiers there were hardly more attentive than their wandering counterparts, Silvin thought they might notice if a complete stranger walked out of the woods towards them.

Suddenly Silvin became aware that one of the soldiers was heading right towards her. He was a burly man with a Dorsean look and thick, matted hair. Silvin froze behind the trunk of a tree. It was plain he had not seen her yet, but if he kept on his present course, he could not miss her.

She looked around. Two paces away, a fallen log lay over a small gap in the earth. A perfect hiding place. She dove into the shadow beneath the log, curling up as the man's footsteps drew nearer.

He stopped several paces away, hidden by the trunks. Silvin heard drawstrings being untied, and then a thick stream of liquid striking fallen leaves.

She sighed with relief. The man had no more sinister reason for approaching than a piss.

"Ho there, Belric!"

The voice came from a near distance. A second soldier, a woman, approached the first. She spoke with the slow but clipped voice of a southerner. Silvin heard the footsteps draw near to the area where the first soldier—Belric, she supposed—stood relieving himself.

"What do you want, Alren?" grunted Belric.

“Our grain stores are low,” said Alren.

“And what do you want me to do about it? Talk to lady Jessa.”

Lady Jessa? That had the sound of southern nobility. Or was it only a sort of joking title? He had not said the name with much reverence.

Alren sighed. “I’ve told her before. Can you nae speak to her on my behalf?”

“She will tell me the same thing I am sure she has told you. She cares little for our food stores. There are more important things going on.”

“And she won’t do a dark-damned thing about them imps, either,” said Alren. “It’s them stealing the grain, you see if it ain’t.”

“I will not see anything of the sort,” said Belric, whose piss was finally trailing off. “That is your job.”

Alren gave a rueful chuckle and said, “Actually, I’m tight myself. I’ll be back.”

Silvin heard the woman’s footsteps draw near. Anxiety spiked in her chest, and blood flooded her cheeks. She struggled to master her emotions, even as she pushed farther under the log.

But she pushed too hard. The log broke with a dull *crunch.* Though it had looked solid enough, rot had in fact hollowed it out. Half of it fell on Silvin’s legs, and she heaved it quickly off her.

Trees still hid her from Alren and Belric, but they had both gone quiet.

“What was that?” hissed Belric.

Silvin looked around desperately. She saw the other half of the log. It was hollow, and just big enough for her to crawl inside.

She threw herself forward, pressing into the moldy space. Mud caked her arms and clothes in an instant, and she felt grubs burst to mush under her hands. Something had taken a shit in the log, and it smeared all down her front. Ignoring it, she crawled in and pulled her legs up to her chest.

The guards approached the hollow. Their steps came close and stopped. Silvin heard the woman laugh with relief.

“Just a rotten old log,” said Belric.

“Those damn imps, I guess,” said Alren. “I juss ‘bout pissed myself.”

“Well, go take care of that in a better place than your own britches.”

He gave Silvin’s log a half-hearted, almost resentful kick. Part of it fell in on her. Silvin closed her eyes as the dirty, moldy wood pattered on her face. When it stopped falling, she opened one eye.

Belric stood just above her, his back turned. Even as she watched, he strode away.

Silvin did not remember gripping the hilts of her swords so tight. Now she released them, watching the blood flow back into her white knuckles. Slowly she felt the flush drain from her cheeks, and her heart stopped pounding under her jerkin.

When she was sure the guards had gone, she slipped out of the log and crept towards the compound.

TWO

Silvin drew near the north wall, where the fewest soldiers wandered about. There she hoped she could climb up and accomplish her first goal, which was to survey the compound and estimate the number of their enemy. After that, she hoped she could find out where they were keeping the boy.

Each corner of the wall had a guard tower, and it was of these that she was most cautious. Once she reached the wall, the tower guards would have a hard time spotting her. But her approach had to be timed just right.

She spent a short while hidden in the underbrush, watching. There was little pattern to their movement, which made things difficult. But at last she thought she had a wide enough window of time.

She leaped to her feet and sprinted for the wall. Her boots came down heavy on the ground, but she took little care to silence them. She struck the wall almost at a dead run, but the impact was muffled by a thick coat of moss and vines that clung to the wood.

For a moment she stood there, body tense, listening. But there was no cry of alarm, no sound of approaching enemies. She sighed with relief and began to climb.

A gentle drizzle started to fall. The plants were as good as a ladder, and Silvin reached the top in a matter of heartbeats. She crouched low and sidled towards the closest tower. Ducking behind its corner, she leaned back out and peered into the compound.

There were guards in the compound, many more than there were outside. She studied them, looking for identifying marks and characteristics. But there was little to be found. They wore many colors and had many shades of skin. They were all similarly armed, with swords and axes and shields that were unremarkable. These were no soldiers of one of the powerful merchant families, nor were they royal servants of some enemy kingdom.

Silvin's heart skipped a beat. Her captain had suspected this might be the work of their ancient enemy, the Shades. So far she had seen nothing to say otherwise.

She took a quick estimate of their number—about a score that she could see, and likely that number again inside the buildings—and then altered her search. Her second task was to find the boy. He would be under guard, certainly, and so she looked for buildings with guards posted out front. The fortress had two, but she doubted he would be there. It was too small to have a prison, and the leader would have stationed herself there—the guards earlier had mentioned their "lady Jessa."

At last she spotted another building with guards out front. It was smaller and meaner, almost a hovel. Silvin focused on it at once. That had to be where they were keeping Rodwen.

For a moment she thought of leaving. She was *almost* positive where the boy was. But the building had windows. If she drew closer, she could see inside. She could be certain.

Slowly, she crept around the tower towards the other side. And then disaster struck.

A door in the tower opened, and a guard stepped out at the exact wrong moment. Silvin had no time to hide herself as he came out blinking in the dim daylight.

He saw her and froze, his mouth open.

"Why, hello," said Silvin.

She drew her swords and hacked into his neck from both sides. The guard dropped before he could even scream.

But the noise of the blades was sharp on the air, and there were shouts from above. Silvin looked up just in time to take cover as one of the guards raised her bow and drew an arrow.

"Dark!" muttered Silvin. She was pressed to the side of the tower, where a slight overhang prevented the guards from firing at her. But they would come down any minute, and she could not try to climb down the wall without exposing herself.

Then there was a thin, rasping roar on the air, and two streaks of light flew over Silvin's head towards the top of the tower.

She was so shocked, she almost stepped out into the open. She caught herself at the last minute and remained pressed to the wall, but when she heard screams from the top of the tower, she risked a glance upwards.

The guards no longer looked down at her. And just above the edge of the tower, she could see bright flashes of light.

"What under the sky . . .?" said Silvin.

She knew she should take advantage of the distraction and run. But curiosity got the better of her. She threw open the tower door and pounded up the stairs, flinging up the hatch at the top.

A scene of madness greeted her eyes. One of the guards lay on the wooden platform, unmoving. His skin was burned so badly that some of it had melted. The second guard was brandishing her bow, swinging it desperately at two tiny creatures before her.

Silvin had never seen imps before, but she recognized them from countless children's stories. They stood three hands tall, with dark brown skin from which protruded many thick spines, like spikes on armor. Their arms were nearly as long as the rest of their bodies, and from their wrists, long flaps of skin swept back to join the skin of their legs, like the wings of flying squirrels from Silvin's homeland. Their faces were flat and stubby with huge eyes. Pointed chins jutted from beneath deceptively huge mouths of sharp teeth. Their long, scaly tails whipped back and forth in rage as they ducked the swings of the guard's bow.

Even as Silvin watched, one of them dodged too slowly. The bow struck the little creature in the ribs. It gave a thin screech as it fell to the wooden platform. The second imp leaped after the first, trying to pull it out of reach of the guard, but a thick boot caught it in the face, and it flew away, stunned.

But the guard's back was turned, and she had not heard Silvin approach. Silvin leaped forwards and stabbed both her swords into the guard's back.

The guard gave a gasp. She tried to look over her shoulder to see her killer, but she could not manage it before slumping to the ground. A pool of blood spread out around her, soaking her skin and clothes.

Silvin looked over the edge of the tower into the compound. The alarm had been raised, of course. Soldiers who a moment ago had been milling aimlessly were now gathering together. Several of them glanced up at her. Silvin ducked back out of sight.

"Dark take them," she muttered.

The drizzle had turned to a steady rain. She looked over at the imps. The second one had helped the first up to sitting. It seemed dazed.

"Are you all right?" asked Silvin.

She realized it might be a foolish question. Did imps even speak the human tongue? The two imps looked at her for a moment, seemingly angry. Then they turned and chittered to each other. If they knew Silvin was concerned, they did not show it. In fact they seemed resentful.

"You should get out of here," she said. She made a shooing motion with her hands, hoping they would understand that, if not her words. "They will climb up here, and it will not go well if they find you."

The imps only chittered to each other again. Silvin shook her head and rose, going to the other side of the tower. She looked over the edge. It was far too high to jump, and she could not climb down. The tower had none of the vines and moss that covered the walls. She would have to run down to the wall and climb from there. But that would not be easy—even as she watched, soldiers pounded down the platform towards her tower.

Silvin turned, resolved to make her attempt regardless. She could hold them at the door to the tower, and mayhap she could kill enough of them to clear a space. If things became truly desperate, she could try jumping from the wall—that might not be fatal.

But as she took her first step towards the hatch, the imps leapt to the top of the tower's low wall. And then one of them looked up at her and spoke.

"Come!" it screeched, beckoning with a thin, clawed hand.

Silvin blinked. "What?"

"Down! Now!" The imp pointed to the ground far below.

"You can speak?"

The imp looked at its companion and shrieked a furious string of words—if she had to guess, she would have said there were many curses. The other imp looked up at her, its yellow eyes large.

"Come down," it said. "With us."

Silvin glanced down at the ground again. "I cannot," she said. "The fall will kill me. I do not have wings like you."

"You can . . . trust." The imp clearly had to struggle to find the words. "You live."

She looked down. The soldiers were close to the tower now. Her delay had made it that much less likely that she could escape by the stairs.

She sighed and closed her eyes. The imps' plan seemed doomed. But even if it failed, she could escape. If she broke her legs on the ground, in those precious few moments before she fell senseless . . .

All she had to do was lose control.

"Very well," she said. "One. Two. Three!"

She leapt over the wall. The imps jumped with her.

In midair, the creatures spread their arms. Their wings flared out, slowing their fall, and Silvin quickly fell past them.

Blasted little monsters! she thought. *This was their plan?*

But then, somehow, she felt herself slowing. The guards on the wall stared in amazement as she fell past them, but moving no more quickly than a brisk run.

Silvin twisted around. Above her, the imps fell still more slowly than she, and both their clawed hands were outstretched. Their eyes did not glow, as a human wizard's would have. But Silvin could almost feel the magic seeping out of them, creating a soft cushion of air that caught her.

Tales spoke of how imps could summon fire, but this was something she had never heard of. The drops of rain all around her hung motionless. Each drop formed into a perfect globe, and Silvin could see herself reflected in all of them.

Her distraction almost made her hit the ground on her back. But at the last second she turned and rolled with the fall before rising to her feet. The imps landed softly on the grass. The larger one looked up at her.

"Come!" it said again. It dashed off towards the trees with the smaller one at its heels.

Silvin did not look back at the compound, not even when an arrow sailed past and stuck in the ground. She sprinted through the rain as fast as she could, and was soon lost among the dark trunks of the Brillig.

THREE

The imps followed no path that Silvin could see, but it was clear they knew exactly where they were going. They ran north for a while, and then without warning they cut sharply east. Silvin almost lost them then, for their small shapes were hard to glimpse among the trees, especially now with the rain. But the smaller one stopped and chittered to catch her attention. Silvin skidded to a halt before turning to follow once again.

They led her to a great oak tree standing in the middle of a clearing. It stood nearly half a span high, its branches reaching out to brush the tops of the forest all around, like an old woman stooping to pinch the cheeks of her grandchildren. Near the base of the tree was a great hollow. It looked like it might have formed naturally, but Silvin supposed the imps could have made it long ago. It did not quite keep off all the rain, but it was a far sight better than standing out in the open.

And then, even as Silvin watched, the imps made it an even better shelter. Each reached out with one hand, and the rain seemed to gather around their fingers. From their upraised hands sprouted two columns, absorbing all the rain that continued to fall from the sky above. Once the columns of water were two paces high, the imps directed them together. The water joined and spread, forming a sort of canopy. When rain fell upon it, it was absorbed, so that the shelter kept spreading wider and wider.

"In," said the larger imp.

Silvin gratefully obeyed. Once she had sat cross-legged between them, she looked up at the water canopy. "That is incredible. I have never seen magic like it."

"Man spells shit," said the larger imp.

She gaped at him, her mouth open. "What?" she said, trying desperately not to laugh.

"Always you say what," groused the imp.

It was all she could do to contain her laughter. She looked at the smaller imp, hoping they could converse without her bursting into hysterics, which she felt might offend them.

"Thank you both for helping me," she said. "It would have been hard to escape without you."

"You will die," said the smaller imp. Immediately it frowned. "You . . . would . . . die?"

"Yes, I might have died," said Silvin, choosing not to correct it. "My name is Silvin. Do you have a name?"

The small imp glanced furtively at the larger. When the larger imp did not react, the smaller imp placed a hand on its tiny chest. It made a sound in the imp tongue that sounded somewhat like *jutur*.

"I cannot quite say that," said Silvin. "Is it all right if I call you Jutur?"

"Yes," said Jutur, baring its teeth. Silvin hoped it was a smile and not a grimace of rage. It pointed at the other imp. "He—" a word that sounded like *drugoth*. "He brother."

"Your brother?" said Silvin. "Well, it is a pleasure to meet you, Drugoth."

"Man voice shit," said Drugoth.

Silvin could not help herself—she gave a brief scream of laughter, quickly cut off. The imps leapt up in shock, and the water canopy above them wavered.

"I am sorry!" said Silvin, spreading her hands to them. "I am sorry. It is only . . . the way you speak. I have never heard anything like it."

Drugoth glared at her, unblinking.

"Why you help?" said Jutur, unexpectedly.

Silvin looked at him, frowning. "What?"

"Always you say what," said Drugoth.

"Us," said Jutur, pointing at itself and then at Drugoth. "You help us."

"We live," said Drugoth. "Man no kill."

"Yes, I am sure you would have escaped even without my help," said Silvin diplomatically.

"But you help," said Jutur. "Why?"

Silvin shrugged. "I had no wish to see you harmed," she said, adding quickly, "though I am sure you would not have been hurt too badly." Drugoth, who had seemed about to say something, looked mollified. "And the people in the compound are no friends of mine."

Drugoth looked at Jutur and demanded something in their own chittering tongue. Jutur answered, and they spoke back and forth for a moment. When they finished, Jutur looked back up at Silvin.

"You . . . hate them?" said Jutur, cocking its head.

"What?" said Silvin. "I . . . no, I do not hate them. But they are my enemies."

Jutur's eyes widened, its shoulders rising. With little knowledge of imp expressions, Silvin could only hope she had not somehow offended it. "You kill but not hate?"

"I . . . sometimes," said Silvin, feeling suddenly put off.

"That is fright," said Jutur in a hushed voice.

"Well," said Silvin slowly, "is it not equally frightening to kill someone *just* because you hate them? I have hated many people in my life. I have not tried to kill most of them. Or . . ." She frowned for a moment. "At least I have not tried to kill *all* of them. If we tried to kill everyone we hated, the nine kingdoms would be full of corpses."

"Nine kingdoms shit," said Drugoth helpfully.

"You man strange," said Jutur, still staring unblinkingly into her eyes.

But Silvin's mind had begun to turn, and now she fixed Jutur's gaze with her own. "Do you hate those people?" she said.

"Yes," said Jutur, its voice dropping almost to a whisper.

"Why?"

"Forest dirty," said Jutur. "Forest quiet. Forest . . . sad?" The last word came out as a question as the imp searched for the word.

"Yes, sad," said Silvin. "That is right."

"But no can kill men," said Jutur. "Not even all imps. We only watch and wait."

Silvin looked back over her shoulder, back towards the dark trunks of the forest. Somewhere through those trees was the compound. And now they knew she was here. She had not worn a red cloak, but they would know she was an agent of the King's law. Who else would come to their stronghold in the middle of the forest, evading their sentries and climbing the wall? From there, it would be an easy thing to guess she was a Mystic. Constables did not conceal their identities, and she wore no red leather armor.

They would know the Mystics were after them. And that would prompt them to leave. As soon as they had recovered from her attack, they would begin making arrangements. Silvin's captain would arrive tomorrow with a force that could take the compound, but it would be deserted. And that was Silvin's fault.

Not fault, she said. *The captain would not tell you that. He would say it is your responsibility. Fault dwells behind. Responsibility waits ahead.*

Because, in truth, it did not matter that the soldiers would leave the compound. What mattered was that they would bring the boy with them.

Such a young boy. Barely seven years old, if she had heard right. He had done nothing.

Silvin clenched her jaw, biting down on a surge of rage.

She turned back to the imps.

"I need to go back," she said. "There is a boy there I have to save. Once I have him, the rest of the humans will leave."

Jutur's eyes widened. "No more sad forest."

"That is right," said Silvin. "Will you help me?"

Jutur looked at Drugoth. Drugoth glared at Silvin, and she feared he would refuse. But after a moment he grunted, "We help."

"All right," said Silvin. "Here is the plan."

FOUR

Silvin crept through the forest towards the southern wall. The compound lay just a half-span ahead.

Where before it had seemed a quiet, lazy place, now the guard had been increased, and the soldiers on patrol were watchful. She could only see one gate from where she stood, and it was closed. No doubt the other two had been shut as well. The sky above was darker than ever, and the sun's meager glow grew ever closer to the horizon. The rain fell thick and heavy now, and Silvin had to raise her green hood against it. She would have to shed it when it came time to fight, for the waterlogged cloth would only slow her down.

Jutur and Drugoth were nowhere to be seen, but if the little creatures had followed the plan, they would be in the woods on the other side of the compound. They had scampered off into the woods first to summon others from their flock. The imps would strike from the north, the same direction that they and Silvin had fled, and where the guards would likely be the most wary. All Silvin had to do was wait and infiltrate the compound as soon as the opportunity presented itself.

It did not take long. No more than half an hour passed before Silvin heard a great commotion from the other side of the compound. It started with shouts from the guards inside. Then there came a loud hiss, followed by a deep *THOOM.*

Silvin blinked in surprise. She had told the imps to start a small fire on the compound's northern end—something to distract, rather than destroy. It seemed Jutur and Drugoth had taken matters into their own claws and decided on a frontal assault instead.

The guards on the wall turned towards the noise. Had they been the well-trained soldiers of a king, they would no doubt have held their posts. But whether these were servants of the Mystics' ancient enemy or no, they did not appear very disciplined. As one, they turned and ran towards the compound's northern end, leaving the southern side unwatched.

Silvin threw off her cloak and sprinted for the wall. She leapt up it as if she were one of the imps. Her hands slipped once on the vines, which were now slick with rainwater, but it hardly slowed her. After reaching the top, she found a ladder down to the ground on the other side.

She had carefully mapped out the compound's layout in her mind, and she remembered the hovel where she suspected the boy was being held. Now she made her way there, ducking and darting between the buildings to reach it. No one barred her path. It seemed all the guards had run towards the disturbance in the north, like a swarm of moths drawn to flame. Mayhap even the soldiers guarding the boy had left.

It turned out that she was not so fortunate. She reached the hovel and crept around it towards the front door. Peeking around the corner, she saw the two guards still stood watch, though both had their heads turned north, trying to glimpse any sign of what was happening there.

Silvin leapt forth, swords flashing. She planted both blades in the back of one of the guards, and she fell without a sound. The other had barely placed a hand on his hilt before she lopped it off. He tried to scream, but Silvin struck him hard in the throat with the hilt of her other weapon. His voice cut off with a sharp gurgle. With one swift kick, she broke open the door to the hovel, dragging the guard in behind her.

She took in her surroundings in scarcely a heartbeat. There was no furniture here, only a pathetic firepit in the center of the room. The windows she had seen earlier were nailed shut with boards, and there was no other exit.

In the back of the hovel sat the boy. His dark skin was further blackened by the same dirt and grime that covered his blue and white clothing, which was of fine make. He stared at her with wide, unblinking eyes. Silvin gave him a grim smile before turning to her captive.

"Who are you working for?" she demanded.

The guard, still cradling the stump at the end of his arm, whimpered and did not even look up at her. Silvin kicked him hard in the ribs to get his attention.

"Who are you working for?" she said again, louder.

"My hand!" he cried. "I . . . please . . ."

Silvin gripped his stump wrist and squeezed. The man screamed in pain.

"Who are you working for?"

"The lady Jessa!" said the man. "She is our leader."

"And who is her master?" said Silvin. "Whence do you all hail?"

The man's whole face twisted in confusion. "What?"

Always you say what, thought Silvin with a grim smile.

She dropped his wrist, and he whimpered in relief. But then Silvin stomped her boot hard on the injury, ignoring his fresh scream.

"To which king do you swear? Are you soldiers of Dorsea? Wadeland?"

"No one! No one!" cried the man. "We are of no kingdom!"

Silvin's pulse seemed to stop for a moment. Was it true, then? Were these the Shades her captain had suspected, that he had been seeking for so long?

"Who is your lord, then?" she said, her voice suddenly hushed in its urgency.

"We have none," said the man, weeping now. "Only the lady Jessa. It was her idea to take the boy. For the ransom."

As quickly as it had come, the thrill in Silvin's breast died away.

Not the Shades, then. Only simple bandits, who had chosen entirely the wrong time and place to try and earn a few extra gold weights.

And to get them, they had been willing to kidnap—and mayhap even kill—a child. A child who had only just reached his seventh year.

Silvin's thrill had gone, leaving only an icy rage.

"The ransom," she intoned. "You took a child from his parents for gold. You killed his protectors. I suppose he even watched you do it, did he not?"

"I . . . I was not there," whined the man. "I do not know."

“Never mind,” said Silvin. “I will not waste any more of my time, nor yours.”

He looked up, hopeful. Before he could speak, Silvin drove one sword into his gut with all her strength. He gasped, and when the breath came back out, blood flowed with it. He collapsed to the ground, fingers scrabbling futilely at the dirt.

She strode past him without a second glance and went to the boy. Kneeling, she drew a jeweled knife and cut the ropes binding him before helping him stand.

“Hello, Rodwen,” she said, her voice quiet and gentle. “I am here to rescue you. Will you come with me?”

He kept staring silently at her. Silvin could hardly blame him. A mind this young was not used to such visions of slaughter and fury, as she knew firsthand.

“It is all right,” she said. “Just stay close, and do not leave my side for anything.”

She took his hand and drew him to the front door, taking a quick peek outside in the rain. The guards still stood clustered near the northern end of the compound, where came the sound of more explosions and a crackling that sounded like lightning. The imps appeared to be unleashing an alarmingly large amount of pent-up hatred towards the humans.

In a moment of madness, Silvin thought of going to join the fight. Together with the imps, she could kill many of the bandits. Mayhap even all of them. They had taken a child. For that alone, Silvin would have happily executed them.

Her control had slipped. Rage had come bubbling to the surface. She forced it away. Her captain had been training her to maintain a balance, and that training had never been more important than it was now.

“Come,” she whispered, and pulled Rodwen behind her as she made for the gate.

They went south, away from the commotion. The gate had been opened a crack—apparently some bandits with a semblance of courage had decided to make a sortie. No one stood nearby to guard it. They were only a few paces away from freedom.

A pale figure stepped through the gate, shrouded in a dark cloak and hood. Silvin skidded to a squelching halt in the now-muddy ground.

Before her stood a lady with a bearing that spoke of leadership. Silvin guessed at once that this was the lady Jessa. Her black hair was cut short, and it stuck out in all directions like the petals of a flower. Her robes were exactly what one would expect to find on a leader of bandits—gaudy and flashy in their purple and gold, but made of thin and weak fabrics that spoke of new and ill-acquired money. But she looked upon Silvin with wary, competent caution, and Silvin knew she was no simpleton. She did, however, look thin and shaken, as though she was recovering from some illness. Silvin hoped that was an advantage.

Then Silvin realized that Jessa carried no weapon.

Another Mystic might have taken this for a good sign, but Silvin was a mage hunter. Her mind raced to the conclusion at once: Jessa was a wizard. No wonder these bandits had rallied around her.

"Rodwen, go back," said Silvin. "Find a place to hide while I deal with her."

She spread her legs, lowering her balance and readying for a dive in either direction until she learned what sort of wizard she was facing. A transmuter would try to get close; a therianthrope would likely transform before attacking; but an elementalist or mentalist would strike from afar, and Silvin must be ready to avoid the blow.

And then agony shot through her leg, making her cry out.

Silvin stumbled, falling to one knee. She looked down at her left thigh. A dagger stuck out from the back of it, half the blade buried in her flesh. It had missed her tendons and veins by only a finger's width, though plenty of blood spilled through the wound regardless.

She looked up. The boy, Rodwen, looked at her. His eyes were as wide and expressionless as ever.

FIVE

Pain and rage flooded Silvin in equal measure. For just one moment, emotion stole all control and overwhelmed her. She fought back to her feet and raised her sword over the boy.

At the last moment she caught herself. Turning her wrist, she struck him with her fist instead of the blade. He crumpled like a flower in flame, falling back into the mud.

A blow struck her from behind—not flame or wind, but an invisible force. Training took over. Silvin rolled with the blow and came up running, looking for cover.

Invisible magic meant Jessa was a mindmage. Silvin raced to devise a strategy. Jessa was not particularly powerful—that much seemed obvious. The spell had been little more than a punch. Still, enough punches could kill. As if to reinforce that thought, another spell struck Silvin between the shoulder blades, and she almost pitched forwards.

At last she reached the corner of a building and dived behind it. That would give her a moment to think. Jessa could not attack again without line of sight.

That would be the key to victory. Silvin had to find some way to incapacitate and then kill the wizard. She would need to go for the eyes. But her flight had taken her a good distance away, and she did not know how to get closer without exposing herself to attack. She had no bow, and she had always been a terrible shot anyway. Bowcraft required an inner calm that Silvin had never been able to attain, despite all her captain's careful training.

Since Jessa was not a Shade, she likely knew little about mage hunters. That might be an advantage. Silvin had trained with mindmages before, and powerful ones. Endless drilling had instilled her reflexes with dozens of tricks. Mayhap a direct attack was best after all. Even if she could not kill the mindmage, Silvin might drive her off long enough to recover Rodwen and escape. Carrying the boy would be no trouble.

But thinking of Rodwen birthed unpleasant anger in her gut. The boy had stabbed her. What was wrong with him? Did he not know she was here to help him? Had he done it out of fear of his captors? Silvin could understand that, though it made her task no easier.

She risked a glance out from behind the corner of her shed. Jessa had been edging around it, trying to get a glimpse of her. As soon as their eyes met, Jessa's flashed with light as she cast a spell. Silvin ducked back in time. Magic struck the building, and she felt the impact in the wall.

Hoping Jessa would need a moment to summon another spell, Silvin rushed out into the open. As she had hoped, it took Jessa by surprise. She fell back, swinging wildly with a spell. It hit Silvin's shoulder, but she had loosened her muscles. She turned with the blow, spinning a full circle without slowing as she ran.

Desperation in her face, Jessa tried to grapple with Silvin instead. The light in the wizard's eyes flared. Unseen bands closed on Silvin's shoulders. But this was one of the first tricks Silvin had learned, and she easily twisted away from the pressure.

She was close enough now to lunge. Her swords flashed, and Jessa dodged a little too late. One blade cut through the gaudy purple cloth, and a small spurt of blood fell to the ground.

Jessa cried out and stumbled away. But the pain seemed to enrage the wizard, and she struck her most powerful blow yet. Her eyes blazed, and the rain turned the glow into a halo. Silvin flew back off her feet, landing hard on her back. She rolled again, but now she was too far away for swords. She retreated once more, hiding behind another building.

"Face me, coward!" cried Jessa, her voice powerful with magic.

"Coward? You stole a child!" called Silvin amicably. But she could barely suppress another burst of rage. *Control. Two deep breaths. In. Out.*

Jessa laughed. "A child who seems to have no wish to leave, judging by the wound in your leg."

Silvin glanced down at it. The leg of her pants was ruined, stained through with blood. But blood loss did not yet cloud her thoughts, for which she was grateful. She hoped Rodwen would not try to attack her again, but now that she knew to expect it, she could keep him from doing further harm.

"I have better things to do than deal with you," said Jessa. "So I offer you a chance: leave now, and none of us will come after you. Stay, and my company will soon finish with the imps. They will fall upon you with more fury than this storm."

For just a moment, Silvin considered it. But if she fled, she would lose the bandits. And there was still the matter of Rodwen. Whatever they had done to cow the boy, he was still innocent. Silvin would die before she would abandon him here.

A fleeting thought crossed her mind. She could release her control. She could let the rage spill over. That would end the affair quickly. It would be easy. Even now, Silvin could feel her anger bubbling just beneath the surface.

But she must control it. If she gave in, the boy would die. She would kill him herself.

Silvin had been silent too long, and Jessa had grown impatient. "Leave!" she cried again, but this time it was a command. "Or I will destroy you with a power you cannot imagine."

That gave Silvin pause. What was the wizard talking about? She risked another look out from behind the building, and what she saw made her freeze.

Jessa stood tall and proud in the falling rain. One hand was outstretched, and in it she held something. A black crystal, almost like a gem, as long and thick as a finger.

A magestone.

Even as she felt the color drain from her face, Silvin's mind worked.

This explained much. It told her why Jessa looked so frail and sickly. And it explained why Rodwen had stabbed her. The boy had not been cowed by the bandits—he was under the sway of Jessa's magic. With the power of magestones, she had commanded him to thwart any rescue attempt.

But why had Jessa not eaten the stone already? This fight would be over. Why had she withheld herself? Especially when she obviously suffered from magestone sickness, and her hunger must be beyond all reason.

One of two things had to be true: she had an iron will and was trying to wean herself off the evil stones, which Silvin doubted; or she had a very limited supply of them. Mayhap the one in her hand was the last one she had.

Magestones. Another log on the fire of Silvin's rage. It boiled inside her, nearly overwhelming. She fought it, trying to rein herself in.

But a sly voice at the back of her mind whispered: if Jessa ate the stone, she would *need* to let go. She would need all the strength her rage could give her.

And with that thought, something in her snapped. The world seemed to grow brighter, as though she could see every detail in her surroundings. Her eyes saw every raindrop in the air as if it were a drop of honey oozing down a window. She felt the fury flood through her veins, overwhelming all rational thought. Her body almost seemed to grow with it, and she felt as if her limbs were made of forged steel, yet light as air.

She sprang from behind the building and charged.

Jessa had barely a moment to look shocked. Her eyes flared with light, and she struck Silvin with all her strength. The blows rebounded from Silvin like gentle kisses from a breeze. Frantic, Jessa shoved the magestone into her mouth.

Silvin's sword followed it a heartbeat later.

The blade pierced through the back of the wizard's head, and the light vanished from her eyes before it could turn black.

The other sword swept around and lopped Jessa's head from her neck. Silvin kicked the head from the end of her sword with a ferocious kick from one heavy boot.

Rodwen stirred on the ground nearby. Silvin turned to him, swords still in her hands. She tensed herself to spring upon him, to drive the swords through his body, to pin him to the ground in payment for the dagger wound in her leg.

He opened his eyes and stared up at her. No longer vacant, no longer unseeing, he faced Silvin with an expression of purest confusion and fear.

The fire in her belly died.

Silvin collapsed to her knees, shaking, heaving, her breath coming in desperate gasps.

"Are . . . are you all right?" said Rodwen.

Slowly the boy got to his feet, nursing his cheek where Silvin had struck him—but then, he likely did not remember that. He came to her, reaching out a hand for her shoulder.

Silvin recoiled, and Rodwen froze. A wave of nausea nearly overwhelmed her. She had almost done it. She had been moments away from it.

"Who are you?" whispered Rodwen, his eyes wide and anxious.

Silvin met his gaze. And then, though it took all her strength, she forced herself into a weak smile.

"Hello, Rodwen," she said. "My name is Silvin. I am here to bring you home."

While he watched, dumbfounded, she cleaned her swords on Jessa's cloak and sheathed them. Then she stood and held out her hand to the boy.

"Come. My friends are keeping these bandits busy, but that will not last much longer."

The relief on his face summoned memories of long, long ago. He took her hand, and Silvin led him from the fortress into the woods, pausing only to recover her cloak from beneath a tree.

Night had come and the compound was long out of sight when Silvin heard stirring in a nearby bush. The rain muffled the sound of chittering, but she still heard it.

"Hello, Jutur, Drugoth."

The imps came leaping out of the bush to sit on a nearby branch. They made themselves a little water canopy to keep off the rain. Jutur tried to extend it to cover Silvin and Rodwen as well, but Drugoth gave a scathing look, and the smaller imp stopped.

"What are—" Rodwen began, his voice a squeak of fright.

"Have no fear," said Silvin. "They are mighty and fell creatures, but they mean us no harm. They have done us a great service tonight, and they are the reason you are alive."

She looked back at the imps. Her words of praise seemed to have had the intended effect on Drugoth, for it looked a little less disgusted with her. But still it did not speak.

"Thank you both, and all your kin, for your help tonight."

"No man help," said Drugoth. "Help imp."

Silvin risked a quick smirk at Jutur, who gave an expression that might have been a smile. "Yes, I think you did. The rest of the bandits will leave this wood before long. If they do not, more of my friends will arrive to clear them out."

"Man brethren shit," said Drugoth.

Silvin squeezed Rodwen's shoulder hard to forestall any reaction. "Thank you again" was all she said.

Drugoth turned and leapt from the branch, spreading his arms to swoop away through the night on his leathery wings. Jutur stayed a moment longer, glancing over his shoulder as if to ensure Drugoth was out of earshot. After a moment, he turned back to Silvin.

"Thank man," said Jutur. "I will remember."

"I will remember you as well, Jutur," said Silvin. "And—if I may? I will teach you a new word. Not all humans are men." She pointed at Rodwen. "Man." She pointed at herself. "Woman. And there are others. But if you meet me again, that is what you may call me."

"Woman," said Jutur, trying the word upon his tongue. "But I will say Silvin. It is . . . it is like sun on trees."

Silvin found it rather difficult to speak for a moment. When she could, she said, "And Jutur is like the strong fire that warms a home."

The imp's expression changed again. This time, Silvin was sure it was a smile. Then Jutur swooped off through the trees after Drugoth.

SIX

Silvin's captain arrived at the town of Tovil the next day, bringing with him a small host of Mystics. Silvin stood outside to meet him. She had left Rodwen in their room at the inn, watched over by the messenger, Robin, despite his protests.

Her captain pulled to a stop barely a pace away from Silvin, surveying her from his horse with pale, piercing blue eyes. She thought they twinkled, though otherwise his face was unreadable.

"Do you have anything to report?" he said.

"A great deal, in fact," said Silvin. "For one thing, I have brought Rodwen of the family Runda safely here. He waits inside for someone to take him home to his family."

Her captain's brows rose. "You were not supposed to attempt to rescue him," he said. "My message to you was rather clear in that regard."

"And I did my best to follow your orders, Captain Adair," she said. "Yet circumstances became quite difficult. And I was trained to adapt."

Jordel of the family Adair swung down from his horse to stand before her, and now he did not try to hide a small smile. "You were so trained indeed, though I fear your teacher was inadequate," he said. "Come inside, and you may tell me the full tale."

Silvin nodded, and he walked past her through the inn's front door. Behind him, the Mystics began to dismount. She knew several of them, and they gave her wide smiles as they came forwards to greet her. A giant of a man clasped wrists with her, and they both squeezed as hard as they could, each searching the other's face for a sign of discomfort.

"It has been some time, Silvin," he said.

"It has, Jormund," said Silvin. "I am glad to see you are well."

"More than well," he said, his grin widening. "As I would be happier to show you later."

"Not until I have had my turn," said Weath, coming up from behind him. She reached out, and Silvin embraced her with a kiss. "How have you fared?"

"Well enough," said Silvin. "But I fear I must disappoint you both—at least for the present. My mood is not as high as it might be."

"But that is just what we propose to fix, darling," said Weath, her smile growing devilish.

Silvin could not help a short chuckle. "Away, both of you. The captain awaits."

She turned, swatting Weath's hand as the alchemist gently slapped her rear. Inside, the captain waited at the common room's back door. He beckoned her to him and then led her to a room, which he had apparently paid for during her brief reunion outside. With him were two guards she did not recognize, and they took up positions just inside the door. Jordel motioned to two chairs, but before they had managed to sit, the innkeeper arrived with a bottle of wine and two metal goblets.

"Only one, please," said Jordel. The innkeeper blinked in confusion, but he took the second goblet away when he left. Silvin reached for the wine, but Jordel forestalled her and poured her goblet himself, placing it before her on the table.

"Thank you," murmured Silvin.

"Of course," said Jordel. "A good deed deserves at least such a mean reward. Now. Tell me why you disobeyed my orders so flagrantly."

Silvin heard the joke in his tone, and so she did not quail before the question. "In fact, I did my best to obey. But I was spotted despite my efforts, and I knew they would remove the boy elsewhere before you could come. That might waste a great deal of time. Or they might have decided to cut their losses and kill him instead. And then, an opportunity presented itself that made it seem prudent to simply rescue him myself. But I am sorry I was not able to do as you first asked."

"You have nothing to be sorry for," said Jordel. "A royal son has been saved from mortal danger, and you yourself are whole. Now, as for those you rescued him from. What sort of force were they?"

She hesitated at the question, glancing at the two guards who stood by the front door.

"You may trust them," said Jordel. "Speak freely."

"They were not Shades," said Silvin flatly, taking no effort to hide the disgust in her voice. "Just bandits. They kidnapped the child for a ransom, nothing more. And they were led by a mindmage abomination."

The room went deathly quiet. Even Jordel seemed taken aback at that news. "I am especially glad you succeeded, then," he said at last. "By all rights, you should have waited for help."

"As I said, that seemed impossible," said Silvin.

"If this abomination is still in the woods, then we should—"

"She is not," said Silvin, forgetting herself for a moment as she interrupted him. "I killed her."

Another long moment of silence stretched. "You did," said Jordel. It was not a question, yet his eyes were inquisitive.

"She was weakened by magestone sickness." Silvin met Jordel's gaze, unblinking. "Her spells had little effect on me."

Jordel raised his chin slightly. "Please leave us," he said quietly.

The guards obeyed without question, filing out of the room. When they had gone, Jordel left his chair and knelt by Silvin's side.

"Did you lose control?" he said. "Did your emotions escape you?"

"I am fine," said Silvin, afraid to look at him now.

"Do not be coy," said Jordel. "Tell me the truth."

Now Silvin's emotions threatened to engulf her again—but this time it was fear and shame that burned within her, not rage. "I lost myself for a moment," she said. "But it was not so bad. And besides, I rescued the boy, and—"

Her words died as Jordel gently took her arm and drew her into a fatherly embrace. As his arms closed around her, Silvin clutched him in return, gripping his red cloak.

"Do not be a fool," said Jordel, quietly and kindly. "I do not ask because I am angry. I am worried. Forget the mission and the boy for a moment. Are *you* all right?"

Silvin gave a few deep, shuddering breaths. "I think I will be," she said. "It will be harder for a while, now. It always is after I lose myself. But I did not entirely give in. When I saw the boy's face . . . he was so frightened, and it reminded me—"

She stopped again as Jordel shushed her, stroking her hair. For a short while they remained that way, and Silvin almost felt she was drawing strength from Jordel's broad, rocklike shoulders, his resolve that seemed unwavering.

At long last he drew back, holding her by the shoulders. Now she did not fear to meet his gaze, and she felt pierced by his eyes.

"I believe in you," he said. "I know you can maintain your control. I have never believed anything more. And I am here if you need me. I will always be here."

"I know it, Captain," said Silvin. And in that moment, she did.

Chasing Moonslight

Riley S. Keene

ONE

The sun rose over the High King's Seat just like it always did, and Aurel of the family Mein tried to ignore it. The breaking dawn, with its blinding first rays that scattered the chill of the lengthening autumn nights, wasn't the problem. Aurel didn't wake with the dawn often anymore, and today was no exception. He had been awake for hours.

His mother had suffered from a form of insomnia later in life, usually only sleeping four hours an evening. Aurel wasn't a young man anymore, and he dreaded the nights where his aging bones and swelling joints caused him to lie awake. But rather than a night of tossing from an ache in the deepest parts of his body, Aurel's sleeplessness had everything to do with his late-night visitor.

There was an assassin in his basement.

Aurel prepared his breakfast in an attempt to go about his normal routine. He told himself he wasn't afraid. She was asleep. And she was injured. She had collapsed in his doorway with a dagger in her shoulder and Eile—the physician he had called to patch the woman's wounds—had pointed out that the woman's right arm was paralyzed.

Eile had also recognized the woman as a member of the Tabarzin, the elite assassins employed by the family Drayden. It had taken a great amount of effort to persuade Eile to leave the situation to him. She had wanted to turn the woman in to the constables, but she hadn't witnessed the simple plea for help that had cut him to the core. An assassin, mayhap, but one who had trusted him to help her.

Aurel took his breakfast downstairs in the shop. Normally he enjoyed his meals in his small apartment, with the fireplace still warm and his favorite blanket drawn over his knees. Now, instead, the cold of the shop burrowed deep into his bones and made his joints swell with stiffness. But it let him keep an eye on the basement door. He took pains to not look at it directly, but he watched it warily from the corner of his eye as he ate and considered his options.

Letting the assassin go free was irresponsible. An unchecked knife let loose upon the Seat would weigh upon his shoulders. But there was something about the woman's plea that had called to him. She was desperate and injured, sure, but he had seen her regret and her penance. The same penance another had once seen in him.

If he called upon anyone to help, they, like Eile, would immediately want to turn the woman over to the constables. So he would deal with it. He would assess whether the woman was truly the monster Eile had painted with her colorful stories of knives in the darkness, or was trapped in an endless cycle of mistakes.

It would be a delicate conversation to have; provoking her risked death. Aurel had no wish to greet the darkness that awaited him, but he had prepared himself for decades.

But for now she rested peacefully, and he had a job to do.

Aurel did well enough that he didn't have to open his shop for the day. Local merchants, businesses, and households had ordered enough commissioned work already to fill his time for the next three weeks. He was pressed to complete the family Aloysia's request before the end of the week. Then there were the new ewers and cups still pending for the Double Grape Tavern. Not to mention the various bits of holloware and cutlery that filled his backlogged workload like gravel along a cobbled path.

But Aurel knew he needed to keep the shop open for two reasons—the first of which was that he was expecting a visitor that evening. He couldn't remember who, and it looked as if he had forgotten to jot it down in his ledger. It would return to him eventually. At least he had remembered that he made plans.

But the second reason was his unexpected overnight visitor. It would be harder for her to kill him if there were patrons in the shop.

Or so he assumed.

And so he lit a fire in the hearth and unshuttered the windows before putting out the angled sign that invited folk inside. While he waited for the hearth to reach temperature, he collected his breakfast dishes and carried them upstairs, only having to pause twice to rest his knees.

When his dishes were dealt with and the hearth was glowing, Aurel began on the family Aloysia's candlesticks. The constant scraping of his file along the seams eventually coerced him into a focused state where his fear and worry melted away.

He was just double-checking the last set of seams when the bell on the front door rang. A customer.

Aurel extricated himself from his seat at his workbench. Even an hour of stillness locked his joints up these days, and he called out to his guest to buy himself a moment. He lurched across the workshop, willing his knees to cease their creaking and stiffness.

"My apologies for keeping you waiting," Aurel said as he rounded the corner. The man there looked up at the sound of his voice, and Aurel was surprised by the youthful face that housed such sunken eyes. The man's dark hair was long and pulled back in a tail, yet stray hairs had escaped the tie to give him a frantic, frazzled look. His clothing was rumpled and creased, though the embroidery and well-tailored cut placed him as a man of money. Aurel was immediately concerned. "How may I help you?"

"Yes, um, you, ah, you are Aurel the silversmith, correct?" Aurel nodded and the man visibly relaxed. "Oh, good. My luck may finally be turning around!" He laughed a little awkwardly. "There are a hundred people on the streets this morning, but not one could give directions to your shop without blundering them somehow." He shook his head and smoothed his hands along the legs of his trousers. "I am Wira of the family Ritonga. I am confident that name means little to you, but—"

"How silly—of course it does not." Aurel nodded with a big smile. He spoke before he fully remembered where he knew the name, but it only took a moment for his memory to catch up. Ritonga was the family name of one of his granddaughter's best friends. "We have not met before, but you must be Chim's father. I've heard so much about her from Mahrit."

Wira blinked a few times, clearly not expecting that answer. "Ah, yes. Thank you. I am Chim's father." He paused, puzzled. Aurel felt a flash of guilt for having interrupted the man's course of thought, but realization returned to his eyes quick enough. "I, well, I am here today because it is Chim's birthday." Wira hesitated, and now it was Aurel's turn to be puzzled. Did the man expect Aurel to extend well-wishes to the girl? But instead it seemed as if Wira was steeling himself to continue. "We are having a celebration tonight at our home. Because of, ah, her illness." He paused, smoothing his hands over his tunic this time. "I am unsure what to do. She is so precious to me. I cannot stand to see her disappointed, but there was just no time and now there is even less."

Aurel held up a hand to stop the endless tide of words. "Please. Calm yourself, Wira. Take your time, but please explain to me what you need and how I can be of assistance."

"Yes," Wira said, drawing the word out with a hissed breath. "That was—you are correct. Forgive me." He took a deep breath in to compose himself. "Mahrit has hardly stopped talking to my Chim about you since you made that lovely ring last month. And now Chim has started talking about wanting her first piece of jewelry now that she is twelve. Soemitro—she would be my wife—has gotten Chim a collection of costume rings and a nice steel bangle for her birthday, but late last night Chim got excited about the potential of having something made of silver." Wira put a hand to his face, running it back over the windswept hairs. "I may have promised her a silver locket to go with the other jewelry. I, well . . ." Wira paused and laughed derisively. "I do not know what I was thinking."

"Ah, yes. I know how fathers can be with their daughters when they want for anything. I made many of my own lofty promises when my two girls were younger." Aurel tapped a finger to his chin. "I unfortunately do not have any lockets made at the moment. However, there is another silversmith to the north side of the Seat by the name of Hitara. She usually keeps a collection of pieces in her shop, and they are quite lovely."

Wira rang his hands together. "Oh, but ... I have no doubt of the loveliness of her work, but Chim has expressed a fondness for your work and yours alone." He looked past Aurel's shoulder into the workroom. "You do not have anything to help?"

Aurel chuckled. "Silver jewelry has grown out of fashion on the Seat, to both my pain and relief. The few pieces I did have left have been sold over the last year. I have no lockets or rings—not even a plain chain made. The ring for Mahrit was created especially for her. I had no idea it would cause a resurgence of fashion among her friends."

"Oh." Wira looked as if he wished to break into tears. He lowered his eyes and toyed with the hem of his tunic. "I do not suppose I could persuade you to create something in time to make me a hero in the eyes of my daughter? Her . . . her illness is getting worse, as I am sure Mahrit has shared. The physicians have started to prepare Soemitro and me for the worst. I fear that she will not see another birthday, and so I hoped to do everything I could to make this one a good memory for us."

Aurel stilled, unsure of how to respond. This day was bursting at the seams already, even without the assassin and his still unknown dinnertime guest. He had to say no. There was just too much to do.

But he could not open his mouth to say so.

The man looked up as the silence stretched on. Aurel's horror and indecision must have been easy to read on his face, because Wira winced as if struck. "Oh, forgive me and my impossible request. I will go to that other silversmith you mentioned. I am sure I will be forgiven eventually for my blunder."

"No, no," Aurel said, suppressing his unrest. "I would not subject a man to the status of villain of his daughter's birthday, sickness or no sickness." He paused, doing some calculations in his head. "I cannot promise it will be my best work, but if I spend the rest of the day on it, I should be able to complete it by the evening."

"No, I cannot ask for such a thing!"

"I said I would help," Aurel said in a patient tone. "I have been where you are with my own girls, and I would hate to disappoint a friend of Mahrit." Aurel grimaced, a bit comically. "I would never hear the end of it."

"Oh, Aurel, you are too kind. Please, come to the party this evening, and present the locket yourself. I am sure it would mean everything to Chim."

"Of course. I shall arrange to be there after sundown. Only, if I could request a favor? Could you please talk to my daughter, Darna, to make sure Mahrit will be there? I am not sure of her schedule at the Academy, but I would hate for her to miss an opportunity to help me present her dearest friend with such a gift."

Wira lit up as if Aurel had asked him to personally invite the High King herself. "Of course! Thank you! Mahrit was already invited, of course, but I will make sure they know to expect you." He smiled at Aurel, and though his face was still sunken and pallid, the edge of stress seemed removed from his jaw and there was less tightness around his eyes. "Oh, you have made my dreams come true, Aurel. I cannot even begin to know how to thank you. But I will find a way."

"There will be time for that later," Aurel said.

"Yes, yes, thank you. I shall see you tonight!"

Aurel managed to keep the warm smile on his face until Wira left, but as soon as the door closed he crumpled against the countertop. It was sheer effort that kept him from slamming his head into the wooden surface. What in the nine kingdoms had he been thinking?

TWO

Aurel struggled to pull himself together. There was too much to do before the evening. He could allow himself to feel overwhelmed when the work was done and the young woman was presented with her gift.

But before he could begin, Aurel felt compelled to check on his guest. The basement door was still shut tight, and he was able to confirm she still rested.

He got to work.

Aurel had the materials he needed on hand, so his first obstacle was the design. Instead of reaching for a blank page of parchment and sketching out a fresh plan, Aurel went to his bookshelves and reached for his old notes. He shuffled through sketches and plans until he reached his much-yellowed notes from his mentor's lessons nearly sixty years ago. They contained exactly what he wanted. The design was ambitious, but classical. A lovely locket, with delicate latticework on the front and an inscription etched onto the back:

A piece of the dream you let me chase.

He had paid for the silver himself all those years ago, creating it in the early mornings and late evenings in his mentor's shop. The locket had been a gift for his mother, given in gratitude for her support.

Aurel touched the flowing script of the inscription, smudging the charcoal. It brought a tear to his eye. The locket had made her so happy, and it had driven his brother to pursue his own apprenticeship.

The locket now rested in a chest in the basement, the etchings and engraving almost entirely smoothed off by the decades it had spent hanging from his mother's neck. It was one of the last mementos he had of her. Aurel hoped, one day, to pass it down to one of his grandchildren—mayhap even Mahrit.

The original design had taken Aurel weeks to complete, but now he had tools and techniques refined by half a century of work. If he started now instead of lollygagging, he could complete it today.

With a determined grimace creasing his brow, Aurel pulled a blank bit of parchment from the shelves and sat down at his workbench to transcribe the plans from the old page to the new. His hands were not as steady as they had once been, and he now used a shorthand all his own instead of the one his mentor had drilled into him. But his mind was as sharp as ever, and the plans unfolded quickly even as he considered what materials he had ready and waiting to be shaped.

He lost himself to the work.

* * *

The familiar sound of his shop's back door opening and closing broke through the fervor of the last hour.

Aurel's first thought was that the assassin in his basement may have woken up and bolted out of the place as soon as she could. But the footsteps echoed into the shop, not away, telling him it was a visitor. He made it about halfway to standing before a familiar figure filled his doorway. The man was tall and thin, with just a hint of the gauntness that had haunted him for so long. He was almost regal in the dark gray robes that marked him as an instructor at the Academy.

"Aurel," Xain said as he swept into the workroom, "please. There is no need to stand on my account, especially if you are otherwise occupied."

"Dean Forredar," Aurel replied, settling back down to the bench as his knees creaked. A deep sense of panic filled him as he thought of the woman in his basement. "I am . . . pleased to see you."

Ever since he had accepted the mantle of dean at the Academy, Xain had made a habit of visiting at least once a week—usually on Marsday, when the students were buried in mid-week exams. Why had he chosen *today* for this week's visit? It was well known that Xain had a long, bitter grudge against the family Drayden, and if he learned one of their assassins rested downstairs . . . well, Aurel did not want to imagine what the consequences would be.

"Forgive me, my friend, as I am rather busy today. Could we—" Aurel stopped when he saw the crestfallen look on the dean's face. "Xain? What is wrong?"

"I do not call upon you for trivial things." Xain shook his head. "It is your advice I seek, and only your advice shall suffice, as you have always known my true heart in these matters." He said those words—*these matters*—with such gravity that Aurel knew at once what he meant.

Aurel frowned, his jaw aching from effort to keep from grimacing. "Very well. I hope you will forgive my rudeness and allow me to work while we talk," Aurel said, returning to the materials at hand. "I have something of a rush on my hands."

"As you wish. I will ... make some tea."

As Xain left the room, Aurel thought about stealing to the basement and once more peeking inside to ensure the woman still slept. But Xain would surely notice him skulking about in his own shop, and how would Aurel explain himself?

Aurel instead busied himself by sorting through the materials on his workbench, but it was idle work that solved no need. He heard Xain ascend the stairs into the living quarters and light the hearth with his firemagic. Soon there came the sound of dishes clinking together, and the smell of fine tea wafted down the stairs. The dean's footsteps followed.

"That is an ominous look," Xain said as he returned, a tray piled with cups and Aurel's battered tea kettle in hand. "Is there something wrong?"

"Wrong? Nothing more than worry for you," Aurel said, aware of just how weak his own voice sounded. He had to control himself, lest Xain suspect the source of his distress. "You seem greatly disturbed by whatever you have come to speak to me about."

"You have the right of it." Xain took a few deep breaths. "I fear that, at any moment, I might burst. And if I speak in public, where I might be overheard, it could be the end of me."

"And this is about . . . your struggles?" Xain had confessed to eating magestones in a moment of extreme need, for which he had been pardoned by the High King, but he had spoken very little of it otherwise. Aurel knew Xain feared the matter becoming common knowledge, and the damage that might do to the Academy, as long as he was associated with it. And now it seemed he was about to speak of it plainly, unaware that they were not entirely alone.

A horrible thought came to Aurel: a vision of the Drayden assassin, awake and listening from the other side of the door. His throat went dry, but he could not warn Xain without acknowledging the woman's presence.

"What else could it be about?" Xain said with a wry grin. "What else indeed." He reached for the teapot and filled both cups. Aurel noticed his hands were shaking. "I know this needs not be said, but please promise that what I am to say will go no further than us."

"Of course," Aurel said, managing to not glance towards his basement.

Xain sighed and shook his head. "What I say involves the Drayden boy, Ebon. If his family were to hear of what nearly happened, they might wish to take me to task for my darkest thoughts. I have barely avoided their hidden knives as it is."

Aurel felt sweat break out across his scalp. If the woman was listening, Xain's next words might seal his fate. But if Aurel told Xain about her, the woman's life was surely forfeit.

Sky above, Aurel thought. *Please let her stay asleep.*

"My duties as dean have done wonders to keep my thoughts distracted," Xain continued, "both from the absence of the Nightblade, and from the voice in the pit of my stomach that cries for the magestones." Xain stared at his hand as it clenched into a fist. "When I see my reflection, I see what I used to be. The hollows in my cheeks. The sunken pits of my eyes. And yet, a part of me believes I will never be whole again without them."

"But you recognize that is far from the truth, correct?" Aurel reached out and put a hand to Xain's arm. "You are more whole now than you ever were with the stones. Look at your reflection when you are with your son. That is when you are truly yourself, Xain. Not with the eyes of an abomination, but with the eyes of a father."

Xain gave a wan smile at that. "Of course I know that. And I tell myself that every time I spoil Erin with gifts. I say to anyone who asks that I am making up for lost time while I was on the run. To myself, I say that I fear Loren may return and need my help once more, and that I will need to leave him behind again." That smile sank and faded, and Xain pulled his arm away. "But the truth is that I am trying to empty my own coffers—to keep myself from having spare coin, because I know what I might use it for."

Aurel fetched his cooling cup of tea and took a sip, prompting Xain to do the same. He could see some of the anger on the dean's face banished by the warm floral tea. "You suffer an addiction, Xain. It does not matter if that addiction is to the black stones, or to liquor, or to any of a thousand other vices. What matters is that you are stronger than it, and we both know it. If showering your boy with gifts is how you stay strong until you are far enough from your worst, then it is what you need."

"I fear I am not getting any farther from it," Xain said with a sigh. "No matter how many days or weeks or months pass, the thought of those hateful little stones follows me everywhere." He took a deep breath and placed his hands flat on the workbench. "It grows harder, not easier, to ignore their siren call. Whenever they appear, they look more appetizing. More necessary. I do not think of all I have accomplished without them, or all they could cost me. I think how much easier things would be with them. How much stronger I could be with them coursing through my veins. How I could bend the world to my will."

Xain stared at his hands. Aurel wished to reach out to him, but the man kept just enough distance between them to make such a thing impossible.

"It would be easy," Xain said, curling his hands into fists. "I could scour the nine kingdoms of all threats. Of all evil. I could turn the Yerrins' own dirty little rocks against them. Blast the Drayden empire to glass. Transform all of Dulmun into a molten-hot river running into a steaming sea."

Xain forced his fists to flatten, and looked up with the saddest smile Aurel had ever seen on the man. "And then you would come for me. The good people of Underrealm. You would see me as evil, as something to be stopped. Even if I never harmed an innocent. And with the magestones running through my veins, you would be right." He paused then, reaching out for his tea with shaking hands. Aurel sat in stunned silence, watching the cup as it reached the dean's parted lips. Before he took a sip, however, Xain smiled wistfully. "Would it be Loren, do you think? Would she be the one who stopped me?"

Aurel swallowed, hard. The dean drank his tea, giving Aurel a brief moment to get himself under control. "The fear in your eyes betrays you, Dean Forredar." Xain looked up, and Aurel nodded. "But you do not fear your own death at the Nightblade's hand. You recognize a darkness in your heart that is not part of you."

"Would that it were true," Xain said sourly. "I have turned my fire on living men before. On Mystics. On—" He paused, choking on the thought. "On Loren. The darkness in my heart *is* part of me. I feared it might be since that moment, but I know it is, now. I made that plain to myself atop the Academy's tower with the merchant children."

"I am sure that you do not mean to imply that you were a threat to the children under your watch," said Aurel quickly.

"Oh, but I was. To Ebon, and to Lilith—that Yerrin girl I have spoken of before." Xain looked to the ceiling, tracing his eyes over the swirls and loops of the bare wood. "Atop the Academy's tower, the criminal Isra had a package of magestones. There were so many." His voice took on a breathless tone. "Ebon and Lilith were the only ones there, and they were exhausted and battered already." He ran a hand across his face, pushing his hair back. "I could have killed them, placed the blame on Isra, and walked away with a parcel of black stones. I almost did, too." Xain gripped his hair tightly. "I told Ebon to destroy them, but he was so slow. So—so stupid. He thought my fire would work against magestones. I almost killed him. Had he hesitated a moment longer, I would have done it. My need for those wretched rocks stoked my anger, and I almost incinerated him right then and there."

"Surely it was just that moment, though," Aurel said carefully. He looked to the basement door again, worry creasing his brow. "A brief weakness is nothing to be afraid of. You said yourself it was your need for the stones and not your true desire."

"Ah, but what is true desire if not the thing we feel when all else fades away?" Xain shook his head, releasing his hair to force his hands to the tabletop again. "My desires felt good. Right. And with the stones in hand I could have turned any of their family to ash in the wind if they sought revenge. They grasp at power, but I would show them what true power is. I would have shown those filthy merchants, with their assassins and their riches, that such things burn as easily as the lives they crush in their wake. I wanted it." Xain looked up to Aurel, the pain clear on his face. "I wanted to kill. I wanted to go to war with their families and strike every one of them dead. I wanted to kill a child—one of my own charges—just because he was a Drayden and because he took longer to follow my orders than I felt was appropriate."

They sat in uncomfortable silence for a moment. Aurel fought hard to keep from glancing at the basement door again. "You are right," he said finally. "Your addiction *is* a part of you. Once it touches you, you cannot get away from it. But it does not define you. Addiction is not who you are. The desire to kill did not come from you."

"But I was—"

"No, Xain," Aurel said firmly. He raised his hand to stop the man's protest. "It was not you. You are a smart man, too smart by far to depend upon violence to solve every problem. Your first instinct was your true desire. What you truly wanted."

"But my first instinct was to kill them. To kill children."

"No, it was not. Your first instinct, when the danger passed, was to demand the magestones be destroyed." Aurel shook his head. "Everything else came after that choice. You made the first move, and your addiction tried desperately to beat you down after. If your first instinct had been to take the stones and lie about disposing of them—or turning them over to the Mystics, or whatever other excuse—then I would say that mayhap your addiction was ruling you. But it does not."

Xain's brow furrowed in thought. He looked down into the bottom of his empty teacup for a long moment of silence.

"You speak of them truly," Aurel continued. "You call them 'hateful little stones' and 'wretched black rocks.' Even when you say the word 'magestones,' you say it as if it is the foulest curse. You can say that you crave them, and that a part of you calls for them in need, but at the bottom of all that, you hate them. You hate them more than anything." Aurel reached out and put his hand to Xain's arm once more. "Your true self, the man I know, if left alone in a room with every magestone in the nine kingdoms, would put them to the torch before he let one pass between his lips."

Xain's chest hitched for a moment, but he nodded. He looked up to Aurel, his face strained and tears near, but his eyes were clear. Resolution danced behind them. "I hope you are right."

"I know that I am. With all that you have now? With how far you have come? Would you trade one moment of your time since your return to the Seat for a whole lifetime with the eyes of an abomination?"

"Never." Xain smiled at this, and it was a true smile at last. "Not even a moment of paperwork at the Academy." He shook his head as if to clear away the anger and fear. "Thank you." Aurel nodded, unsure of what else to say. He went to retract his hand from Xain's arm, but the dean reached out with both hands and grasped it firmly. "I mean it. You are a true friend."

"I do only what you would do for me," Aurel said with a smile. He let his hand slip from Xain's grasp, but only because the dean's hands were still clammy.

THREE

ANOTHER STRETCH OF SILENCE SLIPPED BETWEEN THEM. "I APOLOGIZE," Xain said finally. "I let my fear run away with my tongue. I should not put so many burdens on you. My mistakes are not yours to correct."

"There is nothing to apologize for." Aurel offered his most welcoming smile, and he was glad to see Xain return it, even if the smile was weak on the dean's lips. "You are a friend in need. I am honored that you feel like you can be so honest with me." Tension visibly left Xain's shoulders as Aurel spoke.

"I only wish that I could repay you somehow. This is not the first time I have needed advice and someone to listen."

"If only," Aurel said with a sigh. "Especially today."

Xain leaned over to look at Aurel's sketches and materials. "Is there some noble with more coin than memory who just realized he needs a gift to commemorate his marriage?"

"Nothing like that," Aurel said, forcing the ghost of a smile. "This is a gift for a friend of my granddaughter. It's the girl's birthday today, and her father promised a miracle."

"As we fathers are known to do." Xain ran his fingers through his hair, pushing the dark mass away from his eyes. "It looks as if it will be a lovely piece. She will be awed by this miracle, indeed. Although—" he paused, looking at the aging sketch "—it appears if you have made such a thing before."

"You have caught me." Aurel chuckled. "I am in a terrible rush, and so I am using an old design."

"A smart move, that." Xain frowned at the design. Aurel knew the man had no knowledge of silversmithing, but he was uncommonly intelligent. "It looks as if there are many fine details. I do not envy your task, nor your determination to make the impossible a reality." Aurel glared up at him, and an easy grin crossed Xain's mouth.

"You cannot even guess the half of it." Aurel pointed to the sketches. "The problem is the finer workings. It would be easier to make by starting with a thick gauge of wire and fusing it together, but I already have barely enough wire for the chain I will need to make. I either need to carve it out of the thicker sheets by hand, or waste yet more time making my own wire."

Xain tapped a finger to his chin. "It is a shame you do not still have the original locket. You could save yourself some work there."

Aurel looked at the door to the basement. "I do have it, actually." He almost blurted out that it was in the basement, but he knew Xain well enough to know the young man would insist on barging down there to look for it. "But I would rather not use it," Aurel added, looking back to Xain. "It belonged to my mother. I was hoping for one of my children or grandchildren to inherit it, someday."

"Hm." Xain frowned, looking down at the sketches, but saying nothing.

"I would know that sound anywhere," Aurel said with a laugh. "Speak your mind, firemage."

Xain looked up, lifting an eyebrow. "It just seems unlike you to be so selfish."

"Selfish?" Aurel leaned back, stretching sore muscles. "How is that selfish?"

"I assume you made the locket for your mother," Xain said, and Aurel nodded. "It has meaning for you, and it had meaning for her. But you are not wearing it now." Xain twirled a finger through the air. "It will not have meaning to your children or grandchildren. Nor will it have meaning to their children after them, except as a lump of silver. Their inheriting it is explicitly for you, then, not for them."

Aurel stared at Xain for a moment, but broke eye contact first. He found himself unable to dispute the idea.

"Mayhap your granddaughter would be just as honored for this heirloom to be given as a gift," Xain said.

Aurel thought about that. Mahrit *was* just the type of selfless person to find honor in sharing something so personal with a friend. Her altruistic nature made Aurel proud. Still he said nothing for a moment, instead sipping his cooled tea. The jasmine had bloomed almost perfectly, causing the tea to take on a delicate flavor that was sweet and soothing.

Xain's idea was a simple solution. And one he was surprised he had not thought of. "You are right, Xain. Thank you." Aurel lowered the cup and smiled at his friend. "I am in your debt for opening my eyes to this."

"There is no debt, for I have yet to repay the years you have spent setting me on the right course in matters more important than jewelry. Consider it a small return on *that* debt instead."

Aurel laughed. "The day you consider there being a debt between us is the day I no longer call you my friend." Xain joined in on the laughter, and for a moment all was right.

Xain collected the teacups and piled them on the tray. "I have dominated too much of your time today, however. And I should return to my own duties. I am sure there is some crisis waiting for my attentions within the Academy's walls." The two of them shared a conspiratorial laugh.

The two men embraced before Xain left. They spoke the pleasantries of friends with promises to see one another soon, and then Aurel was alone once again.

Alone, with an assassin.

Aurel stood by the door for a moment. The sun's light through the window told him it was only an hour or two from midday. He had to venture into the cellar to fetch his mother's locket to begin working on it. That was not an enticing prospect. Startling the assassin could be deadly. He would rather she wake on her own, panic, and flee.

But Aurel had work to do, and not a great deal of time.

He heaved a deep breath and took the plunge before he could convince himself otherwise. Aurel swung the door wide, careful to not bang it against the wall, and descended into the basement.

The woman was sitting upright and looking right at him.

Aurel held his breath. She was bleary-eyed, and her weapons were still atop her pile of clothes, paces from her hands. She had only just awakened, and was not about to kill him.

"I am glad to see you recovered so quickly," Aurel said, giving her a warm smile to try to remain calm. His heart fluttered in his chest, and sweat prickled across his scalp once more. "After seeing how much blood was soaked into your clothes, I feared that there would be none left in your body."

"I am sturdier than I look," she responded. She peered at him with her good eye, a piercing look that said she was sizing him up. He was being weighed and measured. Evaluated against whatever values an assassin held dear. "Though I admit, there was a moment where I shared that fear."

"Ah, where are my manners, though," Aurel said as he continued down the stairs, trying to show no fear. If he could convince her that he didn't know she was an assassin, she might be less inclined to view him as a potential liability. "I am Aurel of the family Mein, a silversmith of some renown."

"Of course," she said, nodding. "I have heard of your work."

"I always find it flattering to be recognized." He smiled smoothly and grabbed a stool near the bottom of the stairs. Aurel carried it over to her side so that he would have a place to sit. He didn't want to make her stand up if she wasn't ready for the exertion. "But you have me at a disadvantage, then. You are . . .?"

"Talib," she said sharply. He hadn't expected a family name or other identifier, and she provided none.

Aurel set the stool down and eased himself into it, keeping a respectful distance. "A pleasure to meet you, Talib," he said with the same smile from before. He gestured at the pile of her possessions across the room. "First, let me apologize for the need to remove your armor. The physician who saw to your wound could not easily work around the leather, and she was concerned about infection as well." He then gestured to the simple linen shirt he had helped Eile dress her in. "These clothes were my eldest daughter's. She left them behind when she moved away with her husband. You are welcome to keep them." He laughed under his breath. "They were only collecting dust here."

Talib said nothing, and instead watched him in silence. Her judgment of his every word lingered like a weight across his skin.

"If you worry about the constables who were chasing you down, you can relax." She looked a bit shocked, but Aurel kept his smile warm and nonthreatening. "They stopped by twice looking for someone, but I am no stranger when it comes to recognizing when something needs to be hidden." The tiniest bit of tension left her shoulders. "They had no description of you besides the blade in your shoulder, and so they gave up the hunt before the moons set." He failed to mention that the constables hadn't been terribly insistent, only going door-to-door and asking after someone bleeding, but she didn't need to know that.

"Why?" she said finally, her head cocked to the side. "Why would you hide me if you knew I was wanted by the law? Why help a stranger like that?"

"Would you not do the same?" he asked, mirroring her head tilt. "You looked as though you knew more hardship than most, and it is in my nature to give a moment of comfort to those in need." He laughed once more and leaned back on his stool, straightening his spine before it could complain. "I would think anyone with a good heart would offer a helping hand to someone injured and near to death. Running from the constables or no." He placed his hands on his knees. "Though, truth be told, if it had been the Mystics after you, this situation may have been different." He chuckled. As if he hadn't hidden anyone from the red cloaks.

"I appreciate the aid, then," Talib said after a moment. Aurel tried not to tense when her eyes cut across to her equipment, and to the daggers on the top of the pile. "Thank you."

"I am glad to help. Although . . . well, if you would humor an old man, I do feel the need to ask: there are many reasons a good person might end up on the wrong side of the constable's attention. What happened?"

Talib looked away from the knives and instead watched him a moment. She settled back against the pillows of the cot and leaned her head back to look to the ceiling. "I was simply in the wrong place at the wrong time." She sighed, and silence stretched between them. Aurel watched as her eyes darted to and fro, trying to find her lies along the wooden ceiling. "Some merchant family scion got too drunk in the Empty Cup. He started a drunken argument with another patron. I interfered." Talib paused again, long enough to give a convincing shrug. "He was displeased with someone talking back to him. Things went . . . poorly from there." She reached beneath the collar of her shirt and tugged on a simple silver chain that hung from her neck. "When the constables arrived, it became clear that they would not arrest a goldshi—" she paused and cleared her throat before finishing the unseemly word. "Pardon. A merchant's son. Why arrest him when his family's coin could line their pockets to arrest me instead?"

"I see," Aurel said slowly, nodding even though he didn't believe her. It was a decent story, and one she had likely seen or even lived. But her delivery needed work. Between her clipped language and her clearly uncomfortable tells, it was obvious she made it up on the spot.

But just the same, he didn't dare try and bring that up. "Not everyone has enough of a gift with words to stop a fight, if someone is intent on starting one. It was noble of you to step in like that."

She looked down at him, letting her fingers fall from the chain. A sigh escaped her throat. "I am a little worried about the aftermath of the fight." Her eyes flicked up again, towards the door this time instead of to the ceiling or to her weapons. "I left in a hurry, so I do not know if everyone ended up alright."

"Of course. Your aim was not to hurt anyone." He smiled. She was looking to leave, and that was good for him. He was not inclined to stop her. "It bodes well that you might feel remorse for whatever happened to your other dagger."

His words were a calculated statement. Another bluff. She was suspicious of him. If he played an entirely naive fool, she may have seen through the ruse and ended him there. It was safer to recognize that she had two sheaths, but only one dagger.

Talib fell silent, and her furrowed brow worried him.

The silence between them stretched to an uncomfortable length. Aurel began to fear that if he didn't say anything, it would be the last mistake he ever made.

"I think you have a good heart," he said finally. She jumped at the sudden statement, and he didn't blame her. "That is an important thing. As long as your intentions are good, you will lead yourself back to the right path."

"Thank you for the kind words," she said slowly. "And for the assistance. But I believe I have a lot to do today if I want to avoid being haunted by my actions for years to come."

"Of course," Aurel said with a ghost of a smile. He stood up to hide the sigh of relief. "I hope the next time we meet it will be under more pleasant circumstances." He offered his hand to help her stand.

"I hope so as well." Talib stood without taking the offered hand, but she gave him a genuine smile. "Though I am at a loss for how they could have been worse."

"Do not say such things," Aurel said, forcing a chuckle. "Fate has a habit of surprising us."

Talib smiled in return, a tiny thing that hinted at her unease. She collected her things in silence as he watched. When the bundle was secured in her arms, she ascended the stairs out of the basement. Aurel was tempted to grab his mother's locket before following her, but he decided to walk Talib out. If Xain had forgotten something and returned, or if any of his other various friends had stopped by while he was downstairs, it would be potentially disastrous if she exited the cellar carrying a bundle of blood-soaked clothes without Aurel nearby.

She climbed the stairs almost as awkwardly as he did, but her unease came from not having a free hand with which to steady herself, since one arm held her belongings and the other dangled limply at her side.

"I presume I cannot persuade you to stay for lunch?" Aurel asked as they reached the top of the stairs.

"If it is truly late enough for lunch instead of breakfast, I have lost enough of the day already." She looked to the blood-stained bundle under her arm. "I do feel bad, though, for absconding with your daughter's shirt. If you give me a few moments I can change and return it to you. Although it takes me a bit longer than it used to."

"Worry not—keep the clothing. The shirt fits you better than it does me, after all." He patted his belly and laughed.

She didn't join in his laughter, but she did smile, and that was enough. "Thank you. I appreciate your help. If there is anything I can do to repay your kindness, please seek me out." She bowed her head towards him. "I would be honored for the opportunity."

"I do not accept debts from those in need, but I appreciate your offer. It speaks well of your good heart that you offer your aid so earnestly." Talib smiled softly and turned to head for the door, but Aurel reached out and touched her non-injured arm. "I do have one request, Talib. Mayhap there is something you can do for me."

She stopped and looked back at him, confusion clear on her face. "Yes? What do you need?"

"If I may ask—could I have your necklace?" Before she could respond he continued, rushing to explain his situation. "I find myself in a bit of a bind today. I have need of a chain for a commission and I have none prepared, nor the time to spare to make one. I understand if yours has significance to you and you wish to not part with it. But otherwise, I would be very grateful."

Talib started at him for a moment, unmoving. He stilled as well, waiting for her response. She blinked a few times and stepped to the counter, putting down the bundle of her belongings before reaching up to pull the chain off her neck. It had no pendant hanging from it, which oddly made Aurel feel more guilty about asking for it.

"It feels odd to me," she said at last, the chain dangling from her fingers, "to be giving silver to a silversmith. But I suppose you must come by it somewhere." She handed the chain over without hesitation. "As payment for your kindness, Aurel. I am glad for the opportunity to offer you the help you require."

Aurel pulled the chain close, examining it. He was surprised to find it was of fine make, even if it was a bit tarnished. Why would she relinquish it so easily? But before he could ask, she was making her way to the door. Aurel rushed forwards and opened the door for her, allowing her to move through it while still carrying her belongings.

Talib said no goodbyes, and Aurel offered none in return. He watched her walk down the street until she turned the corner, in case she turned back to look his way, but no such thing happened.

And with her departure, Aurel knew he had no more excuses to keep him from fetching his mother's locket.

FOUR

Aurel was lost to his work.

He had fetched the locket and set about polishing both it and the chain Talib gave him. The repetitive work soothed him, drawing him into a world where his only focus was his task at hand. As soon as they were cleaned, he worked on repairing the locket: he first had to buff out the inscription, and then he moved on to repairing the latticework that had become bent and broken over years of wear. It was diligent, consuming work.

It wasn't until the bell rang at the front door that he looked up.

His mind told him that it should be barely after midday, but the lighting was wrong. It was much darker than it should have been.

Aurel struggled to his feet, fighting stiff hip and knee. The joints were like old floorboards, angry and full of noise about having to be used. His first few steps away from his workbench were painful and awkward as his knees refused to bend and he had to shuffle along instead. They loosened before he got to the doorway into the foyer.

He was shocked to see how late it had become. While the Seat was rarely ever truly dark with so many living on its streets, the outside world was now the faint grey and purple of early evening. The moons would rise soon, and his time would be up.

His guest waited just inside the door, her hands folded neatly in front of her. Her outfit was simple and yet elegant, with polished boots, a nearly floor-length dress of emerald skirts, and topped with a tiny silver hairpin that tied the whole ensemble together. Adara was as beautiful as ever, and poised so perfectly. A pang of guilt lanced through Aurel's chest.

The half-remembered plans. He had been so distracted with first Xain and Talib, and then his work, that he had forgotten about their arrangement. He was supposed to make dinner before she arrived, so that they could eat while they discussed her desires for Ebon's present.

"Adara," he said, rubbing his eyes. "You must forgive me. I lost track of time. I have not even begun dinner yet, and I fear I may have missed lunch as well."

"You poor man," Adara said with a smile, approaching the counter. She reached over and placed a hand to his arm. "Have you had a busy day?"

"No truer words have been spoken, and I still have more to do, I am afraid." He grimaced and looked back into the workroom. "I have a deadline fast approaching—faster than I had originally assumed."

"Worry not then," she said, suddenly chipper. "I know my way around a kitchen, and so I shall cook for you." Adara's smile soothed Aurel's guilt away easily. "You can finish your work and still have a meal with me. To discuss my commission or not, I care little."

"Oh, no, I could not ask such a thing of you. My work . . . my work will simply need to be late, is all." He thought of Wira and Chim, and then of Mahrit, all waiting for him. When he grimaced, Adara laughed.

"I insist," she said, her tone clearly saying that no matter what he might think, this was not up for argument. "Your punctuality is important to you. Finish your work, and let me take care of the meal."

Mayhap it was the forcefulness of her tone, or even the exhaustion that threatened to knock him to his knees, but Aurel relented. "Thank you," he breathed, relieved. "You are perfection itself, dear Adara, and I do not deserve your friendship." He shuffled towards the shop again, then paused and turned back. "Although I believe I may have to ask you another favor." When she didn't ask, he continued. "Your hairpin. May I see it for a moment?"

Adara looked puzzled, but she pulled the pin from her hair and held it out to him. "It was a gift from a client hat I have not seen in a long while," she said. "Is there something wrong with it?"

"Not at all. I only think this could help me with my project." He examined the pin, turning it over in his hand. It had a hinge that could replace that of the locket without him having to make a new one. And the carefully crafted silver flower ornament that adorned it hold a tiny polished garnet in the middle. The orange-red of the gem reflected off the silver petals. The flower would fit over the broken bit of lattice he had worked so hard to repair, and without him needing to continue his efforts.

After finishing his examination, he explained the situation to her. He left out the details of Xain and his magestones, as well as Talib and her knives. But he told her of the party, the sickness, and the promise. When he had finished, she smiled and clasped her hand around his, locking the small pin into his hand. "I would be honored if I could pass along my pin for such a cause. It is a noble purpose, and I am happy to help, even if all that is required is to part with an old piece of silver."

With that said, she climbed the stairs into Aurel's living space to prepare dinner.

Aurel returned to work.

* * *

Little more than an hour passed before Adara found her way into his workshop again. Aurel had removed the old latch and replaced it, and was actively working on setting the flower into the locket's lattice. He looked up when she approached. "Only a moment more," he said before looking back down at the locket. "I am nearly done. I will join you in the upstairs when I am through."

"I should have known better than to expect an artist to stop working to eat," she said with a light chuckle. "Do not take long. If I have to come back down, you risk wearing your dinner instead of eating it."

Aurel laughed. Adara always reminded him of his eldest daughter, who had fled the Seat to live with her Idrisian lover. He missed his daughter, but he didn't have time to reminisce. Unless he wanted to wear fish to the party.

Instead he focused on the task at hand, banishing all other thought. It truly did not take long for him to fuse the silver flower into place, and once it was cooled, the shining silver locket was complete.

There was very little resemblance now to the locket he had gifted his mother. The timeless look of the silver lattice gave it elegance, but the touches added by the hairpin parts—the almost too-dainty hinge and the beautiful silver flower with its central garnet—gave it a youthful charm. As he threaded it onto the chain that had once belonged to Talib of the Tabarzin, he realized that the freshly-polished silver tied the look together marvelously.

The finished work was the perfect representation of his day. All of his surprises soldered together made a piece that was better than what he could have made on his own, without Xain's scolding, or Talib's gratitude, or Adara's generosity.

He rushed up the stairs, in spite of his tired and cranky joints, to show the final product to his waiting guest.

"It is lovely," Adara said, touching it gently to let the light from the lamp dance across the glittering lattice. "Amazing work. And you say you only began this morning?"

"It . . . it has been a hectic day." Aurel settled into his seat, putting the locket to the side of their plates. "I am glad to have completed it in time. I apologize that we will not have long to sit before I must rush out. The party will begin soon and I must deliver this as soon as we have finished eating."

"Nonsense," Adara said with a patient smile. "We will have plenty of time to speak, both over dinner and as I accompany you to the family Ritonga's home."

"You would come with me?"

"Naturally."

Aurel wanted to argue. She likely had much more important things to do that evening. Accompanying him to a child's birthday party was beneath her. But he could see that behind her smile hid the resolution and stubbornness he missed in his daughter, and so he instead decided to focus on the food. He was quick to move the flaky fish and roasted potatoes to his mouth. It was rude to speak with your mouth full, after all.

As they ate, they caught up. Adara told him of a few of events she had been to lately, and she shared word of the gifts she received from clients. But eventually the conversation turned to Ebon, as it always did, and Adara finally started to tell Aurel her idea for his gift.

She wanted to give Ebon a ring, and she knew just how she wanted it to look. Aurel gave her as much of his attention as he could, but his mind wandered. The day's events had left him more tired than he ought to have been, and regardless, he would have to get the description from Adara again later, when he could actually begin his work.

Once their meal was done, Adara went to clean up. Aurel protested, but it didn't matter. "Go and prepare for the party," she said, shooing him away from the kitchen. "I will clean up as you do, and then we can leave together."

Aurel clicked his tongue to the back of his teeth in mock disappointment. "To think, a woman of your stature reduced to cooking and cleaning for an old man like me." He smiled wryly. "What would your parents say if they found out?"

"It matters not what they would say," Adara said, her cheeks red. When he laughed at her blushing, she stomped with one foot. "This is what I choose to do, and neither your words nor theirs will stop me. Go!"

Aurel had no argument for that, and so went into his bedroom and changed out of his work clothes. The trials of the day slowed him considerably, so by the time he had finished lacing up his nice boots and returned to the kitchen, Adara was done with the washing up and was waiting for him. Together they left the shop, putting away the angled sign and locking the door. They walked the streets of the Seat, arm in arm, speaking of pleasant, trivial things to pass the time.

* * *

When they got within paces of the Ritonga home, close enough to see the brightly lit lamps and hear the laughter of those inside, she manifested from the shadows. Talib's approach was casual—just two steps from the alley before she leaned against the nearby wall. But there was something in her stance that caused the panic of the morning to return.

Aurel halted to a stop, and Adara with him. She began to question him, but Aurel shook his head, and she instead looked to Talib. "I did not know Mako's finest worried themselves with the common folk," Adara said with a haughty tone.

Talib looked pointedly at the girl. "Adara. Go inside."

For a moment she seemed intent on arguing, so Aurel interjected. "Yes, please, Adara. Talib and I have a bit of unfinished business, it seems." The assassin nodded, and Aurel's heart turned cold. "I will be just a moment."

Adara looked between the two of them, then turned sharply and continued to the front door of the house. They watched her speak with Wira at the door, and Aurel waved to the man to signify he would come along in just a moment. Wira waved back, and he and Adara went inside, leaving Aurel to face the assassin alone.

"You do not seem surprised to see me."

"I have long known that my meddling would one day be rewarded with forced silence." He squared his shoulders, looking her in the eye. "I only ask for a delay—that I be allowed to spend this night with my family and friends, to share their joy."

Talib laughed, a throaty chuckle that snaked through the darkness. "I am not here to kill you, although I am glad my assumption was correct. You are a clever man, Aurel of the family Mein. Cleverness is a dangerous thing to possess on the Seat."

Aurel blinked at her. "Then why are you here?"

"I have come to relieve your fears." Talib looked away, down the road the way Aurel and Adara had come. "If I did not come, you would have spent nights waiting for me to appear in doorways." She shook her head. "I am leaving the Seat, and I am no longer an assassin. I did not want to torment an old man for his good deeds by keeping my silence."

"What happened? Is everything well?"

Talib looked at him blankly before laughing. "It is compulsive, your need to fix everything for everyone. I learned much of your 'meddling' ways this afternoon, and I commend you for them. Underrealm could use more folk like you." Once more she looked down the street, as if she wished to be elsewhere. "What has happened is between me and my employer. All that you need to know is you will not see me again, as long as I never hear my name upon your lips." She looked back to him sharply. "Ever. I never stepped foot in your shop. You do not know my name. I am nothing to you. It is the only way you will stay safe, from my blades and from those still under the employ of the family Drayden. Do you understand?"

Aurel swallowed hard and nodded. This was a secret he would carry to his grave, like so many before it. Talib appraised him for a moment and then nodded herself. "May we never meet again," she said with a wan smile. She left the way Aurel had come, leaving him to believe she had waited in that alley for some time.

With her gone, Aurel hurried inside. His skin crawled as if a thousand eyes were upon him, and he doubted the feeling would go away any time soon. But he was welcomed to the party with hearty greetings that soothed his worry. Aurel's daughter and granddaughter were quick to approach, and he gave Mahrit the locket for her friend.

"I assumed you would like to do the honors of giving this to Chim," he said with a wide smile. "It is from her father, but I am sure he will not mind."

They approached the girl together. Chim was thin and deathly pale. She was resting in a bed that had been moved into the large living area, propped up against a mountain of pillows. Her smile was slow to form, but when Mahrit introduced her grandfather, and then showed the young woman the present, it became radiant. Aurel's heart warmed at the sight. The girl's hands shook too much for her to work the clasp, so Mahrit fastened it for her.

The piece was lovely by itself, but its sparkling light reflected in the beaming smile upon Chim's face made it a gorgeous work of art. Aurel's hard work and incredible effort wore on him like a heavy weight, but in this moment he wished for nothing else.

"It was all worth it," Aurel said absentmindedly. "I would do it a dozen times over a dozen days to give the world that smile."

"Do what?" his daughter asked, giving him a sidelong glance.

"It has been a trying day, and one worthy of tale." He looked up as Adara approached, a small woman trailing behind her. "Mayhap I will tell it later," he added. Darna looked confused, but nodded.

The woman with Adara was Soemitro, Chim's mother. She had with her a silver ewer of wine, and a handful of cups. Wira joined them, wiping tears from his eyes at seeing his daughter's joy.

Wine was poured and conversation was had, but after about an hour Aurel pulled Adara aside. "You do not need to stay," he said quietly. "I appreciate you accompanying me, but I am sure you have far more interesting places to spend your evening."

"Nonsense," Adara said, taking a small sip of her wine. "You have put yourself through quite a lot to be here, and so I am not convinced anywhere could be more interesting. A man who chases moonslight to accomplish a task for such a cause is a great friend to have." She smiled and looked pointedly around the room. Everyone was having a fine time. There were friends and conversations to be had, and all to celebrate another day of life for a girl who had so few to spare. "There is nowhere in all of Underrealm I would rather be, and I know you feel the same way."

Aurel smiled wide because, of course, she was right.

Blood on the Snow

Rhea Newton

ONE

Tatiana sat by the window and twiddled her thumbs by candlelight, watching the gates of Kalkeane with nervous intensity. Though she did not know it, a long-standing but petty feud was at that moment erupting into a bloody massacre in the castle of Bann Dayne, a mere few spans to the north. And she had been the catalyst.

She replayed the events of that night in her head. What she had done was not strictly against any law, but if Gathran found out . . . the consequences would be severe, mayhap deadly.

The door opened so quickly that she jumped and reached for her knife, but it was only Alder, the Mystic, who had come for her.

"Did it go well?" he asked.

"Just fine."

"And the body?"

"Bron saw it fall in. I heard him roar from across the forest."

Alder arched his eyebrows. "And he did not see you?"

"There is no cavalcade of retainers riding into the city, so it seems he did not."

She peered out of the window just to be sure. The gates of Kalkeane were still shut. The sentry still stood lazily at his post. The wheel of fate continued to turn, uninterrupted.

She smiled as she felt the thrill of freedom creep under her skin.

"You will need to reach Immec by the end of the week," said the Mystic. "Will you manage?"

"I shall be fine," she replied, without thinking. But where there had been confidence and new-found assertiveness a moment ago, there was now doubt; too, the distinct feeling of being lost, after having been trapped for so long that the outside world was a brand-new, intimidating mystery.

"Good." He gave her a feeble smile. "They will be waiting for you."

"Yes, and I cannot keep them. Thank you, Alder, for everything."

"You must not thank me." He raised his hands, palms facing her. "Your deeds and service to the Order will be thanks enough, and you have a lifetime for that."

"Yes," she said again, forcing a smile, "I suppose I do."

Later that evening, in the wee hours of the night when even the owls seemed scarce, a cavalcade of retainers *did* ride into the city, coated in blood and fury. Tatiana was long gone by then, but they did not ask after her anyway. Instead, they sought one Riadrain, of the family Ros.

* * *

Voices echoed through the vast halls of the castle of Bann Dayne, causing Riadrain to shiver nervously. High up, away from prying eyes, the stronghold was masked by the pines that clung to the hillside like fleas to a hound. It was the home of his hated adversary . . . and yet Riadrain was here, eating at the high chief's table.

He fingered the pewter goblet in an attempt to rein in his anxiety. In vain. The red wine sloshed in the vessel as he fiddled with it, and he thought—rather morbidly—that in the dim light, it could be mistaken for blood. Tatiana was nowhere to be seen, which did not help his nerves.

The fire pit blazed with the heat of a hundred logs, more akin to a bonfire than a hearth. The inferno cast a cluster of pulsing shadows on the walls, as the guests supped on the food that had been cooked over it. Roasted turnips, swedes, carrots, and potatoes, sprinkled with a helping of expensive spices from Idris and soaked in gravy and beer. Three filleted trout straight from the Thunderer, coated lavishly in butter and salt. And the main course: roasted mutton soaked and basted in mountaineer's ale, positively dripping with fat and breadcrumbs, which the hungry patrons devoured like starving dogs.

Sometimes it was all he could hear—the slapping of lips and wobbling of jowls, accompanied by the faint crackling and popping of the fire. That part was the worst, when no one spoke. No good tales were ever told of a silent wedding feast. Other times he heard voices only in the dim corners of the room, mutterings of bad tidings and unfinished business, business which Riadrain could only imagine concerned his errant partner. In hours past the castle's hob had played tunes for them on the lute, but now the little creature was nowhere to be seen or heard. Riadrain's family seemed not to have the same qualms as he, and were merrily digging into the fare without a worry in the world.

Across the hearth sat the venerable high chief Gathran, of the family Ronnedayne, now regaling the many guests with a hunting tale from his youth. He was a fat man with an insidious smile. Riadrain liked all of nothing about him.

"Four days! Four days I was alone in that forest. By the sky, it gets dark in there. Such old land, and they say haunted by spirits and Elves and worse. It was poppycock, of course. But my squire begged us to go back, lest we lose our hunting party. Chief Damoine, bless his hide, had stayed behind that morning, and that meant the group was split." He gestured to another man who sat nearby, with a wispy grey beard and sagging cheeks, who seemed half asleep. He must have heard this story many times before. "Now, if there were ever a rule of hunting that my eldmother taught me, it is to never split the party. But I was young and full of fire! Never would I let that beast elude me. The young lad, poor thing, he ate some mushrooms, gave him the cramps. He did not last long thereafter. And so I was alone. For four days, no less!"

He continued the story, loudly enough that nearly all heads in the room were upon him, but Riadrain managed to tune it out.

Where is she?

He had seen her earlier, when she had left under the pretense of relieving herself. But that was before the feast had started, and still her plate was untouched. The high chief did not seem to even notice his daughter's disappearance, so deep was he in his own arrogance.

What foolery this was. Riadrain had been skeptical from the first, but he had allowed himself to be charmed by the promises of this pretty woman. This pretty, absentee woman, with her crystal-clear eyes the color of the sky, and her infectious laughter. No good thing had ever come of a decision made by one's loins.

And not only to give her the promise of his love, but to be wed to her for all their lives . . . it was a daunting prospect. Riadrain was a traditionalist. He liked to believe that love was fluid and cyclical, like time itself, and that to be tied to a single lover was as ridiculous as could be. After all, why would anyone be content to eat only of one dish for the rest of their lives, when the world was so rich with variety? But times were changing. The petty nobles of Hedgemond had realized the advantage of political marriages, and the merchant families found it especially hard to deny a dowry when it came their way. The old ways were dying in Hedgemond, and Riadrain did not like it.

What foolery indeed. What boneheaded, short-sighted greed. Love was natural, and fleeting, and struck like lightning. It did not sit in meeting rooms and discuss the terms of its commitment, sign its name at the bottom of a contract, or happily exchange itself for a coin-purse from the highest bidder. He had loved and lost, and would do so again. And now . . .

Her image flashed across his mind once more. He remembered the way she had introduced herself, how they had spoken, and how they had laughed. And he realized with some shock that love was unbidden, that it was natural, and that it truly did strike like lightning.

He made a decision.

Little did he know that it would save his life.

"Excuse me, Mother, Your Lordship, honored guests. If it is agreeable with you, I would check on my bride. She has been absent overlong, I fear."

Gathran gave him a dirty look, seemingly more annoyed at the interruption than anything else. He waved a hand absentmindedly, and so Riadrain bowed and took his leave. The high chief continued his story.

Riadrain approached the first servant he saw in the corridor and asked for directions to his lady's room. "She is clearly overcome with emotion," he explained, "and I would go to her, so that she might rejoin us at the feast."

The servant complied, giving Riadrain a list of lengthy and confusing directions for how to reach the lady's chambers as well as a fair warning that Pogg was on guard duty that day.

"Pogg?" he asked.

"One of our gabbers," said the servant. "A gentle sort he is, s'long as you don't rile him."

The young nobleman tensed. A gabber guarding the upstairs . . .

And why not? he thought. The family Ronnedayne was more than rich enough. A gentle sort, the servant had said, which was true enough of any gabber. Until they were riled.

Though the servant had been very roundabout in her directions, she had been clear in one thing: the lady's chambers were near the top of the keep. So Riadrain climbed any stairs he could find. Whether by luck or good wits, he found the right rooms soon enough—and with them, Pogg.

The beast was not exceptionally tall—he stood only a few hands higher than Riadrain himself—but he was built like a mountain, with arms the width of tree trunks and a torso that looked as heavy as a warship. From his back grew jagged rocks—as much a formidable weapon as an impenetrable defense. Riadrain saw the twinkle of a gemstone lodged somewhere in the stones, a sign of Pogg's advanced age. His underbelly and face were softer, but by no means soft. Someone not familiar with Hedgemond's fauna might have called him a walking, talking rock, and they would not have been far off.

Pogg stood on his feet and knuckles like an ape, his tiny head staring intently into the darkness.

"You!" he bellowed when Riadrain approached. "You! No go! Beddychambers. Lady Dayne. Pogg guard."

"There is nothing to fear, my friend. I am the lady's . . . husband." The word felt strange upon his lips. "I have come to see that Lady Ronnedayne is well, and nothing more. Is she within?" He kept a generous distance between Pogg and himself. It would do no good for the marriage alliance to fail because his guts had been used by the high chief's gabber to mop the floor.

Pogg hummed and hawed at his request, producing the kind of sound that usually preceded the collapse of a building.

"What humie name?" he asked, slowly.

"Riadrain, of the family Ros."

"Ree . . . ah . . . drain?"

Riadrain nodded carefully. The gabber thought for a moment, as if remembering a long-lost relative.

"Ah! Yes! Lady Dayne, gone!"

"What? Where is she?" Fear began to crawl back up inside him. He had had his suspicions about the lady, but had forced himself to forget them until now.

"Gone! River! Gone Thunderer. Want think. Lady sad. Make Pogg sad. But no time for. Must guard." He smiled, or at least tried to. His teeth looked like more rocks.

"If she has left, then what are you guarding?"

"Uhhhhhh . . . ah! Note."

"A note?"

The gabber nodded enthusiastically. "Lady Dayne say: stay! Guard note. Then . . . hmm . . ."

"Then?" asked Riadrain. It took great effort not to lose patience with these beings, sometimes.

"Hmm . . ." said Pogg, a noise so deep and rattling that it could have been made by an earthquake. "Lady Dayne . . . go . . . say guard . . . Pogg . . . Ah! Now 'member! You go! Read note! Important."

He nodded gravely and then thundered aside, revealing the round wooden door to the lady's quarters.

Riadrain needed no other hints. He hurriedly turned the latch and swung the door open, then leaped into the room. He found the bed itself farther back, and sure enough, resting upon it was a small scrap of curled parchment. He picked it up and read hurriedly.

TWO

Below, in the great hall of Bann Dayne Castle, there was an argument brewing between two women. At first it was just a snide remark, in which the Chief of Rane rather unpleasantly implied to the groom's mother—her counterpart of Glanna—that Riadrain had only been chosen to marry Gathran's daughter and tanist because of the Ros clan's history of belligerency and delinquency, which the high chief intended to stop forever.

Of course, she of Glanna and Ros did not take kindly to these accusations, naming the Chief of Rane a jealous sow who buried her snout in too many people's affairs, and suggested the lady refrain from insulting her betters, lest said betters take offense.

As it happened, she of Rane was the one to take offense, namely at the wording of the Chief Ros' retort, in particular her being likened to a squealing farm animal despite her enviable fitness and physique.

The verbal sparring continued for some time, though most did not notice it, as Gathran was making such a show of his hunting story that no one could have had ears for anything else.

* * *

Sanna was leaning against the wall and fiddling with her sword hilt when the servant burst into the hall, interrupting Gathran's tale once again. She thanked the sky that it was over, at least for a while.

"It-it was the groom," sputtered the servant with some difficulty. "Said it were urgent, s-said to give you this."

Gathran pushed himself away from the table as he stood up, causing his chair to scrape the stone floor with a horrible screech. He threw out his huge, calloused hand. "What is the meaning of this foolery? Give me that!"

The servant handed it over without hesitation. "Said to follow him, to the Thunderer. Said to go quickly, 'fore it's too late."

Sanna winced slightly at the woman's tone. Something terrible was afoot.

The hall fell into silence as the high chief read the parchment, deathly still and deathly quiet.

When he had finished, he merely slumped back into his chair and said nothing. The crackling fire was all anyone could hear. The note he placed gingerly on the table, as if afraid to look at it again.

"May I?" asked the Chief of Rane. Sanna's eyes darted to her charge, who was now reaching tentatively for the scrap.

Gathran nodded silently, and so the lady began to read. Sanna resisted the urge to leave her place and peek over her lady's shoulder. She was a bodyguard, not an adviser. Certainly, she was no snoop either.

Strangely, the chieftess laughed. "Hah!" she cried, "What a terrible ruse! This was their plan all along, my lord! To kidnap your daughter, or worse!"

"What are you saying, woman?" asked Gathran with incredulity.

"I say, my chieftain, that this is not only a forged notice, but a bad ploy. That Riadrain has run off with your daughter. Likely these ingrates will try to ransom her—"

The sharp snap of a hand hitting flesh echoed through the hall, as the groom's mother stood from her place beside the other woman. The Chief of Rane recoiled, clutching her face in horror. Sanna reached for the hilt of her weapon, fingers aquiver.

"Sky curse your unbounded idiocy, woman," said the lady of Glanna, nursing her fingers. "Do you truly believe that my son—"

The Chief of Rane returned a punch to the other woman's stomach, and she doubled over. It proved to be the spark that would set off the wildfire. Near a hundred weapons were drawn in unison as a legion of sworn shields stepped up to protect their charges. Gathran continued to sit low in his chair, as if oblivious to the commotion.

Sanna's heart thumped loudly in her ears, such that she could barely hear what was now being said. She glanced over and saw her bow leaning against the wall nearby. The bow her father had given her once she had come of age. She reached for it, her veins afire, and thoughtlessly nocked an arrow.

The Chief of Rane had freed herself from the table now, standing to face that of Glanna as if to engage in a fight to the death. But the groom's mother remained where she had been, bent over and clutching her stomach. Amidst the din and the chaos, Sanna saw something that nobody else did—the woman's hand, reaching for something small and shiny at her ankle.

Everything happened very quickly after that.

One lady came hurtling for the other, her hidden dagger now revealed and fury on her face; the room's occupants screamed and shouted; Sanna let fly her arrow; Wylthe of Ros, Chief of Glanna fell backwards with feathers sprouting from her chest.

When Sanna would later recall the events of that night, the order of these things was impossible for her to determine. But it did not much matter anyway.

* * *

Riadrain found what he was looking for with very little effort. All he had done was follow the sound of roaring and shouting, until he came across a vast swath of the forest that had been cut away by a gabber gone berserk. As the rider approached, the sound of the creature's cursing and hollering became almost unbearable.

He had to shout to be heard. "Where is the Lady Ronnedayne?"

The gabber did not hear him, but only continued to wail.

Dismounting from his borrowed horse, Riadrain found the largest stick he could lift and threw it like a javelin. The gabber, lost in his throes, did not see it coming, and the wood struck him in the relatively soft face.

"What?" he shouted. "Who hit?"

The lumbering brute swung a rocky arm around as if to strike whatever was there, decapitating another tree in the process. Wood shards flew everywhere, but he hardly seemed to mind. Riadrain was fortunately staying well away.

"Lady Ronnedayne!" He tried again. "Where is she? Did you come here with her?"

"Lady!" he wailed, a horrible, gut-wrenching noise. "Jump!" He tried to jump, which, in reality, resulted in little more than him raising its arms in anticipation. Then he pointed at the river nearby.

Riadrain sank to his knees. The sting of the revelation struck deep, such that he could hardly breathe. He was too late.

The woman who had married him just earlier that day, smiling all the while, had taken her own life. The signs had been there, he thought, that she had never been happy with the arrangement, despite what she said. He suspected there was even more he did not know, concerning her father the chief and his wicked ways. Whatever her grievances, they had driven her to jump into the Thunderer.

Here, where the river narrowed and was channeled between hard, jagged rocks, it carved underground caves and pockets. There were whirlpools and invisible, deadly currents, all just below the deceptively calm surface. This stretch of the river had claimed many a life, voluntarily or otherwise.

Now it had claimed one more. And Riadrain felt as the gabber looked. If rocks could cry, he would imagine that the creature would be doing that just now.

"Dead! Dead, dead, dead! Lordship find out! Kill Bron! Punish!" He threw his head against the nearest surviving trunk as penance. Riadrain barely heard him. "Kill Bron, no! No! Lordship punish! No! But . . . but . . . if . . . yes . . . no see, no hear. Bron leave. Gone. Ladylike. No see. No one. No hear."

I failed her, thought Riadrain bitterly. *Not a day into this ritual and I failed in my oh-so-sacred duty.* It was enough to prove what he had already believed: that he never should have bought into this idea of marriage. And his bride . . . she had died for her father's greed. That was no arrangement that Riadrain wished to be a part of, whether he loved her or not.

Yes, the old ways existed for a reason, and it was time for Hedgemond to—

Wait. What is that?

The sound he heard was the gabber crashing through what was left of the forest with a blood-curdling roar.

"Kill!" Bron cried, "Kill humie!"

The horse whinnied in panic and bolted.

Riadrain, still kneeling on the wet grass, had to dive like a madman to avoid the charge. He threw himself as hard as he could and barely escaped with his legs intact. The beast whirled with impressive speed and came again.

There was no way Riadrain could win this fight, and his only means of escape had fled already. Every dodge was a chance of failure—of death. Scrambling to his feet, he pivoted and pirouetted again, but with scarcely a moment to spare.

An idea struck him. He did not have long to think it over before the gabber came again.

Riadrain positioned himself near the edge of the river, where the rocks were wet and slippery. The waters roiled below him, an acute reminder that one wrong step would spell certain death, whether by shattered bones or filled lungs.

Bron came at him, arms high. Riadrain waited.

The ground shook with each step of the gargantuan legs. Bron's arms came down for an attack—and Riadrain jumped, one last time. One foot slipped on the moss, and his dive came short. He crashed into the rocks, hard, and felt a ruinous pain run up one of his legs.

But the plan worked, thank the sky.

Bron went catapulting past Riadrain's prone form, his foresight clearly not advanced enough to have realized he was being led into a trap. Before he could stop himself, the weight of his immense body carried him headfirst into the narrow chasm between the river's jagged banks. He squealed like a stuck pig, unable to save himself from being swallowed by the rapids.

Riadrain waited, mayhap longer than he should have done, but the pain in his leg was unbearable. When the rockie did not reemerge, he forced himself to his feet and hobbled into the forest.

* * *

Not long after, Gathran arrived on horseback, barking orders to his retainers. Many of them were covered in blood.

Remarkably, Bron the gabber appeared from the river farther downstream, still alive. He found his way back to the chief, and in a move that he probably thought was very clever, told his lordship that his daughter had been murdered by the groom, who had then escaped into the woods.

Though gabbers are not known for their skills in deception, Gathran believed the lie. Or mayhap, as some historians have argued, he only sought an excuse for the massacre that had just taken place in his hall, and Bron provided one without even knowing it.

Thus started the brief but bloody war between the clans of Ros and Ronnedayne, which would claim many innocent lives in the months to come.

Had Tatiana known what events she would effect by pushing that body into the river, she just might have done things differently.

THREE

Rafad of the family Azir was a chancellor of the Mystic Order, a position worthy of respect and admiration, as there were less than fifty such people in the known world. He was born from a line of distinguished Idrisian nobles, whose distant relatives were once kings of that land. He was an experienced commander and duelist, and an excellent mage hunter. And yet . . . he found himself here, in the deep south of Hedgemond, desperately warming his hands by the open hearth. He was not new to this strange and snow-dusted land, not by any stretch of the imagination, but he had yet to truly acclimatize.

This cold autumn morning, he sat hunched over by the flames, shivering, while the rest of the town of Muir Dunn went about their worldly business. The windows were frosted over with the morning's chill, and the sun had only barely bothered to rise. His breath came out as a fine mist.

Tap-tap, tap-tap.

That was Norn's knock.

"Come in," said Rafad.

Sure enough, the leathery old man stepped through the door, a stack of papers in his weather-worn hands. "List of new arrivals," he said, "fresh out of training. You'll be wanting to read the briefs, aye?"

"Aye."

"Right y'are." Norn dropped the stack of documents awkwardly on Rafad's writing desk. He gave the chancellor a sort of sympathetic smile, as if trying to communicate—in the nicest possible way—that he did not envy Rafad's position in the slightest. Then he left.

Rafad did not move for a very long time. It was not only the warmth that kept him by the fire. It was the comfort, too. The comfort of not having to worry about paperwork, which was all there ever was to do in the bitter south, it seemed; the comfort of nostalgia, of a land long-forgotten, of a home in Idris. The soft, sweet comfort of lethargy. But lethargy, Rafad knew, was deadly in Hedgemond.

With a heave and a sigh, he went to the desk.

The list of names was an inky blur. He skimmed over it with as much interest as he could muster, which is to say, none at all.

Karla, of the family Bonn.

Lu, of the family Jiwa.

Tanney, of the family Harrick.

He yawned. *What time is it?* he wondered. The grey sky offered no hints.

Morsin, of the family Hedda.

Tatiana, of the family . . . . No, there was no family name recorded.

He stopped reading for a brief moment, pondering. Bastards were not uncommon in the Mystics. But in this kingdom, they certainly were. The people had a queer—and decidedly more relaxed—way of deciding who wore which name, which very rarely rested upon the institution of marriage. Mayhap this Tatiana was from afar, like him. The thought of it was strangely encouraging.

"Tatiana!" cried a high-pitched, squeaky voice from the rafters. Rafad sat up straight in his chair, blinking fervently. "Tatiana! Nice name. Regal! A good omen, aye!"

A small, green-skinned figure lowered itself towards the desk. It came to hang there, a handsbreadth above the papers, suspended by a strong tail wrapped around a crossbeam. It was not quite two hands tall and sported relatively long, spindly limbs. Its eyes were narrow with dark red irises, and its nose and ears were elongated, almost like an Elf's. But the comparison ended there, as no one in their right mind would equate this harmless little creature to a being of such terror.

The hob picked up the list and scanned it thoughtfully. "Hedda family—naughty. Bad. Want to be rid of errant son, methinks."

"Duly noted," said Rafad, before snatching the paper back. "I appreciate the help, Finnel, but I think I feel a headache coming on, and—"

"Liar," said the hob, crossing his arms.

"—And I would appreciate some peace and quiet. That is all. I will have to meet these recruits soon, and I must be prepared. You know how it is."

"Hmph," snorted Finnel, ascending back into the rafters. "Silly man. Would nae take Finnel's help. Foolish man."

The hob continued muttering for a while, but Rafad was already diving into the reports. Mayhap the next few weeks would be more interesting than he had expected.

* * *

The rain had soaked the prospective Mystics such that it was hard to see each other's faces from underneath their sopping, drooping hoods. They stood waiting for their ride—it was far too muddy to sit. Tatiana's feet hurt, and she suspected the others' did, too.

"Karla, of the family Bonn," said the young woman in front of her, far too happily, while her ginger braids swayed freely in the harsh wind. She would match the red cloak well.

"Tatiana," she replied, unintentionally creating a pregnant pause. Instead of saying any more, she outstretched her hand and shook that of her new compatriot. Karla's grip was firm and hearty, like Father's.

"A pleasure!" cried Karla, raising her voice against the downpour. "So why did you join the Order, if you don't mind my asking?"

Tatiana smiled as best she could. The cold air sent a shiver down her spine, and she found her jaw reluctant to move. "It is a long story," she said, "and not always a pleasant one, I am afraid."

Karla's face grew hard. "Am sorry, truly. You don't have to say if you don't want to. Mayhap we came from starkly different places, but all that matters now is the future. Aye?"

Tatiana nodded. "And what about you?" she said, trying to change the subject. "Why did you want to join?

"Ah!" Karla beamed with excitement. "That's also a long story, though not half so dreary. My eldfather were a constable, in Kalroine of all places! Saw all kinds of madness, he did. Swore on his life there were once a mad mage loose in the city, said it took them weeks to track the bugger down. Mystics helped, of course, he said they were the finest servants of the king he'd ever seen. Knew what they were doing, weren't any folk could say they didn't. Told me that story—the long version, mind you—told me 'fore I were scarce a toddler, and many more times thereafter. I always say it's his fault I ended up here. That and my special talent, of course."

She winked at Tatiana, as if they were in on some grand secret.

Tatiana tensed for a moment, but relaxed when she saw the other woman's eyes glow. A small gust of wind blew the rain out of her face briefly, while ripples ran across a particularly large puddle nearby. Karla flexed her biceps comically.

"Been training at the Academy nigh on seven years, now. S'good to be back home though. What about you, you come from far afield?"

"No," said Tatiana. "Not far."

"Ah. But you do sound a little . . ." Karla shook her head. "My apologies. Should nae pry, iss not my place."

"No," said Tatiana, still smiling gently. "It is not."

* * *

An elementalist, thought Rafad, as he finished the report concerning one Karla of Bonn. *Mayhap she can warm my bones with her fire.*

He turned the page.

The next report was scarce. So scarce it seemed things had been intentionally omitted, rather than just forgotten.

A regal name. A good omen, Finnel had claimed. But Rafad was starting to doubt it.

* * *

The disheveled novices assembled in the small courtyard, the slush of last night's snowfall muddying their boots, and Rafad of the family Azir was first to greet them. He stood straight as a pine, his hands clasped behind his back underneath the long red cloak. His hood was down despite the harsh wind, which meant that even his short hair billowed around his head and in his face. But he stood still, as he should.

"Welcome, my new Mystics," he said, putting a fist to his chest. They responded in kind, some faster than others. "Allow me the pleasure to welcome you here, to our chapter house in Muir Dunn. I am

Rafad, of the family Azir, and I am your new chancellor. I will be overseeing your assignment. Norn is my second-in-command, and will be your guide for the rest of your training—of which there remains little, I assure you. Merely culture and climate training, for the most part. Nothing as rigorous as your journey here, I am sure."

He gave them a light-hearted, hopeful smile. As he expected, some returned it, while others kept to their grimaces. The latter would have the most trouble here, he feared.

"Now then," he continued, as Norn handed him his list. "I will call your names, and when I do, I would like you to step forward, please. Just to make sure that all are accounted for. Karla of the family Bonn. Good, thank you. Lu of the family Jiwa. Thank you. Tanney of the family Harrick. Thank you. Morsin of the family Hedda. Very good. And Tatiana of—Tatiana."

He found the woman in question, still at the back with her hood drawn. She took a tentative step forwards.

"May I see your face, Tatiana?" asked Rafad.

Very reluctantly, the woman lowered her hood. Bright eyes, like aquamarines, stared back at him. They looked worried, mayhap lost. She looked as he had felt, the day he had first arrived in this place. There was a pang of sympathy in Rafad's heart.

"Thank you," he said. "It seems that all are accounted for. Norn will now—"

"Well, well!" cried Finnel, from a pile of crates in the corner of the courtyard. "What d'we have here? A group of newbloods!"

Lu, of the family Jiwa, all but jumped out of her skin when she heard the voice. Rafad groaned inwardly. "Please, Finnel," he said, "Introduce yourself later."

But that was no use, for—as he should have known—no one gave orders to hobs.

"Am the hob of this chapter house!" he declared loudly. "I'll be helping you settle in, no doubt, while Master Rafad is busy with his bookkeeping! Don't look so shocked, lass. Anyone would think you'd never seen a hob before!" He chuckled loudly.

Rafad, having no time for Finnel's shenanigans, left the new recruits in Norn's care. There were other things that needed his attention.

* * *

Later, in the common room, the hob found Tatiana in a corner, alone but for the darkness.

Some distance away, the other recruits laughed and drank to their newfound purpose, her new friend Karla included. But Tatiana was not participating. She was, to her own chagrin, coming to feel a little out of place. So she resigned herself to sitting in the back, away from the fire, fondling the fabric of her new cloak. It was red, like her old one, but lacked the white diamonds.

Finnel appeared quite suddenly, out of thin air it seemed, standing on the back of the armchair she was occupying. He loomed over her like a fearsome specter, casting a long shadow on the wall. But the grin he bore was one of friendliness, not malice.

"Here ye be," he said, "here ye be. All alone, and not to my surprise. What a strange one y'are, Tatiana of no family."

She gave him a blank look. Her own castle had had a hob who had not been that different from this one—small, mischievous, and strangely wise, and she liked to speak in riddles. Tatiana said nothing, sensing he would continue on his own.

"Finnel saw you in the courtyard," said the hob. "Of course you knew that. But Finnel sees more'n the humans do. And Finnel sees more'n he says out loud, Tatiana of no family. O' course . . . everyone has a family *somewhere*, aye?"

"I know what you are getting at, and I would kindly ask you to stop."

"Stop!" he cried, in a voice eerily like her own. "I would kindly ask you to stop. You'll want to be rid of that, mark my words."

She sat up straight. "Rid of what?"

"That horrendous accent," he said derisively. "Can well hear your high birth from nigh on twenty leagues away! Would nae be half surprised if I could plot your birth place to within a single span."

She recoiled slightly. Had it been so obvious? *Darkness take my foolish hide.*

"Fret not, fret not, m'lady, your secret's safe with me. Am the hob of this place, so it's now my charge to protect you, just like all the others. Will nae go gabbing without permission. Don't rightly know why you're looking to hide yourself from the big man, but it's clear you are. Though I will say . . . nothing stays hidden for long around here. Not from him."

She looked around fervently, checking that no one was listening. "What do you mean?"

He chuckled. "Oh, nothing to worry yourself about. I simply mean that he is the chancellor, and the chancellor hears many things. This place was built of wood, not stone. And there are many people here, in a small space. S'all I mean by it, I swear."

Then he gave her a wink and smile.

"What do you suggest I do, then?" asked Tatiana.

"Well," he said, tilting his head to the side, "am an honest creature myself. Can only say that the truth might smooth things over more'n you'd expect."

"I cannot," she said, thinking of what her father would do to her if Rafad sent her home.

Finnel only shrugged. "A right shame, then."

Then he vanished.

"Wait!" she cried, a little too loud. "Stop! I need your help. If you understand my plight, then you must help me!"

A disembodied voice floated down from the rafters. "Never said anything 'bout your plight. Nor about any understanding. Cannae do it for you, you know."

"I know, I just—"

"I gave you my advice, lass. Not up to me what you do with it. Rafad is the right sort o' lad, once you know him well enough. Take a chance. Might be your only one."

"I cannot," she muttered. "I simply cannot take that risk. Do you understand me?"

But he was already gone, and she was alone but for the darkness.

FOUR

Rafad waited for a few days before he pulled the newbloods in for their briefing. That way, at least, they had a little time to settle in and relax before being interviewed.

Most of them took it well. Lu, of the family Jiwa, was a Dorsean girl with a remarkably candid attitude that he did not expect from an outsider. Hedgemond did not seem to bother her the way it did him, that much was clear.

Karla of the family Bonn was a lively and spirited one. Mayhap a little too much for Rafad's liking, but he could not fault her enthusiasm. She might not have known it, but that could keep her alive when push came to shove.

And Tatiana . . . she was ever the enigma.

"And your name is . . . Tatiana?"

"Yes."

"Good, thank you. Your age?"

"Twenty summers."

"Thank you. And whence do you hail?"

That was when she hesitated. He saw her eyes dart around the room for a moment before she spoke. "I am local. From Hedgemond."

"Where in Hedgemond?" he said. "If you do not mind my asking."

"Kalroine," she said.

He frowned. "It says Kalkeane on my report."

"Oh," she said quietly. "A clerical error, mayhap?"

"Mayhap. So you were born in Kalroine?"

She nodded.

"And you trained . . . where?"

"Also Kalroine."

"Very good. Under whom?"

There was another pause. "I do not recall their name, sir."

That caught Rafad off-guard. *Sir?* That was no form of address that Mystics ever used.

"You do not recall?" he repeated. She shook her head. "But you were in Kalroine, yes?"

"Yes."

"Was it, by any chance, Captain Donnoy under whom you trained?"

The young girl perked up. "Yes, that was it!"

Of course, there was no such person as Captain Donnoy.

Old memories, long-forgotten, came rushing to the fore. Memories of a home in Idris, and a flight across the dunes. His mother's corpse, wrapped in a deadly embrace with the assassin sent to end their lives.

He reached for the knife attached to the underside of his desk.

"Are you sure?" said Rafad, gripping the hilt of his blade and leaning over the table.

"Of course she is!" cried Finnel from up on high. "What kind of silly question is that?" He landed on the desk between them with a light thud, his back to Tatiana. He wore a scowl across his face as he stared indignantly at Rafad, despite the good humor in his voice.

The chancellor did not know how to react, so taken aback was he by the interruption.

Tatiana recoiled, but not by much. Not in the same way that Lu of the family Jiwa had.

"Stop frightening the poor girl with your bad jokes," said Finnel, waving his arms around, "It was Captain Donnoy who taught her and she's sure of it. Aye, lass?"

"Aye," she said.

Rafad relaxed for a moment. She did not have the look of an assassin. Nor did she have the look of an Idrisian. But those two facts alone meant little.

For her part, the girl only stared at him with a sort of expectant fear.

"Very well," he said, keeping his fingers tight around the hilt. "That will be all, then."

Hastily nodding her thanks, Tatiana got up from the chair and dashed from the room.

Finnel was still scowling. "Are you truly still worried about hired knives? Here, in Muir Dunn? And you a chancellor of the Mystic Order, no less?"

Rafad wrinkled his nose. "One can never be too careful."

"It's been thirty years, man!"

"The family Camar has a long memory."

Finnel only shook his head. "Whatever your grievances, you leave the young girl out of it. Wager she's had enough trouble already."

"And how do you know that?"

"Finnel is always right about these things. Always right."

* * *

Tatiana packed as quietly as she was able, but it was clearly not quiet enough. No sooner had she stepped outside the door than she found Karla waiting for her in her nightclothes. Though she could not make out much in the darkness, she saw that the girl's arms were crossed.

"What're you doing?" Karla asked. It was a simple question, and there was little inflection to it. Gone was the cheery melodic voice that the newbloods had come to associate with the young elementalist.

"It is as you said," Tatiana replied. "It is not your business." She did not mean for the words to sound harsh, but they did.

Karla did not react. "You're leaving. In the middle of the night, no less."

"I do not deny it." Tatiana moved to pass, her belongings in a bundle under her arm.

But the stereotype of wizards being small and scrawny did not hold true in Karla's case. She was far stronger than Tatiana expected, and easily blocked her from passing in the narrow corridor.

"Am seeing that something is bothering you," said Karla calmly, "but if we're to be sisters then I must ask to confide in me, I must." She sounded completely serious.

"What . . ." Tatiana found herself lost for words. "Why do you care?"

She felt Karla's hand on hers. It was cold, but soft. "Why would I not?" the wizard asked.

"Listen . . . I really must be leaving—before Rafad finds out about me."

Karla chuckled softly in the darkness. "You? Please. He's more'n busy with his own problems. Plain enough to see. Now come on over to the kitchen, and I'll make you some tea. We can talk about it. See if there's aught I can do for you."

"Tea?" asked Tatiana. "What is that?"

"A drink. Nice and warm. Comes from Idris, I think. Rafad's favorite, or so Finnel said. No idea how he gets it all the way out here."

Tatiana found herself being led by the hand. She did not protest.

* * *

Three days later the report came in, exactly when he needed it least. Rafad had hoped to introduce his new blood to the rigors of the deep south over time, but the deep south was not playing along. A courier came by, bearing news of a troubling kind—true Mystics' work, for the first time in months.

And so they would set off on a journey north, at the onset of winter no less, to root out an infestation of satyrs in the hills. Oft was this the way in Hedgemond, where an attack on a settlement was more likely to be perpetrated by feral creatures than any human. After all, the humans did not like to leave their homes during the winter, if they could at all help it.

He expected that not all of his new Mystics would survive the journey. But he could not leave them behind, for they would serve no one sitting by a hearth. And as much as it pained him, he needed to know that his soldiers were hardy and strong, lest they were called to arms against something truly dangerous. Those who he might lose in the coming weeks . . . well, one could say that they were not meant to be Mystics.

He did not like to think that way. His superiors liked to remind him of how tranquil his post in Muir Dunn was, how easy it must be for him. But very few of them understood life out here. Beyond its humble towns, the quiet hills, the rolling snowfields and tranquil pine forests—it was deadly. When the winds rose and the winter's chill came down in earnest, many an elder, child, or sickly villager would be taken. There was always more death than he was accustomed to in the months leading up to Yearsend. Even now, when it was barely Novis, Rafad felt the temperature drop with every passing day. It was why he made every attempt not to get attached to his soldiers.

* * *

"He is very . . . distant," said Tatiana, choosing her words carefully. Rafad was out of earshot, but she did not want to offend anyone else, either. Somehow she had found herself on their expedition, despite having wanted to leave the night of her disastrous interview. She was sure that Rafad knew about her, and yet he had not broached the topic once. Distant was the word, indeed.

"That he is," said Karla, "to be sure. But he's not all bad."

Norn snorted. "He's a hard-working lad. Never sees any recognition for his work, neither. Spurned by the higher-ups, sent here, to the end of the world. Finds it hard out here, so far from home. Thass my take on it, anyway."

"Has he been here long?" asked Tatiana.

"Few years," said Norn, biting a chunk out of his squirrel. "Long enough."

"Long enough for what?" asked Tatiana, unable to resist.

Norn chewed for a while before answering. "Long enough that he's fed up, that's granted. Long enough that he's starting to have regrets, mayhap. Long enough that he's been all but forgotten elsewhere, thass what I'd say. He does nae talk about it much, but I ken how he came to be here. Wanted to get away, that's for sure. Lord chancellor no doubt took advantage of that, used him to fill one of the most remote positions there is. Poor man believes in duty though, so he's never complained about it. Not once."

There was a long silence when Norn finished, interrupted only by the occasional sounds of his jaw moving as he continued to eat.

"And what about you, Whitebeard?" asked Karla after a while. She had taken to calling him that, and he had taken to calling her "Little Imp" for her skills in elementalism.

"Well now, Little Imp," he said, "that depends on whether you're asking how long I've been here, in the Powidd, or how long I've been at the chapter house."

"Both. Either," said Karla.

"Lived in the valley me whole life. Never left Hedgemond neither, not even for a moment. How long have I been a Mystic? A damn sight longer than the chancellor, but don't tell him I told youse." He grinned, and his teeth were red with blood.

"You've never wanted to go further than that?" asked Karla. "See the world, or just a bit of it?"

"Suits me just fine, here," said Norn. "Nothing simpler."

"You've never seen the Seat," said Karla. "You'd pipe a mighty different tune, had you seen such splendor yourself."

Norn shrugged. "Sure it were grand, Little Imp, but in the north, they say the same thing about Hedgemond." Then he changed his voice, elevating his pitch and putting on an exaggerated noble's accent. "The mountains! The fjords! What beauty, what majesty indeed! How wondrous they are! And those snowy forests! A gift of indescribable beauty!" He scoffed. "Beauty is subjective. Y'ought to know that."

Then he turned to Tatiana and Lu—the Dorsean girl was sitting beside her. "Does it live up to the expectations, then?" he asked. "What do youse think?"

"I beg your pardon?" said Tatiana, before Lu could reply.

"I mean, is Hedgemond as beautiful as you thought it'd be?" He smiled, and it seemed he was not joking.

"But I am from Hedgemond!" declared Tatiana, almost too proudly. "I was raised in—" She stopped herself. "Hedgemond. I was raised here."

"Oh?" said Norn, perplexed. "Begging your pardon, I should have known. Iss just that . . . well . . ." He trailed off.

"Do not worry." She smiled awkwardly, and then quickly tried to change the subject. "Karla made a similar mistake."

"Hey now," said Karla with an indignant grin. "Was nae quite like that!"

The other Mystics laughed.

FIVE

Riadrain fingered the scrap in his satchel. Thick, woolen, and red, it had no doubt once been a part of someone's cloak. Someone who wore red.

His thoughts were elsewhere when his commander rode back to give him the good news. "M'lord, are you all right?" she asked.

"What?" he said. "Sorry, I . . . it does not matter. What of Gathran?"

"His army rests by the river," she told him, "just as you said. Very few lookouts. Does nae see as us much a threat, for sure."

"No doubt he expects to reach our lands by the end of the month, and return home before winter sets in. No sign that he is aware of us?"

"None."

"Thank you, Frenna. You know what to do."

He nodded, and Frenna returned the gesture. A moment later she had lowered her visor and was away, riding down the hillside to muster the troops. Riadrain sat alone for a long time, rubbing the woolen scrap between his fingers in a vain attempt to calm his nerves.

As the newsworn and untried Chief of Glanna after his mother's murder, he had inherited her meager lands and levies. If anyone had told him a month ago that he would be out here, commanding a small army in a war for his clan's honor, he would have laughed in their face. Riadrain had never considered himself ruling material, much less fighting material.

And yet he was here . . . commanding an army.

He kicked the flanks of his reindeer and spurred it onwards to join his comrades, ready to descend upon Gathran and his much larger host. Their mounts were not so large—nor so expensive—as Gathran's horses, but Riadrain did not mind. Reindeer had long been loyal and steadfast allies of the Heddish people, and he preferred them to any foreign beast.

If I survive this battle, he thought, imagining that Tatiana could hear him, *I must find you. Mayhap if I do, this nightmare will end.*

Banners and tents appeared in the valley below him as he crested the final hill. They were red, with white diamonds. In the evening's twilight he could barely make them out, but that design was unmistakable now. He was certain that he would never forget it.

With his loyal followers behind him and one hand still in his satchel, Riadrain signaled the charge.

* * *

Sanna bit down into the pork with untempered voracity. It was sweet and juicy, and she thanked the sky for it. Her valiant defense of Rane's Chief had earned her a promotion of sorts, and so she was sitting outside the commanders' tent, eating of their expensive fare. It was a comfort, but not enough to set her mind at ease.

Even now she played back that moment in her head, the moment when something had told her to let go of the arrow—some part of her, deep inside, that she could not resist.

Had it been the right choice?

A horn sounded. Her jaw stopped moving, almost involuntarily. She felt something in the air. *Dread* was the only word she could think of to describe it. And then the horn sounded a second time.

She shivered.

Chief Gathran came out of the tent, barking orders, the fury plain on his face. Without thinking, Sanna found her place by the Lady of Rane, who was struggling with her plate. Her squire complained that he could not see by the torchlight, so she slapped him for his insolence.

They heard the whisper of reindeer coming down the rise, but the snow had muffled the sound greatly, such that Riadrain and his forces were hurtling into the camp before anyone could stop them. They softened up Gathran's clansmen with a hail of arrows and spears, and it was not long before the first screams echoed through the valley. Chaos erupted around Sanna as Riadrain's cavalry collapsed upon their prey with the force of an avalanche.

She drew her sword, though she felt it was much too late. *I suppose this is the end*, she thought, rather calmly. The only thing that worried her was what might befall her father. He was old, and would soon need assistance—

A line of riders burst through the tents, and Sanna was sent tumbling by the antlers of the leading reindeer. A spear came next, striking her hard as the wave of enemies came crashing through. For that moment, all thoughts jumped to the excruciating pain in her shoulder. Somewhere nearby, she heard the chieftess screaming.

All bark and no bite, Sanna mused as she hit the ground. *Good riddance.*

Another rider came hurtling past, and she took a hoof in the chest. *Ouch.* It hurt almost as much as the first hit. She felt warm blood soaking her undergarments. Her ribs were broken, but judging by the pain, her spine was functioning just fine. *Blood loss, then. That's how I'm to go. Not the most glamorous, by any means.*

Her survival instincts, feeble as they were, kicked in. Despite the pain it caused her, she tried to crawl. *Just find somewhere quiet—somewhere to die without getting my head crushed. Nobody wants to be buried like that.*

She found a place behind a tent and propped herself up against some barrels. Then she found the knife in her boot and cut away the thick furs that covered her torso. Sanna knew that the hauberk underneath was too heavy to move, so she did not even try.

She could see the moons clearly from here. They were beautiful.

This'll do.

That night she dreamed many a dream.

She dreamed of the night she had fired that first arrow, only she was a small girl and her father was berating her for her posture. "Not like that," he said, "Keep your arm straight, for the love of Merida." She kept her arm straight and let the arrow fly. Feathers burst from Wylthe's chest as she fell over, the knife in her hand clattering to the floor.

Was she a bad woman? Sanna wondered.

"There's no good nor evil on the hunt," her father said, "only prey or predator. Which are you?"

"Predator," she said, beaming.

Prey, she thought. *A mouse caught in a game of cats.*

Too, she dreamed of a dark and horrid place, of a woman with the smell of death about her and blood on her hands. There were no moons in the sky. The woman argued with a wraith, whose mighty posture revealed him to be a great warrior of yore. He was a spirit of the old barrow-kings, come to take her to the other side, no doubt.

I did my duty, O king. For good or evil.

She smiled.

SIX

It was very cold in the steppes, and even Tatiana was finding it hard to deal with. Somewhere ahead of them in the vast tundra the satyrs lay in wait, though she did not understand how they could survive out here any better than the humans. The plateaus were vast and empty, and there were few trees to cover them from the winds. Satyrs would usually stay away from humans, choosing instead to make their homes in the mountains, as close as possible to the warmth of the hot springs, geysers, and volcanoes. But this particular group had abandoned that warmth and security to descend into the Powidd Valley and wage war upon the humans therein. Why they had left, no one could know, but it did not matter any longer.

Tatiana had seen the destruction they had caused on her way up. Burnt-out villages, charred bones, open graves—and corpses, both human and satyr, preserved by the snow.

It had certainly changed her to see such things. Before she had come up here she had imagined herself running from the Mystics once they were in open country. In the night, whilst it was snowing, so that tracking her would be difficult, and not worth the effort besides. Karla could not watch her forever, after all. But now . . . for the first time in a long time, she felt that she might do some good by staying. And that was enough for now.

The sound of rustling furs jerked her from her thoughts. She had sat alone to eat, and had certainly not expected anyone to disturb her, least of all the chancellor.

He sat beside her without asking, uttering nary a word. She offered him a bite of her meat, and he took it gracefully. There was a long, drawn-out quiet, punctuated only by the faint sounds of their eating and the soft talking of their companions farther away. Tatiana grew impatient, despite her best efforts.

Finally, when they had all but finished the food, Rafad spoke. "I should like to know everything, Tatiana. The truth of how you ended up here, for you are clearly not a Mystic."

She tensed up, her survival instincts kicking in. For a moment her thoughts turned to fleeing once more, running even farther away until she reached another kingdom . . . or something else entirely. But Rafad's voice was not tinged with any malice or malcontent, so she stayed, for now. She was not in any danger, it seemed, despite what she had done.

"Why?" she asked.

He drew a deep breath. "It is my responsibility to look after my Mystics. For that I must know who they are and what they seek in life. I must know if something endangers them. If something or someone were to come looking for you, I must know."

"How do you know that I came from anywhere special? How can you say that I am not a Mystic? I trained—"

"Do not try to lie to me, child," he said, though again, not unkindly. "It is plain enough to me that you did not train at all in our ways. There is no such person as Captain Donnoy. At first I believed you to be an assassin sent by some old friends, but Finnel talked me out of that. I see he had the truth of it, for you would make a terrible assassin. But that does not satisfy my curiosity, nor does it mean you are innocent of any crime. Now, I would ask you for the final time, Tatiana of no family: who are you, and what happened to bring you to me?"

No. Do not send me back.

"Please," she said, "I will leave, and we will forget all about this. I should not be here, you have the right of it."

He smiled faintly. Was that the smile of a friend? Or the smile of a predator cornering his prey? The low light made it hard to tell. "That is quite impossible, and not because I would prevent you—not at all. Rather, because we are quite far away from any shelter or warmth. And I wager that you are no hunter, either."

Of course, he was right. Would she truly rather freeze to death than return to Gathran and endure his ire? She found it a surprisingly difficult choice.

"Let us talk, Tatiana. As we should have done from the start. Let us talk, and then I shall see what we course of action we might take. Together."

Tatiana feared a deception, even now. She knew all too well how easily a silver tongue could hide a blackened heart. But . . .

She remembered, too, Norn's words a few days prior. *A hard-working lad*, he had said, while Finnel had called him *the right sort o' lad*. He had told her to take a chance. Mayhap, just mayhap . . . honesty might bring clemency. What choice did she truly have, anyway?

She took her chance. She told him everything.

* * *

The satyrs came down on them at night. They crossed the plateau like specters—dark shapes illuminated only by the moonslight, which cast long shadows on the pristine snowfields. There was no battle-cry, no warning, just the shape of horned heads on the horizon.

The Mystics drew their weapons and readied their magicks, and joined the beasts in battle outside their camp.

Far away from any keep or castle, any banners or battle-horns, any politics or people, the two sides clashed. It was strangely quiet, so far out here. Quiet enough that the sounds of clashing steel and dying screams could likely be heard for leagues around. But no one could have known who was fighting whom, nor their reasons for doing so, and thus it mattered very little in the end.

The shadows moved like puppets in the moonslight, their silhouettes enacting a macabre dance across the open land, as if the ebb and flow of battle were the rhythms of some long-forgotten song, as if the plateau were their stage, and the sister moons their only audience.

Some others took the time to watch, though much less consistently, as they were oft busy foraging for food and shelter in the snowdrifts. A lone silver fox, at one point, poked its head above the rise and peered over at the battle, but quickly decided to retreat to its den when it saw the dance was coming to an end. It knew to leave well enough alone and not to scavenge where humans could see it.

When all was said and done, Rafad and Tatiana found a wounded Karla writhing in the snow and, with grim determination, worked to save her life. Their conversation from the night before was quickly forgotten. Politics meant very little up here.

The sun rose soon after, and dawn finally broke across the steppes. The early morning snowfall had already buried the bodies, and the Mystics were gone. And if by any chance there was a stray wanderer on a distant hill who might have been looking across the plains that morning—well, they might never have known there was a battle at all.

* * *

The townsfolk of Kalkeane were not happy to see Riadrain, though he had done nothing to wrong them. Like as not, the lies about the massacre in Bann Dayne had dug their claws in here, and he could do little to change that. So he bore the brunt of their anger with calm indifference, while his friend and bodyguard Frenna fought to keep her anger in check.

The city was his, in practice if not in writing, but Bann Dayne eluded him yet. Gathran, having suffered a bruising, humiliating defeat at Riadrain's hands, had fled back to his castle and barred the doors, abandoning even his own city to Riadrain's forces.

Contrary to popular belief, Riadrain cared little for the town. He fought to remove the stain on his family's honor, and to his mind there was only one person who might yet have the power to do that.

The trail began here, in Kalkeane, and that was why he had come. That was why he let them jeer and boo as he rode past, why he ignored Frenna's call for punishments, because he would have something more convincing than lashings and pillories—he would have proof.

Clutching at the red fabric, he entered the Mystic compound.

He was given an icy response, but they received him all the same. Now that he controlled the city, they could not exactly refuse him.

It was not long before he found himself face to face with the chancellor of this chapter, a tall and spindly woman with sunken, milky eyes. He very carefully took the cloth from his bag, placing it on the table before her.

"Is this taken from one of your red cloaks?" he asked.

She eyed it carefully and then shrugged. "It could be," she said. "It is merely a piece of red cloth."

"It was found near the spot that the Lady Ronnedayne went missing."

The chancellor sucked air through her teeth. "So it is about that, is it? Are you trying to clear your name, and pin it on my order in the process? I must confess I do not know why you have come to me, if that is the case. Surely you would do better—"

"I did not kill her," said Riadrain softly. Emotion came flooding back to him unexpectedly, and he fought back tears. "I would like to find the person who did. That is why I need your help. That is why I am here."

She watched him for a long time in silence. Judging him, it seemed. She made a show of inspecting the fabric a second time, though Riadrain could tell she knew all there was to know about it already.

Eventually she spoke. "First of all: this is not a Mystic's cloak." He opened his mouth to speak, but she was quicker. "No, let me finish. Before you say anything else, I will admit that I am intrigued by your accusation. Despite the fact that this is not from one of mine, it may well still be the clue to the late lady's disappearance. You shall tell me everything you know, Riadrain of the family Ros. And when you are done, then we shall see about this conspiracy of yours."

He took his chance. He told her everything.

* * *

Sanna awoke to the scent of death. The pain in her chest was throbbing, but duller than it had been. She heard the sound of boots on snow.

It took her a while to open her eyes. For a while, she was content only to listen. But curiosity eventually got the better of her.

A woman was walking around the tent. She wore gloves and an apron. Blood coated her chest, her legs, and her arms, up to the elbow and beyond.

"Oh," she said. "It seems you pulled through."

Sanna did not reply. The pain was getting worse as her senses returned. The woman handed her willow bark to chew on, and Sanna did so happily.

"Your wound was nae too bad," continued the woman. "Though it took us a while to get to you. The other doctor was nae going to help you. Not until the lord came in to gainsay her."

Sanna wondered who she meant. Who was the lord? Had they won the battle? Did it even matter?

She shot the doctor a quizzical look.

"The new Chief of Glanna," said the woman. "Riadrain, of the family Ros."

Riadrain of Ros. Whose mother I killed. Sanna grinned at the irony.

"What are you smiling about? If he had nae given the order, you'd be greeting the barrow-kings by now."

Of course. He saved my life.

Though it was very unlike her, and though it caused her great pain, Sanna laughed. Long and hard she laughed, until laughter devolved into a coughing fit, and the doctor scolded her for not resting.

Truly, there was no good nor evil. Only death, and those who cheated it.

SEVEN

Tatiana returned to Muir Dunn more fatigued than she had ever been in her life. But strangely enough, the pain in her muscles felt different now. It invigorated her like it never could before. Snow was falling at the time, unsurprisingly, but she could barely feel the cold. Compared to what she had so recently experienced, this was but a chilly breeze.

It was a very unremarkable day—carts were trundling around town as usual, the vendors at the market stalls tried to pawn their wares, and the people went about their worldly business. A lone reindeer stood hitched outside the mystic compound, idly glancing at the passersby. Tatiana found it all quite strange. But then she supposed it was because of the battle.

Anyone who goes through something like that, which fundamentally changes how they view the world—they always find the normal world strange when they return to it.

Stranger still was the man that awaited them at the chapter house. No sooner had they stepped inside to remove their sodden boots than she saw him, warming his hands by the hearth.

“Riadrain,” she whispered, without meaning to.

He looked up, and in that moment of eye contact, panic seized her like a serpent coiling itself around her. She broke the contact and looked around for a way to escape, or for someone to save her. He rose and came towards her.

“My Lady,” he said, reverence and love in his voice. She saw the glint of tears forming in his eyes. It was the only thing that stopped her from fleeing.

The other Mystics were quick to realize that something important and private was happening, and cleared out of the entrance hall as fast as they could. All except Rafad, that is.

“How did you—” She broke off when she saw his leg. He hobbled, using a stick for aid. "What happened?”

“Healed badly,” he said, with a sad smile. “One of your gabbers, actually.”

“What?” she said, still unable to process the fact that he was even here. “What do you mean? What happened?”

“Have you truly not heard?” he asked.

She shook her head. “We have been away. It has been many weeks.”

“There is a war on,” he said.

“What? For what? With whom?”

“With your father. For you.”

She clutched her chest. It felt as if she had been stabbed. She sat down by the hearth, prompting him to join her. “Why? Why would he . . . what did you do?”

Riadrain chuckled, despite how inappropriate it was. “They thought I killed you. Would you believe that? Me? Riadrain of the family Ros, a murderer? They killed my parents. They tried to revoke my lands and titles. I fought a war.”

“You fought a war?” A smile came unbidden to her face, for it seemed so unlike him.

“I won,” he said, but it was clear that he took no pride in it.

“Against my father? Then he is—”

“Alive,” he finished. “Hiding in Bann Dayne. Kalkeane is mine.”

“I am so sorry, Riadrain. Had I known . . . no, I should have known my father. This is my fault.”

“It is too late for that, my lady.”

“Call me Tatiana, please. I ran away from all that, in case you did not realize.”

"Tatiana . . ." He paused to choose his words. "I need you to come back."

Now it felt as though someone had taken the knife embedded in her heart and was twisting it slowly. "I . . . I . . . cannot."

His expression darkened deeply. "What? Surely you cannot mean to stay. I have won the war. If we return home, and you tell the truth, we may still be able to reverse some of this damage. Our marriage will stand; your father will survive, as he will have no choice but to accept that he was misguided. Why would—"

"Please," she said. "The answer is no. I do not wish to return."

He looked down, avoiding eye contact. "I know you never loved me. It was only recently that I discovered the feelings I had for you. But I thought . . . I thought that mayhap you would return, if only for the sake of your father."

She almost laughed. "You do not know him, Riadrain." As tenderly as she could manage, she placed a hand on his. "I know that you think he is a bad person. The truth is that he is much worse than that. It is ironic, actually, that he should blame you for my death. His plan was that I would kill you. Discreetly, after I had borne a child that could be your heir and tanist. That child would have been his puppet, and he would have used it to destroy your clan from the inside. The family Ros would have been wiped from the sagas if he had his way."

His eyes went wide. Even he had not yet realized the extent of Gathran's wrath.

"That is why I ran away," she said. "That and many other reasons."

Riadrain clenched his fists. "I will lock him away. I will throw him in the oubliette and we may move on with our lives."

"Yes," she said. "I already have."

He looked around the room, as if he expected there to be more of it than there was. Rafad was still watching them, though keeping a respectful distance as he leaned on the door.

"You wish to stay *here*? Become a redcloak? No, you must come. Now that I have found you, I cannot let you disappear again."

He was set on the idea, that much was clear. So set, in fact, that she lacked the courage to hold her ground. But she did not need to.

"Tatiana has made her wishes clear," said Rafad. "I would ask that you respect them."

Riadrain frowned. "And who are you to intervene? This does not concern you."

“I have fought alongside Tatiana,” said Rafad. “Together we buried three Mystics. She is my sister now, whether I wished for it or not. And I must look after my own.”

“You know we found the collaborator,” said Riadrain, turning back to Tatiana. “The one who found the cadaver for you, enlisted you into the order without his superior’s knowledge or consent. His name was Alder, was it not? Do you realize that together you are liable for many crimes?”

She could scarcely believe he had said it. Was he blackmailing her? “Please, Riadrain. Do not hurt him. He is a friend. He did only as I asked.”

“And now this one is harboring you,” he continued with a jerk of his head towards the chancellor. “I could send a letter to Kalroine, you know. To the grand chancellor. I could detail all the codes and rules you are both breaking right now.”

Rafad stared him down, unblinking. “But you will not.”

“Is that so?” said Riadrain with an uncharacteristic sneer.

“Yes,” said Rafad. “You will not, because I know your story, Riadrain of the family Ros. Tatiana has told me enough of you to understand how you feel at this moment. But I also know that your heart is pure, and you are not of Gathran Ronnedayne’s ilk. You came here to restore your family’s honor. To exonerate them. You would not be here if you were a person to sully that honor so easily.”

Riadrain looked conflicted for a moment, but it did not last long. He gave a heavy sigh and gripped Tatiana’s hand tightly. “Why do you wish to stay?” he asked in raspy tones.

What came next proved to be the easiest part of the conversation so far. She sat up straight and squared her shoulders to him. “Because I have a purpose here. I feel that I actually belong, as strange as it sounds. Had you come to me a mere few weeks ago I probably would have gone back with you, Riadrain. But now . . . I have seen what the Mystics do, for all of us. Even while we call them outlanders and parasites. The High King’s lackeys, foreign inquisitors, you name it. The tenth kingdom, they say, as if it is some insult. They risk their lives for us, and they receive nary a thank-you. I ran away once, and it was a foolish thing. I shall not do it again, Riadrain. I am sorry.”

He was defeated there, and he knew it. “Very well,” he said, rising from the bench.

He took his walking stick and made to leave without even a good-bye. But she stopped him on the threshold, her hand grasping his and turning him to face her. She placed a strong kiss on his lips for him to remember her by.

"Go in health, Riadrain of the family Ros. I shall not forget you."

* * *

"Why did you stand up for me?" she asked, once they were both sufficiently drunk.

"It is as I said," Rafad replied with a smile. "You are one of us now. Whether I would have chosen it or not."

"I suppose that is a compliment."

He did not reply for a long time. After a while, when they had drained their cups, and the fire was burning low, he spoke again.

"I took a chance on you. Do you know why?"

"No."

"Your story—it is remarkably similar to mine. When you told it to me, and I knew in my heart that you were not lying, I could not easily turn you away. I understand all too well what it feels like to flee your own home."

She nodded and grinned. She felt a warmth welling up inside of her. A feeling that somehow, she finally belonged. She had traveled far to find it, but found it she had.

"Your story . . ." she began, but he waved a hand at her.

"No," he said, quickly. "That is a tale for another time."

A silence followed, but before it became too awkward, he spoke again. "Besides all that, Finnel claimed you were the good type. Now I may be a foreigner, and I certainly am not accustomed to having him around, but I never can say no to him, either. He was right about you."

Above them, in the rafters, they heard a voice. "Always right, I am. Always right, is Finnel! Told youse it'd work out, did I nae?"

The two Mystics laughed together, heartily and easily.

THE HAMMER OF THE KING

BRENNA GAWAIN

ONE

18 Novis, Year of Underrealm 1309

Impenetrable fog shrouded the Isle of Southbreak as they made their approach, just as it always did, no matter the time of year. King Bodil of House Valgun stood at the prow of her flagship, so impatient that she could barely restrain herself from jumping into the sea and swimming the rest of the way, and listened for the calls of the sailors in port that would tell her how far away they yet were. High above them, the glowing orange orbs of beacon torches pierced the mists and announced their destination: Rothton, the capital of the kingdom of Dulmun, and her home. She had been away far longer than she would have liked, and had found herself missing it fiercely.

It was less than six months since the death of her father and her subsequent succession to the throne, and though she had always known that there was a transitory period of unrest in the beginning of every monarch's reign, she was still finding the whole thing more tiresome than she had anticipated. It seemed that nobles in every major city across her nation had been chafing at the bit for a chance to rise up and make a grab for whatever power was on offer. Some of them, she suspected, had not even intended open insurrection, instead meaning merely to test her. She had placed the names of these particular nobles on a list to be revisited later, at a time when she had sufficient breathing room to teach them that it was not *their* place to decide her worth.

The fog parted gradually around her longship's prow as they passed within the bounds of the harbor, the desolate gravel shore as welcome a sight for Bodil as any magnificent feast or homely tavern might have been on any other given day.

The ship's captain appeared at her elbow as the sailors began preparing to lay the ship ashore, seeming to sense her impatience. "Will you be waiting for the ship to be unloaded, Your Grace?"

"No," she replied tersely, and then sighed, thinking of the long ride into the city. "Bring me my hounds, and then meet me on the road when the horses have disembarked. I wish to reach Rothton before the sun has set."

The captain nodded silently, vanishing as quickly as he had first materialized, and Bodil returned to her contemplation of the shoreline, storm-tossed waves of deepest blue lashing against the rocky basalt beach with a ferocity that she felt she understood well after these first months of her reign as king. For every wave that retreated, another would take its place . . . every battle but the first step on the road towards the next.

Frowning, she shook her head, trying to clear the thoughts from her mind. Idly, she let her right hand rest on the head of the hammer that was anchored through her belt, the Hammer of the King of Dulmun. Carried by every ruler since the kingdom's formation, it was both a potent weapon and a symbol. In days of old, elementalism enchantment had lain so heavily upon it that it could freeze lakes and inflict frostbite with a touch, but that had faded away with the years, and its effect was now merely a mild chill. The weapon was heavier than she had always imagined, both in physical weight and in the burden of responsibility, but it was hers now, and that was all that mattered.

"Ship the oars! Brace for landing!" the bosun bellowed from somewhere above her in the rigging, while the captain returned with Bodil's two hunting dogs, Ulsen and Cimric. The dogs strained valiantly at the ends of their leashes, clearly just as eager to return to land as she was.

As soon as she felt the longship's hull come in contact with the rocky ground, Bodil leapt down from the bulwark to wade through the knee-high foam towards the shore, Ulsen and Cimric barking excitedly at her side. The three of them set off past all the sailors and dockhands who had rushed to help with disembarkation, and Bodil at last felt some of the worry lift from her shoulders as she made her way up towards the inviting glow of the torches set along Rothton's boundary wall. It had been far too long since she had seen her family, but at least she was home now.

The captain and four of her personal guard met her some time later. They spent the remainder of the day on horseback, making the journey to Rothton and passing under the high arch of the city gates just as the last tepid rays of the sun retreated back behind the clouds. At this time of year it was seal-hunting season on the shores of the northern half of her kingdom, so the markets were bustling with trappers returned from the catch, leatherworkers seeking good hides, and ordinary folk in search of meat. The absent sun did not deter them, not when bright white seal-oil lamps dyed the grey stone buildings silver, and skalds sang on the street corners, telling stories of mighty hunters of old.

Her troubled thoughts of turbulent politics melted away as they passed into the grounds of the Grand Hall, the promenade lined with banners of the white wave on green, the heraldry of Dulmun, and smaller pennants of black and gold, the colors of her own house, snapping in the wind. Their horses' ears pricked up excitedly in expectation of a warm stable and good food, and Bodil's hounds immediately raced along the wall into the gardens in a clamor of exultation. She did not have the heart to call them back when she, too, was so glad to be home.

The hall itself was sat atop a great mound of earth that had been raised to give it a view out over the rest of Rothton, and tonight, Bodil could already see a welcome party waiting for her at the top of the stairs. It was comprised mostly of various messengers that she intended to ignore, but also her steward, Thargrim, her castellan, Hilrunn, and her son, Esvind. She grimaced at the impressive number of messengers, bristling thick as trees in a forest, and took a deep breath as she dismounted, handing her reins to a waiting groom.

One of the messengers cleared her voice loudly as soon as Bodil was within speaking distance. "Your Grace, if I could just have a moment of your—"

"Not tonight," she growled in response, maintaining her previous pace as she forged upwards past dozens of hands holding documents and sealed letters. "Either leave your concerns with my steward, or wait until tomorrow. Tonight I must see my family."

This seemed to deter most of them, but one, the first girl who had spoken, clambered after her, proffering her scroll insistently. "I assure you, Your Grace, this is a matter of the *utmost* importance, a missive from Lord Breiling of House Tornall. I really must implore that you read it with all due haste!"

Bodil snorted, waving her away more forcefully this time. "Then I suggest you leave it with my steward, so that I may open it after I have dinner with my wife. Nothing, not even a proclamation from Roth himself, passed down through our line and newly discovered, will be read before then."

That seemed to finally shake the messenger loose, and Bodil hastily scaled the rest of the stairs two at a time, hoping she could get inside before any more appeared. The three people she actually wanted to see stood before the doors, and they all bowed as she approached, Hilrunn's flame-red hair standing out against her coal-blackened leathers, while both Thargrim and Esvind wore deep green livery, the same color as the banners that adorned the walls.

She nodded to her two attendants and then embraced Esvind, marveling at how much he had grown even in just the three months she had been gone. He was just over eighteen years old, and he seemed to have saved most of his growing for this year, both in height and in the breadth of his shoulders. She almost did not recognize him except for the round softness of his eyes, for his face had changed shape as he grew into a man fully as well, and it made her heart ache to think that she had missed so much time with him.

"Welcome home, Mother," he said, smiling, as they drew apart. "We all missed you terribly. I cannot even describe what a mess things have been here."

She frowned, inspecting his face closely. Though he was indeed glad to see her, he was also exhausted, and his words were tinged heavily with worry. It would not do to ask him about it here, out in the open, but it was enough to dampen the relief of her return.

"Let us be gone, then," she said firmly, "quickly, before more 'missives of import' are thrust upon me, and you may tell me what you can about it on the way."

"I will bring the petitions that have accumulated in your absence to you after your meal, Your Grace," Thargrim said, opening the great doors before her.

She felt another twinge of disquiet, wondering why there would be a backlog of things that had not been dealt with.

Although it was pleasantly warm inside the hall compared to the biting wind, and it bustled with cheerful servants going about their day, Bodil found herself unable to relax. As they walked, Esvind told her in low tones about the chicanery that he and Alleif had been wrestling with in her absence, from nobles attempting to evade taxes to skalds writing unflattering songs about their family. He explained also about the delegation from the High King's Seat that had arrived, bringing with it a brigade of Mystics and a new ambassador appointed by the High King herself.

"He looks down on everyone," said Esvind, sniffing disdainfully, when Bodil asked him what the ambassador was like. "I thought the idea of ambassadors was to send somebody who knew a culture well, like Aunt Sofina in Feldemar. Apparently the High King disagrees."

Bodil made a thoughtful noise, remembering the ambassadors that had served during her father's time. None of them had been people that she would have considered friends, but they had been professional at least—certainly not the type of people to anger her family like this.

"A new grand chancellor was appointed as well, though," he continued, perking up properly for the first time. "A woman named Falkari—she seems to be a warrior of great skill. She has been very respectful, and I would dearly love to see her fight!"

This, at least, was good news. A good relationship with the Mystics was a great help towards stability, though Bodil did find herself wondering why such an apparently impressive fighter had been assigned to a largely political position. She would have to make some inquiries later.

They had barely opened the door into their family's personal quarters an inch when Bodil's other child, little Eyrhild, short even for her mere five years, came rushing across the room towards her, shrieking excitedly. "Mama!"

Laughing, Bodil gathered her up and swung her around, reveling in the delighted giggles. Eyrhild had not grown as much in height as Esvind had, but her hair was much longer now, and she seemed to have gotten over her phase of hating dresses—at least for now.

"Have you been running the kingdom well in my absence, my little princess?" Bodil teased, tickling her stomach. Eyrhild dissolved even further into fits of laughter, clinging to her tightly and not wanting to be put down.

"Between the two of them, they seem to have your job handled quite well," Alleif said wryly, from a chair on the other side of the room. "We should leave them to it and retire to somewhere with less conniving noblemen."

Bodil went over to her, seeing at once the probable reason why she did not rise: being almost nine months pregnant now, her belly was heavily distended. She was pale and wan, worryingly so, and her words hid the same underlying anxiety that Esvind's had done. Despite this, her warm brown eyes gleamed with joy and relief, and Bodil leaned down to kiss her, managing to get one arm free from Eyrhild to embrace her as well.

"My darling," Alleif said, softly, as they broke apart. "Welcome home."

"Are you ill?" Bodil asked her, concerned. "You and Esvind both seem at your wits' end. Should I call for healers?"

"Oh, no, nothing like that!" Alleif gushed, trying to reassure her with a smile. "It is just—we have been busy!"

"So I heard from Thargrim," Bodil replied, gently, and Alleif sighed heavily, rubbing at her eyes.

"We have barely made it through this last month without you," she said wearily, the façade fading. "I half fear that we will still not be able to hold things together even now."

Bodil looked at her wife's and son's faces, both plastered with fear, and exhaustion, and pain.

"Well," she answered, a chill creeping over her like frost from the Hammer of the King. "We will just have to see about that."

TWO

By breakfast time the next morning, Bodil was in a thoroughly foul mood, having been practically drowning in paperwork and reports for most of the night.

"These petitions are ludicrous," she grumbled, tossing one particularly egregious one onto the table beside Alleif, who was devouring her morning meal of oatmeal and baked ham. "Think of the pettiest possible punishment you can for Brungard of House Hallvar. He wants compensation for one of his sons who died on the battlefield *fighting against me*."

Alleif made a thoughtful noise, opening the letter. "Brungard, you say? He has a son Esvind's age, does he not? We could introduce them, dangle a little power in front of him—unless that is the son you divested him of."

Bodil squinted for a moment, trying to remember, but then shrugged. "It might have been."

"I will see what I can come up with, at any rate. The eastern estates *are* rather overdue for an impromptu tax inspection, now that I think of it."

Bodil grinned viciously, reflecting on how bad the nobles of Southbreak were at hiding their indiscretions, and motioned for a servant to bring her some breakfast of her own. "Where *is* Esvind this morning? He was not in his rooms."

Alleif made a small, thoughtful noise, a wry smile playing across her lips. "I forgot to tell you. I think he is seeing someone."

Bodil raised her eyebrows, curious. "Do we know who? I thought he was exchanging letters with that boy from Dorsea."

Alleif shrugged, still smiling. "You know how teenagers can be. I meant to look into it, but I have been rather distracted of late."

Bodil laughed, gently putting a hand on her wife's belly as the servants returned with more food. "I can imagine."

She sat down to eat, starving, but was shocked when Alleif suddenly reached out and grabbed her wrist, stopping her from putting her spoonful of oatmeal into her mouth. "Wait! That is another thing I forgot to tell you."

She whistled for the dogs, and Bodil gave her a confused look. "Is there something wrong with the food?"

Alleif gave her a concerned look, the look she always had when she knew Bodil would be angry about something. "Several weeks ago, someone—well, they poisoned our food. If it had not been baked fish, and the kitchen mouser had not been hungry before us . . . I shudder to think. So we have been letting the dogs taste things before eating, just to be safe."

The look Alleif gave her had been justified, for Bodil's heart immediately burned with fury, and she banged a fist on the table. "Someone tried to poison you? *In my own house?* Who? I want their heads!"

Alleif sighed, collecting her spoon from where Bodil's fist had caused it to land. "This is another thing I have not had the time or wherewithal to find out. With you home, I hope it will be easier."

This revelation did not help Bodil's already black mood, nor did the fact that half of her breakfast disappeared down Ulsen's hungry gullet. As on every day, however, she had responsibilities to carry out. Chief among them today was a council meeting with as many noblemen as could crowd into one room, her generals, and the servants of the High King who were currently in the city. She remembered Esvind's contempt for the new ambassador and found herself utterly dreading the entire thing.

She made ready anyway, because that was what kings did.

The council was held, as always, in a long room, with sturdy tables forming the shape of an oval, inside which the king would stand and take questions, suggestions and declarations. The more erudite Dulmunsters liked to say that this was because the king was being held accountable to their people, but Bodil knew that at least some of her antecedents had used the open space as a makeshift dueling arena, usually over marriage proposals or trade agreements.

She met Falkari, the new grand chancellor, and the ambassador, who was so instantly unpleasant that she immediately forgot his name. She could see clearly why Esvind had spoken so admiringly of the former; Falkari was a giant of a woman, standing two heads at least above Bodil, with thick muscular arms showing under her red cloak. She had a large nose and an infectious smile, with her honey-colored skin and angular brown eyes marking her as a woman of far-off Idris. The ambassador wore silken robes and looked as if he had never set foot outside a city.

"I am sure you would all like to hear reports from the battlefields near Havnich and the details of stamping out of the rebellion," she began, once everyone's introductions had been made.

Many of the nobles nodded, picking up their quills to take down notes, but one in particular, Lord Breiling of House Tornall, did not.

"Not even six months into your reign, and already an insurrection. Your father would be so proud," he said derisively, smirking at her.

Bodil glared at him flatly, nostrils flaring in distaste. "The last Tornall king was deposed within a week, Breiling. At least I was not defeated."

That elicited a few titters from various other nobles, causing Breiling to sink into a heavy scowl. Happy to ignore him, Bodil moved on. She spoke briefly of the battles and at greater length of the holdings that had been seized by the crown. Several of the attending council members had questions, and she soon found time slipping away under an endless barrage of petty queries that mostly did not seem helpful or relevant. By the time they were finally ready to move on, she had almost forgotten that the High King's new ambassador was even there.

"Well, that was certainly . . . enlightening," he said, smoothly, when it came to his time to speak. "I do hope you will pardon me for bringing business concerns to this meeting, rather than stories of war. My offering today is in document form, as is the custom in the High King's court, but I can read it aloud if the nobles in Dulmun lack the skill for such a feat."

Bodil frowned, not liking the idea of having to speed-read a wordy proposal here in front of him. This was part of the reason that business was presented through speech in this particular forum, to level the playing field, but it would look weak to ask him for more time. She took the document from his clammy hand and pored through it as fast as she dared.

"Yet more export taxes," she mused, causing the nobles to mutter and the ambassador to smile thinly.

"The seas have been so chaotic of late. Merchants require insurance that their goods will arrive unharmed!"

She was surprised by the time she reached the end; she had been expecting hidden injunctions buried in sub-clauses, but it seemed the ambassador was not so crafty as he wished to believe.

"Why, out of all the kingdoms of Underrealm, does Dulmun in particular have to soothe the fears of merchants?" she asked coldly. "There is no mention of any other nation in this document. The Great Bay does not discriminate based on the origin of ships—unlike this tax, it seems."

The ambassador blanched, disgusting her. Had he really been so confident that she would not notice?

"It is most irregular to make such a fuss," he replied snidely, attempting to recover. "As you well know, your only duty to the High King is to obey, not pester her with questions born of your overblown egos."

The nobles took great issue at that, erupting into heated shouting about how preposterous and unfair it was. The ambassador seemed most pleased with this, leaning back in his chair as the cacophony grew, and smiling in triumph.

"Silence!" Bodil thundered eventually, cutting short the rabble.

The cause of all the uproar smirked even wider, clearly enjoying himself immensely. "Why, Your Grace, between your inability to keep order in this room, and all the civil unrest, it is almost as if your presence on the throne is a liability where peace in Underrealm is concerned."

She turned to face him slowly, forcing herself to remain composed.

"Do you have some problem with me, ambassador?" she asked him, bluntly, and he had the audacity to laugh.

"You have always been . . . shall we say, *ambitious*, Your Grace," he replied smugly. "You may have thought that the eyes of the greater world were not upon your actions during your father's reign, but the High Kings leave very little to chance. You are too proud, and too aggressive, to leave unwatched. It may be time for you to learn your place, which is as a servant of your liege."

Bodil clenched her fists, glaring at him. Her very first instinct, of course, was to leap across the table and remove all his teeth, but that would rather have proved his point about her temperament. She did not even know which of her escapades as prince he was referring to, but it hardly seemed to matter; he had clearly made up his mind about the kind of treatment and respect—or lack thereof—that he thought she deserved.

Around the room, she saw many of the nobles exchanging glances as she continued to stare the ambassador down, which was of far more concern to her than any word out of that man's mouth. Having just returned from one insurrection, she was not keen on dealing with another. Right now, she knew she had to make a choice: either bow to this insufferable man's wishes in order to make sure that she did not start off on the wrong foot with Enalyn, and risk her own people believing her weak; or do the opposite, and court her nobles' favor while possibly angering the High King.

Neither option seemed particularly appealing.

"Is that her Majesty's *official* diplomatic stance in regards to Dulmun?" she asked coldly, after a weighty pause.

He made a small amused noise, as if laughing at a child asking why the sky is blue. "She must have appointed me for a reason, Your Grace. What do you think?"

"*I* think you would be wise not to claim to know the High King's mind," Grand Chancellor Falkari interjected, sounding entirely unamused. "I serve her also, and I was given no instructions other than to protect the people of Dulmun, as I would those from anywhere else in Underrealm. I think this grudge against Her Grace you speak of is your own, and no one else's."

Bodil regarded her for a moment appreciatively, but quickly turned back to the ambassador, not wanting to give him a chance to speak again. She had made her decision.

"And I think," she said, very deliberately, as she tossed the taxation documents back onto the table before him, "that your proposal needs some revision. It is untenable, and I will not respect it."

There was murmuring from the various seats full of nobility. Even after Falkari's admonishment they had been strong words, and Bodil was pleased to see the ambassador spluttering indignantly in what seemed to be a combination of worthless bluster and shock that his bluff had been called.

"This is my kingdom," she said clearly, both for his benefit and that of the nobles. "You are a stranger in Dulmun, yet you think you know her ways well enough to eke out of us what you want. But I say this to you now: we do not exist to be tamed, or brought low, for the sake of someone's political career. Bring this document back to me when you can prove that it also applies to the sailors of the other kingdoms, when you can prove that you respect my subjects and their livelihoods, and then I will abide by it."

He looked up at her with some degree of fear as she stood over him, though he attempted to seem unruffled. "You will regret this, Your Grace. Be sure of that!"

"Will I?" she asked, leaning down to stare him right in the eyes. "In the south they say that the pen is mightier than the sword, but we have never liked that saying. You see, the king of Dulmun is a *hammer*."

THREE

There were a thousand things that needed tending to after her long absence, so Bodil spent much of the rest of the day marching between yet more meetings. She spoke with Thargrim about the poisoning attempt and a plan to restrict who was allowed to cook so that she would not have to give up half of every meal to her dogs going forward, she spoke to her generals about the number of casualties they had suffered putting down the insurrection, and she spoke to the royal healers about the injured that had been brought back to Southbreak for treatment.

She was just making her way towards Hilrunn's office to discuss security measures when she happened to see Esvind go dashing past, hurrying off somewhere looking slightly disheveled. She only had a moment to wonder if it was something to do with the person Alleif thought he might be seeing, when he came rushing back and skidded to a halt right beside her.

"Mother," he managed to gasp, trying to get his breath back. "May I ask a favor?"

Somewhat amused, she waited for him to straighten up a little, placing a fond hand on his shoulder. "Always. What is it you need?"

"I have to meet someone, and I—" The look on his face betrayed all the fast thinking he was trying to do. "Would you watch—not from the meeting itself, but somewhere out of sight—and step in if things become . . . dangerous? But only then?"

His words immediately sobered her, and she inspected his face closely, wondering what on earth this could be about. Was he involved with someone who had another, possibly jealous, lover? But that would be a situation best resolved openly, not with words supported by a hidden bodyguard in case of misadventure. She found herself frowning, curious as to whether he was entangled in something else entirely, but nodded. She could hardly turn down a request at the possible cost of his safety while there were poisoners in her own house.

"Thank you," he burst out, relieved, and then passed a hand over his eyes, looking worried again. "And please—I do not have time to explain just now, but please, trust me."

She regarded him gravely for a moment and then nodded once more. "Very well."

He thanked her again, profusely, and then hurried off in the direction of the gardens. She followed more slowly, not wanting to be too close behind him and accidentally be seen.

She trailed him eventually to a small courtyard, set out in the open between two wings of the building, and settled herself beside a window close to the door. They waited a short time until a girl finally arrived, dressed in the same green palace livery, with golden hair and cold blue eyes. Her interest piqued, Bodil leaned as close as she possibly could to the window without being seen.

"—will need some kind of commitment soon—"

The brief snippet of the girl's declaration was all that Bodil could catch, so faint that she wondered if she would even be of any help from this distance.

"—be more difficult, now that Bodil has returned," Esvind responded more clearly as he deliberately guided his partner in conversation closer to where she was hiding, as if strolling casually.

She watched him with interest, for he was not acting like his normal self; he stood pulled up to his full, quite impressive height, and spoke regally rather than in his usual soft tones. He was, she realized with some degree of embarrassment, attempting to emulate her.

"We are hungry for more than words, Your Excellency. We want your mother off the throne, and soon."

It was suddenly clear precisely why he had felt that he might need support, and Bodil narrowed her eyes, memorizing the girl's face. She knew that she should not be surprised to see traitors trying to influence Esvind—she had gone through similar trials during her father's reign—but the sheer audacity of it still rankled her. She was impressed that he had attempted to outmaneuver them, though. Furious, because he could have died *so easily*, but impressed.

"Oh, I agree, believe me," he declared, in response to the girl's statement. "I cannot wait to be king, and fix all the ills that she has inflicted upon our fair Dulmun."

She watched the two of them closely, wary of the girl's every slight movement. Now knowing the stakes that were involved, she wished she had brought a few guards with her. She shuddered to think that if they had not passed by chance in the halls, Esvind would likely have come here alone.

They spoke for some time longer, and Bodil listened to all of it, glad she was there, even though it did not seem her presence was required after all. He gave small pieces of information, little tidbits, from the meeting that morning. The girl gave similarly vague indications of the number of people she was working with, and things they might be prepared to do in the event that Esvind should attempt to dethrone Bodil.

Bodil saw him sag with relief as soon as the girl had left, which was not good—she herself was proof that he could not know who else might be watching him. He had a lot to learn if he wanted to be a truly successful political manipulator. Given his age, however, she hoped that any other unseen watchers might just assume he was inexperienced with the business of treachery as well.

"Do you want to explain all that?" she asked him grumpily, once he had slunk back inside to face her. "How long have you been dealing with this? Does Alleif know?"

He shook his head, holding out his hands defensively. "Not too long! Only a few weeks! And I did not tell Mother anything. I fell rather accidentally into this ring of conspirators when one tried to recruit me, and after the poisoning, I just had to *do* something! But I could not bring myself to put another problem on her plate. I told myself I would have everything solved by the time you came home, but they have been very cautious with me."

Bodil growled at him. "Do you have any idea how dangerous this was?"

"As dangerous as living in a place with enemies trying to poison my meals?" he countered shrewdly.

She sighed, knowing how he felt, and her anger gradually subsided into wry amusement. "You are lucky you did not have Alleif snooping into all this, you know. She thought you were seeing someone."

He made a face, mortified. "I shall have to get better at sneaking."

She grinned at him. "I doubt you will ever be good enough to evade your mother's sharp eyes or her nose for gossip. But in any case, I am glad you have been making headway with your investigations. Both she and Thargrim have had no such luck with their own information gathering."

The grateful smile he gave her was dazzling, and once again she found herself regretting that she had been away for so long. Next time, she thought—if there was a next time—she should bring him with her while she went away. He was almost old enough, being only two years shy of adulthood. It seemed he was ready now to learn to be king, though in her heart she feared that she would not be the best of teachers.

She placed a hand on his shoulder, gently directing him back towards their living quarters. "Come. Let us break this news to your mother and let her take over the scheming. Between the three of us, we will root out this conspiracy in no time."

FOUR

JUST OVER A WEEK LATER, BODIL AROSE BEFORE THE DAWN AND STOOD staring out the window. She gazed out over the city and weighed the hammer of her forebears in her hands. Esvind had spent the past twelve days living up to his promises to convince the girl—and through her, her master—that tension had been sown between him and the rest of their family. He rarely ate with them, instead spending large amounts of time at a manor house outside the city, surrounded by many other conspirators.

Both Bodil and Alleif had been alarmed at how far the corruption seemed to have spread and how much danger he would be in if anything went wrong, but Esvind assured them he had everything under control. Alleif's worrying had made him regret keeping everything a secret far more effectively than Bodil suspected any lectures from her ever could have done, and he had promised them both that it would not happen again. Knowing how impetuously he must have rushed into this business in the first place, Bodil was not really sure if that would hold true.

She turned the hammer over in her hands, wondering how it would weigh against her son's life.

Today they would enact the culmination of their plan; Esvind had managed to convince the traitors that he needed assurance that they would stand with him in his imaginary schemes to seize the throne from her. Cajoling the puppet master who was behind the whole affair into a meeting was just unwise enough a notion that they hoped it would make Esvind seem a naïve fool, ripe for manipulation, and thus lull the conspirators into a false sense of security. With luck, Bodil and her royal guard would burst in to take advantage of that with no hiccups. But always niggling in the back of her mind was the fear that it would instead get him killed.

It was the kind of scheme she would have enthusiastically put her support behind during her father's reign—a scheme both daring and potentially extremely effective—but somehow it felt different now. It was her actions during her father's rule that had led to her being labelled ambitious, both by detractors in Dulmun and also, it seemed, the High King herself. Would Esvind face the same treatment because of today's events? How many spitefully-imposed import taxes laid down thirty years from now, she wondered, would trying to save his kingdom be worth to him?

She knew that he considered the risk of his life worth it, for that was something they already faced. They did not know what kind of numbers their enemies had, and it was entirely possible that neither she nor Esvind would return from this confrontation. If things went awry so badly that Bodil was slain, what would befall Alleif and Eyrhild was unthinkable—if not the utmost dishonor and possibly exile, then certainly ousting and execution. Bodil dreaded the idea that their success might place obstacles in the way of Esvind's future reign, but they simply could not afford to fail. The cost would be far too great.

It was too late to ponder these things now. The meeting would take place in several hours, and she would go there and seek her enemy, and hopefully put an end to the suffocating shroud of fear and mistrust that had been pulled down over her city. It was all there was left to do.

"Did you not sleep?" Alleif asked blearily from behind her, clearly having just awoken.

"I did," she replied, trying to keep her voice light, though she did not feel successful.

She turned away from the window at last and felt her heart lurch at the fear in Alleif's eyes. They had already had several discussions about the possible outcomes of today's battle, but she knew that the fate they both feared the worst was one where their son did not survive.

"Is everything prepared?" Alleif asked, worried, and Bodil nodded.

"As much as it ever will be. The final pieces lie with Esvind."

Alleif made a small noise of concern in her throat, swinging her legs off the side of the bed and attempting to stand up, but Bodil touched her shoulder gently and then kissed her. Kneeling, she took the soft, fur-lined boots that Alleif wore to protect against the cold stone floor, and helped slide them on over her swollen ankles, not wanting her to over-exert herself on top of everything else today.

"We will just have to hope that I trained him well," Bodil said, sighing, as she helped Alleif stand.

"No parent ever trained a child better," Alleif replied fiercely, making her smile, and then embraced her. "Make sure you both return to me when it is done."

"I swear it."

With that, Bodil released her, feeling the cold air on her skin keenly where they had parted, and left the room, steeling herself for the battle to come.

* * *

The inn where the conspirators had agreed to set up the meeting was called The Stout Squire, a relatively high-class establishment set right beside the northern gate of Rothton that opened onto the farmlands beyond. It made sense with what information they had been able to glean about the ringleader thus far; they were likely a noble who did not live in Rothton, and they would not wish to be seen there running this errand if they could avoid it.

They had taken up positions in various houses and buildings around the inn, waiting for the right time to strike. Esvind had entered had some time ago, telling them that he would signal them if anything went wrong, using a small hunting horn that he had taken with him. Bodil, however, was still tense, knowing that if things really did go badly, he might not even get a chance to use it. She strained her ears, listening intently for any sound of something untoward happening inside the inn, while Hilrunn sat beside her watching an hourglass that would tell them the exact time that the meeting was to take place.

She felt her muscles cramping as she held herself at the ready, but she dared not move from her position beside the door. If worst came to worst, Esvind would not suffer from her lack of readiness. She thought to herself dryly that she had been lurking like this surprisingly often lately.

They stood there, waiting, for what felt like an eternity, even though Bodil knew from the hourglass that it was less than a quarter-hour. She felt like she could hear the woodworms in the walls—so the loud thud from a room somewhere towards the top floor of the inn caught her attention immediately. She held her breath, waiting for the sound of the hunting horn, but none came. Moments passed like years, and still she waited, unsure if it was even anything to worry about, until they heard the muffled, grunting sounds of a scuffle, and the crashing of broken glass.

That was all she needed.

"Your Grace, we cannot yet be sure—wait, Your Grace!" Hilrunn exclaimed, trying to catch her arm.

Implacable as the sea, Bodil shouldered past her, out onto the street. "To me!" she bellowed, throwing back her fur hood as she approached the doors of The Stout Squire, shocking the doorman who stood outside. "To me, soldiers of Dulmun! Stand with your king!"

The royal guard burst from their hiding places and converged into formation behind her, the now-flabbergasted doorman simply choosing to vacate the premises rather than deal with what was going on. Hefting her buckler on her left arm, she struck out with one leg, slamming the door open with a single kick, and watched chaos erupt in the common room of the inn beyond.

At least two dozen of the otherwise innocent-looking patrons leapt to their feet immediately and drew weapons. There was only the briefest of moments to consider as the room before her bristled suddenly with axes and knives, but Bodil knew what she wanted to do to these traitors. She charged forward and slammed into the nearest one forcefully, greatly surprising a nearby table of merchants.

Like many close-quarters battles, it was frenetic and vicious. She trapped one conspirator between several chairs at a table, crushing his knees with a blow from her hammer and leaving him screaming on the floor. Many of the other patrons, shocked at seeing her appear, also joined in the fighting. The rebels endured numerous chairs and tankards flung enthusiastically at their backs while they were occupied by the frontal assault of Bodil's royal entourage.

Through it all she pushed forwards, never giving an inch of ground. No matter the cost, she would reach her son.

She knew the meeting was to have been in a room at the top floor of the inn, so as soon as she saw an opening, she shoved through to the staircase. An enemy grabbed at her leg, but she whirled and kicked them down. Upstairs, two guards stood in front of one of the doors, obviously expecting her by the readiness with which they held their weapons. Obliging them, she charged, roaring.

An axe scraped off her shield, and she swung downwards with her hammer, denting one man's helmet and sending him crashing to the floor. The other she crushed between her shield and the wall behind him, hearing the snap of bones as she put her full weight behind the blow.

Without even pausing for breath, she kicked this door down, too, and was immensely relieved to see Esvind standing. There was blood on his forehead and one of his arms, but he held a sword, ready to fight. Across from him, also armed and now sneering contemptuously in her direction, stood Lord Breiling of House Tornall.

Clearly some effort had been made to subdue Esvind—the bodies of two more of Breiling's guards and the upended furniture testified to that—but her pride at his victory was overwhelmed by the wave of disgust that she felt upon knowing her enemy at last.

"*You*," she hissed at him, lunging into the room with her shield raised once more.

Apparently similarly enraged, Breiling hefted his sword and attempted to put up a fight as she bore down on him. He feinted left, trying to trick her into moving her shield and opening herself up, but Bodil had never been a fencer. She barreled forwards, buckler first, knocking him off-balance, and then swung around fiercely with her hammer, smashing it into his forearm.

"Darkness take you!" he howled, as the sword dropped from his now-useless hand, the shattered bones in his arm unable to support its weight.

Esvind came to stand beside her, sword pointing at Breiling's throat, and she lowered her shield, knowing that she had won, even as Hilrunn and several other guards rushed into the room as well.

"I would not be so quick to invoke curses, traitor. They might find you a more worthy target than me."

"You were never fit to hold the throne," he snarled, clutching at his arm. "Look at what has happened to Dulmun already! The High King thinks us ripe for the picking! How long before we bow and scrape before her every whim like Selvan, trembling in fear of her distant army? You will lead us to ruin!"

"And *you* will not lead anyone anywhere," she replied coldly, shaking her head in disgust.

The sneer returned to his lips as he spat at her feet. Before any of them could react, he whipped something out from a pocket of his robes and crammed it into his mouth in a flurry of sudden movement.

Esvind's fist struck him in the stomach and he was thrown to the ground, but Bodil could see that it was too late; yellow flecks of powder glistened on his lips and tongue, obviously some kind of poison. Hilrunn leapt on him and tried to force his mouth open, but he had already begun to convulse. Bodil's blood ran hot with fury as she realized that if Breiling had had his way, Alleif would have died with this same poison in her veins while Bodil had been out of the city. He might even have meant to administer it to Esvind here today, had she not arrived in time.

Growling, she stepped forwards, pulling Hilrunn away, and deliberately put her booted foot down upon Breiling's throat, not wanting to give him the escape of his choice.

"Honorless . . . dog!" he choked, clawing at her leg in an attempt to remove her, as she ground the heel downwards towards the floor.

"Honorless?" she asked him grimly, as his struggles grew feebler. "I am not the one who has lost."

Though his body still wracked with horrible shudders from the poison, and his face had turned a bluish red as he suffocated, he grinned up at her, a macabre rictus of malice that was almost enough to make her pause, the expression of a man dying with the knowledge that he has gotten the last laugh.

"Are you certain about that?" he whispered, with what must have been his final breath.

His body twitched several more times and then went deathly still, and Bodil slowly removed her boot from his neck, chilled to her very bones by his last words.

What had they missed?

FIVE

"I want every inch of his holdings in the north searched," Bodil barked, sweeping along the corridor back towards the stairs, guards trailing behind her like an extension of her billowing cloak. "Every piece of paper, *every* document is to be brought back to the palace for inspection. And someone fetch a healer!"

"What do you think he meant, mother?" Esvind asked, struggling to stay alongside her on the narrow staircase. "Do you think I missed something? Made some kind of mistake?"

She glanced at him briefly, seeing the anxiety in his eyes, and frowned, having noticed how quick he was to take responsibility for their seeming misstep.

"I do not know," she replied, lowering her voice. "But if he truly did slip something past us, then we *all* did not see it. No fault lies on your shoulders, especially since it was you that exposed his treachery here today."

Whether or not he was convinced, she could not say, for at that point they emerged back into the common room, where the confused patrons were milling about and the innkeeper was grumpily demanding to know what exactly was going on, while conspirators in various states of injury littered the floor.

"Get this mess cleaned up, would you?" Bodil said wearily, turning to Hilrunn, who raised her eyebrows slightly but nodded.

She turned towards the innkeeper momentarily, meaning to tell him that the crown would reimburse him for damages, but then stopped stock still suddenly when she heard raucous barking coming from outside the tavern—the barking of her own dogs, Ulsen and Cimric.

She burst outside, barely aware of her own movement, and felt the same chill of terror in her blood as she had at Breiling's final words, seeing not just her hunting dogs, but Thargrim and several of the staff from the Grand Hall as well, clustered around Alleif and Eyrhild. Alleif, somewhat wild-eyed, clutched a sword in one hand, and several of the staff had blood on their uniforms.

"What happened?" Bodil demanded, though some of fear dissipated a little when she saw that they were both uninjured.

Alleif also seemed to relax a little when she spotted Bodil and Esvind, handing the sword to Thargrim. Bodil noted proudly that there was blood along its edge.

"The Grand Hall was attacked. It was not actually all that dramatic—they apparently thought that we would be easy prey. I feared that their presence might mean you had failed here, though."

Bodil ground her teeth, cursing Breiling's name. "Darkness take him and all his kind!"

"I should have known it would be him," Alleif remarked tiredly, as she went to inspect Esvind's wounds. "I take it you dealt with him?"

"Oh, yes," Bodil replied grimly, remembering. "He made some remark with his last breath about a parting shot he had fired, and I am glad to see that it, too, missed its mark."

"A parting shot?" Alleif asked, frowning suddenly. "I . . . oh, no! The attackers who rushed the Grand Hall were dressed in red cloaks . . . I know the Mystics in the city, so I knew it was trickery, but I could not see why, not until now."

Bodil felt her heart sink, thinking of what she might have done if attackers in red cloaks had truly managed to kill Alleif and Eyrhild. "He sought to pit us against the servants of the High King."

"But the grand chancellor seems quite sensible," Hilrunn countered warily. "Breiling could not guarantee that such a plan would lead to strife—if he even knew that the attack would succeed in taking our lives at all."

"No," Alleif replied quietly, a terrible expression of fear on her face. "But if he attacked the Mystics at the same time, under the guise of *our* soldiers . . ."

They all stood still for but a moment, Bodil's stomach turning at the implications of what they had been caught up in, the consequences that would come from the High King believing that Dulmun's own soldiers had attacked her people.

"Get the queen and our daughter back to the Grand Hall, and double the guard!" she ordered, waving Thargrim back to Alleif's side. "The rest of us will make haste to the Mystics' garrison!"

They galloped through the city streets, blowing horns to scatter the townspeople, but by the time they reached the wide, squat building that housed the redcloaks, the front door was firmly closed.

Her concerns growing, Bodil tried opening it normally, then pushing against it, and lastly kicking it in. Unfortunately, unlike the ones at the inn, this particular door did not budge under her assault. It seemed from the sound, rattling in its frame, that it had been barred from the inside. She tried several more times to shake it loose, but got no results, not even angry Mystics appearing to tell her to stop. Grimly, she concluded that her guess was correct, and those inside were indeed in danger.

This was a problem; the Mystic garrison, by its very nature, was designed to be able to withstand attack. How ironic, then, that its defenders were trapped inside by its own safety measures, in need of aid. Neither the high, narrow windows nor the solid stone walls offered any solution.

There were, of course, other entrances, but surely any attackers who had thought to block one door would also tend to the others. She sent several of her soldiers to each of them anyway, just in case, but her hopes were not high.

There will be war for this, her thoughts sang capriciously, as she railed at the door once more. *A war we cannot win. Your son will inherit a kingdom torn into pieces—or a place in the grave beside you.*

She fell back, defeated, and turned to Esvind, who hovered at her side attentively. His eyes shone brightly, full of both fear and the hope that his mother would save them all somehow. It broke her heart to have to disappoint him, but she opened her mouth to tell him to return to the Grand Hall, to let Alleif know to begin preparations for the disaster that awaited them.

As she did so, however, her hand fell once again upon the head of the hammer at her hip, and she froze. Realization struck her like the ringing of a bell.

"Axes!" she barked hoarsely, throwing off her cloak and hefting the hammer. "Bring all the axes you can find! Wood axes, battle axes, whatever is within reach!"

"They will never break through the door in time!" Hilrunn protested, though she did draw her own as the rest of the guards scattered to carry out Bodil's orders.

"I will weaken the wood! Just fetch the axes!" she commanded impatiently, and then set the hammer's stone head against the wood squarely for a few moments.

The enchantment might have been ancient, but it was still there, however faint. And even an ordinary frost could warp a wooden door, given enough time and maltreatment.

She swung methodically, overhand as though hammering at a fencepost, rather than striking outwards one-handed like she did when using it as a weapon. The sturdy oak did not budge at first, but gradually she began to see splinters forming along its surface, radiating outwards from the point of her blows. Again and again she swung, trying to strike at the same place as much as possible, like waves crashing on the shore, relentless, one after another. She was so lost in her exertions that she almost did not hear the cheer that went up from her guards when at last, groaning under the constriction of the sudden cold, a part of the door began to buckle inwards.

"Break it down!" she thundered, swinging again, and four or five of them joined her, hacking at the obstacle in their way like laborers trying to clear a tree on a farm.

Whether the cold had warped the frame that supported it, or whether their axes simply shook it loose through the splintering door, the bar that kept them out clattered to the floor noisily. Bodil kicked at the door one final time, sending the mangled chunk of wood bursting inwards off its hinges like a discarded toy.

"Save the Mystics!" she bellowed, as the soldiers streamed across the threshold, shouting triumphantly. She felt her heart swell when they raised up a war cry as they spread throughout the garrison.

"For the king! For Dulmun, and King Bodil!"

Dead bodies were strewn across the interior of the garrison, with casualties having occurred on both sides. It seemed as though the Mystics had been ambushed during a meal, but they had obviously put up a fight befitting such highly-regarded soldiers. Though battle still raged in various distant corners, most of the noise seemed to be coming from the back, down near the cells. Bodil strode purposefully through the halls, hammer held aloft once more, and many of the conspirators who saw her approach chose to flee rather than face her.

She let them go, for her guards would likely catch them at some point anyway. It was more important to help the redcloaks—and to make sure they did not run crying to the High King—than to stop the traitors, at least for now.

She barged into the corridor that held the prison cells, following the sounds of battle, and saw there a stupendous sight—Falkari, though bleeding and bruised, blocked the hallway with her great bulk, keeping at least ten enemies at bay. Behind her, Bodil caught glimpses of small, frightened faces, and she felt her blood turn to ice. A myriad of cuts decorated Falkari's arms and face, so determined were these vermin to bring her down and enact the murder of innocents for their vile purposes.

Before Bodil could even raise her hammer, an arrow sprouted suddenly from the back of one traitor's neck, and she became aware of Esvind behind her, already drawing back another shot on his shortbow. Buoyed on wings of pride and fury, Bodil charged into the press of them, laying about herself with the hammer and scattering them all. The extra space she cleared was enough for Falkari to manage an overhand swing with her polearm, and the great weapon came down upon an unlucky enemy with the force of a landslide.

Things did not really take all that much finishing up after that.

* * *

"I must thank you, Your Grace," Falkari said later, once things had settled down enough that they had finally convinced her to allow a healer to tend her wounds. "And you, Your Excellency. I owe you both a lifedebt, of that I have no doubt."

Esvind bowed slightly, accepting her thanks, but Bodil regarded her gravely, unsure of where to go from here.

"I am certain you would have done the same for us," she said eventually, and Falkari grinned.

"Of course!"

"Then I will be frank with you. This attack was meant as a double-edged sword: they sought to frame me for the murder of your people, and in so doing spark a war between Dulmun and the High King."

Falkari squinted at her while the healer applied some kind of green paste to a large cut over one eye, the expression on her face somewhere between concern and surprise. "Almost as if someone witnessed the fuss made by Her Majesty's ambassador in the council a week or so ago and chose to try and capitalize on it, would you say?"

Bodil merely nodded, unable to discern whether the Mystic woman believed her or not.

"It is a very good thing that they failed, then," Falkari said at last, a statement with which Bodil emphatically agreed.

"I dread informing the ambassador of what has happened," she admitted, grimacing. "Who knows what he will make of it."

"It is his job only to convey the High King's decrees to far-off kingdoms," Falkari said lightly, shaking off the healer and standing to face Bodil properly. "But as Mystic Grand Chancellor, I am tasked to protect the people of this land, from any ill. No matter the politics between you and High King Enalyn, I am not here on an errand of persecution. I think you want the same thing as I do: for your people to be safe. And so I say, let us be allies, Your Grace. I am not interested in petty bickering."

A wave of relief that Bodil had not been expecting washed over her, the release of the fear that she would have to face some kind of retribution for the day's events. "Nor am I."

"So?" Falkari pressed, extending a hand ready for her to shake. "What say you, then?"

She looked at the woman's outstretched hand, and once again sensed Esvind at her elbow, gazing at her, his pride and awe evident. She thought of herself watching her father, and wondered if this was always how history was shaped, in the small moments that brought knowledge and accord. She took Falkari's hand, and shook it firmly.

"I will do *anything* to protect my people."

THE TIDES OF WAR

LIANDRA SY

ONE

Kara rose from the waves, filling her lungs with the crisp cool air of an unusually chilly morning. Her callused feet struggled with the pebble-ridden sandbank, tripping over shells and stones. At last, she squatted by the rocky shore at the base of Tialara. Nestled in her hands lay the revealing, iridescent gleam of an oyster.

On many days, Kara would seek refuge in Tialara's towering cliffs. Its shadow stretched past the shallow waters and dwarfed the other peaks of the island. With one hand she teased the oyster's openings with her fishbone knife, and her callused fingertips soon began to feel its loosening grip.

Snapping open, the shell revealed a pearl. It shone like a pale, calcified bead. Kara impishly snatched it before hiding it in her oilcloth. It was the third one she had found in a week.

"Kara!" a voice called out.

The young prince clambered back to firmer ground. She thoughtlessly stole a glance at the sky, espying the sun behind its silver veil of thickening clouds. "It is not yet midday," she grumbled to herself as Suki, the clan scribe and royal mentor, approached within earshot.

Suki struggled through the bramble as she walked briskly to her ward. The sand bore the weight of her gait, swallowing her feet up to her ankles as she approached.

Kara, on the other hand, leaped lightly past the rocks, the sand, and onto the gravel-like path from which Suki had emerged, preparing for a scolding. But when she saw Suki's furrowed brows and tight-lipped silence, Kara felt an unease that suffused the air.

The scribe huffed up to a halt before her ward with a look of reproach. "I thought I taught you better," she said curtly.

Kara shot back a stony look. "The summit was not until midday. The rules of hospitality—"

"Someday, my prince," Suki cut in, "you will know better than to rely on trivialities."

The surly scribe nudged her pupil forwards, and the two hurried along through the thorny brambles and treacherous sand towards Clan Mata's village.

"My mother and father?" Kara asked.

Suki said nothing at first, and Kara was somewhat shocked by the silence. "They are already meeting with the emissary in the Kubo," she finally answered curtly.

"And what of this emissary?"

Suki let out a weary sigh and kept her gaze forwards. "You mean to tell me you have been out here fishing for your trifles all morning?" She clicked her tongue at Kara and shook her head.

"Why? Did something happen?"

Again, Suki left her question unanswered as they pushed past the perimeter of the forest. They reached the clearing that opened to the western side of the coast. Kara stopped just before the summit of the hill, patiently waiting for Suki to catch up.

"You will never learn anything playing around those rocks," Suki grumbled. "So far from the village, too! No one goes to Tialara. Even babes know better!"

"We were talking about the summit, Ina Suki," said Kara, careful to add the honorific.

Suki's furrowed brows seemed to give way to a softer and more fearful wrinkle. "The emissary arrived with . . . company," she began hesitantly. "And that is not all."

She tugged Kara by the arm and hastened to the summit of the hill. "Look, there!"

Suki's hand stretched out to the cerulean horizon. There, perched on gentle, shimmering waves, sat a galley with a fleet of oars suspended over the water. Its canvas sails were only partially drawn up to the masts.

"A galley . . ." Kara started, but her own thoughts slipped away from her.

The older woman nodded. "The emissary came with a retinue. Ten foot soldiers and three mages."

"Nao!" Kara said under her breath. "Three?"

Suki nodded. "All depends on this summit."

Kara gazed upon the galley where the High King's flag—a field of white with a golden star circled in crimson—whipped against the mast. "They do not care about the summit," she said suddenly. "Look at the sails."

Her mentor drew closer and squinted.

"The flags show the wind blowing due west," Kara observed. She stepped forwards, watching the sun make its slow climb to its zenith.

Suki watched patiently as her ward pieced together the puzzle. "The tides rise now, but by sundown, the water will creep back into the depths," she said, helping Kara along.

Though Kara stood proud, her fingers coiled with fright. "They do not plan on staying long."

* * *

Lucio contemplated his escape the moment dusk settled onto the horizon. The canoe swayed to a gentler lull, and soon the lanterns lit up like beacons in the encroaching darkness. The small orange lights looked to him like fireflies.

"Ow! Hey!" His hands recoiled as the Wavemount guard tightened the rope to an insufferable grip. "Ease up a little!"

The guard ignored Lucio and left him tied to the mast.

"Is this how you treat your guest, a citizen of Dulmun?!" Lucio resorted to the more official tones of a more diplomatic traveler. "We are at war, you know. The last thing you want is to embroil our kingdoms in conflict just because you found my longboat suspect."

He hoped the mild threat would work on the guard, who had happened upon his vessel quite by accident. Mere hours before, Lucio had had the brilliant plan of circumnavigating the western seaboard trade routes, riding a small gale due southeast. It was an ingenious plan, or so he thought: sneak past patrol routes and land on unattended shores. Little did he know that in times of war, the Chieftains of Clan Mata erred on the side of caution.

Soon the guard abandoned him and resumed his post by the steer. The canoe—a massive and double-hulled tonga—afforded the Wavemount pilot an unobstructed view of both the ship and the sea. His partner, another taciturn guard whom Lucio presumed to be of the same clan, kept to starboard as he scanned the darkening sky. Though the ship was not far off the coast, reading the stars aided many a sailor through treacherous shallows, which were shorn with rocks and wreckage. These threats became invisible during nightfall, a happenstance of nature that did not deter the people of Wavemount. Lucio had heard many tales of the kingdom's expert navigators, for whom the sky was but another map, and they always used it to their advantage.

"I doubt your Chieftain will want to explain this . . . *business* to the King of Dulmun!" Lucio yelled over his shoulder, placing delicate emphasis on his euphemism. "Release me at once!'

The two guards stared at him blankly. When Lucio sank into stoic silence, they exchanged with each other bemused looks. He heard them whisper words in another tongue—Alonian, the ancient speech of Wavemount, whose people proudly held onto the deepest roots and legends of their culture.

"Tignan mo to!" the pilot exclaimed cheerfully. The other laughed boisterously from across the canoe. Even the waves seemed to lap at the ship's hull in a shared fit of amusement.

"Tigil, tigil na!" the other retorted, slapping his knees in good cheer.

Are they . . . laughing at me? Lucio's cheeks flushed. With thick dark hair and skin of warm brown complexion, Lucio could have passed for any sailor of Wavemount origin. But clad and armed like a Dulmun pirate and sailing on a meager longboat, he seemed strangely out of place in the neutral waters of Alonia.

The guards paid no mind to Lucio's seething silence, contenting themselves with their already fading trails of laughter before quickly brushing off a slight tear and ambling away. There, from the back of the hull, their hushed conversation was barely within earshot.

The captive, meanwhile, snuck a glance at the horizon. The reddish trace of the sun had all but disappeared. The sky was a dome of dark blue, speckled with only small glimmers of pale light.

A new moon, Lucio observed.

He craned his neck as far as he could around the mast and saw from the corner of his eye that the guards were now in rapt conversation. Whether they bickered or joked, Lucio could not tell. Their Alonian was intermixed with the common tongue of Underrealm.

Now is my chance.

Lucio maneuvered his hands as best as he could, bound as he was under the rope. His focused eyes glowed in the impending darkness. From under his breath, he murmured incantations as ancient as Alonia itself.

"Look! The water!" The pilot shouted.

The waves lapped more vigorously against the hulls of the canoe. The two Wavemount guards panicked as they scrambled to draw the sails and steer to calmer waters. But the waves kept surging towards the boat, rocking it back and forth.

"Quick! The sail!"

But the two struggled to stay balanced as the waters grew more violent. By the time the pilot grabbed hold of the tiller, a gale had snapped the knots, releasing the sails to the fury of the wind.

Under cover of the havoc, Lucio sprang into action, wrestling to gesture with his hands.

"The prisoner!" the pilot cried out. "He is casting a spell!"

The smell of ash permeated the air as Lucio's flame singed through the bindings.

"Well, gentlemen!" he jeered with a self-satisfied grin. "I wish I could say it has been a pleasure, but—"

A javelin cut through Lucio's speech and splintered the center of the mast.

"Get him!"

The other guard leaped to his feet and unsheathed his sword. Lucio readied another spell, but the swordsman swung before he could speak. Lucio fell to the deck, then rolled away as the guard lashed out with his blade again. The steel landed mere inches from his face.

The guard's sword stuck in the wood of the canoe. Lucio jumped to his feet and raised his hand. Sparks lit the night, and fire blasted the swordsman off the boat. It was not until Lucio heard a splash that he realized he was winning.

"You will pay for that, brigand!" the pilot yelled. He grabbed another spear and launched it at Lucio. Lucio dodged it by a hair as its pointed end cut through the sleeve of his doublet.

"Your friend *should* know better," he taunted with a smirk. "Who brings a sword to a fire fight?"

The pilot let out a guttural cry and leaped at Lucio with another blade, landing atop him. Lucio struggled, feeling the cool flat of the blade against his throat.

"I will *end* you," the pilot snarled.

Lucio's vision blurred against the dark sky, and his arms flailed about for another chance at life. He heaved as his chest constricted, and a numbness started to set in. His fists pounded on the wooden planks until his fingers landed on the pommel of a discarded blade. Lucio grasped it with renewed strength. A desperate cry shot out from his lungs, and he struck the pilot's head with the pommel, throwing him off.

Lucio's opponent crawled towards his weapon. He wanted to yell, to cry out any incantation, but he could only blurt out unintelligible sounds. His opponent rose to ready feet as Lucio heaved from the weight of crushed ribs.

I have to get out of here.

He looked around with desperation, and a suggestive breeze seemed to beckon him into the inviting waves.

The pilot was readying to strike once more. Lucio rolled to the edge of the deck. He waved a hand and murmured the beginnings of a spell.

With a sigh, he felt jets of water envelope him. The bluish depths—darker than the night—engulfed him, and Lucio felt his body carried away as if in a dream.

TWO

THE HIGH KING'S EMISSARY, WALTER RODHAM, SAT BEFORE THE PYRE with a delighted grin. Across from him, Chieftain Yue and her husband weathered the emissary's appeals with sullen solemnity. To the left of Chieftain Yue, Kara and her mentor, Suki, hovered in subdued silence.

It was customary for the hosting family to treat their guest with a welcome feast while regaling them with the sights and pleasures of Wavemount hospitality, but the summit they had all been waiting for had begun days in advance, without representatives from any of the other clans.

"I am afraid that is just not possible," protested Chieftain Matang. He looked at his wife as if pleading with her to agree with him. "You cannot ask us to offer you a hostage—"

"Not a hostage!" Walter interrupted. "What an unpleasant and vile word! The High King has nothing but the best intentions for Wavemount."

"But what you are asking of us is—"

"What the High King is asking," the emissary bellowed louder. The echo startled even Chieftain Yue, whose unyielding countenance betrayed none of her husband's fears. "She is asking that the people of Wavemount show and prove their loyalty in these dangerous times of war."

"You are asking," Chieftain Yue persisted, "that we represent all of Wavemount before any of the other clans have arrived." A cool, impenetrable calm settled over the room as Chieftain Yue sat poised. "That is unfortunately not possible."

Kara watched the exchange as one would a battle. Each word fell like a strike, each retort hastening to a parry. Her presence there was redundant, for the prince was merely a Chieftain-in-training, but she found excitement in the artful ways with which her mother dexterously sparred with the High King's emissary. It was clear from the way he shifted in his seat that it took great effort to hold his tongue and wait his turn.

"In the meantime," said Yue with a generous smile, "we ask that you consider what we have done for the High King in these . . . trying times."

Chieftain Matang nodded proudly. "We have supplied your troops with food. We have provided you with ships. The people of Wavemount have shown nothing but loyalty."

"Yes, the High King has always appreciated these valiant efforts. I assure you wholeheartedly, the High King has only Wavemount's safety and protection in mind." Something about the way the emissary grinned with almost theatrical deference was unnerving. As he spoke, his smile dissolved, and his brows wrinkled as if in deep concern. "The war has cost the High King's Seat and the kingdom of Selvan countless lives and resources. To ensure the welfare of all of Underrealm, Her Majesty must achieve a decisive victory against Dulmun."

"And giving you our leaders will ensure victory, how?" Chieftain Matang blurted out with thinly veiled rage.

Walter, who had been sitting awkwardly on the cool and damp ground, smiled and affected more patronizing tones. "High King Enalyn seeks *advisors*," he enunciated the word with impatient care. "To be an advisor, stationed on the High King's Seat, is the greatest honor."

"Honor?" Chieftain Matang retorted. "Where is the honor in—"

Chieftain Yue, who had receded into the margins of conversation, held up her hand to still Chieftain Matang, eyeing the parcel unrolled before them. It bore the High King's stamp, along with the terms meant to exact their show of loyalty.

"You are right," she said suddenly. Kara turned to her mother, visibly shocked. "We have arrived at an impasse."

Walter looked as if he was ready with a rejoinder, but he let out a placating sigh. "In that case, what answer should I bring the High King?"

Both Chieftain Yue and Matang exchanged harried glances. The barely suppressed threat loomed over them all. Chieftain Matang curled his fists.

"You have heard Chieftain Yue," he said, straightening his posture. "We cannot arrive at a decision without the consent of the other ruling chiefs."

Rodham's varnished mask of pretense shattered. He folded his hands together as if in resignation. "I am afraid that time is what the High King does not have. We are at war—"

"And you are asking us to endanger our people," Chieftain Yue snapped back. "Is this how the High King rewards her loyal subjects?"

Kara looked on, playing with complete fidelity her role as a dutiful heir. But her mother's sudden outburst was hard to bear, and even worse was this emissary's intractability. She knew—*somehow*—that every gleam of his eye was a sign of his carefully thought out ploy to lure her mother and father.

The main doors burst open as if by tempestuous winds, washing with the pale light of midday. Laki, the village courier and lieutenant of the royal guard, ran in with a local soldier. "Chief!"

Kara recognized the other man to be a guard she had encountered often during her dives off Tialara. The two figures approached the pyre, revealing the soldier's poultice-covered arm. Reddish burns and greenish ointments checkered his skin. Kara was inexperienced in war, but she knew well the wounds inflicted by magic.

"Speak," demanded Chieftain Yue, unfazed.

Laki shot an apprehensive glance at the emissary. "Pardon the intrusion," he said warily. "But we must speak with you and Chieftain Matang immediately."

"Whatever concerns the safety of Wavemount concerns the High King," Walter said ungraciously.

Kara tightly wound her fists, which were clasped with irrepressible rage. "The High King once contented herself with our crops, our ships, and our riches." She raised her head as if to look down on the emissary. "Yet when we suffered, our affairs were somehow unworthy, our wars petty. Why does she choose to meddle now? Why embroil our kingdom in *her* petty wars?"

A hush swept the room. Chieftain Matang sat speechless. Even Suki woke from her stony silence. Laki and the guard seemed to have vanished into the margins of the Kubo, and suddenly their ill news dwindled in the face of the implied treachery their prince had uttered.

"Forgive my daughter." Chieftain Yue's voice cut through the silence. "She is young, and has much to learn in the art of ruling."

But the damage had been done. Walter bowed his head in acceptance of her apology, smiling with the knowledge that Chieftain Yue now had to make a concession.

"Laki, please share with us your news," said Yue.

"There has been an attack," he blurted. "Kupe—a seaguard stationed along the coast of Tialara—apprehended a pirate who claims to be a citizen of Dulmun."

"Claims?" said Suki.

"Yes, Ina Suki," Laki bowed his head as he explained. "He wore the clothing of an outsider and proclaimed impunity as a citizen of Dulmun, but . . ." The words drifted as Laki looked to the soldier, Kupe.

"He looked Alonian, Chieftain," Kupe said, addressing the couple before the pyre. He remained stalwart and rigid despite his obvious wounds. "He could have been a kinsman from a neighboring clan. What is more, he is a wizard." Kupe stepped forwards and brandished his burned arm.

Kara watched Walter Rodham attentively. He seemed to shrink into his own thoughts, uncharacteristically surly and reticent.

"Where is the prisoner now?" asked Chieftain Matang.

Kara saw Walter's eyes light up. Something about this Dulmun pirate burned through all his pretenses and illusions.

"He escaped to the water last night," answered Kupe. "If he survived the rocks and the treacherous waves, he cannot be far from the cliffs of Tialara."

Chieftain Yue looked to her daughter, "You know those cliffs well." Her tone was cool, yet severe. "It is time you lead your people in Wavemount's defense."

"I volunteer my soldiers of the High King," Rodham chimed in. His mood seemed to have undergone a sudden transformation, and he smiled at Kara. "We will send out patrols near the forest. If High

King Enalyn's devotion to her subjects is in doubt, please allow me the opportunity to persuade you."

Unable to refuse, both Chieftains nodded in acceptance.

THREE

The sand felt hot against Lucio's cheek. As the sun rose, the tide tugged at his boot, beckoning him back into the icy waters below. Lucio sputtered out a cough, and his eyes opened to a sky bathed in gold. Another set of waves pushed and pulled him with more force, momentarily drowning him before receding back into their calm. Lucio gasped and shook for air.

He rummaged in his vest and felt the rugged shape of a leather-bound scroll beneath the fabric. "Oh thank—"

His words faltered as his lungs seized for breath. It took several more moments of breathing the still air and shaking off sand before Lucio rose. With the dossier still intact, the mission—and its reward—remained his priority.

Moving along the shell-carpeted beach and onto the bramble-weed-laden path, Lucio was more sure-footed than he expected. Wave-mount had always been rumored among northern pirates to have treacherous terrain. Its coasts boasted perilous cliffsides, its seas were fickle, and its people left much of the forests largely unscathed.

Fortunately for Lucio, he had *some* guidance. He thought of the moments buried deep in his childhood, a time before he had known the cruel sea. At the time, he had not known his mother's lullabies and stories would guide him into dangerous territory.

In Ancient Alonia, it was said powerful mages shaped the land with the sea.

He unsheathed his sword, cutting through defiant vines and upturned roots barring his way.

They nourished the land, and the forests grew to protect it.

Towering trees with leaves as large as paddle boats draped over him. Sunlight flickered through the foliage. His feet knew the way, spurred by the memory of his mother and the tales he had once so voraciously consumed.

The dossier felt heavier in his vest. Lucio had stolen it from a Selvan galley months before. It looked like nothing but bookkeeping—pounds of grain, days at sea, loads of cargo. Yet Lucio knew it was worth more than the goods it listed. The information it contained could engulf other kingdoms that had hitherto remained neutral in the war.

Lucio's instructions led him through the forest to the sacred groves. There, an agent would retrieve the dossier and reward him for his efforts.

The plan was simple enough, but a slight hunch—that things could *always* go wrong—nagged from the back of his mind. His hand felt for the dossier in his vest again. A mist had enveloped the path before him, and soon even the sun could barely cast its pale light into the maze of green.

* * *

Kara considered her life as a prince incidental, a formality she merely maintained. She breathed most freely during a hunt, when her limbs moved with ease and her thoughts flowed with the chorus of crickets, birds, and brooks that littered the ancient forest.

So it came as no surprise to her that she was the first to find signs of the escaped pirate. On the eastern side of the woods were torn branches and splintered roots. The tall, spindly trunks of the trees bore scars from a blade. Only an outsider would force their way with violence.

Aie! She cursed to herself. Kara felt her stomach sink when she realized where the outsider's tracks led. *Several leagues more, and he will reach the sacred grove.*

The prince strung her bow and quickened her pace. Her feet wove around the jutting roots of the forest, following a path that only people of Alonia knew.

The grove itself was not particularly special to an outsider. Why the prisoner would be heading there was beyond Kara's imagination. As she blurred past the scenery, her thoughts ran fast and wild with speculation.

How would he even know to go there?

The clang of metal exploded in the air and stilled Kara mid-dash. She jolted to a halt, searching for the source of the sound.

A stillness followed in the wake of the noise, but Kara felt more disquieted than ever.

I have to hurry.

* * *

Lucio cut through the last vine and entered a clearing. A line of trees encircled it, and in the middle stood a giant moss-covered tree with branches weaving upwards like latticework leaves. Around it was a sea of grass and fern that grazed his knees.

A stranger hooded in an orange cloak stood motionless by the tree, barely concealed by its serpentine branches.

"You are late," the stranger announced, audibly irked.

Despite the long flowing cloak, Lucio could tell the stranger had a thin, lurching figure. And by the looks and sound of him, Lucio guessed the agent was Alonian.

"I ran into a bit of trouble," Lucio offered with a hint of sarcasm. He approached slowly, cautiously. Politics was a high-stakes gamble, and Lucio knew better than to believe his journey over. "Do you have it?"

The cloaked stranger muttered inaudibly before stepping out into the light. His hand reached into his robes and uncovered a small burlap sack. "I hope it is worth your . . . troubles. Hand over the dossier first."

Lucio let out an exasperated sigh as he unveiled the scroll and offered it.

The other snatched it and, in the same dexterous motion, threw the sack. It fell behind Lucio with a thud. "Take your prize," he said blithely.

"A pleasure." Lucio feigned a reverent bow, letting his hand weave the air as if to a highborn lady. The stranger ignored him, focusing on the parchment.

Lucio shrugged before turning and walking to the sack. It was light to the touch—almost empty and airy, given the impact it had had. For a moment Lucio was seized with terror at the thought that it was empty. But he dug his hand inside, and there he felt it. The unmistakable weight of a ring. His fingers brushed against the proud sigil of Dulmun.

A light and airy feeling overwhelmed Lucio, and for a moment he felt lost in the cloud of his own joy. *It's here.*

The crunch of grass broke the silence. Lucio caught sight of a shadow and the pointed end of a dagger.

Lucio instinctively drew his sword and deflected the other's blade before dodging to the side. Both men dropped their prizes as they overbalanced—but Lucio exaggerated his stumble, scooping up the dossier out of sight of the agent. The ring was farther away—it would have to wait.

"What is the meaning of this?" Lucio cried.

"Chieftain Lourang sends his regards," the stranger said gleefully. He took advantage of Lucio's fumbling stance, lunging once more. His hilt struck Lucio's throat, knocking him off his feet.

His hands clawed at his neck as coughs rattled his lungs. The agent moved towards him and raised his dagger once more, this time aiming the tip at Lucio's heart.

"Do not fret," he said. "Your troubles end here."

Lucio clamped his eyes shut as he heaved, in dire need of breath.

In the darkness, he heard a high-pitched whistle and a burst of wind. The agent let out a sharp cry as he fell back.

Lucio looked up. The agent writhed in agony on his back. An arrow had pierced his hand.

A figure emerged from the enshadowed woods. The agent snarled at this new foe and threw his dagger. The figure evaded his attack and called out in Alonian, to no effect.

"W-wait!"

Both of them were deaf to Lucio's plea. He struggled to get to his knees and ready a spell. His eyes burned with a fiery glow as he flailed his hand in the air. Fire licked the grass between the two figures, missing both completely. But as the smoke settled, a shadow emerged from the whirlwind of dust. A kick to his neck sent him flying back once more. It took all Lucio's strength to breathe. The chilly air felt like a knife burning through the sting of his throat.

"Who are you?" the stocky blur of a figure demanded.

Lucio tried his best to look up, but his hands still clutched his throat. All he managed was a dry, hoarse cough. Finally his blurred vision steadied, and he was suddenly confronted with her harsh, interrogating gaze. She was an Alonian woman armed with a longbow. Lucio saw no sign of the agent.

"So *you* are the mage." She kept her bow drawn, an arrow pointed squarely at his face.

Had Lucio been in better condition, he would have mustered up a laugh. But his throat still stung from the blow, and his body seemed to give in to the exhaustion of his limbs.

"W-wait!" he coughed out, raising his hand as a plea.

She raised the bow and struck him with it. His skull throbbed with pain, and Lucio sank away from consciousness.

* * *

With Laki's help, Kara checked the ropes for the third time, tightening them once more for good measure. The prisoner's hands were bound with hemp rope, woven with the intricacy and expertise needed for sailboats. A ripped piece of fabric served as a makeshift gag—a measure taken for dangerous elementalists.

Her horse was a tall and proud beast, who bore his burden without complaint. As they walked on, from time to time Kara would halt for a rest, unwilling to risk injury to the animal as they navigated the winding and stony paths of the old forest. As they trudged on, Kara's attention returned to the small burlap sack. The silver signet ring within bore engravings of silver waves—the insignia of Dulmun. Small emerald gemstones lined its grooves, evoking the color of sun-lit waves rising with the tide. It was beautiful, and the mysteries of its origins and purpose piqued Kara's curiosity no end.

As for the prisoner, he wore outlandish clothing akin to the attire of foreign sailors. Yet his olive-hued skin and warm black hair were the marks of an Alonian. It was not unheard of for her countrymen to abandon their home and seek ruthless adventure on the open sea. But Kara recognized his accented speech from Dulmun, and he had none of the tattoos that Alonian mages earned upon completion of their training. The threads of the mystery unraveled further the more she pondered them, and yet Kara could not help herself.

"Prince, the prisoner is waking up," Laki warned.

Indeed, Kara noticed him fidgeting. The rocking horse and the sudden jolts from missteps along the rocky trail brought a tired groan as his eyes started to flicker open.

"Halt," she commanded.

Laki pulled the reins and coaxed the horse with soft, droning tones. Kara drew her fishbone dagger from her boot and rested it on the prisoner's neck. She waited patiently as he slowly regained his senses.

"Quiet." Her tone was calm yet foreboding. "Nod your head if you know what *this* is." She nudged her knife closer to his jawline.

The prisoner nodded without the slight trace of panic in his eyes, though she could see his bewilderment.

"Good," she said curtly. "When I found you, you were fighting someone. Did you know him?" Kara kept her face stony and blank. Her mother had always told her a good leader lulls and coaxes, illusive and persuasive as the calm sea.

The prisoner shook his head.

"Do you know what this is?" Kara held up the sack before his eyes.

She watched as he eyed the burlap sack with suspicion. A bead of sweat fell from the tip of his nose. The protracted silence unnerved the horse, which started as if to begin a trot. Laki pulled the reins tighter and murmured harsher words.

They exchanged furtive glances. Kara could read Laki's worried expression. Soon they would be forced to spend the night under the trees, and then Walter Rodham's patrol would come searching for them. A pit in her stomach told her the prisoner could not be trusted with the High King's emissary.

She pushed the burlap sack closer to his face. "The man you were fighting . . . did he give this to you?"

This time the wary prisoner nodded slowly.

Kara paused. "That man . . . he bore the facial markings of a warrior from Clan Koura. Did you know this?"

Again the prisoner nodded.

He was cooperating, but Kara could only distrust such a gesture. He had everything to gain in this exchange, and she had everything to lose.

She shook the sack containing the ring as if reassuring herself of its weightless presence. "Answer truthfully," she said, pressing the dagger with her other hand so it grazed against the lump in his throat. "Do you know the High King's emissary? A petty nobleman with a Selvan accent?"

Laki started as if woken from sleep. He looked at her and whispered harshly, "Prince!"

Kara ignored him and watched the mage more intently.

His gaze darted between the two of them. Before long he yielded yet another nod.

"Does he have anything to do with your dealings here?"

The prisoner bobbed his head again.

Laki edged closer to Kara without letting go of the reins. He whispered close to her ear. "We do not know if we can trust him, Prince."

Though she turned her head to acknowledge Laki's warning, she kept a vigilant gaze on her prisoner. His answers offered nothing but *more* questions. Kara closed her eyes and sighed deeply, feeling both exasperated and frail. She wished nothing more than for her parents' wisdom in this matter. But she was alone, and one false move could be the end of their perilous game. She thought of the galley, of Walter's forces prowling the coast in search of the prisoner, and the revelation of betrayal. Strange tides had visited Wavemount's shores, and Kara had no choice but to act.

She opened her eyes again and handed Laki the Dulmun ring in its burlap sack, whispering in Alonian. "Take this with you to the Tialara Cliffs. Hide it in the grotto, beneath the rocky waters. Make sure no one sees you."

Laki cast another wary glance at the prisoner before accepting the pouch from Kara and hiding it in the vest of his doublet. In exchange, he handed her the reins.

"Kulia, my prince."

Laki sprinted into the forest.

"Laki is a loyal servant of my family," she said to the prisoner, who remained surprisingly complacent. "He will hide your precious ring and keep it safe for me."

Kara grabbed the rope tied to his wrists. She slid her dagger into the gaps of the knots. "Cast one spell, make one wrong move," Kara glowered as she made her threat, "and you'll never get it back."

With a flick of her wrist, she cut through the bindings and let the hempen rope fall to the ground in pieces. The horse neighed, as if in protest of her recklessness.

Kara cut the bindings on his feet. "You will aid us in apprehending the Koura warrior, and more importantly . . ."

The prisoner looked at his wrists, which were raw and reddened from the constraints. He rose up from the saddle and sat frozen in disbelief.

". . . you will come back with me to my village. There, you will explain to my mother and father all that you know, *especially* about your dealings with the Koura warrior." Kara gave him a helping hand off the saddle, and soon the two stood eye-to-eye on solid ground. "What is your name?" she asked.

The prisoner still appeared disturbed by her trust, and he had a keen eye. He was watching the dagger by her side.

"So I help you," he began, speaking his first words since the attack, "and I get the ring back?"

A smile crept to her lips. She knew there was a madness in her plan, but it was a madness she had long ago embraced. She found it in her dives, the moments spent in the cliffs, the thrill of getting lost in a hunt. Trusting a pirate to save her people was another risk she was willing to take.

"You have my word." Kara held out her hand to him.

The prisoner still looked at her with dogged suspicion. "*After* I get the ring back," he said, "will I be free to go?"

For a moment she was ready to offer him freedom. Yet she knew something of the guiles of brigands. "That will depend on the nature of your information and the judgment of my mother and father. As Chieftains of Clan Mata, only they can decide your freedom." She did not miss the pained expression that immediately swept over his countenance, so she hurriedly went on. "All the more reason for you to help us, especially if we really *do* have a traitor in our midst. Keep to your word, and I promise to help you with all my power."

The prisoner was visibly dissatisfied with her answer. His mouth curled into a frown, but he had to be aware of his position—battered, exhausted, and lost in a foreign land. He bit his tongue before heaving a sigh of resignation.

"My name is Lucio." He took her wrist with a firm grasp.

But before she could answer him, a thunderous explosion burst in the air.

The two looked around, bewildered. Kara rushed to the nearest Kauri tree and climbed its moss-covered trunk. Another loud explosion thundered in the distance, and even the trees seemed to quiver. The prince scanned the forest where it dipped to the coastline.

A column of smoke rose from the valley before the sea. The plume of black ash rose from the village Kubo. Kara felt her heartbeat stagger as she searched desperately, but her eyes strained to see any sign of life. Behind the smoke waved a white flag with the familiar red-centered star, shimmering in gold.

FOUR

When Lucio first met Walter Rodham, it was in the meager establishment of a seaside tavern off the coast of Selvan. Lucio had been marauding and harassing trade routes in the area for two months. That day, he was capping off his success with a celebratory and solitary drink in the hopes that he would soon sail safely back home. Little did he know that within seconds of his finishing the third flagon, a nobleman would walk into the unseemly establishment bearing the offer of a future Lucio could not refuse.

"Why me?" he had asked then.

To which Walter Rodham offered a sallow and knowing grin. "You have a special connection to the place."

Rodham's words bore heavily on Lucio as he trailed Kara through the forest. He struggled to keep up, for Clan Mata's prince tread the winding trails with ease. But it was the fire before them—and the menacing column of smoke looming over the trees—that haunted their fledgling and uneasy alliance. The two stopped in a clearing near the edge of the forest. Between the trees came the vermillion glow of the towering fire.

Lucio watched bleary-eyed from behind an overgrown thicket. A large dome-like hall jutted from the center of rice paddies and huts. The burning structure—the one Kara called the Kubo—dwarfed everything around it. Even from a distance, the fire's heat struck harshly against his face. Lucio could hear the flames crackle as they consumed beams, posts, and fronds until nothing but smoke rose to the sky.

"I am sorry," he said sheepishly, feeling the emptiness of the gesture. Kara merely watched, stunned, her mouth agape. Lucio saw in her face the shock and dismay of one lost in a nightmare.

"The people . . ." she suddenly muttered.

Lucio looked at her, dumbfounded, from his side of the thicket.

"I do not see my family or . . . *anyone*." Kara rose from her low crouch, risking exposure for a better look. The pirate, however, kept to his cover and waited silently for her report. "Lucio, there is no one!" she exclaimed.

No one? The fire raged indifferently as the two searched for signs of life. A catastrophe of such scale would not go unattended, or so Lucio thought. And where were the perpetrators behind it?

"Do you see the emissary and his retinue?" she asked hurriedly.

Lucio conducted another cursory scan before shaking his head.

Kara crouched, clutching the thorny leaves of the thicket, lost in thought. Lucio kept to his silence, feigning another glance for the sake of it, looking for another way out.

"Look! Over there!" he called out. Shadows skirted the edges of the rice paddies. One of the figures wore a deep red barong like Kara's. "I think it is one of your men."

Kara brightened as she spotted them. "Laki! He and his crew are headed to the port." But suddenly she grew troubled. "Come on!" she beckoned Lucio. "We need to follow them."

"W-wait!"

Lucio followed haplessly as Kara bolted after the courtier. They skirted around the village, putting a great distance between them and the burning Kubo. Lucio found it odd how Kara seemed unperturbed by the inferno raging in their periphery. As row houses and huts receded for the clearer horizon of the sea, soot and ash drizzled from the sky. A cloud of gray smoke hovered over the air like a heavy and stifling fog.

"Hurry!" Kara called under her breath. They snuck behind a row of stalls near the gates of a square.

This must be their market, Lucio observed. Every stall was abandoned, flies and myriad insects keeping vigil over the neglected wares.

“I see Laki . . . and look!” Kara whispered.

Ahead of them, Laki and several warriors furtively stole into an emptied pavilion.

“Citizens of Village Mata!” A familiar voice woke the deathly silence of the square. Beyond Laki and his crew, Lucio noticed the Selvan galley docked ominously close. There, a muted throng of Wavemount villagers gathered before a makeshift dais. “I come before you with tidings of treachery and deceit!”

“Kara, look,” said Lucio, nudging her shoulder. The flag of the High King waved proudly over the wooden dais. In the center stood Walter Rodham, whose portly figure bore the gravity and solemnity of the High King herself.

“No . . .” Kara paled as her eyes fell on the figure next to the High King’s emissary.

Lucio followed her gaze. “Who is it?” he asked.

Her eyes trembled, and her breath stilled. She thoughtlessly jutted out from where she hid, crying out a desperate plea. “Father!”

* * *

Kara felt the ground crumble beneath her. She heard the emissary’s grave words, but their meaning eluded her. The pounding of her heart clashed with Rodham’s deafening shouts. Panic overwhelmed her, like a tide flooding the land, drowning everything in its wake.

“This man is harboring a Dulmun fugitive! A traitor and enemy to the High King!”

Disbelieving gasps and plaintive cries rang out. The people stirred, and soon the emissary’s soldiers had to encircle the riled crowd.

“What is more, he has *helped* this fugitive escape!” The emissary stepped aside as three cloaked mages brought forth a man wearing a familiar orange cloak. His arm was wrapped in a poultice, crusted brown with dried blood. “This man is the messenger and servant of Chieftain Lourang of Clan Koura! He has offered his aid and support in the apprehension of the Dulmun enemy in this kingdom.” Walter scanned the crowd and saw their faces aghast. “But do not take my word for it! Come forth, my friend, and tell your story.” The emissary stretched out his hand, inviting the agent to take his place in the center of the dais.

The Koura agent stepped forwards with a grim resolve.

“My kinsmen! I am Nanue, servant to the mighty Chieftain Lourang of Clan Koura. It is with great suffering that I reveal to you . . . Lord Rodham, loyal emissary of the High King and friend to our people . . . I am afraid what he says is true." Nanue turned from the crowd as if in agony. "War has reached our shores! A Dulmun spy took cover in the forests of Wavemount!" The crowd watched Nanue, enraptured and enraged. "We found him in the sacred grove bordering our two great territories. Lord Rodham was there, and he offered to escort the prisoner back for trial and judgment before the High King. But this traitor and his daughter conspired with the enemy! He has betrayed Wavemount; his family has betrayed us all!"

"Why would they do this?!" A voice called out from the throng of people. Faces turned, looking for the source.

"Who dares take up the reasoning of a traitor? Who dares understand the madness that commands one to betray their own kingdom?" Nanue raised his bandaged hand and brandished the wound to the audience like a sword. "His daughter attacked me, and together they spirited away the pirate. They conspire to wage war against the High King *as we speak!*"

The gathering rose to a pitch, shouts filling the docks with impenetrable noise. The emissary's soldiers struggled to contain the crowd. Many pushed back, throwing fruits and wayward rocks at the soldiers.

Lucio was shaking Kara now, and she could hear the muffled noise of his voice. But her eyes were fixed on the proud and solemn figure of her father. He stood on the dais as if trapped on a solitary rock, braving the tempestuous waves of the ocean.

Where was her mother? Where was Suki? Kara's limbs had seized with terror.

"Kara, we have to go!" Lucio was shouting. "We have to stop them now!"

But she was deaf to his pleas. The emissary's guards took her father away from the dais in chains and disappeared into the chaos.

"You have heard the truth!" shouted Walter above the noise of the crowd. "We will leave with one of your chieftains, so that he may stand trial before the judgment of the High King!"

A member of the crowd cast a stone. It thudded against the emissary's proud face. Walter stood speechless and wide-eyed.

"Outsider! Outsider! Outsider!" came shouts from the crowd.

"Quell this rebellion!" commanded Walter, throwing back his cape as he left. The three cloaked mages followed him, Kara's father in tow.

"Kara!" Lucio grabbed her by the shoulders and shook her out of her trance. "Laki is preparing some men to fight the soldiers! Now is our chance!"

The people burst through the wall of soldiers like a flood, and the clash of metal filled the air. Laki jumped into the fray with his crew, and the riot erupted into a battle.

"Over there!" Lucio motioned towards the pier beyond the fighting. The emissary and his retinue were headed towards the galley.

Kara climbed over the stall and made to dash across the growing distance between her and her father. But a hand stayed her.

"Buy me some time," Lucio said. "Shoot your arrows! Do . . . do something!"

He sprinted off, leaving her in a haze. Just before Kara could call out to him, the pirate splashed noiselessly into the ocean. A westerly wind gently nudged her to the direction of the galley, where Walter was preparing to board.

"Hey!" Kara called out. She used her hand to make a sharp and high-pitched whistle. Several soldiers and some of Rodham's retinue turned to her direction. "*I* am the traitor you want!"

Kara drew an arrow and strung her bow. Her muscles tensed as she strained to pull the twine. The westerly gale blew behind her and guided her aim. She squinted her eye for a sharper focus on the orange cloak that flew in the wind.

"Over there!" shouted one of the cloaked mages.

Kara fired. The arrow flew the half-span and struck one of the mages next to the emissary.

"Get her!"

But as the emissary called to his soldiers, a figure emerged from the waves, barring passage to the galley. Lucio sprang from the depths, his eyes aglow. He folded his hands together and yelled an incantation in ancient Alonian.

A wave rose before him and crashed onto the pier. All Kara could see was the silvery glow of the mage's eyes and the receding waters of the dock. The battle in the market square paused as the people watched for survivors.

* * *

The water pulled Lucio back, but he clung to the edges of the dock.

When the waters receded, he pulled himself up as his lungs choked out leftover seawater.

That was sloppy, he thought, barely able to rise. He did his best to search for the chieftain.

"Impressive." A woman approached, clad in a leather cuirass and orange cloak. The weight of her heavy boots thudded on the pier. "Perhaps lacking in discipline, but nonetheless impressive."

Lucio scrambled to his feet. "Oh, for the love of—who are *you*?" He wiped sweat from his brow and took a fighting stance.

She chuckled to herself, eyes afire from beneath the shadow of her hood. "The dead have no need for my name."

As she waved her hand, a white flash blinded Lucio before pale blue lightning burst from the air. He leaped without thinking, hoping against hope it would not strike him.

Thunder shook the sea. Lucio fell to the side of the pier, close to the merciless waters. Fire now snaked around the floorboards and the ropes tying the wooden columns together. *The level of control* . . . Lucio flailed around in an attempt to escape another attack. Lightning was an art he had barely practiced. His opponent, on the other hand . . .

The woman clicked her tongue in reproach. "I wonder," she said devilishly, "how many leaps and rolls you have in you before you finally give in."

Lucio backed to the edge of the pier. The playful tide beckoned him. He sighed and breathed in what he could of the air as he readied himself for an escape.

An arrow pierced the wooden plank where the cloaked mage stood. She and Lucio both turned towards the dock, where Kara stood with bow in hand. She drew until her weapon quivered from the tension. "What kind of coward fights the injured and the weak?"

She loosed. The cloaked mage sidestepped the shot and menaced Kara with another lightning spell.

Kara bolted for her escape. "Lucio! Run!"

With a few words, another set of sparks lit the docks like a beacon. A whip of lightning burst its way towards Kara.

But Lucio's feet were still rooted to the pier. He took a firmer stance and folded his hands for another spell. Flame shot at the cloaked mage, who deftly turned and canceled it.

"We are done here!"

Lucio risked a glance at the galley. It had cast off, and Walter

Rodham stood on the deck. A mage held the Chieftain. The cloaked mage turned to Lucio with a bright yet devious grin. She jumped into the sea, the waters carrying her to the ship.

"Father!" Kara called out as she ran past the flames on the dock, ash and soot raining on them.

Lucio held her back from boarding a longboat. "It is impossible! We need help!"

"No . . . no!" She shook her head, wringing her black hair. Tears welled in her trembling eyes. "My father . . . we failed!"

The battle carried on behind them. Smoke and ash filled the market square. The sky, reddened with sundown, was streaked with the black smoke from the inferno. Laki was issuing commands. But Kara could only fall to her knees as she sank into utter hopelessness, without even the will to save what was left of their home.

FIVE

Suki watched in bitter silence as her ward kept to her downcast stupor. The healer was just finishing up wrapping bandages around Kara's arms, delicately applying soothing oils and ointments to treat the burns. Chieftain Yue sat silently nearby, gazing out into the window towards the endless line of the sea. Another healer tended to the Dulmun prisoner.

Suki had entered just moments before. She had been dealing with the townsfolk and the royal guard while the royal family was reeling from this most grievous loss. They spent most of the evening putting out the fires, and with the help of the village's few mages, they had managed to save half of the homes. Now it was time to pull them back from their sorrow.

"I received a report from Laki's scouts," she began timidly. She raised a scroll that bore all the details, but neither mother nor daughter moved to receive it. "Some of the schooners were able to catch up to the galley. They are tracking it from a distance as we speak. Your sailors await further instruction."

Chieftain Yue turned towards her. "And what instruction could I possibly give?" She sighed and sat on a stool beside her daughter. Wrinkles formed upon her brow, and her jaws appeared gaunt as she spoke. "We are at war with Dulmun; we are at war with the High King; and Clan Koura is somehow behind all of this. What could they possibly want?"

The scribe watched intently as the Dulmun prisoner seemed to bite his tongue. She noticed his eyes fall to his vest.

"They want this," he said suddenly.

Both the chieftain and her daughter looked up at him, puzzled by the sudden announcement.

The boy rose and reached into the pocket of his vest, producing a small, leather scroll case.

"It is a dossier," he said. "Walter Rodham paid me months ago to steal it from a Selvan ship."

Suki whipped past the healer and snatched the dossier from the pirate's hands. She eyed him suspiciously as she unrolled the scroll. "This is . . ."

Both Yue and Kara looked to her with impatience. Even the healer paused in his ministrations.

"It is a *schedule!"* Suki blurted out in disbelief.

Chieftain Yue paced to her side and snatched the dossier from the scribe's hands. Her eyes wandered from one edge of the scroll to the other, reading the words with harried wonder.

"Not just *any* schedule," Lucio cut in, rising. "It is the schedule of a certain trade route . . ."

Suki watched as Chieftain Yue looked up from the scroll. The wearied ruler fell back on her seat, shaking from the revelation that had dizzied her mind. "It is a schedule of *our* supply routes from the High King's Seat." Yue lowered the scroll and turned to address her scribe. "It has everything: cargo, lists of barrels of grain, nara lumber, cotton . . ."

She let the words falter as she contemplated the missing pieces of the puzzle. Suki tried to still herself as question after question fermented in her mind. The older woman looked to her leader for the answers. *Why would a Selvan nobleman, emissary to the High King, steal this information for Clan Koura? What is more . . . to use a pirate with Dulmun allegiance . . .*

Kara leaped from her seat and paced to the center of the room, limping slightly. "Do you know why Walter Rodham and Clan Koura are conspiring together?"

Lucio shrugged.

"A spy," Suki chirped with a hint of a smile. "The mages that worked for the emissary, and the Koura warrior who calls himself Nanue . . . they all wore an orange cloak."

Chieftain Yue scrunched her brow. "You are saying the emissary is *also* a spy in league with these mages?" She then turned to Kara and Lucio. "What else do we know of him?"

"Nothing more than that he is a petty nobleman, born from a lowly family teetering the precipice of poverty," Lucio offered. "When I met him, he was a rising star in the High King's court. He caused quite a stir."

"And he could solve all his problems selling that scroll to Dulmun." Suki brightened as the pieces started to cohere. "The information on this scroll is enough to bring down support lines—maybe even starve the High King's armies in Feldemar. It could mean her defeat."

"And Clan Mata's as well," added Chieftain Yue. "Chieftain Lourang has resented our privileged position as negotiator with the High King's trading emissaries. I should have anticipated his treachery."

"But his plan failed," Kara cut in. The four of them now huddled in a circle as the healers stepped out.

"And?" Suki waited for her ward to complete the riddle.

"His failure means he has to cut his losses and prove his innocence. What choice does the High King have but to reward his loyalty for uncovering a treacherous plot in the unlikeliest kingdom?" Kara's eyes shone bright, not with excitement, but with fear. "My father will be that proof. We have to bring him back. We have to intercept the galley and rescue my father before he reaches the High King." She clenched her fists together and wrenched her eyes shut, hobbling towards Lucio with a guiding hand from her mother.

"What then?" Lucio asked, somewhat bewildered. "The High King will still have questions about what happened here, and if we rescue your father, it would be *your* word," he said, looking at Kara, "against Walter Rodham."

"We still need to apprehend the traitor," Chieftain Yue interjected. "Nanue is aboard the galley with my husband. If we get to them both, we can make him confess and force Chieftain Lourang to reveal himself to High King Enalyn." The aged chieftain looked to her daughter. "For that, you will need a good fighter," Chieftain Yue smiled, placing her hands gently on Kara's shoulders, and then turned to Lucio, "And an even *better* sailor."

* * *

Kara's gaze fell on the gentle waves before the shores of Tialara. The pink streaks of sunrise brushed against the silvery wisps of night. The dawn's early fog soon broke its trance over the ocean and let in the first rays of light.

"You ready?" Lucio asked as he boarded the tonga.

It had taken much haggling and negotiating, but Kara could not have been more grateful for Lucio's assistance. She had lured him, in the end, with the promise of freedom. Kara's thoughts raced to the Dulmun ring he coveted. It was still safe in the secret grotto, and there it would remain until he fulfilled his oath.

"Give me a moment," she said, turning to face the sea-battered rocks. Her eyes grazed over every crevice and wind-lashed corner of the peaks. She memorized the patterns of moss as they crawled up the rocks like persistent vines, unfazed by the devouring waves. She breathed in the last breath she would draw from her homeland. It tasted of salt and smelled of the stormy seas. "I have never left home before," she mumbled.

Lucio positioned himself by the bow of the canoe. He gently pushed off into the slow but rising current. Above them, the sail remained flat, waiting for the gales of an ocean adventure. Kara hopped on as the canoe started to float away. She quickly grabbed hold of the tiller.

"How did you feel when you left home?"

The seasoned pirate breathed in the air and let the breeze gently nudge his body forwards. The sun bathed their vessel in a golden sheen, and soon the bluish dome of the night sky gave way to a cerulean blue. Yet even as the sun rose, distant stars shone bright, like beacons to a sailor lost at sea. "I was sad. But I told myself what my mother used to say whenever I left home. She always told me, *'A child of the stars is never lost.'*"

With those words, he tugged the rope of the topsail and led it to a northeasterly wind. The canvas followed, pulling the canoe towards deeper waters. The Alonian prince looked up at Lucio's silhouette, her thoughts were fixed on the wisdom he had unveiled to her. Kara had heard it before, a proverb originating from the ancient families of Clan Koura.

Their canoe followed the trail of seagulls hovering over them, and soon the vessel sped with the wind out of Wavemount's bay and into the sea.

THE LEGEND OF CABRUS

ANTOINE BANDELE

ONE

When the sun went down, there were parts of Cabrus that no one went to. Those afforded the luxury of choice retreated into a lambent inn—or, if they were especially privileged, their own private homes in the wealthier northwestern district. Even the beggars knew it was best to find a well-lit corner where the ground was not too cold for sleep. Anything was better than going down to the slums that the ill-fated and impoverished called home.

But even as nobles and travelers alike withdrew from the stench of the dark alleys, Enu skipped along the cobblestones into the forsaken district. The boy wore a smile that stretched from ear to ear, a single tooth missing from his front. His teeth shone bright in the moonslight, contrasting against his dark skin. Through the gap in his teeth he whistled a tune, a melody that matched the clinking staccato of coins in a sack he held tight within his grip.

He knew Auntie would be pleased with what he had tucked away in his hand. Today he had filched more coin than he ever had since she found him abandoned near the Wyrmwing Inn. Enu could only imagine what kind of award he would receive. Maybe she would give him a sweet, or mayhap his first choice of a blanket instead of the cold floor.

Most of all, Enu wanted a smile. That was all. Auntie had the best smile, a beam that reminded him of his mother. That's all he remembered of her: kind, hazel eyes, a warm voice, and a grin that warmed his heart. Like his mother, Auntie had a way of making him feel wanted.

Two rights, then a left, under the bridge, smell for the shit, and through the wooden door, Enu thought as he skipped and hummed down the alley. That was the way to "Auntie's place," as the older boys called it. Enu had gotten lost on his first day. He had made a left where he should have made a right and ended up meeting an unfriendly crowd—another group of beggars and thieves who rivaled Auntie's boys. They had made him empty his pockets and then taken all the coin he had swiped. When he had returned, Auntie had been none too pleased, and she had forced him to sleep on the floor near an open window. It had taken him a week to get over his cough.

But today would be different.

Enu turned the correct corners, avoiding questionable individuals. Most of them paid him no mind, too drunk to ask for a spare coin. Even if one of them had jumped at him, Enu knew he could outrun them. His legs might have looked like twigs, but they were quick.

At the last turn, Enu used his nose to find Auntie's place. It always smelled of pig, though Auntie never had pigs. When he caught the scent, he looked to where the cobblestones disappeared into an expanse of dirt and straw. Most travelers walked past the small house; to them, it was no more than a hole in a wall that could easily be missed. But Auntie and the other boys waited beyond the door hanging off iron hinges.

Enu could not contain himself, rushing to the door with a wide grin on his face. But his steps and smile faltered when he noticed Auntie standing at the threshold with another boy: Gem. Her favorite.

Enu's eyes fell to Gem's hand. Clutched between the boy's fingers were at least four sacks. The jingling of coins was unmistakable as Gem lifted his take for Auntie to examine.

It matters not, thought Enu. *He has only got bronzes and silvers, I bet.* But as Auntie pulled the coins from Gem's sack, they all shined gold.

It cannot be real. He must have fakes. The second time Enu had gone to work for Auntie, he had unwittingly brought fake coins that he had traded with a conniving merchant. It had seemed like a great deal:

two gold weights for one loaf of bread. But when Enu turned over his earnings to Auntie, she bit into the coins and found them to be fakes. Enu slept outside in the cold that night. It took him a fortnight to get over his cough.

But as Auntie bit into the gold weights now, her teeth left tiny marks. They were all as real as could be. Enu frowned down at his sack of coin. Auntie wrapped Gem in a warm hug and whispered something into his ear.

Enu swallowed past the lump in his throat and sighed with slumped shoulders. He hid his own sack of coin behind his back. Instead of moving forwards, he took two steps back into the shadows, away from Auntie's candlelight.

"Oh, Enu," Auntie said to him. "What do you have for me, my love?"

Enu shook his head. He did not want to disappoint her with his pocket money. But he could not deny her, either.

"What is that behind your back, my sweet?" She wore a mild smirk. It looked lovely, but it was not the true smile Enu had been hoping to see. He bit his lip and shook his head.

"Come on, move." One of the older boys pushed him forwards. Enu stumbled right into Auntie, falling to the ground at her feet. When had the other boys arrived? Now Enu would be embarrassed in front of them as well. How could he have thought he had enough coin for Auntie's purse?

"Show me what you have." Auntie helped him up and extended her hand.

Enu brought forth the single sack of coin between his hands. Auntie lifted the sack and examined the coin inside. There were but two silvers and two dozen bronzes.

"At least they are real this time, Enu. You should be proud." But Auntie's voice was cold, and her lips thinned in what Enu had come to recognize as her version of a frown. "Tomorrow I expect more, do you hear?"

Enu nodded furiously. Auntie gestured, indicating that he was allowed to enter the dwelling. Enu cupped his hands in one another, his head held low.

After he crossed the threshold into the sleeping quarters, he looked for his friends. He bet they had brought in more than he had. But he could not see them anywhere, which meant they were not here; the room was not big. There were at least two scores of children who lived in the house, with only twelve beds to go around—though Enu would not have called them beds, exactly. They were more akin to loose collections of straw thrown about the ground. Enu had arrived early, so he took his first pick of one next to the window with a view into the alley, making sure to avoid the open and broken floorboards near the middle of the room.

Enu lay down and daydreamed about how to earn more coin the next day. More boys returned from the day's work until there were only two cots left. He knew his friends would have wanted him to save them a spot, but Enu did not want to bother the older boys. If he left his favorite cot now, he might not get it back.

What was taking his friends so long? Hassan had been working on something for weeks now, and Nicolás had always done well for himself. Mayhap they were still about the city streets, making their last rounds. Omari had planned to serve as lookout for some older boys who had been planning a robbery all week. Enu shook his head at the thought. He should have gone along. Their take was likely going to be larger than his own, but the job had sounded too dangerous for Enu's liking.

Suddenly his friends stumbled into the hideout, all of them out of breath—and without any coin. Enu did not get out of his cot, but he craned his neck to see if his friends would be punished. Auntie did not often hit the boys. But the boys did not often come back to her place empty-handed.

Though none of Enu's friends came with a reward, they could not stop yapping at one another and making animated gestures. What had them so chipper? Enu thought they would have been as downcast as he was without a coin to their names, yet they all acted as if they had had the night of their lives. Even as they turned open empty pockets, even as Auntie scolded them in her cold-mannered way, they still went on about their conversation like nothing had happened.

"You have disappointed me today, boys," Auntie said. "You will not like what happens to you tomorrow, if you do not improve"

When his friends reached the sleeping quarters, Enu waved them down. "Where were you lot?" he asked them.

All of the boys spoke over each other. Enu could only make out bits and pieces of what they said.

"—he has the breath of a dragon, I say—"

"His whole body is covered! His whole body! You had to see it—"

"The man can fly—"

The one word Enu could make out between them all was "ghost."

"He was like a crimson ghost," Nicolás said, his long, curly hair bouncing as he pulled Enu from his cot. Enu made no protest. Many thought Nicolás was a girl because of his hair, but he was the biggest and tallest of them.

"A ghost is what I'd call him, too. He had red wings, and he could fly high in the sky," said Omari, who had a black eye that was almost hidden under his dark skin.

"He is a beast, I say," Hassan said as the candlelight reflected in his grey eyes. "His whole body was like an animal's hide. Nothing could touch him!"

Gem, who had been walking by the group, stopped and shook his head. "That was not some flying beast, or whatever foolishness you just said. That was just a constable, or a Mystic. You lot have much to learn about Cabrus—though if you live long enough, I suppose you shall figure it out eventually, as I have."

"We know enough," Enu snapped. Gem shrugged and walked towards one of the cots near the room's edge. Hassan's eyes were dewy with his daydreaming. Despite his sharp words to Gem, Enu had to admit that all their stories sounded a bit far-fetched. "Did you mean to say the man wore armor? Folks like that always do, if they mean to fight."

"No, no!" Hassan shook his head vigorously. "His entire body was thick, like a beast! He must have been one of those body-changers. What do they call them?"

"Weremages?" Nicolás suggested.

"Yes, one of them."

"So what happened, then?" Enu asked, eager to hear the tale.

"Do you know Old Man Robert?" asked Hassan.

Omari shook his head. "You were not trying to swindle him again, were you?"

"It would have worked, if not for the Red Ghost!" Hassan said. "I wrapped myself in rags, so he would not recognize me, and pretended to be blind. I knew today was the best day to try it, because Old Man Robert gets his pay at the end of every week. And I was very good today. Even *I* thought I was blind! I did just like Auntie told me to—it is better to focus on something than nothing at all when you are playing the part of the blind. So I kept staring at the mole on Old Man Robert's cheek. It looked like I was following his voice, the way blind people do.

"I have been telling him my 'life's story' for days. A week ago, I puffed him up with a tale about my mother getting us enough money to travel to the Seat."

"You could never afford a trip to the Seat," Omari scoffed.

"Of course not," said Hassan.

"He also does not have a mother," said Nicolás.

"Neither do you," said Omari.

"Will you lot shut it?" said Enu. "I want to hear the story." Enu turned to Hassan and nodded, his hands pressed into his chin.

Hassan returned the nod. "Thank you. So then I told him my mother had been robbed near the Wyrmwing, the day before we were to leave. I said, 'I never liked to see my mother cry, so I took it upon myself to show those robbers a lesson.' Then I did my hand like this." Hassan clenched his hand into a fist and shook it, looking slightly to the left when he did it, to sell the lie of his blindness.

"Then I said, 'I found the thieves with my mother's coin. They were spending it on cheap ale. So I went straight to them and demanded her coin back, but they just laughed at me. Then I tried pushing them. But their leader was this giant of a girl who had eyebrows that never ended. She knocked me across the head, but I did not fall. I kept my chin up and I hit her back, right in the stomach. But that got her in a rage. A *real* rage. The next thing I knew, she turned to me with a ball of flame in her hand and slapped me right in the face. And that was the last thing I ever saw.'"

"And the old man believed that?" Nicolás said with a raised eyebrow.

"Well, Hassan does have those grey eyes, like some blind people do," Enu said.

"Auntie calls them 'slate,' not grey," Hassan corrected. "I also painted the skin around my eyes to help the lie."

"You tried to pass that off as a burn mark?" Omari pointed to Hassan's face, which only had a few skids marks of red.

"That is part of the rest of my story. Listen." Hassan leaned forwards for effect. "When I told Old Man Robert that I was trying to earn money so my mother could see her sister on the Seat, I had him in tears. I did not look him in the eye, of course, but I could see the tears coming down his cheek."

"I am surprised you did not break face."

"Shut up, Omari." Hassan's eyebrows furrowed. "As I was saying . . . the old man was in tears. Then I told him, 'I do not need much, sir. Only a bronze will do. I am sure the others in Cabrus can help me with the rest. They say this city is the kindest in Selvan. I use to believe that, too, until what happened to my eyes.'

"Then he told me, 'Do not fret, young one. I will get you the coin you need.'" Hassan made his voice deep and ragged. "So he started digging into his bag. I could hear the coin. There was a least a stone's weight of it in there. I had him in my clutches. I even saw the coins he was going to give me: five gold pieces. Five! But then it happened."

"What? What happened?" Enu leaned forward.

Hassan jumped up with his hands spread wide. "A fire blast the size of a wagon came out of nowhere! I went flying back, Old Man Robert went flying back. We both fell down and saw a firemage running down the street, and just behind her was the ghost. It was dark, but no one could miss the red wisps that roiled behind him. The firemage kept hurling fire at him, but the ghost did not even try to dodge them. He faced the flames head on. And guess what happened?"

"What?" Enu said with wide eyes.

"Nothing! The fire bounced off of him like wind. I got up and followed them as they kept fighting, and I saw his skin. It is dark brown and thick like—like a bear without fur! Then the ghost turned around, and his eyes glowed orange, like a demon from the dark below. The firemage ran off again, and the ghost took off after her. I could not get a better look than that."

"And what happened with Old Man Robert?" Omari asked.

"Oh, him. He was scared out of his wits. But when he calmed himself down, he noticed I was not exactly blind. He put his coin back in his pocket straight away and told me I should be ashamed of myself, or some such thing, and then he walked away. I tried to tell him that I had never said I was entirely blind."

"But you said that firemage was the last thing you ever saw," said Nicolás.

"Oh, right." Hassan blushed. "I suppose that *was* a mistake."

"You are a liar!" Omari pointed his finger right between Hassan's eyes. "The Crimson Ghost is not some bear-man with brown skin. If anything, he is half dragon."

"Oh? How do you figure that?" Hassan crossed his arms.

"Because he could fly!"

Hassan shook his head. "I saw him, and he did not fly."

"Maybe your eyes do not work after pretending to be blind," Omari shot back.

"Is that where you got a black eye?" Enu asked. "Did you run into the firemage, too?"

"No, nothing like that. I did see the firemage, but the older boys gave me the black eye," Omari confessed.

"Why would they do that?" Nicolás said.

"Because I was supposed to be their lookout," said Omari.

"Why did you not?" Nicolás asked.

"I was doing well. The alley was empty the entire time, until the Crimson Ghost showed up. I saw the firemage first, running as fast as a storm. I thought she was just a pickpocket, because she did not cast any fire at first. But then I felt something at my back, so I turned. When I looked up, I saw the Crimson Ghost flying down on great red wings. Then he soared around the corner, and I lost sight of him."

"And then you left? To pursue him?" Hassan said.

"Do you take me for a fool? Flying man or no, I was not going to leave the others."

"Then why did they give you that black eye?" Enu asked.

"Because the firemage came back. Just a short while later, she came down the alley in the opposite direction—but this time she saw me. By the way she was looking at me, I knew she did not mean me well. I whistled to the other boys like I was supposed to, but she already had me by the collar, and she pressed a finger of flame to my ear. She began to turn round and round, shouting to the shadows.

"'Come out, wherever you are!' she said. 'I will burn the boy if you do not give up this chase.'

"And then *he* showed up again. And I saw him before the firemage, because he came from the skies again. He hung there for what seemed like forever before flying down and kicking the firemage right across her chin. She turned me loose, and I found cover next to the inn. She fled, and the Crimson Ghost flew after her, dodging the flame she threw back at him. Then, just as they both turned the corner, Petyr and Jon showed up at last.

"They were empty-handed, of course, and plenty angry. I tried to explain to them about the ghost and the firemage, but they would not hear it. They said it was a poor excuse for a story. That is when Petyr gave me this." Omari thumbed to his right eye. "And Jon gave me this." Omari lifted his shirt, revealing black and blue blotches around his ribs.

"I do not understand." Enu shook his head. "Why did they not go back in and continue the job?"

"If they were thinking clearly, they would have." Omari pulled his shirt down. "I even said as much as they were beating me. That just made them even more angry."

"I wish I had seen him fly. He did not do anything like that when I saw him." Hassan frowned.

"But if he could absorb fire, as you said, why did Omari see him dodging?" Enu asked.

Omari shrugged. "I do not know about all that. I saw what *I* saw."

"Those are fair tales," Nicolás said. "But they are *nothing* compared to what I saw. I think you are right, and the Ghost *is* half dragon—but not just because of his wings or his skin. It is because he can breathe fire."

Enu threw his hands up. "Now I *know* you are lying!"

"No, no, he has a point," Hassan said. "His skin is thick and tough because it is dragonskin, not bear skin!"

"And when I thought I saw a cloak, he was unfolding red wings!" Omari added.

"But that does not mean he is a dragon." Enu shook his head.

"Wait until you hear my story." Nicolás sat forwards in his cot. "I was headed back home when I saw him. And I can tell you that I had even more coin than Gem brings in."

"Let me guess," Omari said. "You lost all of it by the end of the story?"

"Shush," Nicolás said. "I let you tell *your* tale. As I said, I was headed back with a sack of gold that would have made the king himself want to kiss me. But as I went, I thought I saw a building on fire up ahead. I was about to turn around and take another route, for I did not want to take any chances with my coin—"

"Or your life," Enu interrupted.

"That, too. So I was about to turn around, when I realized it was not a building fire at all. It was a battle! I could not see much at first, but I saw balls of flame rolling into one another. And then the firemage was blown back."

"The same firemage we saw?" Hassan asked.

"I expect so. She wore her hair short, and she was a bit short herself."

“That was her,” Omari said.

Nicolás sat forwards again, nearly falling out of his cot. “She almost flew right into me. Her clothes were all singed and burnt on the edges, and her skin was covered in blisters. I had never seen a firemage burnt by her own magic before. But then I realized she had not burned herself at all, because the next figure to come out of the flames was the Crimson Ghost. And you may not believe it—well, mayhap you two do.” Nicolás pointed to Hassan and Omari. “But that is when I saw him breathe fire!”

“So he *is* half-dragon.” Omari said.

“And a mighty one, at that!” Nicolás said. “Every time the firemage hit him with a blast, his skin lit up. Then he blew back the fire right back at her. It was like she was empowering him.”

“That makes sense,” said Omari. “Dragons are supposed to be immune to fire. It stands to reason that it makes them stronger as well.”

“Where did you hear that?” Enu asked. “I have never heard of a dragon being immune to fire.”

“If you had ever actually left Cabrus or opened a book, you would know it. It is common knowledge,” Omari said.

“Common knowledge to who, a dimwit?” Enu said. “I read better than any of you. You cannot tell me dragons are immune to fire when that is not true.”

“Reading the sign to the Wyrmwing Inn, does not count, Enu.” Omari shook his head.

Enu balled a fist. “Alright, so he can breathe fire. Did he beat the firemage, then?”

“No. The firemage had skill beyond magic,” Nicolás continued. “When she realized her flame would not help her win, she stopped casting it. I was just behind her, so I could see everything. The Crimson Ghost started coming at her while his skin was lighting up with that orange glow—I expect that was his skin absorbing the fire. And just as the ghost came to within a few paces of the firemage, she drew a dagger and swung out at him. She struck well, too, right across his chest. But it did nothing. His hide was too thick. What is more, the ghost drew a weapon of his own—a great longsword.

“The pair of them began fighting anew. The Crimson Ghost had the firemage beat in strength, so she fought him with speed. Every time he brought down his blade, she was two steps ahead, landing blow after blow. But she never pierced him. At last she must have realized that if she continued the fight, she would tire out. So she turned to her magic again, but this time, she did not attack the ghost directly. She cast a ball of flame at his feet, which swelled into a wall of fire. And when the wall dropped, she was gone. The ghost ran after her—ran, and did not fly."

Omari shrugged. "Mayhap he was tired."

"Mayhap," Nicolás nodded.

"I do not understand," Enu said. "How did you lose your coin, then?"

Nicolás swung his feet over his cot with a half burned sack in his hands. Near its bottom, the sack was singed black. His trousers were also burnt on their left side, the side of his knee showing through with minor burns. "It must have happened when she threw her last fire blast."

"Even if your coin dropped through your sack, surely it would have been on the ground for you to retrieve," Omari said.

"Oh, they dropped through, all right. Right through a sewer grate. I spent the past hour trying to find them, but they had all washed away."

Hassan plugged his nose. "So that is why you smell of pig shit."

Omari shrugged. "He always smells like that, though."

"None of you said anything until I mentioned it," Nicolás said.

"I never get to see anything in Cabrus!" Enu exclaimed. "You would think the life of a pickpocket would be more exciting."

Suddenly, somewhere in the distance outside, metal clanged against metal. The sound reverberated through the window of the room, followed by the unmistakable sound of flames roaring into the air. Enu rushed over to the thin window near Nicolás' cot, squinting his eyes, but he could see nothing in the dark alley.

"Did you hear that?" He turned to his friends. "What if the Crimson Ghost is out there?"

Omari waved his hand dismissively. "I have already seen him. I nearly died on his account. That firemage is dangerous."

"I want to see him!" Enu said.

"We are already in trouble with Auntie. Sneaking out will not help that," Hassan said.

"You do not want to go out because your stories were all lies."

"How can we all be liars if we all saw him doing the same things?" Nicolás asked.

Enu scowled. "Then you are worse than liars. You are cowards."

Omari clenched a fist. "Take that back."

"Do not make me get Petyr and Jon on you," Enu threatened.

"I am no craven," Hassan said with a puffed chest.

"Then why have you been trying to fool Old Man Robert? Are you too afraid of more dangerous work?" Enu stood toe-to-toe with Hassan until the boy backed down.

"Alright then, Enu," Nicolás said. "Let us show you the Crimson Ghost."

TWO

Sneaking away from the Auntie's place took no effort at all, for she was busy punishing Petyr and Jon for failing their burglary job. The boys could hear it through her wooden door.

"Wonderful," said Omari. "I will get a second beating from them, and then we will have our hides tanned by Auntie."

"Quiet. I cannot hear if we are close," Enu said as he led the group down the streets. The moons shone bright in the sky, giving light to the slanted rooftops of the inns and taverns. Enu crouched low, walking as though the cobblestones of the street were eggshells. They had lost the trail of the fight, but Enu was determined to find it again. Mayhap he was chasing a myth, but he could not allow himself to sleep without at least trying to see the Crimson Ghost for himself. His friends, however, were far less motivated, limping behind him with a complaint for each step they took.

"We will never find them like this," Enu said. "We need to take to the rooftops."

"And break our necks? I think not!" Hassan exclaimed.

"Fine. I will meet you all around the corner, then. I just want to get a better look of the courtyard up ahead." Enu started to scale the side of a building.

"We will see you there," said Nicolás, "if the firemage does not get you first!"

Enu quickened his pace as he reached the rooftops, jumping the narrow gaps between the buildings as he neared the courtyard. After the third building, he found what he was looking for. First he saw an orange glow reflecting on the courtyard's cobblestones, then the silver sheen of a sword. A large man swung his blade at a smaller woman with short hair. The woman's hands were sheathed in flame. Enu had found them! The Crimson Ghost and the firemage were doing battle—and a mighty battle it was.

But the Ghost was . . . losing.

The firemage ran circles around him, using the courtyard fountain as cover and then vaulting off them when the ghost attacked her. Twice she kicked him in the head, one foot after the other. Yet the Crimson Ghost hardly reacted. He took the hits as though in a daze.

Why did he not fly? Enu looked for the Ghost's wings but soon realized he had none. The red at his back was merely an ordinary cloak, now burned and singed from battle.

The firemage cast flame at the man's chest. Then Enu saw that his skin did glow a very slight orange—but it was only enchanted armor, not the skin of a beast or a dragon. As the flames died, the man stumbled back, wincing in pain. The armor hardly seemed to protect him at all.

He certainly did not breathe flames. No half-dragon wielding the power of fire, then. He swung an ordinary longsword, if a fine one. The Crimson Ghost was no beast with insurmountable strength and resiliency. He was not a ghost at all ... simply a man, and one who looked thoroughly exhausted and spent beyond reason.

His friends had been right about one thing, though. The firemage did have skill beyond magic. She worked her dagger around the man's blade as though he were swinging a tree trunk. Somehow the firemage was still fresh, and she seemed to be playing with her foe.

Enu clenched a fist. "Come on. Fly away, Ghost. Fly!"

But the man never flew. Enu looked more closely at the red that billowed behind him. It was truly nothing more than a cape. Part of him had hoped it only looked like a cape, or mayhap that there were wings hidden under it. But the man never took to the sky. Enu had to admit, though, that the enchanted armor was impressive. Each time a flame struck it, strange symbols lit up and reflected in the man's eyes.

That must have been the "demon" eyes Hassan was talking about, Enu thought.

Each time the strange symbols lit up, flame flew back towards the firemage, though they sputtered and fell to the ground each time. Through squinted eyes, Enu could see how one might think the man breathed fire, had the redirected flames been stronger. And he did vault rather high, using the fountain and the surrounding walls to gain the high ground against the firemage—but it looked nothing like flying to Enu. Worse still, the man looked sluggish, his jumps half-hearted and his sword swings lackluster.

This man did not look powerful at all. Enu had expected a formidable, towering man, someone who could challenge an Elf. But Enu saw men like this all the time in Cabrus or on the Kingsroad. He was no more extraordinary than any other. He bled, and he tired.

Even as Enu watched, aghast, the firemage disarmed him, and the man's sword clattered to the ground. With three quick moves, the firemage cut into the man's wrist. He fell to one knee, defeated. The firemage cackled with menace and spoke words that summoned a flame above her palm.

Come on. Get up, whoever you are. Do not let her hit you so easily, Enu thought.

"I must say, Jordel," the firemage chuckled, her voice carrying across the courtyard to Enu, "I have never known anyone more persistent than you."

"Even if I fall, my men will find you," the man called Jordel said. Enu thought the name hardly suited him. He looked like a Brock, or a Griffin, or mayhap a Demetrius. Jordel sounded like the name of a poet, or some noble Enu would target for a pickpocketing run.

Still, even in defeat, this Jordel showed no fear on his face—just pure and simple fatigue. He faced death like it was nothing to be afraid of, as if the firemage were about to put him to sleep. Had it been Enu, he would have tried to scurry away into the shadows or distract the firemage. But Jordel seemed almost content.

If someone who had no powers could be so brave, maybe Enu could do the same.

With light feet, Enu climbed down the building into the courtyard. Where were his friends? They should have met up with him by now. Enu pushed the thought aside as he trotted up behind the firemage.

"The armor," she said. "I would like it back."

Enu knelt down next to Jordel's fallen sword.

"You will have to take it from my corpse," Jordel said plainly, his face still a statue. "Indeed, I am too weary to take it off on my own."

Enu lifted the sword, which was lighter than he expected.

"It was difficult for me to create it. I would rather not ruin it, and I know it will not withstand another blast," the firemage said.

Enu lifted the sword above his head. For the first time, he met Jordel's eyes. The man did not change his expression as his gaze drifted back up to the firemage.

"Do what you will," Jordel said.

The firemage pulled her hand back, ready to fling her fire straight into Jordel's face. Enu heaved with all his tiny strength as he brought down the long blade across the firemage's head.

He had expected the sword to cut through her skull. Instead, the flat of the blade smashed into her, bringing forth no gore. The firemage fell forward, limp and motionless, but still alive.

Enu dropped the sword at his side, looking down at his hands. Had he really done that? Had he saved the Crimson Ghost, the myth his friends had spoken so highly of?

Jordel lifted himself up and dusted the ash from his armor. "That strike was true, young one, though the turn of the blade was not."

"I am sorry, lord. I have never swung one before. I would have killed her if I knew what—"

Jordel held up a hand. "I am glad you did not. One day, mayhap, you will find that taking life comes with a price—one I am pleased you will not yet have to pay." Jordel stretched his back before bending down to lift the firemage over his shoulder.

"Who is she?" Enu asked, handing Jordel his sword.

"A thorn in my side that I am finally rid of, thanks to you." Jordel smiled. Butterflies fluttered in Enu's stomach. For once someone had given him thanks, not because they thought him a joke or something pitiable, but because he was helpful and appreciated.

"The woman said something about your armor," Enu said.

"It is enchanted—by her, as it happens," Jordel said. "It is what protected me from her attacks tonight. But the enchantment has been fading. A shame, really. I could use something like it in my line of work. Mayhap when I wake her up she will explain how it works, though I doubt it."

"How did you do it?" Enu asked. "How did you face her down without any powers yourself?"

"Many years of broken bones and bruises. More than my fair share of pain." A smirk crept onto Jordel's lips. "Experience, child."

Enu perked up. "And could I gain such experience? Do you need a squire?"

Jordel gave another kind smile and then rubbed the top of Enu's kinky hair. "I think you have done enough for me tonight. Go back home to your mother and father. Tell them you have done good work in the king's name."

Jordel flung a sack of coin into Enu's hand. Enu felt the weight of it in his hands and then opened it to check its contents. There were at least a dozen gold weights within it.

"Thank you—" Enu looked up from the sack but Jordel had gone. In his place, Enu could see his friends squeezing through the mouth of a tight alley.

"We heard the fire blasts! What happened?" Omari asked with wide eyes.

"Did you see the ghost?" Nicolás' asked.

Enu's mouth could not keep up with everything in his head as he recounted the tale. His friends did not believe him, of course, but then Enu lifted up the sack of coin in his hand.

"What is that?" Hassan asked.

"He gave it to me as a . . . reward, I suppose." Enu shrugged.

His friends bombarded him with another set of questions, still in disbelief that Enu could save someone like the Crimson Ghost. But just over their shoulders, Enu saw a red cloak dip into a dark alley.

Even if no one believed his story, he knew in his heart that he was an urchin of the streets that had saved the Legend of Cabrus.

THE SUNMANE PASS

GARRETT ROBINSON

ONE

8 Arilis, Year of Underrealm 1313

Damaris of the family Yerrin rode with her guard through the Sunmane Pass, near the back of the procession. This high in the mountains winter had not yet gone, for snow still covered the mountains in thick drifts. But servants of the Dorsean king tended the road well, and so the snows did not hinder Damaris' progress.

And that was well, for she was being pursued.

Loren of the family Nelda, Nightblade of the High King, had chased the merchant down out of the kingdom of Feldemar into Dorsea. If Damaris' soldiers were right in their reckoning—which they would be, for Damaris worked hard to foster competence—Loren was only a few days behind them.

And so she would remain, until Damaris wished to receive her.

Despite the chase, and what she knew must lie at its end, Damaris was content to enjoy the majesty of the pass for the time being. The mountains, shrouded in their wintry robes of white, loomed tall and grim above the party, with the sun casting its rays onto the folds of the land to turn them golden. The air was just warm enough to melt the surface of the snow, which refroze in places to become a glistening coat of ice. It gave the impression that they rode through a mighty palace of glass and gold.

A shout went up from the head of Damaris' little column.

The riders pulled to a stop. Two guards pressed close on either side of Damaris to shield her. But she bade them away with a wave of her hand and kicked her horse to a trot, pushing towards the front of her party.

"What is it?" she said. "Why have we stopped?"

But all the guards had their attention on one of their number who had pushed forwards away from them. The guard—a woman named Wami—moved towards a patch of shadow by a small rise in the land. And then as Damaris looked again, she saw that it was not a patch of shadow at all, but a figure sitting by the side of the road. They wore a dark green cloak, the hood of which shadowed their face. Beside them was a shield on the ground, and they leaned on the haft of a short spear with a wicked, barbed head.

"You there!" said Wami. "Who are you?"

The figure stirred, as if they had been sleeping and the shout had awakened them. The snow crunched as they shifted, raising their hands to cast back their hood.

It was a woman. Her black hair was cut short, and her skin, though somewhat pale, had been darkened by many leagues of wandering under the sun. That wandering showed, too, in the stains on her cloak and the fading of her boots. Her round eyes were hard and lined by much care, and her arms were thick with wiry muscle.

"I am no one of consequence," she said. "Only a wanderer. Who are you?"

Wami straightened in her saddle. "Watch your tongue."

"Alas, it is not long enough for me to see it well," said the woman.

Damaris smirked, even as Wami bristled. Then Wami turned and, with some surprise, noticed her lady at the head of the column. She turned her horse and came to Damaris' side.

"Is there a problem, Wami?" said Damaris. "We are in quite a hurry, if you have not forgotten."

"I have not, my lady," said Wami, bowing her head. "But I saw this woman sitting by the side of the road, lurking, as it were, and grew suspicious. She could carry information of our passing."

Damaris leaned around Wami to look at the woman. "So might anyone. We have passed others on the road."

"Yet few who looked so suspicious," said Wami.

The woman met Damaris' gaze, apparently quite calm. Damaris nudged her horse past Wami's, ignoring the guard's sharp gasp of protest as she came out into the open. She stopped a few paces away from the woman.

"My guards think you look suspicious," said Damaris. "Are they right?"

"Suspicion is created here," said the woman, placing a finger to her temple, "and is often born of guilt on the part of the suspicious party. Those who have little to hide rarely suspect the motives of others—especially chance strangers on the road."

Damaris maintained her smile, but inside her something rankled. Upon a time, she had quite enjoyed finding strangers with quick minds and quicker tongues. But the Nightblade had quite spoiled that enjoyment.

Still, past experiences had little bearing on the present. There was no reason to waste time—and possibly the lives of some of her guards—in order to kill someone when there was only a slim chance it might prove necessary.

"Many times we find wisdom on the tongues of strangers," said Damaris. "Forgive my companion. The Sunmane Pass has not been gentle to us, and every shadow begins to seem threatening."

The woman studied Damaris for a moment before nodding slowly. "That can happen. I, too, find it a darker world than it once was. Safe travels."

"And to you," said Damaris.

She walked her horse back to Wami and tossed her head towards the road. "We have wasted enough time. Ride on."

"But my lady," said Wami in a low voice, so the woman could not hear. "The party we have left behind could—"

"I have given my order," said Damaris. "You will obey it. The party we have left behind may eliminate any need for secrecy, after all."

Wami did not argue again, but she looked hard at the spearwoman. Damaris could feel her unease. "As you say, my lady."

* * *

Mag watched the small party ride off, snow flying up from their horses' hooves. Their dark green cloaks soon vanished around the next bend in the pass. She waited a few heartbeats as the air settled into silence.

"Tiss, Oku," she said softly.

The great brown wolfhound trotted forth from behind the hill. Softly he whined, pressing his head to her hand.

"Stop yowling, you great idiot," said Mag, scratching him behind the ears.

Rarely did she meet a party on the road that was so ready for a fight. Mag was well-traveled enough to recognize them as Yerrins. But she could tell, too, that someone was hunting them, and that they had ridden south from the kingdom of Feldemar, where their family had the greater part of their holdings.

And the women who led them, though she had not been a fighter, was both clever beyond reckoning and fearsome beyond doubt. That, too, had been clear.

Mag sighed, got to her feet, and walked back to camp with Oku trotting at her heels.

Before long she came to a cleft in the mountainside, and she passed through it to the alcove where Albern and the old man were waiting for her. Albern was seated, but he looked up at her with interest, and Mag noted that his bow was close at hand.

"I heard hooves," said Albern. "Who was it?"

"No one of great import," said Mag. "Only some travelers. They were Yerrins, and they did not seem to like the look of me. I cannot understand why—I wear a green cloak, the same as they do."

The old man chuckled. Albern, too, smiled, but it seemed somewhat forced. "Yerrins, were they? A caravan?"

Mag shook her head. "Only some riders."

At that he frowned. "Odd to see them in the pass at this time of year, if they are not moving goods. But these are strange times."

Mag thought of their last few months together. "Strange, indeed."

"You call these strange times?" said the old man. His sightless eyes seemed to stare just past Mag's shoulder. "I have seen days that would boggle your young minds. Have you ever seen an army of Elves descend upon a city?"

Albern and Mag stared at him.

"Have you?" said Albern at last.

The old man sniffed. "Of course not. But it has happened, and I know an excellent tale about it."

"I am sure we shall enjoy hearing it," said Albern. "Why not tell us once we are back on the road again. I will ready your horse."

"That would be most welcome," said the old man. Oku trotted over to him, and he patted the dog's head. "Even Oku wants to hear the story."

"And he shall," said Albern. "Mag, you should rest while I ready our things."

Mag nodded, though in truth she had barely heard him. She was still thinking about the Yerrins. Something about the encounter had troubled her.

At last she placed what it was. They had been *Yerrins.* That merchant family was the richest in all the nine kingdoms, and perhaps the most powerful. Yet someone pursued them. Mag recalled the whispered discussion between them—they had been debating whether or not to attack her. No doubt they feared she might bring word of their passing to someone behind them on the road.

But who was foolish enough to chase Yerrins?

* * *

Loren of the family Nelda nudged Midnight with her heels. The mare nickered, picking her way up the eastern end of the Sunmane Pass.

Her party stretched out behind her—all except Shiun, who led the way. The children, Gem and Annis, rode together on one saddle. They would soon have to find Gem his own horse—the boy grew by leaps and bounds, and he was nearly too big to share a steed already. Behind them was Uzo, his spear strapped to his saddle.

And behind Uzo, Chet brought up the rear, slumped in his saddle. His head hung low as he stared at his saddle horn.

He had not looked her in the eye since Yewamba.

Now they were riding into the Greatrocks again. After much thought, Loren had decided that she rather disliked the mountain range. On her first journey through its southern peaks, she had ended up losing her friend and mentor, Jordel. And only days ago, she had infiltrated another stronghold in the mountains, but this time in the northern kingdom of Feldemar. Damaris had escaped her, she had been shot with an arrow—she rubbed at the wound, which still pained her—and Chet . . .

Chet had suffered worst of all, and it was Loren's fault.

But they would find Damaris soon. They were not far behind her, and Shiun was a peerless tracker. They would capture the merchant and deliver her to the King's justice, and then they could go home—or to Ammon, which passed for home these days. And then, mayhap, Chet's healing could begin in truth.

In the meantime, Loren only had to make sure that he came to no more harm.

Shiun stopped her horse so suddenly that Loren almost collided with her. The Mystic had bent low in her saddle, and after a moment she dismounted, stooping to inspect signs in the snow. Loren saw many tracks beside the road, but this was a well-traveled place. She could not see anything special on the ground—but then, she did not have Shiun's skill.

"I believe they stopped here," said Shiun. "See where the hooves of horses have paced back and forth, and recently?"

"I cannot see it, though I believe you," said Loren. "A midday meal, mayhap?"

"Mayhap," said Shiun. "But they have not done that before. I think they have been eating in the saddle."

"We share something in common, then," said Gem. "I would give much for a hot meal." Annis shushed him.

"What do you think they stopped for?" said Loren.

"I do not know," said Shiun. "There is nothing around that I can see—no spring to refill their waterskins, no bloodstains from an animal they shot and carried with them. They may only have had a hurried counsel. If that is the case, we may need to be watchful."

Loren suppressed a shiver. "Do you think they will have laid a trap for us?"

Shiun looked up at her. "It is possible."

"Let them," said Uzo. "It has been days with hardly any sign of anyone else upon the road. I would relish a chance to use my spear instead of riding these endless leagues."

"Mayhap a few of us should ride ahead," said Loren. "To scout the safety of the road before we press on too heedlessly."

"That would take a great deal of time," said Shiun. "A scout could hardly move any faster than we have been, and then we would spend all the time it would take to double back and fetch those who remain behind, if indeed the road ahead is clear. It would give Damaris a much greater lead than she already has."

"That may be her aim," said Annis. "My mo—Damaris is clever, and she has been hunted before. She may have left false marks, hoping to throw us into doubt about our course."

"I say we ride on," said Uzo. "Do we have another choice?"

Loren looked to Shiun, whose mouth twisted. "I think Uzo is right. But we must be especially watchful now. If Damaris means to turn and ambush us, she could not ask for a better place to do it than the Sunmane Pass."

"We will be watchful," said Loren. "Lead on."

Shiun nodded and mounted, taking the lead again. Loren motioned the others forwards, sparing a quick smile for Chet. He did not meet her gaze, and if he saw her smile, he did not return it. Loren felt her spirits sink.

It will be all right, she told herself. *We will soon catch Damaris. Then we will return to Kal, and everything will be fine again. Fine. I will not lose anyone else—the way I lost Jordel, and Albern, and Mag.*

* * *

Zash returned from their scouting walk in the mountains. A narrow path had revealed several interesting turns in the land, as well as a uniquely stationed cliff. That had been the last thing Zash needed for their plans, and they had carefully noted it for use at need. Now it only remained to finish preparing for the Nightblade's arrival, which should be no more than another day off.

"Hurry, friends," said Zash with a smile. "The day's winding on, and what would your lady say if I told her you'd been lazing about, eh?"

The four Yerrins scowled in reply, but they did not stop levering the heavy boulders into place. Zash had some idea what the guards thought. They did not appreciate Zash's low speech, a relic of southern childhood. Nor, indeed, did they enjoy receiving orders from anyone outside their own clan, much less a child of the family Caelon.

But Damaris of the family Yerrin, at least, was wise enough to know a useful tool when she saw one. She had ordered Zash to ambush the

Nightblade, and she had ordered these Yerrin guards to follow Zash's orders. They would obey, even if they were a bit grudging about it now that Damaris could not see them.

Zash, for their part, doubted that Damaris expected this ambush to succeed. The merchant had only left behind five guards, meaning the Nightblade had the greater numbers. If Damaris truly meant to kill her, she would have stayed and committed her full party of more than a dozen.

No, Damaris probably thought Zash would merely delay her foe. But that did not bother Zash much. They would attempt the task they had been given. It would be enjoyable, and it would not be dangerous—not for Zash, at least. As for the Yerrin guards . . . well, Zash did not have high hopes. The guards, naturally, assumed they were *meant* to succeed, that they had been left with a task they were *supposed* to complete. When fools clung to such assumptions without question, Zash did not waste much time lamenting their predictable fate.

The last boulder finally shifted, one half-roll depositing it in just the right place. From there, they would be able to push it over the edge of the ridge to land on the floor of the pass, a half-span below them. Two others were lined up beside it.

One of the Yerrins stood back from the boulder, wiping her brow with a thick and meaty hand. She glanced up at Zash with somewhat less animosity than the others. Zash had not learned her name, or had forgotten it.

"What is next?" she said.

"What's next, *laird?"* said Zash. "Forgive me, but I'm only recently come into my good fortune, and iss still so sweet to hear it upon another's lips."

The woman rolled her eyes, but Zash thought there was a twitch in her lips. An ambitious member of the family, mayhap? One who wished for an estate of her own, one day?

"What is next, then, laird?"

"It sounds as sweet as I'd imagined," said Zash with a smile, "though that may have much to do with the speaker. Next, we cross the pass and do the same thing on the other side. The boulders have got to fall from both north and south, and we'll split ourselves up so that when the Nightblade's close, we strike simultaneously."

Another of the Yerrins snorted. He was a thin and reedy man with a rather pathetic wisp of mustache. "You mean to split us up? We are already outnumbered."

Zash raised an eyebrow. "We won't be outnumbered once we crush a few of them under falling rocks."

"Only some of them are even armed, and most of them are children," said the man. "They could not withstand us."

"First you complain that we are outnumbered, and now you say they have too few warriors to resist us. Which is it?"

The man's scowl deepened. "Are you too much of a coward to bring the fight to them?"

Zash guessed that was supposed to be an insult, something to stoke their passion and make them speak in anger. It did not work. Their smile broadened to a grin. "Oh, sweet child. Why bother fighting? Wouldn't you rather just win?"

The man looked at them incredulously. "How do you mean to win without fighting, you fool?"

Zash said nothing, but only kept up their smile. The man snorted louder than before and walked away towards the path leading down into the Sunmane Pass proper. Two of the other Yerrins followed him. For a moment, it was only Zash and the Yerrin woman who had spoken before. She looked at Zash hesitantly.

"May I ask another question, laird?"

Zash ran pale, thin fingers through their short, flaming red hair to muss it slightly. "You may, though I cannae promise to please you. My answers seemed to infuriate your friend."

"You mean Toka?" said the woman, shrugging. "Call him an acquaintance, rather than a friend. He has never shown great wit. But my question is this: on our way through the pass, I saw many sections of the road more precarious than this. There are places where it shrinks to only a few paces wide and runs along the side of a mountain. Would it not have been better to start our rockslide there, where the rocks might fling the Nightblade into a chasm?"

Zash cocked an eyebrow. "A simple guard who pays attention? Incredible, as well as invaluable. But the parts of the road you describe wouldn't have worked. Even if we could've climbed them in time—and we couldn't've, for they were sheer cliff faces—like as not, the rocks would have rebounded from the mountainside, bouncing clean over the Nightblade's party. Here, we *know* the road will be blocked."

"Could not the Nightblade avoid the landslide?"

"Aye, you could be right," said Zash, appearing to consider it with pursed lips. "How might you do so?"

The Yerrin folded her arms and frowned, as though she had an answer but suspected Zash's question was a trap—which, indeed, it was. "I would turn around and go back the way I had come."

"And thass when I'd drop the second landslide behind you—the one we'll be setting up on the other side of the pass."

Comprehension dawned on the Yerrin's face. "They will be trapped."

"And we'll be above them, bows in hand. Easy pickings."

The Yerrin smiled and shook her head. "You did not tell us that part of the plan."

Zash shrugged. "I rather thought that being in charge meant I didn't have to explain myself."

The Yerrin chuckled. She stooped to lift her cloak, which she had discarded due to the sweat of her work, and threw it over her thick arms. "Fair enough, laird. We had better catch up to the others."

"I suppose we'd better," said Zash. "What's your name, by the bye?"

The guard cocked her head. "I am Hadi of the family Yerrin."

"A long day's work awaits, Hadi. We'll all be sore and tired when iss time to pitch our tents at night. "You're welcome to skip the bother and share mine. To be well rested on the morrow, of course."

Hadi smiled at her. "Of course. I think I will take you up on your kindness, laird."

"Excellent," said Zash. "Let's be off, then."

Not a complete waste of time after all, then, thought Zash, keeping their gaze on Hadi's rear as she led the way down the path.

TWO

9 Arilis, Year of Underrealm 1313

THE EASTERN END OF THE SUNMANE PASS WAS JUST OVER A DAY AWAY, but Mag's disquiet had not left her since she had met the Yerrins near its western slopes. She did not know exactly what she feared lay ahead, but she remained wary as they rode on.

And so it was with some alarm, but little surprise, that she spotted footprints in the snow, crossing back and forth across the road. They rose up into the mountains on both sides, vanishing along little paths that led along the slopes. In this part of the pass, the mountains came down to form a narrow valley with the road running through its center. There were great boulders above, as well as smaller piles of rocks running up the heights, all of which would be excellent places to hide. She could not be sure, but she thought she saw the signs of stones having been moved above them.

"What do you suppose has happened here?" said Albern, who had reined in his horse just behind hers. Behind them both, the old man slowly turned his head back and forth, listening for what he could not see. Oku whined as he sniffed the ground.

"I do not know," said Mag. "But there is something going on here. I think there are more Yerrins, and they are planning an attack."

Albern pulled his bow from its saddle harness. "Where?"

"Above," said Mag. "But stay your hand for now. They cannot be planning to ambush us. They did not know we were coming this way—I gleaned that much, at least, from the ones I saw farther west."

"Mayhap they are attacking someone of ill intent," said the old man cheerily. "We ourselves have seen many evil wanderers in the nine lands these days."

"We have, but I count the Yerrins among that number," said Albern. "The last Yerrins I met would have killed me, if a powerful firemage had not ridden by my side. I do not know how often you have encountered the children of that family, but they are rarely far from strife."

The old man's bushy white brows leaped up. "You could easily say the same of us—and in fact I have, often and loudly."

"Too loudly, as I have told you," said Mag. She turned to Albern. "I mean to go find out what they are up to. Fall back a bit, and find a safe place to hide him."

Albern's face grew stony. "And let you go off alone? We should both find a place for the old man to hide, and then we can seek out the Yerrins together."

"You know I will return," said Mag. "Two will hardly be better than one in this case, when I am only scouting."

His mouth twisted, though he knew she spoke the truth. "At least take Oku with you," he said. "It would make me feel better."

"Very well," said Mag. "He may be able to sniff out more than I can on my own. But go, and quickly. I want to be able to take my mind off you and keep it with me where it belongs, if things should come to a fight."

"I thought you were only scouting," said Albern.

"You know what I mean. Take my horse."

Albern looked to the sky as if searching for support. Finding none, he shook his head. Mag handed him her reins before pulling her spear and shield from their harnesses. Albern led the old man away, though he looked back at her more than once while he rode off.

"Oku, tiss," said Mag. The wolfhound trotted behind her as she started up the slope of the southern mountains.

She stayed a good distance away from the path so that she could hide easily if she needed to, but always in sight of it, so that she could keep an eye on the footprints. Whoever had made them had walked the path several times, going up and down the path on some errand or other. Beside the path, little trails in the snow showed where small rocks had skittered down the slope after being disturbed. But she could not tell whether the final journey had been up or down, and whether the Yerrins were above her or on the other side of the pass—for she was certain it *was* the Yerrins.

And then a sound echoed through the pass, coming from a great distance away.

Mag froze. The sound had been a high laugh, and it struck some chord within her—a distant memory that now seemed like a dream. A tremor struck her heart, though she did not know why.

Oku nosed at her hand, seeming to sense her disquiet. "Shush," she whispered, though the hound had not made a noise.

Cautiously, Mag stepped to the edge of the path so that she could see the road below. She had to know whose laugh she had heard. It certainly had not been the Yerrins—likely it came from whatever unlucky travelers they were planning to attack.

And then a party appeared around the eastern bend in the road.

Mag stopped dead on her feet as if spellstruck.

Six figures made up the party, riding on five horses. Near the back of the line was a dark man with a spear, and at the front was a short, Dulmish-looking woman with a bow. Mag did not recognize either of them.

But she knew the other four riders. She knew them as well as Albern, Oku, and the old man. Gem and Annis, riding together on one horse. Chet, bent over his saddle as though weary and in pain. And Loren. Loren of the family Nelda, Nightblade of the High King, leading her friends through the Sunmane Pass. It had been Gem's laugh that Mag had heard.

Why?

No, *how?*

How could it be that Loren was here, just at this moment? Had Loren arrived two days later, she would have come to the pass after Mag and Albern had already left. Had Mag and Albern not been delayed in Calentin, or had they chosen to ride due east, they would never have been here in the first place. What was Loren even doing here, so far from Feldemar, where she had been bound the last time Mag saw her?

It seemed impossible. It *was* impossible.

Yet there she was, plain as the sky above. Mag even imagined she could see Loren's startling green eyes, though the distance was far too great for that.

For a moment she wanted to run down the slope, to sprint into the pass and drag Loren from her saddle into an embrace. She wanted to clutch the children to her chest and never let them go, to see Chet and find out why he looked so miserable. Despite the impossibility of it all, Mag thought she should have known. She had wondered who would be a great enough fool to hunt Yerrins. Loren, sky bless her, was just such a one.

Then, as suddenly as she had wished to run into the open and greet the children, the desire vanished. The Yerrins still hid nearby. It was clear now—they meant to ambush Loren and her party. And Loren clearly had no idea.

And then Mag had another thought.

What if she *did* greet Loren? What if Loren saw her here? What if she brought Loren back to the camp?

What if Albern saw Loren again?

Albern had never wanted either of them to go on this hunt. He wanted to join with others who had become caught up in the great conflict threatening Underrealm. Though he spoke rarely of Loren, it was clear he thought of her often. Mag did, too, though she hid it well.

But if Albern saw her now? Loren rode west. Mag and Albern rode east. Would Albern leave the children again? Or would he want to go with them, no matter Mag's wishes?

All these thoughts flitted through Mag's mind in an instant. And then she came back to herself.

Loren was here. So were the Yerrins. Things would come to violence before long.

Almost as if in answer to her thoughts, she heard the scuffing of a boot on stone somewhere farther down the path. It had to be the Yerrins.

Mag looked back west down the pass. To where Albern waited with the old man.

She made her decision.

* * *

They were now in a part of the pass where the base of the mountains joined the road on either side. It was a relief to no longer be riding along the edge of a cliff, but the gentler landscape had brought them no peace. Shiun kept turning in her saddle, clearly uneasy as she searched the landscape around them. Uzo rarely moved his hand far away from his spear. The children, too, had caught the tension in the air. Gem kept trying to tell jokes, but they seemed weaker and weaker, and his laughter grew higher and higher in pitch, until it rebounded from the mountainsides all around. Only Chet remained unchanged, but that was no comfort, for he slouched dismally in his saddle.

"Shiun?" said Loren. "What is it? Something seems wrong."

"I do not know for certain," said Shiun. "There is something in the air. I hear fewer sounds of birds and animals than before."

"Yet the land is gentle here," said Loren. "Surely if someone wanted to attack us, they would have done it before, where the road was narrow and perilous."

"That is what one would assume, yes," said Shiun. "And yet I keep seeing signs that may be nothing, but may be something. Tracks of animals that have come too close to the road, as if they were disturbed out of some hiding place. And now the signs we saw yesterday are much on my mind."

"Yet it seems our decision now must be the same as it was then," said Loren. "Ride on, but cautiously."

"And it is caution that makes me warn you now."

Loren frowned and glanced at Chet. He had not stirred at their conversation. It sickened her to think of leading him—and all of them—into danger. But they could hardly turn around and ride away now. Not without admitting defeat, which she would not do. Damaris had to pay for what had happened to all the nine kingdoms—but to Loren's friends in particular.

"Is there another way?" she asked Shiun. "Mayhap we could climb higher, or use some path off the main—"

Her words fell to silence as a deep rumble started under their feet. The horses nickered anxiously. They all looked sharply around for the source of the noise.

"Nightblade!" cried Uzo, pointing up.

There, high above them, rocks came tumbling down from the mountains.

"Landslide!" cried Loren.

Chet's horse screamed in fear and bolted ahead—directly into the path of the falling rocks.

"No!" Loren spurred Midnight hard, and the jet-black mare darted forwards. Shiun cried out a warning and followed.

* * *

The valley floor was covered with snow, but that did not stop dust from filling the air, cast down from the mountain heights. It obscured all view of the road and the travelers upon it. The landslide had fallen just where Zash had planned. Even better, the Nightblade and at least some of her companions seemed to have ridden *towards* the falling rocks, rather than turning around.

"A fair result," said Zash. "Can anyone see them?"

Toka scowled at them. "Can you?" he asked.

But Hadi leaned forwards, peering into the settling mess. "I think they—there!"

Zash saw them at last: three figures, on foot and leading their horses away from the pile of boulders that now blocked the pass.

"Sky!" said Zash, grinning. "Things are even better than we hoped."

"They escaped the slide," said Toka.

"But look there." Zash pointed. "The party's divided, and soon the three in the rear will be trapped by the second slide. We can pick off the Nightblade with ease, then turn back to finish off her friends."

"Should we head down towards them, then?" said Hadi eagerly.

"Yes," said Zash. "Down the path we climbed to get here. Unless I'm much mistaken, they'll find it and start to climb, hoping to rejoin their friends. Thass where we'll ambush them."

Hadi nodded and turned to Toka. "Come on, then. With me."

Toka's mouth twisted, but he seemed to prefer receiving orders from Hadi than directly from Zash. He rose to a half-crouch, still hiding behind the rocks where they had taken cover, and began to follow the Yerrin woman. Zash made to follow, but then they stopped, head cocked.

What was wrong? Something seemed . . . missing. Incomplete.

Zash glanced down at the Nightblade again. She and her two companions were still moving away from the fallen boulders, and just as Zash had guessed, their course would carry them to the bottom of the path leading up. Zash turned to look at the other travelers, the ones who had been trapped on the wrong side of the fall.

Then they realized the problem. The second landslide had not yet been set off.

"What happened to the others?" they said, not even meaning to speak out loud.

Hadi and Toka turned back. "Who?" said Hadi.

"The others across the pass. The second landslide."

Both Yerrins turned to look, though of course they could see no more than Zash could. The pass was too wide, and the rest of their party would have been obscured by rocks, if they were there.

But Zash had the distinct feeling they were *not* there. Not alive, in any case.

"Mayhap they could not get the rocks moving," said Hadi doubtfully. "They were large."

"Not too large," said Zash. "We readied them to fall in the first place, remember?"

They glanced down. Loren's other companions had successfully turned back and led their horses away from the fallen rocks. They had already passed the place where the second landslide was supposed to come down. They were safe, unless Zash came to finish them off.

But then, Damaris had only given instructions for the Nightblade. Why waste extra effort?

"Well, let's not spend our worries on them now," said Zash at last. "The Nightblade is more important, and it would be rude to keep her waiting. Come."

Zash strode straight past the Yerrins, letting them fall into step behind. But despite a projected air of confidence, Zash was far more worried than they would have wished to admit.

There had been a plan. Outside factors always interfered with even the most careful schemes, but it was rare indeed for the steps not to be carried out at all.

What in the dark below had happened to the other landslide?

THREE

Mag pulled her spear from the body of the final Yerrin with a wet *shunk.* Blood dripped from the spearhead, steaming where it hit the snowy ground. A few paces away, Oku stood over the body of another green-cloaked warrior, bristling and growling. The dog had crushed the woman's throat, and her eyes were glassy in death.

From a quick survey of the area, Mag thought she understood what the Yerrins had planned. Many rocks and great boulders had been arranged on the edge of the ridge, where they could easily be pushed into the pass below. The first landslide had missed Loren, but it seemed there was supposed to have been a second. That would not happen now that Mag had stopped it, but she doubted that Loren was entirely out of danger.

She stepped up to the edge, careful to keep herself concealed, and surveyed the road below. Loren's party had been split. The children and the dark, unknown Mystic were heading east. Loren, Chet, and the other Mystic were trapped to the west. It looked as though they were searching for a path that would lead them back towards their companions. Even now they made for a path that would lead them up the slopes of the northern mountains.

Mag suspected there was another party of Yerrins in those peaks, just like the group she had found here. If that was true, Loren and her friends were walking into a trap.

"Oku," she whispered. The dog came trotting over, and Mag knelt to scratch him behind the ears. "It is not safe here. Go back to Albern. Kip!"

Oku jerked, taking two hesitant steps away, but then stopped. He looked up at her and whined.

"Go to Albern. Kip," she said firmly. "Kip!"

The wolfhound dropped his tail between his legs and slunk off, back down the path towards the floor of the pass. Mag sighed. She would rather have had Oku's nose with her, but it was too dangerous. Mag knew she would return from a fight unscathed. The same might not be true of the hound.

She looked down again. There did not seem to be any threat near Annis and Gem, and they were accompanied by a Mystic warrior. Loren, on the other hand, looked to be climbing straight into the arms of her enemy. And Mag remembered Northwood. Evil had sought out Loren, and only Loren, caring little for those by her side. Mag doubted much had changed since that day. It had not even been a year ago, though it felt like something from another lifetime.

The steep slope below her ran straight down to the landslide. Mag stepped over the edge and half slid, half fell towards her friends.

* * *

Loren led Midnight forwards, keeping close to the flanks of Shiun's horse just ahead. Chet followed, jumping in fright whenever the settling landslide made another noise.

"Are you all right?" Loren asked him again.

"F-fine," he stammered. His teeth chattered as if from the cold, though he had seemed warm enough before the rocks fell.

"We will find our way back to the others," she said. "Do not worry."

He nodded, but his shaking continued.

When the rocks had stopped falling, they had called out to Uzo and the children. No one had been hurt, for which she thanked the sky. But they could not try to climb over the fallen rocks; Shiun had forbidden it, saying it was far too dangerous. Moreover, a landslide was often followed by other, smaller falls, so they could not remain where they were. Loren had ordered Uzo to lead the children away from the slide, while she and Chet and Shiun tried to find a path that would lead them back east.

Loren's pulse had been racing ever since the slide, but Chet was far more frightened than she was. It was his terror that kept her from asking Shiun a question that burned within her: had the landslide been natural? Loren doubted it. She thought of the strange tracks the day before last, and then the feeling in the air that had put Shiun on the alert just before the rocks fell.

But if the Yerrins had thought to catch her party and crush them beneath the falling rocks, that ruse had failed. And since they had seen no sign of anyone nearby, Loren hoped the Yerrins, if they were here, had given up and retreated, trying to outrun their pursuers once more.

If not, they would soon find out.

"Do you see anything?" said Loren.

"I think so," said Shiun. "There may be a path ahead."

"May?"

Shiun looked back and gave her a wry look. "I am not familiar with the Sunmane Pass, Nightblade. Forgive me if I do not recognize every corner of these mountains at first glance."

"I only mean," said Loren, flushing, "that I am worried about another slide, or . . . well, anything else we might find here."

The Mystic's brows rose, and she gave the slightest of nods. It seemed Loren was not alone in her worries that the landslide might not have been natural.

"Well, we shall certainly keep our eyes open," said Shiun.

"We did that before, and a mountain almost fell on us," said Loren.

"But because we were watchful, it did not," said Shiun. "Come. The bottom of the path is not far."

As they drew closer, Loren finally saw what Shiun had spotted. The nearly-sheer sides of the mountain ahead became gentle, running up through a gap in between rocks to form a little path leading east. If the path continued on that way, it would take them straight back towards their friends.

They had almost reached the path when arrows came flying through the air towards them.

Loren gave a cry and dived behind a low rock. Shiun took cover a few paces away, and Chet was quick to follow Loren. Another volley of arrows whistled past, clattering off the stones around them or plunging into the snow. Loren counted three of them. Three archers, high above. They would fire as soon as Loren or the others showed themselves again.

"We should run!" said Chet, voice quavering.

"We cannot," said Shiun. "There is no cover the way we came. We would be entirely exposed, and they would kill us at once."

"Which begs the question, why did they not do so as we approached?" said Loren. As ever, she was surprised by how calm her voice sounded in the midst of the fight, when her heart thudded with terror that something might happen to Chet. Even her hands were steady as she fished in a belt pouch for her bowstring.

Shiun's eyes flitted back and forth, the way they did when she was thinking quickly. "My guess is that they only got into position a moment before we appeared," said Shiun. "Otherwise they would not have missed in the first place." She risked a glance above the rock, ducking immediately as three more shafts rebounded from the rock. "That means there are not many of them—the same ones who started the landslide must be the ones shooting at us. I think there are three of them."

"As do I," said Loren.

Beside her, Chet groaned. Loren took deep, slow breaths as she nocked an arrow. Their foes—Yerrins, no doubt—had the high ground, preventing their retreat. They could not retreat to the center of the pass, and even if they did, an immovable wall of fallen boulders now blocked the way back to their friends.

They were trapped.

* * *

"Hold," said Zash in a low voice. "Wait till they show themselves more plainly. We have many arrows, but they're not limitless."

"Why would they show themselves? They know we will only kill them," hissed Toka, who was beginning to annoy Zash more and more. They should have assigned him to the team on the western slopes. By all appearances, that team was now dead, which would have been a blessing if Toka had been among their number.

"They can't hide forever," said Zash. "Stay here. I'm going to make sure the others haven't found some way to approach."

And see if I can spot what happened to the others across the pass.

Something had not gone according to plan, and Zash hated that feeling. They specialized in simple but unpredictable schemes that stood little chance of failure. It was the core of their reputation—and what good were they without such a reputation? It was how they had come by their lairdship, after all.

Zash slung their short bow on their back and loped off, back up the slope to a point where they could see the pass more clearly. Once they reached it, they shielded their eyes from the sun and peered away south to where the other Yerrins should have been.

For several long heartbeats, they saw nothing. Then they caught a flash of sunlight on metal.

It was a bracer. A bracer on a Yerrin arm, poking out from behind a rock.

The arm lay unmoving.

"Dark," spat Zash. It was as they had suspected. The others were dead. Zash had not predicted something. Thoughts of wild beasts flitted through their mind, but they quickly discarded it. Elite Yerrin guards would not have been overcome by something as simple as wolves, even if such creatures were common in this part of the Greatrocks, which they were not. Nor were satyrs or harpies to be found near here.

No, there were other humans here. Enough of them to overcome three highly trained, well-armed and armored Yerrins. But who would even have known—

Zash's thoughts cut short as their eyes caught movement. Their gaze fell down to the boulders that now blocked the pass.

A figure in a green cloak scuttled across the rocks. A woman, it seemed, though it was hard to tell from this distance. On her back was slung a shield, and in one hand she carried a spear. Even from here, Zash could see the glisten of fresh blood on the spearhead.

One woman had killed three Yerrin guards? Zash felt a quick stab of fear in their gut. The lady Damaris did not employ weak or foolish warriors. Even if this woman had taken them by surprise, she must be a powerful warrior to have overcome them. Unless she had had help, but Zash could see no one else nearby.

Possibilities flitted through Zash's mind, each one coming with a solution that was quickly discarded. Zash could flee. But if they alone survived, that would not leave them in good standing with the family Yerrin, which would mean trouble down the road. And if Hadi or Toka were captured, they could reveal much about Zash and Damaris that should remain secret. Too, Zash's gut twisted at the idea of leaving Hadi behind.

Next came the thought of ambushing this new wanderer. But Zash and two Yerrins could not keep the Nightblade pinned while also fighting this new threat.

Another landslide, this time to crush the newcomer? They had no time.

There seemed no easy answer, and their fear continued to grow. If this wanderer had killed three Yerrins, seemingly without injury, she could kill three more.

And then Zash noted something odd.

The green-cloaked wanderer was moving very strangely. She flitted from cover to cover as if trying not to be seen—except she was entirely exposed from above, and she had to know it. She was not trying to avoid being seen from Zash's position, then. But where . . .

It came to Zash in a burst of insight. The wanderer kept looking west, towards where the Nightblade was pinned down. She was hiding from them, not from Zash and the Yerrins.

New possibilities emerged. Why would this be? The wanderer had attacked the Yerrins. Was she not an ally of the Nightblade? It did not seem so. Was she, then, afraid of the Nightblade?

That was a *very* interesting idea. Zash tried to think how they could turn it to their advantage. They recalled the path up which the Nightblade was attempting to climb. In their mind's eye, they saw the side path that led, not far off, to a unique little cliff.

The rest of the plan came together very quickly after that.

* * *

Mag was close now. Close enough to see Loren, Chet, and the Mystic woman whenever she ducked out from cover. It meant she had to move more cautiously, and therefore more slowly.

A cliff stood ahead of her. It was steep, but not sheer. Mag thought she could climb it in short order. If Loren and the others could stay alive until she reached the top, Mag could strike the Yerrins from behind and kill them quickly.

And then? How would she get away before Loren found her?

One problem at a time.

She reached the bottom of the cliff. One by one she found handholds and footholds and was soon several paces high. The slope was even gentler than she had thought. She was going to make it in time. Just a few moments more—

Hssst

An arrow flew by, just a few fingers from her shoulder.

It startled her, and her feet slipped. For one terrifying moment, she dangled by her fingers before her body slammed into the rock wall. She barely held her grip.

Quick as she could, Mag got her feet situated again and risked a glance up. At the top of the slope stood a stranger. Not a Yerrin, by the looks of them. Short, flaming red hair, and clothing of black and muted blue. Mag took in all the details in one quick moment before pressing herself to the cliff again. Another arrow whisked by. It passed harmlessly through Mag's cloak, which flapped in the wind that blew through the pass.

"Dark," she cursed into the rock.

She could not try to climb again without exposing herself. But Loren was still pinned down, and it would not be long before the Yerrins moved in for the kill.

Mag turned her head this way and that, looking for an idea. She glanced east down the pass, but no one was there—Loren's party had gone, and they would not come back this way.

She looked west and froze.

Far, far away, figures moved towards them. Two people on horseback, leading another horse by the reins.

Albern had finally tired of waiting for her, and he was coming east to find out what was wrong.

Panic set in. She had no time left. Albern would see Loren unless Mag acted *now.* She tensed herself to make a desperate spring, a reckless bound up the cliff to attack the stranger with the flaming hair.

And then she stopped, squinting. There was Albern, and the old man, and her horse.

But where was Oku?

The dog's ferocious barking sounded on the air. Like a hellskin beast from the darkness, Oku came dashing from the rocks below Mag. He struck the bottom of the cliff and raced straight up, his feet scrabbling on the stone but slowing not at all.

"Oku, no!" cried Mag. "Kip!"

But the stranger atop the cliff seemed completely taken aback by the wolfhound's appearance. No arrow came flying, and it was barely a heartbeat before Oku had reached the top of the cliff. Mag heard the stranger cry out, and she heard Oku's savage voice as the wolfhound lunged.

Mag entered her battle-trance. All doubt, all worry vanished. She no longer cared about Albern's approach. There was only the enemy above her, the allies below, and the spear on her back.

She nearly flew up the slope. Soon she had gained the top. Oku stood there, legs spread wide apart, fur bristling. At his paws lay the stranger's bow, snapped in two by the wolfhound's incredible jaws. The stranger stood several paces away, looking at Mag and Oku in horror.

"I do not know who you are," said Mag, her voice emotionless with the battle-trance. "But you had best ready yourself for death."

The stranger turned and sprinted through a gap in the rocks with incredible speed.

"Tiss," said Mag, slinging her shield off her back. She bounded after the stranger, Oku just behind her.

FOUR

Zash pelted away from the woman and the wolfhound. The dog had been another unpleasant surprise, but this time not fatal to the plan—as long as the damn beast didn't catch them while they fled. But it appeared to be following at its master's heels like a good beast, which meant Zash had a chance.

They stopped at a bend in the path. Turning back, they drew a dagger from their belt and readied it. As soon as they heard footsteps approaching, they threw the blade. It missed the woman, but that was intentional. As it *clanged* on a nearby rock, the wanderer ducked back, pausing for a moment, and the dog stayed with her. It bought Zash exactly as much time as they needed.

Zash came running to where the Yerrins still waited, loosing occasional shots at the Nightblade and her friends below. They pressed against the rock, out of sight of the Nightblade, and hissed to draw the Yerrins' attention.

"The plan's changed," they said. "Toka, hold her here a little longer. Hadi, come with me to flank them."

"As you say," said Hadi, shooting to her feet at once.

"No!" cried Zash, reaching out one hand.

An arrow pierced Hadi's neck from behind. Blood flew from the arrowhead, a few drops of it spattering Zash's face.

Zash's outstretched hand closed to a fist. They drew it back, as if trying to pull Hadi away from the arrow. But it was far too late for that. She crumpled to the ground, eyes wide and staring at the sky, fingers clawing at the arrow.

Hadi, you dark-damned idiot.

"Well," said Zash, voice thick as they drew another dagger from their belt. "Dark take all of it, then."

They threw the dagger into Toka's face. The dagger pierced his eye and went straight into the brain. His body went limp, slumping to the ground before his expression could even register surprise.

I'd rather you not have died, either, thought Zash sadly. *But you'd have gotten us both killed, whether I left you or tried to bring you along.*

They stepped forwards, keeping partially concealed. There was the Nightblade, peeking out from behind a rock. The Mystic nearby was drawing another arrow—it was she who had killed Hadi.

Zash made sure to be seen by both of them. Then they ran.

* * *

Mag skidded around the corner, coming to a halt.

Two Yerrins lay dead on the ground. One of them had been shot, and the other had a dagger in his eye. Both held bows. These were the ones, then, who had kept Loren pinned down. That meant Loren was safe . . .

. . . or did it? The redheaded stranger was nowhere to be seen. Another path led off to the side. They must have gone that way. Did they plan to attack Loren from a different angle?

"Oku, tiss!" Mag ran down the side path, making sure to stay out of sight of Loren, who was now below her.

The path dove straight into the mountainside, where it ran through a narrow, twisting passage with sheer stone on either side. Mag strained her ears, trying to detect any sign of the stranger attacking. But there was nothing. Soon the path emerged into the open again, where a small, natural platform sat in the side of the mountain. The platform ended in a cliff—this one sheer and impossible to climb. Below were only trees.

On the edge of the cliff stood the stranger, staring straight into Mag's eyes.

"Well, hello," they said, voice musical with a southern accent. "It's a pleasure to meet you, wanderer."

Mag raised her spear. The stranger had a sword, but it was sheathed. Mag's eyes narrowed as she searched for a trap.

"What are you doing here?" she demanded. "What do you want with Loren?"

The stranger's brows rose. "The Nightblade?" they said. "You know her by name, then. Why don't you ask her yourself? She and her friends are coming down the path just behind you. Can't you hear them?"

Mag jerked in surprise. It was true. There were footsteps coming down the path behind her, echoing loud between the sheer rock walls. All the color drained from her face.

"Yes, I thought you'd be less than pleased at that," said the stranger.

"What are you playing at?" said Mag. "You were trying hard enough to kill Loren. Why give up now?"

The stranger shrugged. "It seemed clear to me the Nightblade wasn't fated to die today. I've never been one to fight when I can win, instead."

Mag scowled. "You think you have won? You are trapped."

"It certainly seems so, doesn't it?" said the stranger. "Yet the Nightblade will be here any moment. And now that I think of it, I'm of a mind to let you deal with her. Ta."

The stranger stepped back off the edge of the cliff.

Mag leaped forwards, trying to stop them, but too late. The stranger vanished between the branches of the trees. Worse yet, from the sounds coming up the passage, Loren was only moments away. Oku was already sniffing at the air, whining at the smell of the approaching party—strangers to him, of course, for the wolfhound had never met Loren.

She made her decision.

* * *

Zash stepped off the cliff.

Their stomach lurched as they fell into empty space. Tree branches struck them, slowing their fall. One particularly thick branch thudded against their ribs, making them grunt.

And then they reached the slope. It was almost as sheer as the cliff higher up, but it was made of smooth, almost polished rock, and it soon became a gentle ramp. Zash went sliding down it, letting it bring them to a gentle halt.

They stood up, probing where the branch had struck. The ribs were likely bruised, but not broken. Zash stepped away from the end of the slide and waited.

There came the sound of tree branches breaking high above, and then a body sliding on rock. The green-cloaked wanderer slid into view a moment later, and just behind her was the wolfhound. They both skidded to a halt.

"I thought you might come this way," said Zash.

The wanderer was on her feet at once, brandishing her spear. The wolfhound growled, bristling by her side.

Zash raised both hands at once. "I've no quarrel with you. And I could tell you didn't want to run into the Nightblade any more than I did. Thass why I led you down here."

"Led?" snapped the woman. "You jumped off a cliff."

"And I knew I'd live," said Zash. "Just as you must have guessed, for you followed me. Now we're safe, for the moment. See those tunnels?"

Zash pointed left and right into caves that ran into the heart of the mountains on either side. The wanderer glanced in both directions, but her spear did not waver.

"What about them?"

"I'm off that way," said Zash. "It will take me through the mountains and far away east. But you can follow that tunnel over there. It will take you west, away from the Nightblade, and also give you a place to hide until she passes you by."

The wanderer scowled. "You expect me to let you live? After you tried to kill the girl?"

Zash shrugged. "I mean her no harm any longer. I was hired to ambush her here. I tried, and I failed. Now I'm all alone, and hardly foolish enough to try again, for I'd rather live. Can you respect that?"

A long moment of silence passed. Zash sighed.

"What about your hound?" they said. "I'd wager he can smell when someone means you harm. He's ready to attack if you tell him to, but he's hardly even growling any longer. He knows I only want to leave. Trust the beast, if you can't trust me."

For the first time, the spear dipped, though only by a few fingers. The wanderer glanced down at the dog. Zash had spoken true enough. It had stopped growling and was now curiously sniffing the air.

“Get out of my sight,” said the wanderer. “And remember this day if you are ever again hired to harm the Nightblade. She is under my protection.”

“I will remember it,” said Zash. “And I hope that, the next time I’m hired for a fight, it puts me on your side and not against you. Sky bless your road.”

Zash turned, thudding their heels together, and then sauntered towards the tunnel that would take them east. They did not even glance back to see if the wanderer watched them go.

FIVE

Loren burst out of the narrow path between the two cliffs to find a small, natural platform in the rock. It ended in a cliff, with the tops of trees just a few paces below.

No one was there. Loren had thought she heard something—she had been certain of it. But now . . .

"Loren?" said Chet.

"Shhh," she murmured.

Loren took several careful steps towards the edge of the cliff. Once she reached it, she leaned forwards to look down. But there was nothing except the trees.

Behind her, Shiun spoke quietly. "Nightblade?"

Loren turned towards them both. "Nothing. Let us return to the main path. I think it will lead us back to the others."

Shiun nodded and turned, heading back down the rocky passage. Chet hesitated for a moment, studying Loren with anxious eyes before heading off after the Mystic. It was several long moments before Loren realized that Chet had finally met her eyes. A curious warmth pulsed through her, as though her heart had pumped it.

She took one last look at the cliff. Something twinged at the back of her mind—a sense that she was missing something.

But surely, if it was very important, her dreams would have revealed it to her.

And now she had to return to the children. Loren turned her back on the cliff and followed Chet down the path.

* * *

Zash stood on a rise, watching. Below them, the Nightblade reunited with the Mystic spearman and the children, who ran forwards to bowl her over with an embrace. The sun was just beginning to set, and even as the party spoke animatedly about the adventure that had befallen them, they started readying their tents to make camp for the night. The next day, Zash knew, Loren would take them back up the path that would lead them west, pursuing Damaris into the western reaches of Dorsea.

A vague idea danced across Zash's mind. They could form another plan. They could probably succeed this time, without the Yerrins to hold them back.

But they had given their word to that wanderer. They would have to report their failure to Damaris. Not now, but some time in the future, when they could guarantee their own safety. It would be unpleasant all the same, but Damaris knew of Zash's skill and value. They would be in no great danger.

Zash gave the Nightblade a final salute and turned away from the edge of the rise. And as they strode away, they murmured under their breath, "We'll meet again."

* * *

Mag found Albern near sunset. He stood near the fallen boulders from the landslide, and his brow was creased with worry. On one side of him was the old man, still on horseback, and on the other side was Mag's own steed, its reins held tight in Albern's fist. Oku came bounding forwards, leaping up at Albern and trying to lick his hands. But Albern gave the hound only a cursory scratch behind the ears before turning to Mag.

"What under the sky happened here?" he said.

“I would guess it was a landslide,” said the old man helpfully. “And if even a blind man can tell, I wonder why you cannot, young one.”

Albern ignored the poor joke, keeping his gaze locked on Mag’s.

“Well, he is right,” said Mag, raising an eyebrow. “You can see the rocks for yourself.”

“Mag,” said Albern in a warning tone.

“Oh, all right,” said Mag. “There were some Yerrins as well. But they will not trouble us. I saw to that.”

Albern’s eyes narrowed. “What were they doing?”

“I do not know,” said Mag. “They attacked me before we could strike up a conversation. But there were only a few of them, and no great conspiracy. Now, come. The landslide blocks the way forwards, but I found another path. It is a tunnel into the mountain, and it will carry us out the other side, where we can rejoin the main road.”

And of course, the tunnels would avoid the higher path—the one that Loren would take, once she had rejoined the others.

“But let us not ride too much longer,” said the old man. “I am already weary. Mayhap we can rest in this tunnel of yours.”

“We can,” said Mag.

“Good, good,” said the old man. “Now, Albern. You were telling me about this song of yours. It is about that Mystic friend of yours, yes?”

“I . . . yes,” said Albern. “Yes, it is. I am somewhat stuck on some of the lines.”

“Well, tell me, tell me. I have learned enough songs through the years to be of some assistance, I hope. Let us hear what you have.”

Albern acquiesced and began to lay out his verses. But as they rode on, he kept stealing glances at Mag. It was clear in his expression that he thought something was wrong. And of course, he was right. And Mag could not tell him so.

I cannot come with you, she thought. *Darkness take me, Loren, I cannot come with you. And I cannot tell him.*

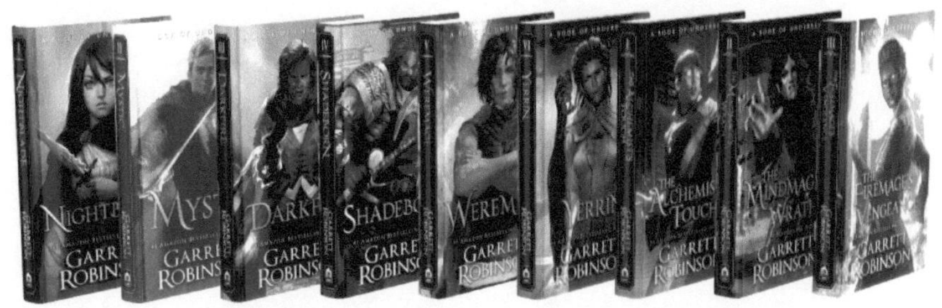

KEEP READING

The tales you've just read are stories from across the nine kingdoms of Underrealm. But the world doesn't end here. There is a broad and ever-growing selection of novels of Underrealm, penned by the authors in this collection, as well as others.

A brand-new fantasy world is waiting for you. But it's up to you to take the first step.

Find all the works of Underrealm at:

Underrealm.net/Books

THE AUTHORS

ANTOINE BANDELE

Antoine Bandele was born and raised in Los Angeles. Son of a kinesiologist, he was supposed to be the first major league player in the family, to the point his father forced items into his left-hand so he could become a southpaw pitcher (who have natural curve balls).

But in high school he took a new path—the pursuit of the creative arts. Whether writing stories, drawing comics, or directing home movies, he's always had his hands in creating something.

After flirting with the film industry, majoring in Multimedia at California State University Northridge, he eventually found an audience on YouTube where he accumulated 100,000 subscribers before taking on another new pursuit—indie publishing.

When he discovered there were very few African fantasies based in the continent's deep folklore he decided to (instead of waiting) write the books he wanted to read himself, starting with *The Kishi* in 2018, based on the real myth from the Kimbundu people of Angola.

Now Antoine is embarking on a journey to build an entire world around a mythical continent he calls Esowon in the, get this, Tales from Esowon series.

Antoine lives in California with his girlfriend.

Antoine can be found on:
FACEBOOK: facebook.com/youtubeantoinebandele
YOUTUBE: youtube.com/antoinebandele
INSTAGRAM: instagram.com/antoine_bandele
TWITTER: twitter.com/antoinebandele
GOODREADS: goodreads.com/antoinebandele

E.L. DRAYTON

E.L. Drayton was born and raised in the Bronx. As the daughter of a former high school English Teacher, her single mother taught her how to read and write before she even started school. She quickly picked up reading and understood books well beyond her age, so her passion for writing came as no surprise.

She went on to college and studied psychology instead of taking the expected route of literature or creative writing. Not taking any formal writing courses, however, never deterred her from her goal. In fact, it made her want it more. She spent countless years building a library of books from all sorts of genres to learn from those she considered to be the best. All throughout her years of writing, she never lost her thirst for knowledge as she read others' works of fiction.

Deciding to become an independent author was something she'd always wanted.

She's working on her own universe, Stonehaven, with many books planned. Also, an illustrated novel series called Twin Crossing.

You can find her online here:

WEBSITE: ELDrayton.com
TWITTER: @EricaDrayton

BRENNA GAWAIN

Brenna Gawain was born on the same definitely extinct volcano where she still lives today. After spending years of being that child that brought books to family gatherings, everyone was apparently still somehow surprised when she made plans to try and make a career out of writing.

Brenna has a background in almost every kind of art imaginable, from classical music and theatre to writing for video games and dance. She has studied information technology, archaeology and sound engineering at postgraduate levels, and her passion for writing is as broad as her interests in other fields, ranging from horror to fantasy to science fiction and back again.

The chance to work with Legacy Books was a dream come true, for both Brenna and her cat, who greatly appreciates the warm laptop that she writes on.

RILEY S. KEENE

My name is Riley S. Keene and I'm a fantasy author.

Well, okay. That's kinda a lie.

Riley S. Keene is actually the pseudonym for a husband-and-wife writing duo, also known as Robert and Kristen. They live in the Pacific Northwest and enjoy the rainstorms, lack of sunlight, and excess oxygen that come with living in that part of the U.S.

Robert is a Pacific Northwest native who has a degree in Applied Mathematics and Computational Sciences. He has a love for video games and a dislike for pretty much everything else. Robert is in charge of writing the first draft for all of our books.

Kristen was born and raised in a town outside of Philadelphia. She has a degree in Multimedia Design and works full-time as a marketer for a Seattle engineering firm. She loves gloomy weather, good books, food made from animals, and spending time with Robert. Kristen is in charge of outlining and editing for all of our books.

Our ultimate goal as an author duo is to write entertaining fantasy novels that are inclusive but not preachy. We strive to include as many cultures, settings, and characters as we can without relying on stereotypes or tropes. Doing so requires a lot of research and hard work—and we're the first to admit that it's never as in-depth as we would like. So we encourage you—if you find something in our book that doesn't represent a lifestyle, culture, or setting correctly, please use the contact form and send us a message. We'd be happy to be educated. It's kind of our thing.

RHEA NEWTON

Rhea Newton is a British-Irish writer, gamer, and linguaphile. As the daughter of travel-hungry and restless parents, she has lived all over the British Isles and Ireland, but she was born in London, in 1995.

Having moved home a great many times, she was a solitary child, and from a young age she began imagining and concocting far-away worlds, ancient lands, and sprawling stories. A love for RPG games solidified this interest, and it wasn't long before she had taken this hobby to new lengths. Since university, she has been steadily building up a catalogue of half-finished books and over-ambitious series, finishing her first full-length fantasy novel in 2017.

After her novel caught the attention of Legacy Books, she has been working with them to create fiction for the world of Underrealm, from short stories to a multi-book series, releasing in 2018.

In the meantime, Rhea is also a writer for the critically acclaimed Skyrim mod, Beyond Skyrim: Cyrodiil, the pre-release of which was Beyond Skyrim: Bruma.

Like a true millennial, she lives at home with her ever-patient, long-suffering mother, just on the outskirts of London.

GARRETT ROBINSON

Garrett Robinson was born and raised in Los Angeles. The son of an author/painter father and a violinist/singer mother, no one was surprised when he grew up to be an artist.

After blooding himself in the independent film industry, he self-published his first book in 2012 and swiftly followed it with a stream of others, publishing more than two million words by 2014. Within months he topped numerous Amazon bestseller lists and formed his own publishing company. Now he spends his time writing books and directing films.

A passionate fantasy author, his most popular books are the novels of Underrealm, including the series The Nightblade Epic, The Academy Journals, and Tales of the Wanderer.

However, he has delved into many other genres. Some works are for adult audiences only, such as Non Zombie and Hit Girls, but he has also published popular books for younger readers, including The Realm Keepers series and The Ninjabread Man, co-authored with Z.C. Bolger.

Garrett lives in Oregon with his wife Meghan, his children Dawn, Luke, and Desmond, and his dog Chewbacca.

Garrett can be found on:
TUMBLR: garrettauthor.tumblr.com
TWITTER: twitter.com/garrettauthor
BLOG: garrettbrobinson.com/blog
FACEBOOK: facebook.com/garrettbrobinson

LIANDRA SY

Liandra Sy received her M.A. in English from New York University and is currently pursuing a Ph.D. in English Literature from the University of Pennsylvania. She was born in Quezon City, Philippines, before immigrating with her family to Queens, New York. She has written scholarly works on seventeenth and eighteenth-century British literature, with an emphasis on race, empire, and colonialism. Her work deals mostly with the broad genre of prose fiction, especially with what many call today "the early novel." Liandra now lives in Philadelphia, PA with her supportive and loving family, Ben and Luna.

ERIC UGLAND

Eric Ugland ran away from Seattle to join the circus. And then he came to his senses and moved to Manhattan. Now he's a novelist in Los Angeles. Don't worry, it doesn't make sense to him, either.

Want to see what other nonsense he gets up to? You can check out EricUgland.com, or follow him on Twitter @Bodegazilla, or on Instagram @Bodegazilla. And then you can totally ask him why he wrote this in the third person.

CONNECT ONLINE

FACEBOOK

Want to hang out with other fans of the Underrealm books? There's a Facebook group where you can do just that. Join the Nine Lands group on Facebook and share your favorite moments and fan theories from the books. I also post regular behind-the-scenes content, including information about the world you can't find anywhere else. Visit the link to be taken to the Facebook group:

Underrealm.net/Nine-Lands

DISCORD

Do you do The Discord™? We've got an awesome server where you can hang out with other fantasy nerds, writers, video game fanatics . . . basically the best people humanity has to offer.

Underrealm.net/Discord

THE BOOKS OF UNDERREALM

To see all novels in the world of Underrealm, visit:
Underrealm.net/books

THE NIGHTBLADE EPIC
NIGHTBLADE
MYSTIC
DARKFIRE
SHADEBORN
WEREMAGE
YERRIN

THE ACADEMY JOURNALS
THE ALCHEMIST'S TOUCH
THE MINDMAGE'S WRATH
THE FIREMAGE'S VENGEANCE

TALES OF THE WANDERER
BLOOD LUST
STONE HEART
HELL SKIN

CHRONOLOGICAL ORDER
NIGHTBLADE
MYSTIC
DARKFIRE
SHADEBORN
BLOOD LUST
THE ALCHEMIST'S TOUCH
STONE HEART
THE MINDMAGE'S WRATH
WEREMAGE
THE FIREMAGE'S VENGEANCE
HELL SKIN
YERRIN

www.ingramcontent.com/pod-product-compliance
Lightning Source LLC
Chambersburg PA
CBHW031958040826
48979CB00043B/1689/J
* 9 7 8 1 9 4 1 0 7 6 5 8 3 *